STORM
FROM THE
EAST

ALSO BY JOANNA HATHAWAY

Dark of the West

STORM
FROM THE
EAST

Joanna Hathaway

TOR
TEEN

A Tom Doherty Associates Book

NEW YORK

STORM FROM THE EAST

A Tor Teen Book
Published by Tom Doherty Associates
120 Broadway
New York, NY 10271

www.tor-forge.com

Tor® is a registered trademark
of Macmillan Publishing Group, LLC.

The Library of Congress Cataloging-in-Publication Data
is available upon request.

ISBN 978-0-7653-9644-0 (hardcover)
ISBN 978-0-7653-9646-4 (ebook)

Our books may be purchased in bulk for promotional, educational, or business use. Please contact your local bookseller or the Macmillan Corporate and Premium Sales Department at 1-800-221-7945, extension 5442, or by email at MacmillanSpecialMarkets@macmillan.com.

First Edition: February 2020

Printed in the United States of America

0 9 8 7 6 5 4 3 2 1

For my mother, who teaches me both courage and grace

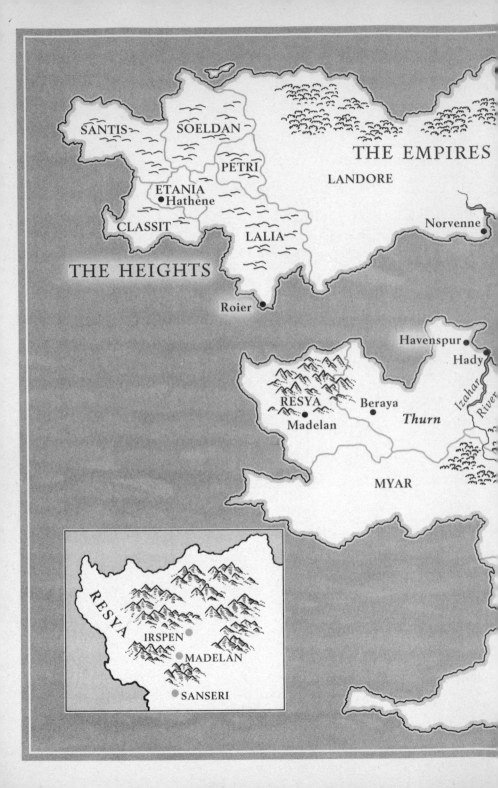

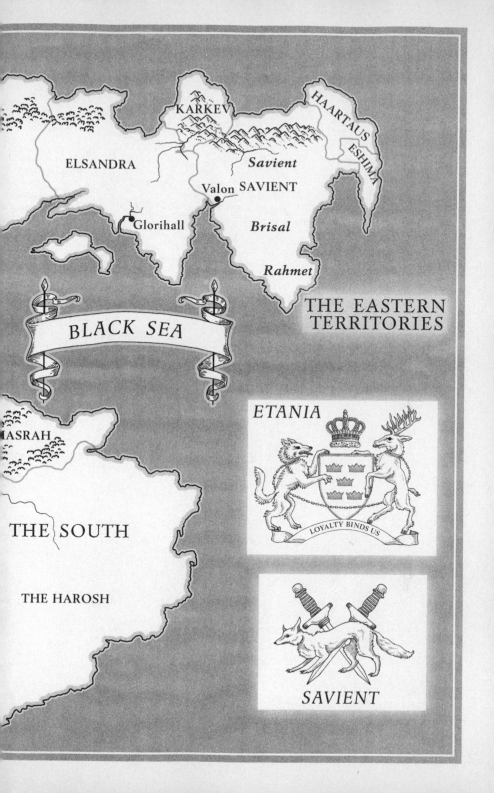

KARKEV

HAARTAUS

ESHIMA

ELSANDRA

Savient

SAVIENT

Valon

Glorihall

Brisal

Rahmet

THE EASTERN
TERRITORIES

BLACK SEA

ETANIA

LOYALTY BINDS US

MASRAH

THE SOUTH

THE HAROSH

SAVIENT

STORM
FROM THE
EAST

War is not the story of generals, or even of kings.

The sniper learned this long ago, that it is the smallest and most forgotten—by the ink headlines, by the march of history—who comprise its greatest ranks. Which is why she kneels, now, beneath an open window, the cool steel of her rifle wedged between shoulder and collarbone, the world before her partitioned by two perfect crosshairs.

There is power in her hands.

Feverish morning sun dampens skin, muscles cramped against hard floorboards, curtains drawn to hide her within their shadow. She peers through her glass scope at the military outpost far below, at the sandbag-protected encampment stirring to life with a dozen friendly shouts and foreign cigarettes.

These men are lonely, easy. Dull. Festooned with badges that make them believe their story is the most glorious one. They don't care that their mothers wear stolen diamonds sifted from streams by nameless, bone-tired peasants. They don't see the rivers stained red by the plundered copper used in their ammunition and aeroplanes, the children and animals left with poisoned water on thirsty tongues. And they'll never understand how this land once was long ago—fertile with fruit and crops and dreams. Yet still they come. Conscripted, perhaps, or compelled by misplaced patriotism, constructing their reasons along the way.

And she has done the same.

The young man behind her mutters, "Which one first?"

That's always the question. Which one. But to determine that, she needs to follow the evidence, find the right path, study their strange rhythms piece by piece. Through her rifle scope, she can see that the commanding officer wears a wedding band, gold flashing in the sun as he writes his reports. Another soldier has shoulders too narrow to be declared old enough for war; his friend, too many grooves in the face to be young enough. Still another is fishing cigarettes from his pocket like they are desperate jewels, oblivious to the deadly streets around him. To the death breathing at his neck.

"The one who's most innocent," she replies, her index finger warming the curve of the trigger.

She hears her comrade grimace. She knows her rules make no sense to him—never have—but he doesn't understand the meticulous nature of this pitiless job she commands, the way she must study each living corpse, the way she must decide how it will happen. He only fires and runs. Fires and runs. But she? She inspects death straight in the face, guarantees it even, and so, the most innocent should go first. No time for panic, for fear.

Grit cakes her parched throat as she studies the olive-clad figures. They can't see her. They wouldn't see her, even if she stood a foot from them. She is, in their eyes, a girl erased. A girl smudged from the map with a single formal decree, then traded—along with two hundred thousand others—for a few invisible border lines, deemed a worthy sacrifice by someone behind a faraway desk. Over the years, she's been marched through heat, snow, rain. She's been ordered to sleep in this tent, then walk to that camp, then to wait only one more year, and always they dangled the hope of "home" before her like a mirage. But at the end of it all, she's learned she's only one thing to the men writing the headlines, and that is this: a nameless girl.

Only one girl of many, many, many.

"*Sinora,*" her father said to her, the morning he was jailed for simply trying to feed his four children, *"your name means 'ever proud,' and don't you think I chose that for a reason?"*

No. She didn't think he had, nor did she feel terribly proud. Not for a long time. She remembered, faintly, the little farm they'd once had, the memory of her father very young, bespectacled, leading her through a garden of sage and jasmine, among trees of tender apricots. Her hands touching fieldstone walls bursting with violet capers. But those gentle reflections are long gone, replaced by the day she faced a pair of sweaty, puerile soldiers who stole her favourite horse and threw rocks at her, who kept her father in prison simply because they could, and who reminded her—in every way they knew how—that she was expunged from the only story that mattered. Their story. The remembered one. But in the end, they failed at their game, because after she left them she was still on her feet, still standing, and she vowed that never again would anyone take from her that which she did not willingly give first.

She was above them all—they simply couldn't see it yet.

She is truly above them now, crouched in this window, the sun pressing high, and her comrade shifts closer, his strong arms braced against the peeling wood. Though she doesn't glance left, she can imagine him leaning there. Perspiration dripping from sleeves rolled to his elbows, across defiant tattoos and fair skin.

"Just pick one," he says, impatient.

He is always impatient. With the world, with her, but she remains fixed on her scope. "If the right one is here," she replies, "I could end this forever. Chase them back across the sea in shame."

"Don't get ahead of yourself."

There's a grin in his voice, a wry taunt, the familiar way they always push each other—back and forth, back and forth—and she thinks, *I have one hundred and eight kills with this rifle. I am far, far closer to my victory than you are to yours, Dakar.*

Because every single one of her bullets is building a new

story, growing bolder, inching her to the top of their high command—these generals and kings and monsters. These arrogant conquerors. It's only a matter of time, and he's the only one who understands this relentless strategy she clings to, who knows what it's like to have the taste of revenge coating your tongue every minute of every day, to despise fate for setting up this world of impossible imbalance, because he, too, has been erased. He, too, has learned how to rewrite himself into the margins of history.

Though for him, she suspects the margins are only the beginning.

She drags her rifle left, to the low-ranking soldier still fishing in his pocket, his focus distracted, his smile small. She finally sees it's not cigarettes at all, but a baby bird tucked away. The young soldier—hardly older than her—feeds the tiny creature faithfully.

There's the first, then. The one deserving the quick, merciful death, and she shifts, nearly imperceptible, sensing her comrade's familiar smile. It slips across her own lips in reply, the sort of smile that only two survivors can share at the prospect of action, at rebellion in the face of the powerful, a cold relief that billows up from somewhere in the hollowness of their insides.

They are equally nameless—but, in the end, they will win. Because she knows the true secret to victory. She learned it the day her father had his little farm of tender apricots stolen out from under him: that if you take a man's pride, you take his life. Death of a different kind. A quiet draining of the will to live. Cut by cut by cut. And now she will return the favour, bringing the twin furies of justice and revenge together in the sight of her faithful gun, burning away all guilt, a story which will be told eternally in four sharp flashes.

This time I take, Sinora tells the world, *and you will remember it.* She pulls the trigger.

I

GOD OF WAR

1

❧ AURELIA ISENDARE ❧

Etania

Our palace is sharp with autumn's chill. The boilers in the cellar hiss to life, radiators ticking in every parlour corner, but creeping cold still permeates the arching halls of home. A wintry breath snakes between double doors, jeweled chandeliers, marble alcoves. The high ceilings and endless rooms swallow warmth, hearth fires burning brightly in defiance.

My mother is as defiant as the flames. She sits at her mahogany desk, dressed in a wool coat trimmed with ermine, and I stand at her left shoulder, seeing every twitch of breath in the slender expanse of her throat. It's the only thing that belies her calm. Beyond the large windows, the faithful mountains rise, their peaks gone brown, spindly leaves clinging in scarlet patches.

Lord Jerig places a white paper on the desk. "Your Majesty. Let justice be dealt."

He waits obediently before us, as do the other men of her Royal Council, and even her brother, my uncle Tanek. A little herd of men hungry for retribution. From where I am, the decree is easy to read. A simple paper, with elegant script.

Ink words holding death.

"For betraying Etania, the kingdom of our true hearts, and aiding in the coup against Her Majesty, forsaking the honourable legacy of His Late Majesty Boreas Isendare—who, in good faith,

crowned Her Majesty to rule until our Prince is of age—the follow-
ing shall forfeit their life in payment for their shameful crime."

It's only been two months since that awful night when these
men attacked my birthday masquerade, a fragment of our own
people revolting against us and claiming my mother murdered
my father for the Etanian throne. It's still fresh, still frightening
inside, and sometimes I catch myself counting the steps to each
door or window in a room, scouring for an escape—anything to
get away from the clatter of bullets, the plumes of smoke rising
into the night sky. Something deep within me has been left
small and fearful. I want this over. I want this hateful thing
ended forever. And yet, I can't stop reading the names on the
paper.

Twenty-five names.

Elegant, precise, dead.

Mother tucks a strand of hair behind her ear. The raven black
is twisted into a regal chignon, but another cut of grey strikes
the dark. "Yes, let justice reign." Her firm voice lilts with its
lovely Southern accent.

She scrawls her looping signature, the first from our family.

My father, the late king, worked hard to ensure the death
sentence was a laborious verdict to pass. He didn't believe in
handing out death like God. My mother, in only eight weeks,
has undone that. She introduced a new law to the Council—
"guilt by absence"—and they voted in quick favour, the entire
kingdom left shaken from that night. We don't have the true
culprits who plotted this treason against us, only the secondary
men who are either too fiercely loyal to confess where their
orders came from, or too fiercely threatened into silence by
their superiors. But now they will hang regardless, bearing the
guilt of their absent leaders.

Mother kept only one of Father's rules. The one that says
each royal must agree before life is taken, each royal signature
on the warrant.

So, here we are.

I'm next, and I know what they all see—a seventeen-year-old princess, the perfect reflection of her foreign-born Resyan mother with a flicker of traitorous doubt on her face. I can't hide it. Guilt slips between the cracks as I read those names. They're real people, with families and homes and hearts, and while I despise them for what they did, for trying to hurt my mother and shattering the sanctuary of my home forever, I also don't want to take life again.

Once was enough.

Mother looks over her shoulder at me, and there's gentle prodding in her eyes. We've discussed this too many times over the past month, the importance, she says, of making this decisive statement, so no one will ever try to steal from us again. I don't want to disappoint her. I don't want to imagine how she would look at me if she knew the truth, what I've already done.

I reach for the fountain pen and sign.

Jerig offers an indulgent smile at me—his tiny moustache spiderlike above thin lips—then slides the paper to Renisala, who stands at my left.

My brother's signature is the one they're truly waiting for. Their nineteen-year-old prince who is mere months away from his crown. They've heard his eloquent speeches denouncing this severe sentence, this abject rejection of everything Boreas Isendare stood for. But my brother has been overruled by fear—and our mother. He had no choice but to surrender to popular opinion, and now he stands on Mother's other side, the picture of everything noble, uneasy at the prospect of executing men for simply believing an idea. His dark hair is brushed smooth, his hazel eyes fixed on the paper.

His hand rests against his tailored suit, unmoving.

Jerig shifts awkwardly, glancing at the Council, and Mother turns to face Reni. The clock has the nerve to tick rather loudly as my brother continues to stare.

Somewhere down the hall, a muffled radio address talks of peace, glorious peace, since Savient's war in Resya has been

denied. The Safire Commander's impossible claims against my
mother's homeland—"the Resya problem" as they call it—
were soundly overruled by the Royal League's verdict this
summer, and surely reason and good sense will overcome
these trying times, lead everyone to a brighter dawn of trust
and reconciliation.

Peace for all.

Before us, the death warrant still taunts.

"Your Highness," Jerig begins uncomfortably, then stops.

What is there to say to a prince who defies his queen? Reni's
eyes lift, but they don't settle on Jerig, or Uncle, or even Mother.
They look beyond the flock of men, to the oil painting hung
above the gilded bronze of the crackling hearth. It's our royal
ancestor, Prince Efan, waging his victorious battle for the
North, centuries ago. Kneeling in silver armour, Efan holds his
helmet in humble acceptance of his divine victory. His regal
face is lit by three rising suns, and his black stallion sprawls on
the ground nearby, arrows poking from its chest and hind.

Earlier this morning, Renisala looked at me across our breakfast tea, and asked, "Do you think you can dream your own
death, Ali?"

It was the strangest question he'd ever uttered. One that
came, seemingly, from his musings over the history of Efan—a
prince who once foresaw his fabled victory, every detail of it
envisioned, from the flame-tailed horse to the three suns. Over
the past month, my ever-pragmatic brother has developed a
habit of waxing philosophical about the nature of fate, and it's
a surprise to everyone, since he's always been more inclined
to simply take what's his. Perhaps he's kept this under lock
and key for all these years, only now, at last, tapping into the
full realm of the deep spirit Father left him. Weighted with
responsibility, longing to imbue everything with some shred of
nobility.

I feel obligated to be firmer. I have no patience left for myth.

I nudge Reni's foot with my own, behind Mother's chair

where no one can see, and his gaze shifts to mine. The storm of regret churning there mirrors the one I've hidden from sight. My sweet, sweet brother. All of his rules and reasons can't save him from the true weight of taking life. It's final—it hangs over your soul like a shroud, an endless bruise that throbs with sudden words and thoughts and even the way someone says your name. Cheerful, because they don't know the blood on your hands. It's hell, forever.

But still I nod at him, because Mother knows best, and today, justice must come.

His shoulders straighten. "I'm sorry," he says regally. "I simply wanted to read the names again."

"*I'm sorry.*"

It's not Reni's voice I hear in my head now. It's the boy I love, his apology whispering against my neck, and I'm back in that lonely place with only him, the palace splintering round us, both of us reaching for each other's warmth. Seizing that precious moment that was ours before it all went wrong. My beloved Safire pilot who agreed to aid me in blackmail against his General Dakar, then kissed me perfectly as the royal forest burned—and he thought to beg my forgiveness. For what? For being afraid? For not knowing how to save us? Athan Erelis betrayed his own uniform to become my ally that night. I told General Dakar that I ordered Athan to help me, that Athan had no choice, but what if that wasn't enough? What if someone signed a warrant for Athan's execution just as I signed one today? Guilt by absence?

Is that why I haven't heard from him since then?

My cold hands tremble, that tiny, fearful thing in me gnawing afresh as Reni signs his name and the entire Council exhales with relief. They don't need to worry. My brother is everything they could want in their future king—compassionate where possible, just when necessary. Strong and gentle and good.

I'm the murderer.

I'm the one who killed my own cousin.

The necessary signatures over, everyone smiles, like executions are proper business. Uncle Tanek's consent doesn't matter, since no blood of Prince Efan glitters in his veins. He's only a quiet, foreign phantom following his royal sister who was gifted her dying husband's crown, and Reni passes the warrant across the table to Jerig. At last, it seems finished, the sentences to be carried out immediately, ropes placed round necks and life strangled away. Yet I feel no relief, no joy, because nothing's over, nothing's done, and the worst might yet come.

"Peace," the radio broadcast assures, *"between all our great nations."*

Only I know what that truly takes.

2

Savient

It's been over two months since the Royal League ruled against our war in Resya, but the sunset wharf before me tells a different story. Standing on the walls of an old citadel, I count three torpedo boats floating in the murky water far below, mounted anti-aircraft guns gleaming on the forward and aft decks. Earlier this week, they only had a single turret. Now they've multiplied to four, and everything's encased in armour. On a nearby carrier, hidden beneath netting, twenty fighter planes sleep, camouflaged wings and flanks painted forest green.

The quiet conspiracy of our war machine rousing to life.

Trying to ignore that unpleasant reality, I focus above the deceitful harbour, on the multicoloured sky still honest and raw and mesmerizing. Tiny pricks of light appear, the first stars, and I challenge myself to find at least ten while they're still pale and barely detectable. Soon enough they'll be enemy planes. Barreling out of the dusk light, guns ablaze. The faster I can train myself to spot danger in the sky, the better pilot I'll be.

Also, it's a nice excuse to stargaze.

"How's that letter coming along?" Cyar enquires, leaning on the bulwark beside me. "Your page still looks mostly blank."

We've been hiding out here for over an hour, me with a fresh sheet of paper in hand. Usually Father relies on speeches and toasts and contracts for his wars, businessmen made to feel important and essential. But since no one in the North can know we're about to invade a sovereign kingdom, he's been forced to employ a different tactic. Instead of a proper war rally, he's let my brother Arrin host another kind of spectacle—a reckless party that outshines any arms deals being signed backstage.

It's turned, more or less, into a drunken cabaret show.

I squint up at the sky. "Six . . ."

"Stop avoiding this, Athan. You said you'd do it before I took leave, and now I'm back, and there's still nothing."

"Just let me get to ten."

"If you don't write something, I will."

"Seven . . . Eig—"

Too late. Cyar whips out his own notebook and begins penning something for me.

"I swear," I say, "if it's about snakes or sunflowers I'll—"

"No, that's my thing. Get your own."

He scribbles away, then passes it over and looks at me with a very Cyar look—a bit earnest, a bit smirking. His thick black hair's all mussed from the sea wind, which means mine probably looks even worse.

I glance down.

The letter's two lines long and barely legible.

Ali,

Your eyes are lovely and beautiful as night.

My name is Athan Dakar.

"Wow," I say. "You definitely got my handwriting."

"I've been copying notes off you since we were eleven. Besides, you write like a blindfolded drunk."

"No, this is simply drunk." I gesture at his scribbles. "To get *blindfolded* drunk takes a special talent in penmanship, one which I've been perfecting for years."

I try to grin, to make all of this funny, but it's not. Cyar knows it. We can hide out here forever, but I'm still the unwelcome traitor in my own family, the one who lost us an entire

STORM FROM THE EAST

coup meant to ruin my father's oldest enemy—and the girl I love is quite firmly on the other side.

If she knew the truth, she'd hate me forever.

Cyar yanks the page back. "Eighteen years spent making sure no one can understand you, and now you can't even tell her who you really are. There's a lesson here, I think."

An amused snort startles us both. We turn and find my sister Leannya spying from the citadel doorway behind us, uniformed in Safire grey, blonde hair pinned back. It's still strange to see her like this. Like when she was a kid and would wear Arrin's officer cap for fun. "He has a girlfriend, then?" she asks Cyar slyly.

I jump down from the chilly bulwark. "No point," I announce to them both, before she can pry something out of him. "We're going to war and I'll probably die, and besides"—I glance at Cyar—"I can't put anything in writing right now. Censorship. Loose lips. All that. Let's get back inside where it's warm."

Leannya frowns at me. "I came out to hide with you."

"Not possible." I link arms with her. "If there were three sisters, you might be able to disappear, but unfortunately, you're the only one. And also—wait." I stop and glance up at the brilliant sky one more time. It's getting darker now. The stars brighter. "Nine . . . Ten! That was too easy, but I'll count them."

"You're my strangest brother," Leannya says seriously.

I smile—I've perfected it by now, anything to undo my traitor status—and steer her back inside the square door of the old fortress, Cyar following. The hallway is stone-damp, music echoing ahead, and when we push through the wide doors of the armoury-turned-banquet room, we're greeted by the wild herd of Arrin's officer corps. The smoky air is charged with brandy, liqueur, and the smooth brass of a raucous band. A rather scantily clad girl from Rahmet warbles away on a small stage, her words slurred as she grips her metal microphone like it's the throttle in a dogfight. A wine-filled smile radiates across her brown skin. Arrin's cap dangles sideways on her head.

Somehow, his cap always ends up on someone else.

Father's maintained a solitary corner of decency in the back, seated with Admiral Malek, Colonel Evertal, and other older, more dignified leadership. Most of them are wearing their "youth will be youth" expression, but Commander Vent, a new addition, sits beside Father, clearly unimpressed. He'll be leading one of the army groups in Resya, in support of Arrin, and he's decidedly not one of my brother's biggest fans.

This party isn't helping.

"Who the hell thought this was a good idea?" I ask Leannya.

She shrugs. "Not me, but at least the reports in the papers will be fabulous. *'Savient's favourite son, hero of Karkev, lights up Brisal!'* Who's going to notice that?"

She nods to where a gallantly smiling Evertal—a woman who only smiles during times of great political necessity—escorts a business-suited man out of the room, to quieter places where war contracts can happen. This is how it works. Father buying bullets for his secret war while Arrin's star burns bright and furious as distraction.

And so far, the charade's working. Both here and abroad. Our local papers have turned the King of Resya into a cartoonish caricature of every terrible thing Savient despises. A spoiled royal who feasts while his people suffer, feeding selfishly off Southern unrest. It's the same argument that garnered popular support for our last war in neighbouring Karkev.

Of course, no one knows the King of Resya isn't the only one feeding off Southern unrest.

My father's cornered that market already.

"Hey little darling, you're back!" a young captain crows, staggering by and reaching for Leannya with a stupid smile.

I'm about to push him off—she's only just fifteen—when she extends a firm hand to him. "Congratulations on your glorious demotion, Lieutenant."

He gawps at her hand, then at her face, unsure if she's joking. Then he wobbles off.

I nod. "Not bad."

"I'm getting practice with these bootlickers. Now, time for me to continue impressing the navy. Kalt said he'd help me, but God knows where he is. Good luck, Athan," she adds with an ambivalent salute in my direction. "Glad you don't have a girl-friend."

I give a questioning look. That's rather ominous, and I'm tempted to follow her, but then I realize Father's up from his table and striding towards me, an unfamiliar uniformed man at his side. There's a smile on Father's face.

A smile?

At *me*?

New plan. I need to get the hell out of here. I need to run right now and—

"Athan, I've been looking everywhere for you," Father calls, which is definitely a lie. "You haven't met Colonel Illiany, have you?"

I've spent three quarters of this thing hiding outside, and he knows it. But better play along. Father's tolerance of me since Etania is dangerously thin.

Cyar makes a stealthy escape, and I force the fake smile I've become excellent at. "Good evening, Colonel."

The well-built man has white hair and a sallow face, but his eyes hold a perceptive glint. "Your father speaks very highly of you, Lieutenant. Graduating with top score from the Air Academy, and two planes already shot down in Thurn. Your brother must be grateful to have you in the sky for his campaign."

"Thank you," I say, though he'd have to ask Arrin that.

"Colonel Illiany is our new governor in Karkev," Father explains, gaze stressing the gravity of this to me. "He was an essential benefactor in our victory there."

I think it's safe to assume "benefactor" means willing sup-plier of weapons, paired with a nice dose of betrayal to his own corrupt nation—the one we voluntarily settled with tanks and planes last spring. If Illiany's here now, praised by Father, then who knows what he gave up for the honour. Family and comrades. Blood loyalty. He's a turncoat, but at least he was a turncoat for us.

He and I might have that in common.

Father waves at a nearby table where a blonde girl sits alone. "Athan, please make Illiany's daughter, Katalin, feel more welcome."

I nod obediently. Anything to show Father that I'm cured of my rebellion. Anything to get my cards back. It's the only way to protect Ali, Cyar . . . everyone. Even myself.

Determined to get this over with, I head for the Colonel's daughter. Her hair is as fair as snow, with skin to match, and black gloves cover her hands, clenching a wine glass. I should be good at this, after Etania, after Ali . . .

No, not now. Can't go there.

But I wish.

I struggle to hold my smile. "May I sit down?"

"Do Safire ask?" she replies, her cold Savien words heavily accented.

I'm not sure if that's permission or sarcasm, and now what? Do I make napkin animals again? I know how to make Ali smile at me—not this stranger. And truthfully, Ali's joy is the only one that matters. She could be the last girl in the world to ever smile at me and I'd be perfectly happy to the grave.

I take a seat anyway. "Is this your first time in Savient?"

"Yes."

"Do you . . . like it?"

"I like Karkev."

"I've never been," I say, hoping she'll realize I had nothing to do with my father's three-year campaign in her homeland.

I'm guilty by association only.

She glares, but there's a nervous flit to her gaze, flickering around this stuffy room of perpetually violated personal space.

"It doesn't seem like you want to be here," I suggest, trying for honesty. Or maybe an escape. I'll take anything I can get. "We could go outside, count stars—"

"No, I must be in this place. I have no decision."

I'll assume she means no choice.

"I know what that's like," I admit. "Why are you here, then?"

"Marriage."

She watches Arrin with unhidden disgust. He's reappeared to take the spotlight, his sandy hair plastered to his forehead, the singing girl latched on to him now, both laughing in drunken abandon on the stage. Everyone cheers. If only Arrin could actually dance. None of us Dakar brothers excel in that department.

"Who's getting married?" I ask, distracted by the rising shouts.

"Me," she replies, like it's a death sentence.

Suddenly, the picture comes into a bit more focus. Her scowl at Arrin, the reward Father certainly feels he owes Colonel Illiany who helped us win the rich oil fields of Karkev. No. He wouldn't. Father's not like that. He doesn't believe in those kinds of things . . . But maybe? If he really owed Illiany enough? I remember what Kalt told me about the unification with Rahmet years ago. This wouldn't be the first time Arrin was offered as reward to someone's daughter.

Why not?

He's a twenty-five-year-old military genius with an entire nation to inherit.

And a terrible dancer.

Katalin looks fairly ill. I'm beginning to think she might have a fate worse than mine. "Are you all right?"

"I *hate* your brother," she says to the table.

She'd better learn to keep that opinion quiet—like me.

"Listen, Lieutenant." She looks up. "I forgot your name."

"Athan."

"Yes, Athan. Have you seen a field with mine?"

"You mean a minefield?"

"Yes, but after? After the boom?"

I shake my head, unsure where this is going.

"Be happy then. Pray you never." Her blue eyes fix on me. "I heard you like mountains, and Karkev has beautiful mountains. Please do not make me stay here."

There's a painful memory in her plea. Her fair hair, her desperation. She reminds me of Mother.

She reminds me of me.

"You're marrying my brother?" I ask bluntly.

She narrows her eyes. "No."

"Oh." I offer a tentative smile. "That's good."

"You."

"Me?"

"Not him. *You*."

What the hell?

"You're marrying *me*?"

"Sorry to be the bad news," she whispers viciously, glaring again.

We face each other, me horrified, her defensive. "This . . . can't be right," I say, stumbling. "No one told me."

She laughs bitterly. "I have learned today, too."

"Excuse me."

And I leave her. Don't care. This doesn't make any damn sense, not at all. Father doesn't do this. Arranged marriages are what old-fashioned kings do. Not us. Fury drives me back across the room, through the drunk crowd, straight for Father, but Kalt's lanky frame nearly collides into mine, heading me right off.

"Don't," he orders. "You'll sign your own execution warrant."

My middle brother is entirely sober, of course, every piece of his brown hair carefully gelled. Not a button out of place.

"You knew about this?" I demand.

"No. Well, a bit." He pushes me into the nearest corner, out of earshot, not that there's much point. There are only about seven other people in this room who can still count to ten properly—and they're all sitting at Father's table. "I'm sorry. This should be me. But . . . for obvious reasons, it's not."

"No, this should be *Arrin*. But he's too much of an ass to make it work."

An unexpected arm seizes me, wrapping roughly around my shoulders. "I'm not an ass," Arrin intervenes, joining our little huddle, all sweat and liquor. "Though you need to look on the bright side here, Athan"—he glances at Katalin, who's still staring at the table—"like those extraordinary breasts."

I imagine putting my fist into his nose. He's drunk enough, I stand a chance.

Across the room, Leannya's buttering up some naval officers, Admiral Malek as well, but she catches my eye between her nods. Her expression is pure innocence, and I know, then, who fed Katalin Illiany my secrets. Who said I liked mountains.

I glare at my brothers. "Why didn't anyone tell me about this?"

They're silent, and I realize I'm on probation with everyone—not just Father—since Etania. Kept away from plots in case I end up sabotaging them. I think I'm even more annoyed about that, since it's not like I didn't also save Arrin from being exposed before the Royal League as a war criminal. I made the photographs of his supposed crime disappear. I defended all of us. I've said it enough to Father, I believe it entirely.

No one else seems to.

"Listen," Arrin says with astonishing diplomacy, given his current state, "you're only ever going to see her on leave. Just let Father give his thanks to Illiany and pray it comes to nothing in a year. Maybe you'll even be dead then." He grins.

Kalt nods. "Arrin's right. Not about the dying part, but don't ruin this one. Illiany won us nearly half of Karkev."

"No, that was me," Arrin corrects. "Illiany did maybe a corner."

I turn my back on my oldest brother. I'm seeing red. It's no surprise that Illiany wouldn't want his daughter anywhere near Arrin. Arrin's turned his exceptional immorality into a saving grace. I beg Kalt instead, the one who might listen. The one who should be next in line for this duty. "Couldn't you just pretend to like women?" I ask hopefully. "Until it comes to nothing?"

Kalt stares at me, affronted. "*No*. And it's not like you have anyone."

"I'm not so certain about that," Arrin replies with a dark smile, and Kalt raises a brow. Arrin waves at the door. "To the city! Let's get drunk."

"Aren't you now?" Kalt points out.

"Not enough."

And with that, Arrin's marching off, apparently abandoning his own party.

I cross my arms, refusing to obey, and Kalt's expression mirrors mine. Laughter erupts from a nearby table of my fellow flyboys—all slammed except for Captain Garrick Carr, who sits with an untouched drink in front of him and a mute acceptance for whatever his first officer Ollie Helsun's doing near the stage. I just want my stars again. Far, far from here.

But Kalt sighs and puts on his cap. "No, let's go. He might try to throw himself off the damn pier."

Well, it wouldn't be the first time.

I don't know why I follow. Maybe I'm tired of being on the outside, hiding on walls and waiting for fate to find me. Or maybe I like seeing Arrin at his worst, because then I somehow feel better about myself. Neither reason feels very noble, but I follow him anyway from one drinking hole to the next, collecting samples of whatever's most expensive, and we end up on some remote stretch of the wharf. All three of us, so knocked through a bottle we can't even walk straight. There's a moment where I think this might be a bad idea, that if Father finds out—which he will—we'll all be executed at dawn.

But then I think a bullet in the head might be better than marriage to Katalin Illiany of Karkev, and I down another shot.

"The navy is your greatest asset," Kalt argues with Arrin as we wander. "Fifteen of my destroyers can deliver more firepower in an hour than a thousand of his damn planes."

He stabs a wobbly finger at me, and I smack it with my bottle.

"Great," Arrin replies, teetering on the granite ledge of the wharf, sea waves heaving below. "But you're mostly paddling around for days on end. Fishing on your little ship."

Kalt begins to protest, but I cut him off. "Pilots are the greatest asset." I hiccup. "What other weapon can get behind enemy lines?"

"Seventy-five-millimeter shells," Arrin offers.

"Shells with no ounce of . . . brains or intuition. Load me up with bombs, then you'll get some damn firepower!"

I finish with a triumphant miming of explosions, and Arrin stops walking. "Hang on—you can put *bombs* on those fighters now?"

"Of course," I say, like he's stupid, but it's ruined by another hiccup.

Arrin turns to Kalt. "He's better drunk. Actually sounds clever."

"Without my little *ship*, your army wouldn't even make it to Resya," Kalt retorts, still stuck on the earlier offense.

The whole world lurches suddenly, and I flop down onto the cold stone.

Everything spinning.

"Oh God, we killed him," Arrin says, and something pokes me in the side. "Hey, Athan. You've got to die by a bullet, not a bottle. Father said that to me once and—wait." A hand snatches my wrist. "Is that my watch? What the hell, Athan!"

Kalt snorts. "He stole it years ago."

"You little thief!"

I don't even care anymore. The sky's whirling with stars above me, impossible to count. A wondrous place that could be up or down or sideways right now. I'm grinning just because. Steal those stars. One, two, three, four . . .

Eventually, Arrin and Kalt become so far gone they actually start to get along again, and shivering snippets drift over to me—their memories of stealing leftover drinks from Father's soldiers long ago, getting sick, blaming it on a cake Mother made.

"You have a sailor boy?" Arrin's hazy voice questions, and Kalt mumbles something in reply. "Folco? Folco *Carr*?"

Of course it's Folco, I want to say, if I wasn't spinning so much. *Who the hell didn't see that?*

I realize I miss it like this. A family that almost feels like a family. Maybe I can forget the truth. For an hour. For a night. I don't have to look at Arrin and see those photographs Ali showed me of the dead kids shot in Thurn. I don't have to imagine a minefield in Karkev, pale bodies mangled in the pale snow. I can just see my brother. Pretend it's another life, another world. A better one.

The moon above me blinks pleasantly in and out of focus, smiling down on laughter, memories, secrets. Slapping waves. Time twisting. Then the lights reflecting on water spiral outwards, little sparks in the black. Little fiery planes with wings lit up like matches at 3,500 feet.

I freeze.

Not tonight.

Please.

I reach for Ali desperately, anything to forget, to keep them away, and mercifully she curls near, pressed warm in my heart, her sweet smile more powerful than 3,500 feet. She's too bright. All the stars in her dark eyes. A thousand promises to count.

I return her smile, because she's here.

I feel her.

And I have to tell her who I am, but not with a stupid letter. She deserves my words, my voice, my mouth. I have to get to her, and in the fractured home of frantic dreams, I walk to her. I walk and I walk down an abandoned hall while the broken walls shrink on every side. No sign of Arrin or Kalt. Only Ali, waiting for me on the other side of that door. I know it, but I can't reach her, and panic grabs at me, the fiery planes exploding, the children dripping blood, the hours stretching into weeks, years, centuries, and then suddenly, it's only been a moment.

My eyes fly open to grey light.

I push up onto my elbows, disoriented.

Dawn.

Arrin's already wandering down on the shoreline, and Kalt leans against the cement post of the pier beside me. "We're a matching pair," he observes, eyes ringed red. "Impossibly in love."

"I'm not—"

"He told me the truth about Etania. About the princess. You're an idiot."

I'm too bleary and hungover to launch a defense.

"But don't let him trick you." His eyes fix on Arrin, who's looking for something, maybe a place to be sick. "He's hiding worse."

Kalt doesn't say anything else after that, loyal in his own way—or else vindictive—and the sun appears above the city at last, brilliant and blinding. Arrin holds out his hands, like he's determined to keep the day from starting all over again. Like he can hold it back just a while longer, to be tired and drunk and alone a few more hours yet.

But he can't.

And the eastern sun climbs.

3

⊰ Aurelia ⊱

Hathene, Etania

The week after the executions, our palace is silent and still, as it has been since the coup. Courtiers mourn the ones who were killed that night—Lord Marcin especially, since he was my mother's favourite advisor, and my father's boyhood friend. A man raised alongside a prince who never once spoke in envy or hungered for more.

But his daughter is different. She's made of another bone, filled with restless dreams, and we've spent these silent weeks as constant companions, both of us scared to be alone, both of us left untethered.

Longing to escape the persistent chatter of death, and the newly returned Ambassador Havis, I take Violet to the stables, to its safe realm of leather halters and creaking metal latches, the place that has always felt like my true home, but before I can lead Ivory from her wooden stall, Violet pushes past me. For the first time in her life, she throws her arms round my mare's neck—this creature she's never adored the way I have—and hugs tightly, her face buried in the sweet-smelling mane, grieving, surrendering to the exquisite gentleness of a horse.

I watch her a long moment and, as always, my guilt is a hot ember in my chest. Her father, her only family, was murdered at my masquerade, and the immense grief has turned her against herself, evenings spent second-guessing final decisions and last words.

I understand it too well.

"I'm sorry, Violet," I whisper. "I'll never forgive myself for what happened."

I haven't spoken this aloud yet. But it feels like time, at last.

Slowly, she releases Ivory and faces me, tears caught behind long lashes. A plain wool sweater hugs her luxurious curves, her rich auburn hair hanging limply against her hunched shoulders. "Oh, sweetheart," she says softly, "it wasn't your fault."

"No, a lot of things are my fault. Too many things. But I'm going to make it better. I promise."

Tears now hover behind my own eyes. I feel them, finally, after all these weeks of silent emptiness, a well of shame opened up and poured out at last. The apologies don't need to be made only to Violet, and that's why I have a mission before me. A plan. I'll take the photographs of the executed children and share them with the Royal League—the photographs from my cousin Lark which I used as blackmail against General Dakar, the vicious crime his own son carried out in Thurn—and perhaps there will be justice. I can undo my wrong of using them to save my family. I can make amends.

But Lark?

He'll never come back, no matter who I tell, no matter how many apologies I make, and my heart aches—never-ending.

Someone clears their throat nearby, interrupting our shared sorrow. I turn and find Reni standing in the alley, an uncomfortable expression on his face. For a long moment, his eyes are on Violet, searching for something I know he won't find. I've read the letters from her much older Safire officer, Captain Garrick Carr. He begs her to meet him in Landore, in its grand capital of Norvenne, says he'll meet her there and make good on his promise to find her an audition at the royal opera. Someone willing to sacrifice on her behalf. Someone who would break an order to get to her.

I only have the fading memory of a hurried kiss.

I shake myself from that pang, resisting the unbidden jealousy.

"Ride with me?" I ask my brother instead, to end the awkward stalemate between him and Violet. I'm not sure there's anything worse than watching two heartbroken people with old love hanging between them.

He nods, well aware this means I've more to share with him privately, and Violet honours the exclusory request. She touches her ivory hand to my amber one, then walks gracefully past Reni, avoiding his hopeful look. I know it isn't cruelty on her part. It's necessity, because in her fragile state, one sweet word from him might undo her resolve for her new beginning, far from here.

Reni's gaze fiddles with the alley floor a moment, his embarrassment evident.

"Get Liberty and we'll race," I suggest, to rescue him from himself. A familiar challenge, from days long ago, and I muster a smile. "I'll meet you by the gardens."

He nods, striding down the alley for his stallion, and by the time our horses are saddled and ready, a faint twinge of joy struggles to resurface in my chest, restive after these painful weeks. The air's crisp, the forest beckoning with lingering scarlet and gold. Liberty and Ivory dance beneath us impatiently. They're burning for this as well.

"To the meadow and back?" he asks, knowing our old routes.

By his lighter tone, I think he needs to be out here as badly as I do, chasing this mountain wind stamped into our souls.

He raises a gloved hand. "Ready, set . . ."

On *go*, we leap forward, Ivory untangling beneath me, the grass swallowing her hoofbeats, mane flying. I laugh into the fierce breeze, overwhelmed by the magnificence of it. The madness. We gallop over the river bridge, Liberty pounding at Ivory's side, more solid and muscled, at least a hand higher.

We're neck and neck as we head onto the wide, smooth path away from the palace.

With a smile, I half halt on the reins to warn Ivory, then press with my right leg. She obeys joyfully, darting off the trail in a sharp left turn, into the stark underbrush of the forest. It's another challenge, a shortcut to the meadow, and I expect Reni to follow. To accept the dare. But instead, the shadow of Liberty disappears into the distance, and it's only Ivory and I cantering onward, following the river, its swirls of black tinged with golden silt.

The colour of my eyes, Father used to say.

The place Athan and I explored together.

I allow myself a brief fantasy, conjuring the sound of his voice, the memory of him when we tipped our boat over and I was suddenly in love with the way he looked all wet—blond hair darker, grey eyes glimmering with captured water droplets, damp shirt sticking to shoulders and chest and arms. A sweet temptation of details. The outline always makes you wonder about the sketch in full colour, what's waiting below to be discovered. . . .

We hit the meadow in record time—Ivory tossing her nose happily at the beckoning open space—then turn and double back for home at an equally reckless pace. We're soon storming past the usual finish line, hidden behind the palace, where Mother can't see, and coming up behind the stables.

Reni is nowhere in sight.

Only dull grass and honey-coloured stones to greet us.

We've actually won—the first time in five years of rivalry!— and Ivory snorts, seeming to sense our victory as we hide within the elms, to give Reni the illusion of triumph before surprising him.

I glance at the trailhead, waiting.

It takes far longer than it should, and when Liberty finally appears, the truth arrives as well. They canter into the open at a careful pace, both horse and rider scanning the lumpen ground like it might reach up and bite them with teeth. My exultant joy dissipates. This isn't the same pair who charged through the Royal Chase last summer. Back then, they had no fear. They were both equally brave, Liberty leaping anything Reni pointed him at.

No longer.

I skirt behind them, hidden in the trees, then squeeze my heels into Ivory again. We gallop up as if we've only just arrived, breathless and sweating.

"You won!" I announce with a grin. "I knew the shortcut was a bad idea."

Reni looks over his shoulder at me, face pale and clouded. "That was a foolish move, Ali! You know there are holes off the main trails!"

"I was careful."

"And what if careful isn't enough?"

He's still rattled, taking no satisfaction in his victory, and I'm startled by his ashen cheeks. The genuine fear caught in his eyes. "I simply want to enjoy every piece of home that I can," I reply, softer. "Every perfect moment before it's gone. You understand that."

Reni's expression eases slightly. "I do. But you don't have to go through with this engagement, Ali. There's no reason to accept Havis's proposal, no matter what you might think. I'll speak for you."

"It's only for a time," I say, trying to reassure him as much as myself, but fresh bitterness returns. Reality can't be outrun, not even in this place I love with my whole heart. We're different now. All of us.

My brother clearly wants to press further, as he has these past weeks, but he already knows it's a fruitless offer. Deep down, I think he suspects that whatever happened the night of the coup is too dark for even him to stop. The things I did, the secrets I hold. The reason I must now go deal with our faraway family in Resya. Instead, he stares up at the rounded mountains, the same way he stared at Prince Efan's painting, like he might divine some mystical message there, in the rocky outcroppings and empty sky.

"It's all going to work out for the best," he tells me. "Havis has returned from Resya with good news. Everything that happened this summer will be forgotten. The Royal League rejected the Safire petition for war and your precious lieutenant will be safe. That's what will happen. You'll see."

The promises fall easily from his lips, because he has no idea what he's talking about.

"And the Nahir revolt?" I ask. "You think it will simply disappear across the sea if we ignore it long enough?"

"Well, perhaps if Seath were a bit more reasonable, a solution might be easier."

"And perhaps Seath is the *most* reasonable one," I tell him sharply, longing to add more, to tell him about Lark's mission. The mission that has now become my own. But my brother isn't ready for anything else, because to him, Seath of the Nahir means chaos and unrest. A silent enemy whose revolutionaries stir violence in the valuable territories the North claimed a century ago, sending young Northern soldiers back across the sea in caskets.

But he doesn't know that our cousin Lark was also Nahir, and Lark was *good*. He wanted peace and justice, the same as I do, and his sister in Resya will have answers. Lark knew the truth that no one else in the North does—that Seath is old and weary and wants to negotiate, and my mother can give him that chance. She's both Northern and Southern at once, the only one who could stand before the League—as their equal, with a crown on her head—and share the dark reality of what's happening to the people of the South. The lies and deception, the children murdered by Northern guns. She could bring everyone to the table of negotiation, invite justice once and for all. I'll finish Lark's mission like he asked me in his final letter.

I simply have to get to Resya.

But Reni throws me a pointed look. "Please don't turn into Mother right now, Ali. Controversy won't help our position, not after these executions."

His cold words are a reminder of which stance I supported before the Council.

The one in opposition to his own.

Before I can answer, though, a shadowy figure emerges from the stables. Ambassador Gref Havis. Tall and draped in a heavy tweed coat, he waves at us, a cigar glowing in his leather-clad hand.

Ivory tenses beneath me, sensing my own dread.

"Your beloved betrothed, freshly returned to you," Reni observes to me flatly. "Good luck with it."

And just like that, my brother's trotting Liberty away, leaving me to this fate I refuse to back down from. It's mine alone.

By the time Havis halts before Ivory, he's popped his collar to cover his ears, his feet stamping at the ground in chilled annoyance. He's a long way from the warm, lush mountains of Resya.

I raise my chin. "Is this an ambush?"

"Far too cold for that," he replies smoothly. "All of me is frozen, which gives you a decisive advantage."

I slide down from the saddle for the face-off. He's sporting his usual half beard, dark along his jaw, and smelling strongly of bergamot. Where Lark was shorter, with a clean-shaven face and an earnest countenance, Havis is roguishly attractive, wielding height and a sly presence that smirks in the corner.

I miss Lark—too terribly much.

"Be straight with me," I tell Havis. "Does my cousin's father believe it was suicide?"

I sound bolder than I feel. I don't let Havis see the pounding desperation in me to hear him say yes. To hear him say he's told no one about my terrible act, that he'll never mention it again, that I can't be a murderer because murderers must feel it in their hearts and I never wanted Lark dead.

But Havis only shrugs. "The truth won't change, Princess, no matter how many lies we decorate it with."

"You're right, Ambassador. Because I didn't kill him. You dealt the final bullet." My accusation works, and Havis looks a bit thrown, as if he hadn't expected I'd work out this little fact. "You put that gun to . . ."

I can't finish the sentence. It's scoured into my memory, the pistol against Lark's head. The earsplitting crack. The horrific scattering of blood and stars know what else. How easy and how monstrous death can be at once.

"Then it seems we both murdered a diplomatic ambassador," Havis relents after a moment. "We're in this together, Aurelia, and there's no going back. We take this one to our graves. If even a whisper gets out, they'll be telling our story for years to come—the bullet that launched an entire damn war, do you understand?"

I nod, seeing in Havis's measured precision the tenuous politics on every side. I killed a Southern ambassador who was also a revolutionary. If the truth slipped out, I'd have both the kingdom of Resya *and* Seath of the Nahir seething for amends. And yet I've also just gained a fraction of terrible power over Havis. It's in his cautious gaze, waiting for whatever move comes next. I'm not the same princess who faced off against him last spring. He knows that better than anyone.

"Take me to Resya," I say firmly. "To the capital."

"Why?"

"That isn't for you to know. In return, I'll accept your marriage proposal officially. I'll tell my mother only the best things about you. You'll stay in her good favour and have yourself a princess after all."

Interest grows in his gaze. He's a man of opportunity. And I'm an interesting opportunity.

But then he grins. "Actually, I don't want a little girl for my wife."

My cold hands make a fist, ready to hit him, to make him, for once, do the thing I expect, the thing I need. "Now you reject me? You don't want a stained gift, is that it?"

"I fired the killing bullet, not you."

I reach out and grab him tight. I feel like I'm all alone in a shifting place, nothing certain, and the one person who has an answer to it is as complicated and fickle as a mountain spring.

"You need to take me," I say, hating the desperate plea in my voice. "You're the only way."

He glances down at me, his brow rising quizzically. "What a strange world this is. Did you ever expect to be begging me to marry you?" He removes my hand from where I'm gripping his arm, putting space between us again. "Fine. I'll get you to Resya. But be warned, you might not like what you find."

"It's too late for that."

And it is. I see Lark standing in front of me, blood sputtering from his neck, his gaze a look of stunned betrayal. A question—*why?* He was the one who taught me how to fire the pistol. He taught me himself at the target range, not far from where Havis and I now stand.

My cousin. My friend.

I feel my vision wavering.

Tears.

"We'll go," Havis continues, peering down at me with evident concern now, "but first I have some news that might brighten your day. As it happens, I've arranged a parley in Landore, to bring Resya and the Safire to the same table. It was my king's wish that I do my part to set this business from the summer straight."

I blink away the sting in my eyes. "A *parley?*"

"Yes. General Dakar has already agreed to it, and as of this morning, so has your mother." He taps his cigar, embers scattering. "Though I think the Landorians are more interested in turning this into a ridiculous arms display. We'll take what we can get."

I can scarcely comprehend it.

A chance for peace.

For reconciliation.

STORM FROM THE EAST

"The General won't be there, though," Havis adds quickly, "so don't get any ideas. It will be his son."

My mouth falls open. "The *Commander*? No, he can't possibly—"

"Never. It's one of the other ones. The captain in the navy. The best option for this."

Havis sounds genuinely confident, and I remember he once told me this other son was the practical one, the one with the most sense. Which means he's trying to shift the right pieces into place, the right players. Ones who might listen and be reasonable. . . .

Stars. He can be useful!

Havis offers me his hand politely. "I suppose this make us allies?"

I ignore it. "Regrettable ones, if so."

He laughs, glancing to Ivory, patting her gently instead. "Pretty mare. But we'll get you a better one in Resya."

The dismissive comment reminds me of the truth. His handsome smile, his confidence, his quiet affection for horses—it's all a ruse, and I can never trust it no matter how contagious it may be. Havis strides at the edge of this complicated world, observing the chaos as though it will never hurt him personally. What a luxury he holds. To care for nothing, not truly. But I have far more at stake in this game, and our alliance will only last as long as Resya.

I take Ivory's reins, shoving past him.

"I don't want your damn horse."

Because once we're in Resya, I'm leaving him behind—for good.

4

Valon, Savient

Father never mentions our drunken night.

I'm sure he knew where we were. It's not hard to figure out when all three sons disappear together, staggering back at dawn. But he doesn't say a word, his steel focus entirely on the war he's about to launch. And as quietly as the loaded ships are sent out to sea, I send my first letter to Ali in months, the one I've been prolonging.

Both my letter and the ships share one unfortunate feature.

We're not exactly honest.

The ships' deadly cargo of tanks and artillery are bound, on paper, for our Landorian-approved army base in the territory of Thurn—conveniently located right next door to Resya. We've spent the past five months helping them "settle" the insurrection in Thurn stirred by the Nahir, a military presence that my father won through cold-blooded deception.

An insurrection he also secretly watered with arms.

Now, these ordinary supply routes are ones the Northern royals will expect. Nothing suspicious which might alert them to our amassing invasion force. And in a twist of my own precarious fate, I'm summoned to the main campaign briefing by Admiral Malek. It's the kind of elite gathering I'm not usually invited to, and it feels, for some reason, like a trap. But there's no turning down the grim-faced Malek—rather terrifying as he is—so I show up to Safire High Command, the stone building foreboding in the night lamps, a ghostly fortress. As I'm heading up the steps, I find another member of my family already being hauled out by Colonel Evertal.

"I'm in the army now," Leannya protests. "This is my right!"

Evertal looks down at her, exasperated. "Hardly. You're still in school and far too young for this."

"You helped Arrin when he was my age. Don't deny it."

"Exactly right," Evertal replies wryly. "And I can only handle one of you at once. Good night, little wolf." She glances at me, still stuck on the stairs in front of them. "Lieutenant."

She shuts the door on Leannya's indignant face.

My sister spins, a scowl wrinkling her nose. "She swore to let me in, Athan. She's a damned liar!"

Evertal might have promised, but I suspect there's a very good chance she caught one whiff of Father's displeasure in that strategy room and quickly reneged on whatever pact was made. He doesn't like Leannya involving herself—one of the few things he and I actually agree on.

"Try again for the next war," I offer brightly.

"Stop making jokes, Athan. It isn't right that he's sending all three of you at once and I can't even do my part. He gives me *nothing*."

She's talking about Father, and there's no choice but to distract her, to keep her from nurturing this bitter anger that has no resolution. Look at me. The weeks since the Etanian coup have been full tilt and I've been left adrift at the edge. His silence is the worst void. You just have to put on your most obedient face and say nothing except what he wants to hear, then hope you might win the stalemate.

"Since you're staying, perhaps you might watch over Katalin?" I suggest. "Teach her some Savien. Be a friend?"

"I don't trust her. I feel sorry for her, yes, but she hates us."

"Then there's your mission. Make her an ally."

My sister walked into that trap too perfectly. She grimaces, well aware what I've done, but spying on my frosty Karkevite girlfriend at least holds some level of intrigue. The possibility of secrets and hidden agendas.

"Excuse me," I say, gently pushing her aside, "I'm due to this death parley."

She relents with a sigh, but nudges my shoulder in solidarity as I pass.

Once through the door, I'm hit by a smog of suffocating smoke. Cigarettes burn as shoulders hunch over maps, fingers rattling through papers, the room filled with low conversation and strains of bravado. Everyone integral is present—Father and Malek and Evertal. Commander Vent and Arrin and Kalt. The Air Marshals of both the bomber and fighter squadrons. The Commodore of the fleet.

All of them—and then me.

Also Folco Carr. Not sure how he managed an invite, but there he is, seated in the corner, smoking, quiet as a red-haired fox.

I find a place as far off the main stage as I can get. Arrin gives me a brief nod, but Father offers nothing, and I'm suddenly not sure whose order brought me here.

A trap.

The briefing starts like usual, everyone staring at a map while the person in charge—in this case, Arrin—points and lays it all out. According to reconnaissance flights, he says, there's only one stretch of Resya's coast suitable for an amphibious landing, where the mountains recede slightly—and it's armed to the teeth. With the rising fear since Arrin's speech to the League when he pushed for military intervention, and the growing instability in Thurn, the Resyans have stepped up their defenses, walls of artillery fortifying every feasible invasion point. But they're focused mostly on their border with Thurn, because even they can't imagine someone being mad enough to simply storm in off the sea in plain sight of those who ruled against war.

Apparently, they haven't met my brother.

"It's a two-pronged attack," Arrin informs the room. "Both land and sea. We need their strength divided. Myself and Army Group East will be coming in from Thurn, while Commander Vent and Army Group North will use the fleet to come in from the coast. We're running an entire operation across the Black"—he waves at the map, at the vast sea between Savient and Resya—"and speed is paramount. Both armies will drive south and link up in the city of Irspen. Then it's on to the capital."

"I get to hit the fortified coast?" Vent enquires with no subtle sarcasm.

Arrin glances at him. "Losing your nerves of steel already?"

"Not me, but my divisions might, Commander. What if the Resyans have tricked us with—"

"Lieutenant," Arrin interrupts, "what's our most vital asset in this war?"

Silence. Feet shifting. I realize very late that there's only one lieutenant in the room and Arrin's looking right at me. Everyone else, too. Folco's expression is minor sympathy, like he knows I was trying to lie as low as him.

"Fighter planes?" I say, hoping this isn't going where I think it's going.

"With bombs?" Arrin presses.

"Yes . . . ?"

"Thank you, Lieutenant. And where would you put those fighters with bombs?"

Everyone stares. Father cocks his head, like he didn't expect this either. "Ahead of our lines," I venture. "A coordinated attack, since we can go higher than those mountains and also lower and faster than the bombers."

"There you go," Arrin says to the room. "No more letting the fighters play their own games up at 18,000 feet. I want planes down low where I can see them, and then I want the rest so far behind enemy lines that I can't. I want them targeting everything: bridges, trains, bunkers. A total destruction of enemy supply lines. Precision bombing to lead the infantry divisions. It's a new age of war, and fast, overwhelming air power is going to make this invasion possible."

The head of the fighter squadrons looks stunned. "But the ground fire and flak could—"

"It's what the army lives with every day," Arrin interrupts. "Welcome to combat."

No one can argue with that logic, but it also means a lot of fighters won't come back. All of air force leadership looks at me like I've just shot them in the back.

I'd like to tell them I was drunk and didn't mean to do any of this.

Arrin thrusts onward. "We open this with the naval fleet pummeling the coast and a round of bombing. General Windom has secured an island for the bombers to launch from and they can swing over at night, I presume?"

The Air Marshal of the bomber squadrons nods hesitantly. "Yes, sir."

Arrin snaps his fingers. "Good. Commander Vent, you get one night of spectacular firepower from the fleet and the bombers, then when day breaks you send four fighter squadrons ahead of your divisions and hit the beach running."

It's like Arrin's mouth can't keep up with his galloping thoughts. When he realizes everyone is still staring, half stunned, he holds up a hand, wiggling his fingers. "Let me make this clear: naval barrage, planes, soldiers, tanks. In that order."

Vent looks unconvinced. "And your Army Group East is simply waiting in Thurn to see if my opening gambit works?"

I realize, then, this might also be revenge on Arrin's part. He's bestowing Vent with what could be the worst thrust of the war, and now I really want to know the old drama between them.

"Neither will be pleasant," Arrin replies, an edge to his voice. "I don't get an entire fleet to barrage the border. When we invade, the fortifications will be fresh. Take your pick."

Vent's jaw ticks. "What if you don't make it to Irspen? What if those 'fresh fortifications' hold you back?"

"I'll be there. Give me two weeks."

"*Two weeks?*" Vent's laugh is incredulous. "You're hoping for the best at every stage! Let's not forget our little rebel friends in Thurn. God help us if they decide to put on a show in Resya."

With that, Vent's found his crowning moment of defiance. The tiny room of elite military staff stumbles to a stunned, collective silence, cigarettes and pens paused in frozen hands. Everyone here knows the truth—that we've armed the Nahir behind the Landorians' back, the quiet exchange of guns and bullets and even planes—but it's never spoken aloud like this. It's a classified state secret. A necessary evil for the greater good. Not a threat to be wielded against anyone named Dakar.

"Commander Vent." Father's voice is low. "Are you no longer so invested in your role for this campaign?"

"General, I'm asking legitimate questions. I've been in Thurn, and I know the damage they can do for the sake of our pretend show and—"

"There's no need for questions," Father interrupts. "In fact, forget Army Group North. You'll take the Seventh Armoured instead and provide support to my son."

Vent's mouth falls open.

"Colonel," Father says.

He doesn't look at Evertal, but she knows he's addressing her. She puts out her cigarette quickly and stands, walking through the gathered uniforms to the map. "Yes, General?"

"Take North."

She nods.

And just like that, Arrin's been outfoxed. Perhaps it's a long overdue punishment, for all those parties that have teetered too close to the edge. Or perhaps it's only an inevitable twist. My father loves to make people sacrifice, and Evertal is nearly closer to Arrin than Mother ever was. She raised him to this, trained him.

And now she's inherited the revenge that was meant for Vent.

Arrin slaps the map. "No, I'll take North."

Father raises a brow. "You want the coast?"

"It was my idea."

"Very well." There's a flicker of dark amusement on Father's face.

I watch as my brother paces, his brain rapidly taking stock of his new situation, determined to make declarations and keep them. I can practically see him searching for a way to be the best. To not let Father win.

I don't know why, but it's kind of pitiful.

"Commander, you only have four squadrons for taking the coast," I observe, eyeing Moonstrike squadron's place on the map, on the border with Thurn. The place Garrick and Cyar and the rest of us have been shoved by air force brass.

Arrin glances over, as if my chair just spoke. "Your point, Lieutenant?"

"Our fighters carry a single load each."

He looks confused.

"They're not *bombers*," I say bluntly. "Why don't you put Moonstrike in the sea assault as well, concentrate more fighters ahead of the landing?"

I might have just volunteered Garrick for this nightmare, but since I'm probably already dead, what difference does it make? Hopefully Garrick doesn't go back to hating me entirely.

Father gives the barest nod.

Initiative.

"Yes," Arrin mutters. "That could be helpful."

It's not quite a compliment, but something, and at least now he knows our fighters aren't miracle weapons. He's going to need a lot of us if he plans to beat Evertal to his target city of Irspen. And as I watch my pacing brother, I can't help but wonder if he came up with this whole thing while drunk off his feet on a lonely stretch of shoreline.

An endless night, racing the sun.

Since Father's silence means approval, no one else contests. Boots shuffle out the door. Vent takes his wounded ego and a fresh cigar. Only a few remain, and Father drops a folder on the desk in front of Arrin, who quickly busies himself signing away our fates.

Then Father motions for Kalt. "You're going to Norvenne," Father informs him. "The Landorian royals want a summit and we have essential communiqués which must be retrieved from Resya. Distract them and buy us time."

"For how long, sir?"

"Until we have those documents from Havis in hand."

Kalt shifts, a hint of concern flashing. Contained. "But I'll need to return to the *Pursuit*." He gestures at the map. "The fleet will—"

"Yes."

"You don't need the *Pursuit*, then?"

"No, I do. But you're no longer on the *Pursuit*."

There's a brutal pause. I feel the fist of that declaration on my own face.

"Not on it?" Kalt repeats, his voice holding a trace of panic.

He's been on that ship for five years. He bleeds for that ship. And Folco's there.

"I'm transferring you to the *Warspite*," Father explains. "Once you've finished the parley, you'll be reassigned."

Folco fumbles his cigarette, then retrieves it from the wood floor quickly.

I've never seen Kalt pale, not quite like this, and my anger flares hot on his behalf. I remember finding him and Folco on the *Pursuit* last summer. They're happy—they get along well, quietly in the background—and only one person would meddle with that for no other reason than because he *can*. I glare at the source, furious that I actually felt sorry for him a few minutes ago. But Arrin won't look up. He's signing papers.

I want to drop him onto a mountain and light him in flames.

Helpless to the order, Kalt backs away from Father, and Folco stands. They leave together.

Father motions for me next, and I walk over, struggling to douse the anger. "You see how it is here," Father says to me. "Your brother is the God of War, and what he says, you do. When I'm not there, you never question him. Do you understand?"

He doesn't mean Kalt.

"Yes, sir."

I see exactly how it is.

Once everyone's trickled away, only a haze of smoke left behind, I stand in front of Arrin, who's still seated at the desk. I want to grab him and tell him what a bastard he is. I want to tell him he has even less loyalty than me, betraying the brother he used to love. It was always Arrin and Kalt. Sneaking their bottles, a thousand stories I'll never know. But he stops what he's doing and looks up.

His eyes hold no defense.

"My whole damn invasion relies on you idiots in the sky," he says, "so you sure as hell better keep up to me."

II

ALLIES

Dear Athan,

I'm not going to mention the fact that I still have no address from you and my stack of waiting letters daily grows. I'll spare you this time. Instead, I'd like to tell you that I'm currently flying in my very first aeroplane—and <u>I positively hate it.</u>

What is your expression right now? Entirely horrified? The earth below is far too small and with all this rattling and occasional swooping from side-to-side, I rather feel this could be the last letter I ever write you. How do you do this every day? How do you find this fun?!

I suppose it must be the sky. The shaking metal and ungodly height aside, the sky itself is a truly breathtaking sight to behold—I won't deny it. The clouds are sun-dappled and smudged together, like paint on canvas, and the colours keep growing richer the closer we come to sunset. I feel I could lose myself right into the feathery swirls. A heavenly kingdom that goes up and up and up . . .

So, for you alone, I might endure this experience again in the future.

If you insisted.

I should point out that flying isn't the only thing I'm willing to weather for your sake, Athan. I've also displayed a remarkable resistance to each argument made against my affection for you (of which my mother has many) and have only come out more convinced of it. You see, she thinks that what *we shared this summer was only an infatuation and she's glad it's over. She's glad I've chosen to be reasonable and move on, because (she says) unless you choose to remove your uniform and never wear it again, I'll only be hurt in the end. You'll already be dead. A boy who can be ordered and broken.*

But she doesn't understand how I can't even bear to think that! Your mad love of this hideous flying aside, the idea of you dead is like the roots of my very soul being torn up. Even if we someday outgrow this "infatuation," I know it won't ever truly be over, not even when I'm old, because you'll forever represent the spirit of the very sky to me. No one can kill the sky. No one can shrink it back down to the earth. I need to believe there are some things in this world which can't be stolen from it. Some wild and breathless realms, too high to touch, even by war, and you are one of them—always.

Now look at all these poetics you're missing out on.

Send me an address. Please.

Ali

5

⊰ AURELIA ⊱

Norvenne, Landore

"And who, pray tell, is this obnoxious one? Some king who died *twice* in battle?"

Havis's sardonic question is muttered under his breath, prompted by a nearby statue of a rather large and vainglorious rider on horseback. It's mottled by age and salty air, as are the giant carved lions towering over the marble pavilion we stand on, the Black Sea sprawling before us. Both Havis and I have been entirely forgotten by the huge crowd gathered on this balcony. The bloated pageantry of the day is dazzling in its scope with banners fluttering, instruments playing, and what seems to be an entire naval fleet lurching through the waves below. Destroyers, cruisers, battleships. It's a grand show of death in the harbour, and everyone else is riveted, none more so than King Gawain of Landore, who's quite happy to remind everyone of his supreme reign on both land and sea.

There's only one true empire left in this world—and it belongs to him.

"If it was possible to come back from the grave and enjoy a second glorious death," I say drily, "a Landorian would find a way to do it."

Havis snorts. "Or perhaps any Northern king in general."

A volley of shots explodes from a ship, ringing in my ears, and the crowd applauds happily.

"There used to be ruling queens," I inform Havis over the

noise. "Before Prince Efan. I'm fairly certain it was a much better time."

"You clearly don't know the same women I do," he replies with a grin.

I roll my eyes, glancing over to where Mother and Reni are keeping vigil with King Gawain and his gaggle of Landorian officials. The King beams beneath a regal beard and wolfish brows, puffed up on the sight of his own splendid navy. Mother is patiently enduring it all, nodding at his monologues from time to time, an unreadable mask on her face. And Reni looks appropriately intrigued, smiling often, though since I know he's mostly here to meet with Gawain and establish himself as the soon-to-be King of Etania, I'm not convinced how genuine his enthusiasm is.

And then there's the General's son. He's tall and thin-faced beside Gawain, dressed in a grey Safire uniform with red stripes on each shoulder, appearing impassive to the display in the harbour. Dark chestnut hair matches his father's, his pale cheeks ruddy in the breeze, and from what I gathered in the few moments of introduction before this show began, he operates with a dull, nearly monotonous voice that's so unlike the Commander's it defies belief. Since Havis and I are now relegated to our place on the sidelines, under the guise of a happy couple betrothed, I can only watch from a distance. It's a miserable charade. But at least we can comment on the entire spectacle without being overheard.

Leaning against the pavilion's railing, I venture with, "Do you still think the General's other son is the more sensible one?"

Havis copies my repose. "Why do you ask?"

He's clearly suspicious, and has been since I insisted he take me to Resya, but I resist his wary appraisal. He can't yet know of the wild, new idea that sprouted in my head during our flight here. If there's even a whisper of a possibility that the General's second son is the more reasonable one, as Havis suggested, then he might hold value for the mission Lark has left in my hands. An unexpected opportunity.

"In these weeks since the coup," I reveal carefully, "I've realized that exposing the truth is quite a powerful tool. The night of the masquerade, something happened which altered the course of the nightmare. And it wasn't with a gun."

Havis tilts his head. His black hair's windblown, strands beginning to curl at his neck in the damp air. "What did you do?"

"Not me," I lie, since he still has no idea what took place in the throne room, my blackmail against the General. "But my brother, he rallied a whole kingdom with only a radio address, and—"

I'm interrupted by a thunder of propellers overhead. Two full Landorian squadrons of fifteen aeroplanes fly past, and from the western sea, an enormous battleship appears, cutting through the waves despite its impossible size. Heavy and squat in the middle, it's over twice the length of any other ship present—and fiercely decorated with giant guns.

Its presence earns an eruption of applause and whistles. The *Northern Star*. The Landorian fleet's flagship is often featured in countless newspapers and pranced about like a prize horse before the cameras, but seeing it in person is something else entirely, and my stomach turns with strange dread. It seems large enough to swallow the coastline whole.

When I glance again at Gawain, he's grown rosy cheeked with satisfaction, nudging a bearlike balding officer who's appeared beside him. They both, rather indiscreetly, investigate the General's son to catch his reaction.

Captain Dakar reveals nothing. In fact, his gaze—part perturbed, part disinterested—is so magnificently his father that it eliminates any doubt about where he came from.

"That's General Windom," Havis says, nodding at the balding man. "The Saviour of Thurn or the Butcher of Thurn, depending on who's telling the story."

"Butcher?" I repeat.

He shrugs. "Rumours. Or maybe not. I dare not mention them here. But this ship they're so proud of, I'd wager it alone is worth the cost of your palace. There's a lot of money sitting in this harbour."

"You sound intrigued," I observe flatly.

"No. I don't deal in arms, Aurelia. That's not going on my conscience." He gestures at the *Northern Star*. "This damn creature could unleash twenty tons of deadly steel in a single minute, with a firing range of seventeen miles. You'd be sunk before you even saw it coming! It's a ship of death. And if I had to guess, I'd imagine it's meant to leave a rather strong impression on anyone Safire who might be watching."

I raise a brow. "They want to impress the General's son? Are they worried?"

"Worried might be an understatement. And impress is too friendly."

Everyone else cheers again as the monstrous battleship blasts its horn, reverberating off the pavilion walls, and Havis gives me a dark smile. "What were you saying about the truth being a powerful tool?"

I glare at him. I know he doesn't believe my words are enough to tackle this brewing tension, but that's because he doesn't have the imagination for it. He doesn't care the way I do— desperate, in the deepest place of my heart, to find a better way forward.

And this is why he'll never win.

"You'll see soon enough," I reply between gritted teeth, glancing at the Captain, more determined than ever to do what I must. "And friends in high places are always helpful."

Havis shakes his head. "Stars, Aurelia. The General's son isn't going to play for *you*. Never expect anything in return from the one who has the most to gain."

I look out at the steel-coloured sea, a dozen deadly ships swirling in the harbour, and I know what I might accomplish with this alliance. It's the promise of atonement for my sin. The promise of a world where horror cannot be unleashed without consequence. Where justice—not power—reigns and never again will children be shot before a damn wall.

"Perhaps," I say, turning from Havis, "I'm the one who has the most to gain."

6

Valon, Savient

Without any fanfare, our warships glide out of harbour and into the Black Sea. Here and then gone, bearing weapons and men and tanks, their hulls emblazoned with names like *Triumph* and *Victory* and *Fury*.

On the night Father orders the *Impressive* south, the night of my scheduled embarkment, the Moonstrike squadron assembles on the pier near an aircraft carrier called the *Intrepid*. The dock bustles with activity, glassy black water catching sparks of light from flashlights and cigarettes as our fighter planes are secured carefully onto the runway of the massive ship. Major Torhan, our old instructor from the Academy, is waiting for us. He's been promoted to Group Commander for our sector of the campaign, and he greets the arriving squadron pilots with a curt nod. They all graduated from his school, the very best. Captain Lilay of Lightstorm—the sole woman to hold the rank, tiny and serious with a gleam of chin-length black hair— Garrick Carr, Ollie Helsun, Sailor, the rest of the Moonstrike pilots we've been flying with since last summer. But Torhan doesn't meet anyone's eye as he makes count, simply checks off names on a clipboard.

"Lieutenant," he greets me, his efficient presence reassuringly familiar.

"Congratulations on the promotion, sir," I say quickly, since this is an impressive rise—from heading the Academy to commanding battle squadrons.

"Thank you, Lieutenant. Now bring your first officer." He nods at Cyar. "There's someone to meet before you board."

I share a glance with Cyar, then shrug and follow Torhan like the old days. No questions asked. To our left, the *Intrepid* lurches in its berth, taunting me with the promise of cramped days at sea. "Since you're on track for your own squadron, Lieutenant," Torhan says over his shoulder, "it's essential—particularly in war—to find you a non-commissioned officer to train up as well. We usually try to promote from within the squadron, but in your case, we thought it best to assign someone with genuine talent to complement your own. And straightaway."

I stop looking at the ship. A bit of suspicion coils. "Who is it?"

"Trigg Avilov."

I rack my brain, sifting through the other pilots who graduated last spring. I didn't have many friends among them, but I knew their names. All the ones who claimed top score after testing and joined the fighter squadrons as officers in training. No one was named Avilov.

"Did he graduate a different year, sir?"

"No, no." Torhan stops. "He never went to the Academy."

Cyar looks dumbfounded. I'm sure I do, too.

"He's a remarkable pilot," Torhan continues firmly. "Truly talented. We haven't promoted him yet, since he lacks the Academy qualifications, but I'm hoping under your guidance on the frontlines he'll be there soon enough. He's your match, Lieutenant."

Suddenly, I'm thinking not to like him. Petty, yes, but the praise irks.

"Then why isn't he in line for a squadron?" I ask, not caring how it sounds.

Torhan pauses. "He doesn't have quite the same instincts for leadership. Not yet, at least. Why don't you meet him?"

He points to a brown-haired kid about our age lounging on the ropes, bag at his feet and uniform unbuttoned most of the way. He's alone, staring at the *Intrepid* with a standoffish gaze. Taunting the salty beast right back.

"Avilov!" Torhan calls.

The boy stands—rather slowly—and saunters over. With his uniform sleeves rolled up, his tanned forearms show off tattoos, shadowy in the lamplight, and he stares at us while we stare right back. This entire thing is as bizarre and unexpected as my engagement to Katalin.

Torhan says he'll leave us to get acquainted before we board, and I'm fairly certain he senses the awkwardness. He loves to make the most of uncomfortable situations. Encouraging growth.

I offer my hand diplomatically once we're on our own. Cyar does the same. Trigg accepts both with an off-kilter grin, the kind that doesn't warm me any faster.

"Where did you learn to fly?" I enquire. That seems a good place to start.

"Flew cropdusters on my family's farm in Brisal," he replies. "My uncle contracts with the navy and saw my talent. Had me test for the Air Force. They were so impressed they put me through a quick summer course. Got to do lots of those"—he mimics a circle with a hand—"what do you call them?"

Good God.

"A wing-over?" I suggest.

"Yes. That. A hell of a lot of fun, and they said I had the best damn aim they'd ever seen." His grin radiates something very close to smugness. "Can't wait to try out a real twenty-millimeter cannon."

Cyar frowns. "It's not so easy when another plane is firing back at you, rookie."

A bold jab, considering Cyar's never even shot anyone down yet, but I don't let on.

"Don't doubt it," Trigg says, not seeming a fraction worried. His eyes take in Cyar, the copper skin darkened after nearly a month at home in Rahmet. "Be honest, ace, how much did *you* pay to be his first officer?"

Cyar appears blindsided. "I'm sorry?"

"A Rahmeti kid with the General's son? You're here for a reason. What is it? Higher wage? Quicker promotion?"

I'm not sure who looks more appalled by the suggestion—me or Cyar.

I want to throttle him, but Cyar's better than that. "We've been flying together since the beginning, and I graduated with *second* highest score at the Academy. I'm here for myself."

His clipped reveal makes Trigg pull a face that's either genuine surprise or veiled mockery. "Right. Though it's not like first place was a surprise going to *him*."

He says it like I'm not even standing there, and I'm actually speechless.

"Listen," I finally say. "You can't just—"

"Oh, don't worry," Trigg interrupts. "I get it. For the record, I didn't want to be assigned to you either. I've got a friend in the Skypirate squadron. That's where I asked to be. You really think I'm excited about being wingman to *you*? I sure as shit am not! It's a goddamned suicide position, benefits aside."

He adds a few more creative curses after that, the kind Arrin would find endearing, then stomps for the gangway.

What the actual hell?

"Hang on," I call, marching after him.

"I'm requesting a transfer," he announces. He doesn't look back. "And I'm hungry."

"You won't get it."

"They don't have food on these ships?"

"I meant the transfer."

He turns. "Well, god*damn*."

The sailors on the dock pretend to keep loading things, but I catch them grinning at one another like the nosy rats they are. Gleeful at the unexpected nighttime entertainment. Trigg's in over his head if he thought there was even a chance of transfer.

And just like that, the preposterous situation finally comes into better focus.

A test.

"You think you're the best?" I hear Father asking me. *"You think you can handle anything? Then here's the first member of your squadron. A farm kid with no formal training, no Academy wings—and he might even be better than you."*

It's exactly what Father would do. After all, he did make me train under Goddamn Garrick Carr.

I cross my arms. "You got yourself into this. You volunteered."

"I know." He glares at me, as if it's my fault. "And you have no idea how important this is to my family. I need this."

His hand fidgets near one of his tattoos, a rabid-looking squirrel, and the gesture's childish enough it flattens my hostility slightly. Sometimes I forget. I forget what it's like for everyone not born into my family, the ones like Cyar, who join up not because it's in their blood, but because to be a Safire officer is to have a prestige and status that probably doesn't exist anywhere else on the flat, dusty farms far from Valon.

And I think it cost Trigg something to admit it to me.

"You have good aim?" I ask reluctantly.

"The best."

"Then we'll be glad to have you." They aren't the words I want to say, but I say them anyway.

"Thanks, *Captain*," he replies, not even trying. A crinkle of smugness reappears. He eyes Cyar again, in the distance. "Besides, you need some Brisali talent to balance your future squadron out."

It finally clicks.

Savient. Rahmet. Brisal.

The three united regions of our nation.

I sigh. "I hope your aim is as good as your mouth, Avilov."

"Definitely, Captain."

"Don't call me that. I'm a lieutenant."

Trigg grins again, fully restored. "But not for long, Captain." He glances behind me. "And hey, I think your papa wants to see you. If he gives you some good money for the crossing, let me know. I love playing cards!"

I turn, and sure enough, there's Father standing beside a black automobile parked along the pier. He waves for me.

"Ask for at least a hundred," Trigg whispers right in my ear.

And just like that, Garrick Carr has lost his title to God-damn Trigg Avilov.

7

Norvenne, Landore

Nighttime at Gawain's home is overwhelming in its opulent silence. A palace far larger than our own, filled with endless, twisting halls and glittering mirrors, and I've become disoriented twice already. In my guest room, shadows darken the gilded frames and wood-paneled walls, soft lamplights tickling brass trim. Somewhere, Reni's attending a diplomatic function with Mother—no doubt hoping to achieve a private audience with Gawain—but I feigned an illness to avoid the entire thing. I'm truly not in the mood to entertain Havis in front of everyone again, and more importantly, I need to determine how I'll get the General's son alone.

I have six days.

And that needs a strategy behind it.

Nearby, Violet studies the local train schedules, preoccupied because she's going to make her escape at last. I invited her along to Norvenne under the pretense of giving her a change of scenery, but secretly, it's a chance for her to stay here until her Safire Captain comes to make good on his ardent promises.

While she dreams up her new future, I sit by the window, mulling over what to do next. Havis's observation during the naval display has me worried, his unsettling and urgent suggestion that Landore is growing suspicious of Safire ambition. Though the Royal League's verdict against the war in Resya proved Gawain's inclination to protect his royal brother, King

Rahian, I still can't rest easy, because I know the lurking truth—
that even if Rahian himself doesn't support the Southern revolts against Landorian power, his kingdom still holds Nahir
sentiment like the Safire Commander claimed. It held Lark.
Who knows how many other Resyans profess allegiance to
Seath? And what will Gawain do when he discovers that?
Endorse a Safire intervention after all? Or will he try to take
matters into his own hands, shoving the Safire out of the
way?

Stars.

Everything feels perched on a precipice! It can't get to that
point of heated confrontation. There must be a way to diffuse
the situation. Instinctively, I touch the amber stone at my neck
for reassurance, the one Athan gave me. Outside my window,
the glamorous streets of Norvenne sprawl lamplit and ethereal,
an elegant sea of tiny sparks beneath the moon, and I count the
rising stars above, imagining I can use them to map my way
back to him, to some place where only he and I will be, far
away from this madness, only us.

I pull out paper and pen.

"This is really a rather long time for you to be silent," I write as
fervent distraction, *"and I'm beginning to think you do, in fact,
have a girlfriend in Savient. She's discovered us, hasn't she? You're
home and now in trouble. I have it half in mind to come there myself and duel her with pistols."*

I almost add that I have good aim, then am horrified by my
own dark humour.

*"No, I hate the very idea of guns. Instead, I think I'll have to lure
you back through other means. Might a kiss work? Or two? I promise with a bit of practice, I'll become quite good. There's nothing I
can't improve on when I put my mind to it. In fact, if you'd let me
practice on you, I'd put even more than my mind to it."*

I feel my cheeks tingling, confessing things I'd certainly
never say aloud to him, but it feels safer in ink, unspooling
these lovely ideas that have tempted me ever since his mouth

captured mine during the coup. A desire I can't stop, not even with the looming uncertainty on every side.

A giggle interrupts my most lurid thought mid-sentence.

I cover the letter with my elbows, mortified, and Violet beams over my shoulder. "Don't stop. It's getting good!"

"You're such a spy!"

"No, it's perfect. Though maybe you could mention his—"

"Ssshh!" I order, ending the letter exactly where it is and signing quickly. When Athan and I began writing each other in the summer, back when I had an address to send these to, I started adding a little extra heart buried in the flourish of my signature, though I'm not sure he's ever noticed. They're like my kisses on the seal—a secret, just for me.

I frown at the grin still on Violet's lips. "You have more to add?"

She holds up a small brown package. "Heathwyn had me bring this for you," she confesses. "She hid it away for a week, but felt too guilty to keep it any longer."

The plainness of the package connects to Violet's guilty expression, and I snatch it, overwhelmed to find familiar, untidy lettering.

Athan's messy scrawl.

Stars, my governess is a crafty one! She's determined to keep herself innocent of this friendship my mother disproves of, but I'm already delirious from the words I haven't read, imagining the way they'll taste, drinking them up, dizzying with relief. I tear open the letter, reaching in and finding a photograph. My smile nearly aches. After two months, the sight of Athan Erelis, even in black and white, is infinitely better than my fading memories. It's a portrait. He's serious—too serious for him— but it's his face, in uniform and Safire cap, epaulets and insignias across his chest that mean things I don't know. I only know they make him look older, more important. I wish he was smiling in the picture.

I turn it over, and the back says, *"Eyes on the horizon."*

There's another paper in the package and I pull it out, desperate for the words, the words that are everything I need. . . . But it's a sketch. Athan's usual style—dark shading where he pressed down with his charcoal, parts smoothed away with an eraser—of a kestrel holding a crown.

It's the Resyan royal crest.

Disappointment grows, and Violet's face mirrors mine, the realization that there are no other papers. No letters. It's only a portrait of him and a sketch—a sketch that makes no sense. It isn't something poetic or tied to us. It isn't our mountain. Our shared story. It's simply . . . a crest. I sit down on the bed, heart heavy, clutching the photograph, and drop the package beside me unceremoniously. It hits with a thud.

Confused, I reach in deeper, my fingers grazing something smooth and cool.

I tug it out and open my hand.

A bullet.

It gleams merrily beneath the lights, like it's happy with its dark purpose, and I stare at the portrait, then the Resyan sketch, then the grey bit of lead sitting in my palm, trying to see what Athan is saying. Trying to understand . . . And then I know.

I know.

I look up at Violet, horrified. "When did Heathwyn say this arrived?"

She frowns. "A week ago?"

I don't explain anything else. I simply run for the gala about to begin.

8

Valon, Savient

Father has me sit in the automobile with him while the final cargo is loaded onto the *Intrepid*. It's beginning to rain, a dreary night fog pushing in from the sea, and for a long moment, he's focused on some transcript in front of him—reading, his usual way of making everyone else seem like an afterthought even after a direct invitation from him. By the faint smile on his face, I'm guessing the cable's from his Landorian ally, General Windom. Windom devised a perfect distraction for us today, luring everyone in the North away from the scent of war, buying us time while we prepare to invade. His parade of Landorian ships culled all the deadliest ones from the Black for a weeklong display in Norvenne.

And I have to admit, it encourages me to know Windom is still on our side, unafraid of the historic gamble we're about to make. He believes our allegations against Rahian—and he's happy to see the man deposed. Maybe this war will be short and easy after all. A brief nightmare, and then escape.

Freedom. Mountains.

Ali.

"You look excited to leave," Father finally observes, seated at my right. Apparently, I'm smiling a bit. "Arrin left today on the *Impressive*, and I hope to God he stays there until we've at least secured the beachhead."

"He's bold, sir. Not stupid."

"Usually." Father studies my face. "What do you think of Katalin Illiany?"

Of course this isn't the friendly goodbye I'd hoped for. There's always something else, and it's a cruel place to begin, since he still hasn't admitted the truth to me—that I'm the bait and reward. But I keep my face obedient. "Arrin said her father won us a corner of Karkev. They were good allies for you."

"A corner? It was a hell of a lot more than that. Listen, Athan," he says with cold precision, and I know I'm going to get a lecture I don't want to hear. "War is never the final goal. We want to see these regions thrive independently again, build a lasting alliance. But we're also the outsiders. The victors. They need their own leader at the helm, someone who's loyal to us. That's who Governor Illiany is in Karkev." He pauses, glancing at the closed car door. "And that's who Seath will be for us in the South, once we've finished there. Do you see what I'm saying?"

I nod. A powerful and loyal ally in the South is the ideal for my father. No costly occupying force necessary. Just blissful trade of wealth for years to come, Seath and my father crowning themselves as the new kings of the modern world.

"Karkev isn't Savient," he finishes. "Marriages and family connections mean something there, at least for the time being."

And with that, he's acknowledged my status as bait without actually saying it.

"For the time being?" I ask, grasping that single sliver of hope.

He gives me a look. "As long as it's deemed necessary."

Maybe a longer war is better.

For me.

"Sir, may I be honest?" I ask hesitantly.

Father's expression narrows, and it's clear he doesn't quite know what to expect from me these days, the star traitor. "Yes. If you'll stop looking at me like a kicked dog."

I quit the ingratiating act. "I'm not trying to be Vent," I

explain preemptively, "but I keep hearing stories from Thurn, and I know the Nahir are doing a good job of pretending to be our enemy. I know it's fake. But it's also real."

It's real, because I remember the bullets hammering my own wings last summer. An entire charade I was oblivious to—but it had deadly consequences.

3,500 feet.

"They're not going to bother us in Resya," Father replies. "You don't need to worry. You just need to fly."

Wouldn't that be nice?

"But I'm supposed to keep pretending they're our enemy," I press, "even though they're *not*?"

"You'd better, or I'll put a gun to your head myself."

I think that was his attempt at a joke, barely, and I must look pathetic enough because Father frowns, shifting on the leather seat. "Son, I know war is hell. I've lived it myself, in the thick of it. But this world has endured royal arrogance long enough. A true change is essential, for the greater good, and any sacrifice will be worth it. We'll keep the Nahir as our perceived enemy for as long as it remains helpful, so that these kings are always scared of the shadows. But once we have Resya, there will be no more royals in the South—the first step towards independence there. Seath has ensured that Rahian will be found as guilty as we said he was, and even better, his guilty trail with the Nahir will lead right back to the Queen of Etania." He smiles thinly. "Sinora won't slither her way out of that trap as easily as the coup. Another game ended. At last."

I ignore his deeply gratified expression, this vision of his greatest enemy's downfall. "Seath has evidence against her?"

"More than you can imagine. I told you before—their quarrel goes back far longer than mine, and even I don't dare step into it."

I struggle to follow, my brain working to fit these moving pieces together. I believe my father's trying to do something right in the South for once. Give it freedom, a chance to recover from decades of imperial trespassing. But it's a mad way to go about it, allying with Seath, and I can only see two versions of the future, neither of which are particularly appealing for me personally.

One has us invading Resya, an entire kingdom resisting our advance—war unlike anything I've yet endured—and at the end, Rahian is convicted of aiding the Nahir revolution, a trap which entangles Sinora Lehzar to her doom as well. Two guilty royals. Traitors to the North. And I lose Ali altogether, because I'm the pathetic son of the man who ruined her mother, a man who's now happily controlling Resya, his first territory in the South, while his ally Seath is one step closer to removing all Northern royal influence from the region.

The other version has all of the same war horrors, except in this one, the Landorians consider our invasion of Resya a massive betrayal after their League verdict against it—never mind what Windom says—and they come to their fellow king's rescue. We're forced to fight the greatest empire in the entire world, plus their allies, and it won't be a short war. It'll be a duel to the absolute death. And I still don't have Ali.

Sometimes, I wish I was actually Athan Erelis. I wish I knew none of this and just had to fly.

"Do we have an understanding then?" Father asks me expectantly.

I nod, even though we don't.

I need cards back.

"Good. Then that's the last I'll speak of this." He means I better stop asking questions. "And I do hope the Princess honours the understanding she and I made as well."

My stomach tightens. "What?"

He waves. "With the photographs from Beraya. I'm not sure whose idea that was"—he gives me a pin-sharp look—"but regardless, she'd best keep her side of the bargain and hide those forever. It would be a shame to try both mother and daughter before the League as defenders of the Nahir."

It takes me a horrified second to rally my voice enough to speak. "She'll honour her word, sir."

"Sinora's daughter?" Father gives me a disbelieving smile, then checks his watch. "I believe the *Intrepid* leaves in twenty minutes. Good luck, son." I reach for the car door, but Father puts a hand on my shoulder first. "And don't let Arrin off that ship before they secure the beachhead."

At least he's worried about one of us.

9

Norvenne, Landore

I'm not entirely sure what I'll do when I arrive to the reception, since I already announced I didn't wish to attend, but here I am anyway. Not to mention, I was supposed to strategize my first encounter with the General's son, a flawless negotiation, but all of that's gone up in smoke and I don't care. I'll march right up to him if I must.

Music murmurs from behind the elegant doors of the grand ballroom, the sight beyond familiar to me—tables dressed in ivory, crystal goblets shimmering, footmen tiptoeing here and there amidst candelabras and jewels and false laughter. And I, Aurelia Isendare, Princess of Etania, shall march inside and demand an audience with the duplicitous Captain Dakar while decorated in nothing more than my nightdress.

I steel my nerves to do it, determined, but another door, farther down the hall, bursts open abruptly. I startle, overwhelmed by the sudden urge to throw myself behind the nearest potted plant.

This was a truly terrible idea!

But then—stars in heaven, it's the *Captain*. He's moving with impressive speed away from me, his uniformed shoulders hunched, and right behind him trails a young woman with radiant red hair.

Taking this as a sign from Father above, I chase after them both.

I can't hear what the woman is saying, but it's evident she's in pursuit as well, and whatever she's trying to share, the Captain refuses to listen. After an animated display of hands on her part, followed by the unfortunate verdict of "You're just like your brother!" she spins on a heel and clicks the opposite way down the golden hall.

The Captain stares after her, then pushes through a pair of double doors to an outdoor balcony.

Guilty dog.

I race after him, reaching the doors—all glass, so the view of the Black remains glorious—and shove them open. Outside, a few brave guests stroll in the night air as I hurry down the walkway, arms wrapped about myself, checking every alcove, finding him finally at the farthest end. He's smoking alone with desperate dedication.

"Captain Dakar!" I call, more bitterly than I intend.

He turns with a start. Surprise pinkens his cheeks in the palace glow, and I try to measure my frantic anger, the words on the edge of my tongue that I'd like to hurl. I won't win information by accusing him off the cuff. I've observed him carefully all day, listening to him speak for peace on his father's behalf, watching him avoid everything on his meal plate that was once alive—just as I did—and I believe there's something reasonable, something softer, hiding behind his vague front.

But where do I begin?

"Princess Aurelia," he says, looking at me like I've pulled a gun on him. He stamps out his cigarette quickly. "Can I help you?"

Only one neutral option presents itself, and I wave at the distant sea pathetically. "This is nice. I've never seen it before."

He appears as unimpressed by my observation as I am. "Never seen what, Your Highness?"

"This."

"The sea?"

"Yes."

"*Never?*"

I shake my head.

"How could you . . . ?" He looks at a loss for words, apparently unable to fathom a kingdom like Etania, entombed by rock and pine. "Well, you've missed out. It's the only way to travel, I think. No one truly wants to be in the sky, and trains are bound to one track. But on a ship, you—"

He stops, as if realizing he's talking too much. Instead, he fiddles to put his leather gloves back on. He has lovely hands.

"You can have your cigarette," I offer nobly. "I won't mind."

He hesitates.

"Please," I say. "You were out here enjoying your favourite place in the world and I interrupted you."

The Captain gives me a sidelong glance, narrowed green eyes so like his father's, holding a vague depth—and who knows what else. Clever secrets I can't read. But he retrieves another cigarette from his wool pocket and lights it with haste, taking a long, luxuriating drag, smoke twisting from his nostrils. "My favourite place, Princess?"

"I doubt anyone joins the navy if they don't like the sea quite a bit." I pause. "Unless your father made you? Or perhaps you joined to get as far from your brother as possible?"

An inch of amusement appears. "No. You're right. I like it quite a bit."

Encouraged by this crack in his reticence, I say, "Does Savient truly want peace, Captain?"

"Yes. I've spent the entire day telling everyone—"

"I don't want what you *need* to say. I want the truth."

He looks at me sharply. Perhaps he hears the doubt in my voice, and his mouth flattens in suspicion. "Why do you think we want war? Did someone tell you differently?"

His voice is wary, and I shake my head. I don't dare implicate Athan. Perhaps the Captain's telling the truth here, or at least his version of it, and I'll only annoy him further, pushing like this.

I change tactics. "No, I don't think you want war. But I think everyone else does."

He raises a brow.

"I think that war is profit for many," I explain, "whether here or in the South. They like the show of it. The fancy ships and the rich business. But someone once told me that peace can be the better gain, and that's what I believe."

"I see."

"May I ask you another question?"

He nods, a fraction more curious now than hesitant. Like I'm some odd phantom that's appeared on his shoulder and needs to be explained.

"If someone meant to execute young soldiers in battle—boys, really—would you intervene?"

At first, I think he'll say nothing. I'm making quite a large gamble. But then he shrugs. "I suppose I'd say we need all the facts first. Who are we talking about? Rebels? Conspirators? Were they—?"

"Never mind that. They're children. What would you do?"

"I'd say it isn't right to execute the underage, and the rest should be given a proper trial."

I smile, relieved. "Yes, exactly! I feel the same. Though I believe there might be some in your family who feel differently."

He hesitates, the kind filled with suspicion again. "Is that so?"

"Listen, Captain," I say, leaning forward, trying to keep him focused on me. "You clearly want to do what's right. And I know your father does too. It's your brother who threatens to ruin the Safire name, chasing war and his own glory."

The cigarette freezes between his lips.

He must know what the Commander has done, the crimes hidden away. He must also see what I've come to realize—that there *is* someone who wants war in Savient, the one who declared his case before the League this summer. The hot mouth who's trying to *make* this war happen.

That's why Athan sent me his veiled warning. I ordered him to never go to war again without telling me, and this was the best he could do. We were fools to think the Commander would stop after his campaign was denied by the League. He hasn't stopped—he's simply trying again, devising new evidence to convict Resya with, readying his army. And perhaps only one person can stop him.

His own brother.

"What is it you're asking of me?" the Captain finally says.

"I wish to go to the League and set new rules of war," I reply as calmly as I can, the way Lark always talked. "Rules that must be obeyed. I know for a fact that a crime has taken place in Thurn, a crime that I have photographs of, and if those photographs were exposed . . ."

I trail off, letting us both imagine the Commander shamed before the entire world.

A criminal.

A warmonger.

"Dear God, Princess," the Captain says, stunned. "You don't know who you're dealing with."

It's an echo of what Athan told me during the coup, that if I reneged on my word and exposed the photographs, the General would find his vengeance. But I'm sure that's the overblown fear of a low-ranking lieutenant. Athan might have had to worry about the noose, but certainly not the General's own son. And more importantly, there's something gentler pressing up through his careful eyes, something honest and cautious. Familiar somehow.

It's time to jump in entirely. I have to leap for it. "Everyone in the North knows your brother is reckless, Captain. It's whispered in all the royal courts. Why, even here I overheard someone calling him a rake for what he did with Gawain's daughter last summer. His reputation is hardly sound, and I have the photographs that would prove them right. Not to mention, my brother knows of other crimes in Karkev. No one believes the complaints of the defeated rebels there, but if a royal and the General's own son stepped forward? Presented the evidence? My brother would do it. You'd have a king on your side, Captain. A *king* to speak for you."

I realize, almost disbelieving, that his head is cocked, listening.

"We could do this," I press, "and then you'd be the one to inherit Savient. Hasn't the thought ever crossed your mind?"

He blinks, the spell suddenly broken, and takes a step away. "This is some old royal scheme, isn't it? A younger prince betraying the crowned prince for a throne?"

"Not at all," I say quickly. "But in this modern age, not every eldest born is suited to rule, and we have to be clever in the ways we get the right person in power. We need to use politics."

"And you'd have me throw my brother in prison for this?"

"I doubt it would need to come to that." I pause. "He could simply retire?"

We share a look, and I think we both know that "retiring" the Commander might not keep him out of the papers. But it would be better than this. Once the Commander is removed from power, the threat of war will go with him.

The Captain sighs. "You shouldn't be saying these things to me, Princess."

"I have no choice. I believe you might be the best of your family."

It's another leap, hoping to endear me to him, and a fracture appears again. A wry smile on his pale face. "I'm not so certain you think that."

I don't understand his words, but his brow succeeds in furrowing deeper, considering my wild offer, and I pray that I'll reach him. I need him. A king aligned with the Safire before the League would truly bring change. A chance to ensure that if there ever must be war then there will also be trials and fair deaths, no children ever again placed before a wall like unholy target practice.

And it will be even more dramatic when I bring Seath of the Nahir to the table.

Peace at last—everywhere.

The Captain glances down at me. "And when would you . . . ?"

"Soon," I say. "I'm headed to Resya on personal business, but when I return, we'd have to begin quickly. I'm not sure what other ideas your brother is concocting."

I try to sniff for any reaction, any hint of mobilizing armies, but the Captain only pulls out another cigarette, lighting it. "*Resya*, Princess?"

"It's a family matter."

"But it . . . isn't a safe place."

"I promise it's not as terrible as your brother would have you believe. In fact, I—"

"Darling!" a familiar voice calls. "What the stars are you doing out here?"

It's Mother. She's nearly to us, her dress catching in the breeze, bare shoulders wrapped in a blue velvet stole. "Havis said he saw you in the hall. I thought you were in bed ill?"

She studies me, my nightgown and my long hair gone frantic in the salty air, then the General's son—her expression shifting to something sharper.

The Captain, for his part, smokes a little faster, evidently knowing his chance has come to an end. "I'd best get inside," he tells us both, savouring one last taste, then tossing it over the rail. He offers Mother a stiff nod. "Your Majesty."

She returns it slightly.

"Good evening, Captain," I say. "And thank you for your time."

He smiles, a very tiny thing, but still a smile. Then he stalks off down the walkway, and Mother turns to me. "What was this about?"

"I was being a diplomat," I reply firmly.

"With regards to?"

"Resya."

She lets out a sigh, staring at his retreating figure, and I feel suddenly cold, the sea wind at last crawling across my exposed skin.

"I'm afraid of what's to come," I admit. "I don't know if I can believe anyone's promises here."

She looks at me, her face gaunter in the palace lights. Her gentle arms draw me close. "Nor do I, but never forget the truth, my star. I will protect you, no matter if there is peace or war or whatever lies between. I always have."

She leans down to kiss my forehead—like I'm a child again, small and restless at midnight—and I surrender to it, holding on to the sun of my mother, a warmth against my skin even as the night presses down on every side, a taunting chill of worse to come.

10

The Black Sea

Our sea-crossing is swift since we're moving at a reckless speed, racing the clock. The metal passages are cramped with the scent of burning fuel from whirring engines deep beneath our feet, and everyone aboard the *Intrepid*—the Moonstrike and Lightstorm squadron pilots, their mechanics, the crew of this massive carrier—waits on edge. Perhaps even the four well-armed destroyers trailing in our wake. Our Safire flotilla is completely spread out, to avoid arousing suspicion, and an unsettling awareness hangs across the grey water, the awareness that the Landorians might, at any moment, discover our ruse for war and seize our ships—or worse.

"This carrier's the perfect target," Trigg informs Cyar and me on the third day. "We're so heavy, they had to strip away all the protective armour to ensure we'd be able to keep up to the rest of the fleet." We gaze at him in horror, and he grins. "My uncle's with the navy, remember? I know a lot about this shit."

Trigg's commentary ruins any sleep we hoped to have. We can only pray the men and women up on the bridge don't misjudge and put us right into the guns of Landore's *Northern Star*, because thanks to endless meandering monologues from Kalt, I know that ship is lethal. Nearly equal to the *Impressive*. And quite frankly, drowning to death while trapped in this tin can is not the best exit from life I've envisioned.

But in the end, the greatest drama of the trip is when nerves get the best of the normally sober Garrick Carr and his drunk self is sick all over the forward deck, a violation of ship policy which Ollie Helsun nobly steps in to take credit for. By the time we halt in the warmer waters off the coast of Resya, there's an uncanny calm all around—nerves aside. The faint outline of mountains appears a hundred miles off, but there's still no sense for how many of our ships are actually gathered here.

The Resyans are certainly growing suspicious. Their constant reconnaissance flights prove it, no longer convinced we're docking in Thurn to the east, and it's only a matter of time before they call the ruse and wire their friends in Landore.

Perhaps only hours.

I busy myself getting reacquainted with my plane. My mechanics, Filton and Kif, fuss with me as fighters sit on the wide carrier deck, gleaming with the squadron symbols and mottos.

Moonstrike: *First into the fray.*

Lightstorm: *With eagle eyes above.*

Eastwind: *Silently into the sun.*

In a last-ditch effort at distraction, I produce two rum bottles for Cyar and Trigg, parting gifts from Katalin—whether to wish me well or wish me dead, I'm not sure. We hide behind my fighter, and Cyar lets Trigg choose which one to drink first, but Trigg just stares at the contraband items.

"They're Karkevite," I explain. "Katalin suggested the blue one first."

Trigg still stares, like I'm holding a trap that might bite his hand if he reaches.

"Hurry up! This isn't a trick."

Trigg glares at me, a bit of heat on his cheeks. "Not thirsty, Captain."

I'm about to point out that we're all sweating, the Southern sun beating down on metal and skin, when Garrick swings around the nose of my fighter. There's no time to hide anything. Cyar and Trigg scatter, and I offer up the blue bottle to him lamely.

Garrick rolls his eyes. "For you, I'll pretend I didn't see this."

In other words, he'll pretend he didn't see this, and I'll pretend I don't know that it was him, not Ollie, who threw up all over the pristine wood deck of the *Intrepid*.

He ignores my conciliatory bottle, offering me metal tags instead. They're the ones for around my neck, the not-so-subtle reminder that someone, in the very near future, might be needing this tag to identify the charred biscuit on the ground as me.

I accept them warily.

ATHAN DAKAR is stamped in big letters.

Confused, I quickly check the other one, and sure enough, they both say Dakar, not Erelis. Last spring, Father didn't want to put me in any unnecessary crosshairs. He gave me Mother's unknown name as protection, so that everyone in Landore and Etania and Thurn would ignore me. Not anymore.

"These could save your life," Garrick explains, sensing my thoughts. "If you're captured as a Dakar, they might play the game instead of shooting you."

I glance up. "I doubt my father would play a game over me. And I think they'll shoot me either way."

"He's not going to let you die."

I wish that could inspire some kind of hope. But it doesn't. Not even Garrick looks entirely convinced, and I have no idea what my father wants for me. As an Erelis, I'm nothing. As a Dakar, I'm everything. Both are weapons for him to wield in his plot—and I don't know where the safest place is anymore.

"You know what your problem is?" Garrick asks. He sounds a lot more like an officer when he isn't moaning in his bunk, clutching a photograph of his Etanian sweetheart. "It isn't pride after all. I thought it was, last summer. But it isn't. You just think too damn much. You need to silence it up here." He knocks me on the head. "If you want to be as good as you can be, you've got to—"

A roar of deafening propellers cuts him off. Above us, a fighter skims 500 feet up, engine cackling in glee, trailing white vapour. It's low enough to see the twelve black kill marks on the flank from Karkev and Thurn—and the nightmarish cartoon fox smirking on the nose.

For the first time in days, I grin.

"What the hell?" Garrick asks. "He's supposed to be on the *Victory*!"

We both know who it is. There's only one pilot with that distinct fighter, and I sprint forward as the lone plane curves lower to land on board. Everyone—even the sailors—stares as it catapults down, careening to a spectacular, screeching halt on the frighteningly short carrier runway.

Fuming in the sun, sputtering flames, it's a very apt show for the captain of the Nightfox squadron: *We spit fire.*

I don't even hesitate. I'm at the cockpit as it opens, and the officer I've longed to train under since Academy days appears. Captain Thorn Malek. His smile is bright against dark skin deepened by months spent in Thurn, patrolling supply routes for the Landorians and defending them from Nahir attack. He ignores the mechanics buzzing around his busted plane, zeroing in on me, and his infectious smile grows brighter.

"Athan!" It's always my name. Never a title. "Thank God I picked the right carrier to crash into!" His muscled frame hops to the ground, his radio set dragged off a sweaty brow. His strong arm claps my shoulder with affection. "It's good to see you, kid!"

"What the hell happened here?"

"A bit of gymnastics over our enemy. Got sent to scout their defenses on the coast, and they radioed me to keep my distance. So I did what we all would do—told them I couldn't speak Resyan and went in for a closer look!"

"They fired at you?" I ask, stunned. The Resyans really can't afford to be seen as provoking anyone. Not with the position they're in.

"Do you blame them?" Thorn replies. "They see the writing on the wall." He moves me to the far side of his fighter, lower-

STORM FROM THE EAST

ing his voice from the mechanics. "And between us, I'd bet the big show starts tonight. We've carried this thing for as long as we can. Now it's time to face the music." He pauses. "And I don't think this is going to be a quick surrender either. They'll be on the defense, above their own homes, and God knows they'll fight like hell to defend it. I would."

As usual, he sees straight through me. My unspoken hope for a short war. He's always known how to read me, even back when I was just the little kid brother Arrin and Kalt had no time for. It's why I've always wanted to fly with him. He can keep up with any of the cocky aces, running them gamble for gamble, but inside he's gold. Honest and good. And unlike every other squadron captain here, he understands me in the way that matters. He knows what it's like to serve with a hefty last name. To have a father in power and be caught between worlds.

"Don't go too low in your plane tomorrow," he continues, and he looks more like his father as he says this. A face that can be quietly intimidating through sheer soberness. "Your brother's mad idea is going to be deadly. We're going to lose pilots."

"Too late for that," I reply. "I'm in the first wave."

"Not anymore. My Nightfoxes just got plucked to be the third squadron going ahead of the divisions."

I stare. "No. *Moonstrike* got plucked."

They did, because I volunteered them.

Thorn smiles. "Apparently the God of War did some shuffling around. You're back off the hook, going up with the bombers instead."

At that, something hurts in my chest—a confusing mess of anger and disbelief. I volunteered for this hell, the whole thing was my idea, more fighters for the main assault. And Arrin's pushed me right back out again. Away from the worst of it.

I'm not sure if I should be furious or touched.

Thorn grabs my shoulder lightly. "Quit worrying, would

you? I'd rather it was me than someone else. I can do it right. By the way, saw your brother last night on the *Impressive*."

"Please make sure he stays on board until we have the beachhead," I recite glumly. "My father would appreciate that."

Thorn chuckles. "I served with him in Karkev and I don't think anyone could stop him from disembarking early, even if they wanted to." I must be staring out in alarm at the distant convoy where the *Impressive* waits, Arrin quite possibly plotting to join his own siege, because Thorn's hand waves in front of my face. "Hey. You got any food not from a tin can here? It'll be at least an hour before they fix my plane."

This time, his obvious distraction chafes. I'm not eight anymore.

"Everything naval is cheap, expendable, and comes in a tin can," I reply pointedly. "Like us."

Thorn raises his hands. "Oh no. Athan Dakar sarcasm. I've really entered the flak field now."

I resist a grin. "But . . . there might be illegal rum."

"Forget the food, then. You ever seen five battleships unload a barrage?"

I shake my head.

He smiles again, but it doesn't quite reach his eyes this time. "Then you'd better get a little drunk, Charm. You won't be sleeping tonight."

11

Norvenne, Landore

The evening we see the General's son off to his aeroplane, the setting sun is hidden by clouds. I've hardly spoken with him since our nighttime meeting, left outside this swirl of diplomacy which stubbornly remains the realm of men—and my mother. Windom departed as quickly as he arrived, pulled away by some urgent business in the South, and the rest of the time was spent drinking wine and marveling at the naval display along the docks. Now the Captain is bound for Savient with our Resyan settlements to encourage this fragile peace since summer, and it's Havis who passes him the leather briefcase.

I'm determined to ensure some kind of promise of my own.

"I hope we'll continue these discussions," I tell the Captain politely, searching for some assurance that he sees my deeper meaning. No war from his brother. Only a future which holds something better for him and the world alike. "There's no need for trouble when we have everyone at the table and a favourable way forward."

He gives a curt nod, bundled up in his long wool coat, Havis's briefcase now in his hands. "Perhaps," he replies, equally polite. He looks down at me, breath misting. "And please choose your next steps carefully, Princess."

His soft words are a flicker in the cold, then he's striding for his aeroplane.

The others head back inside to warmer halls, but I linger at the edge of the aerodrome, watching the Captain's plane rise up and merge with the iron clouds, disappearing.

Havis also watches, his empty hands fidgeting, as if he misses the briefcase he's so often held. "Looks like we're going to Resya, Aurelia. Tonight."

I turn to him, stunned. *"Tonight?"*

He grimaces, agitated in the drab light. "If you truly want to work for peace, then we need to go now. Are you with me?"

For a moment, I can only register how strange urgency looks on him. It's always hard to determine if it's real. Is he telling the truth? What if Havis is the one who has the most to gain here? But I'm also certain he's drawn the same conclusions as I have—that the Commander is still scheming somewhere in the shadows, trying to get his war however he can. Racing us to the end.

And I have to head him off with a better negotiation.

I nod. "I'll do anything, Havis."

"You shouldn't say that. Not yet. Meet me out here in an hour?"

I'll have to sneak away from both Mother and Reni, but I'll find a way, and we march back inside together as if nothing's the matter.

Violet, my only true ally, helps me pack, a few simple blouses and skirts and dresses, then she shuts the trunk for me, her hands shaky on the clasp. Her green eyes peer up into my face, knowing so little of my mission, yet knowing enough to fear. "You're brave to do this, Ali. Braver than me."

I muster a smile, fighting the realization that we're saying goodbye. Perhaps for a very long time. "I might actually be rather witless," I confess. "But I love you, Violet."

She kisses my cheek. "I love *you*. And I'll be waiting here when you return and everything's made right. We'll always be strung together like stars, no matter how far or wide we go. I promise."

This I believe, a tiny warmth in my chest that I need right now.

Before I can begin to question my own sanity, I pick up my trunk and haul it awkwardly for the door. Usually someone grapples with it for me. I don't look backwards, hurrying down the soundless evening corridors of this strange palace, longing to say goodbye to Mother even though I know that would sabotage the entire thing. She'd place me under house arrest, for certain. Possibly banish Havis forever. A funny laugh bubbles up inside me. I could frame Havis tonight—an ambassador kidnapping a princess—and be done with him forever. But now that I have the chance, it feels as far from what I want as actually marrying him.

Havis, my regrettable ally.

"Making your escape?" a quiet voice asks behind me.

I spin. Reni's shoulders are already lowered in surrender, a sad expression on his face. He's been preparing for this moment for weeks, despite his insistence that somehow, someway, he might undo whatever dark thing happened the night of the coup.

But even a prince can't undo death.

"It's now or never," I reply firmly. "Havis insists."

"Be careful."

I nod, looking up into his troubled eyes. They hide the words he's decided not to say, the final protests against his only sister's venturing off into a precarious world that's far from here. "Violet's staying in Landore, Reni. Please help her catch the train she needs. I know it's hard for you, what she's doing, but she needs—"

"I'd do anything she asked."

He doesn't hesitate, his voice honest, and I know he's going to let her leave. He's going to let her leave the same way he's letting me leave. Some deeply tender part of him has been roused since the coup. Weighted with responsibility, desperate to love well. Mother always said I had my father's heart, but she was wrong.

It's Reni.

How I wish I could explain better what I hope to do! How I wish I could show him what Lark showed me—the innocents killed by Northern guns, the terrible injustices that extend back decades. I long for Reni to see more than just a map, divided between North and South, practical lines on an earth he's never walked. I want him to see the invisible hearts, like Lark's.

But he can't. He's in another realm entirely, a Northern prince in line for the throne, and right now he's more worried about how he'll look before the world if he defends the wrong cause and implicates himself before he even has a crown.

Please give Reni a sign, Father. Let him see his blood of two worlds is a great power to wield, not a hindrance to erase.

But there's no whispering reply, and Reni offers me a book instead. Gold letters embossed on the front: *An Introduction to Savien.*

"I know how badly you wanted to study at the University," he explains. "I promised you a tutor, but perhaps you can teach yourself for now?"

The beautiful gift is so unexpected, I reach for him, wrapping my arms round his strong chest. We hold each other close, fighting the distance to come. "Watch over Mother while I'm gone," I plead into his neck. "I don't trust anyone except you."

"I will."

"Do whatever you must to protect Etania."

"I will."

"To protect her."

"I will." He pushes me back, looking into my face. It's the way he says it this third time, the same and yet different. "Send my regards to our family in Resya. I hope I might visit myself someday."

They're polite words, but I don't think he believes them.

And it dawns on me, in this moment, that he has his own secrets. Things trapped on the tip of his tongue, things he can't tell me—or won't. I know when he's hiding, and this is the same boy who gave Athan Erelis a black eye for daring to speak back to him. All of that energy still surges inside, desperate for focus.

Where does it end?

I kiss his cheek then will myself to simply head for the aerodrome, to leave him. I make it only a few steps before I stop. I glance back and Reni still stands there, a silhouette, the hazy hall glow cutting his form and slashing the dark.

He's there.

I'm here.

Gentle fingers try to draw me back, but I push from their invisible grasp, and turn for the hushed darkness of the aerodrome and Havis's waiting plane.

III

RESYA

12

It begins like distant thunder.

In the inky dark, a starless night makes the sea and sky indistinguishable as our Safire fleet descends on the coastline with rage. The *Impressive* and four other battleships unleash their full arsenal. Artillery guns. Heavy cannons. Long-range shells. It's fireworks in every direction, exploding under my skull, streams of fire clawing at Resyan defenses. The beautiful shore before us lights up like dry brush, and it's too damn easy. A barrage of incendiaries. Alloy and white phosphorous. Mountains and men, reduced to rocks and teeth.

A steady drone high above moves like a swarm of unseen wasps. Twin-engine medium bombers from the nearby island. Loaded with hellfire, they're on their mission to disintegrate enemy lines far behind the coastal defenses our battleships rage against.

There's a flash of bright yellow in the distant smoke. A bomber caught by flak, disappearing to the ground, to nothing. Bones and flesh and metal all melted together at once. Another and another. Flash after flash after flash. Brilliant as noon sun.

Eight lives in each . . .

This is what strategy around a map becomes. All those words. Those empty numbers. Now they're death, raining down, and my hands are desperate for my throttle. Forward—

fast! Anything but being left here to watch, helpless in the maddening dark, miles out on the sea.

An explosion hits too close to us and I shove my hands over my ears. The *Intrepid*'s engines growl urgently beneath our feet, trying to lumber backwards, farther out of range. But it's not quick enough. A shrill whine plunges overhead, the far side of the deck erupting into flames. A fighter shoots through the black sky.

Not ours.

"Mad bastards are flying at night!" someone shouts.

An alarm sounds, but the *Intrepid* is too heavy to react. A sitting duck for the enemy planes. One Safire destroyer charges to the rescue, cutting through the waves right in front of us with fiery grace. The *Pursuit*. Kalt's old ship. Its anti-aircraft guns pound at the sky, finding their mark. The Resyan fighter above chokes down in smoke—right into the turret of the nearby destroyer *Fury*. We're all frozen on the deck, watching in horror as the wounded *Fury* falters briefly, like it's equally stunned by the blow, before one of its ammunition caches alights. The middle blows skyward. Pieces of hull scatter, separating apart, the destroyer rolling beneath the waves, sixteen hundred tons of iron and blood swallowed in the space of a held breath.

"Pilots inside!" Torhan yells.

Our carrier's batteries fire more frantically now, raking the sky for these mad, brave Resyan fighters. Defending their own, like Thorn said. Sailors race to put out the flames and pilots dart behind port doors, but I'm not quite quick enough, too busy staring at the rippling waves where the *Fury* was. A hand shoves me through. I turn to find Torhan's furious face near mine. "Get the hell inside, Lieutenant, and be ready to fly at first light!"

The iron door swings shut, explosions echoing, the orange hell disappeared.

They lock us into suffocating darkness.

War.

13

I wake somewhere over my mother's homeland.

Groggy, I peer out the round window of our aeroplane, finding the endless sea has at last been replaced by green earth like a tender jewel. Even in the pre-dawn light, the luminous mountain peaks are lit by the sinking moon in the west, ghostly clouds—or perhaps mist—coiling round the highest points, where the dense forest grows pinched and thin.

I rub my eyes, trying to clear the strange smoky haze.

It remains.

Tendrils, like ominous fingers, reach towards our aeroplane.

"Good morning," Havis greets at my left.

I straighten sharply, mortified at the idea of having slept beside him. It's far too intimate for us, but it's too late now. I put ample space between us again. "Those are peculiar clouds," I observe, trying to look farther behind the aeroplane, to find the source of the billowing mist.

"Possibly from the sea," Havis replies, though he sounds strangely unsettled.

We lower, curving round the side of a mountain, and my belly dips with the plane. I try to take deep breaths, focusing on little details below. Winding roads and motorcars darting beneath the trees. Then cement blocks appear, grey amidst the green, and it doesn't take long to identify the ugly truth—

bunkers. The square-shaped blisters of war I've only ever seen in newspapers, carving deep into the earth. Reni has always said that mountains are the greatest armour a kingdom can wield, the reason our kingdoms in the western Heights were spared the conquest of the old Empires, and it's a shock to see Resya so blatantly militarized. Mighty guns pointed at the sky.

At us.

I push back from the window, suddenly feeling too exposed, vulnerable.

"Relax," Havis says wryly. "You're on the right side."

I try to let that reassure me as another hour passes, the mountains spreading out in every direction. At the front of our aeroplane, the pilots begin conversing together in the still-darkened cockpit, headsets on, agitated. Though we can't hear them over the propellers' rhythmic thud, it's clear something has gone wrong.

"Are we nearly to Madelan?" I ask, meaning the capital.

Havis grunts an alarmingly vague noise as we lower rapidly, the gusting mountain winds shaking the small aeroplane. One of the pilots glances back at us, clearly scared out of his wits.

"Shit," Havis says.

He's never used such low language in front of me. "Is the engine dead?" I ask, hoping I sound calm and official, not petri-fied.

"The propellers are still whirring, aren't they?"

"Yes."

"Then of course the damn engine's working! This might be worse than that."

He doesn't elaborate further, leaving me to sweat profusely as the earth rushes up to meet us—far too fast—and then there's an enormous bump and I actually yelp aloud, Havis gripping me tight as we hurtle down the tarmac, brakes hissing, stench of smoke souring the air.

All at once, we've stopped.

I let out a shuddering exhale, the propellers spinning to stillness, and I glance outside to find a shadowed tarmac lit by lamps. It's a swarm of frantic activity. Well-dressed families haul luggage as they make for small aeroplanes—ladies in heels, men in tweed suits. Children follow in dresses and caps, carrying alarmed pets in their arms. One even holds a towering birdcage.

"What the stars is going on?" I ask.

Havis doesn't need to answer, because in the swelling silence of our aeroplane, the pilots have ripped off their headsets and turned on a radio. It emits crackled words that echo darkly in the tiny space.

"... and so we do repeat that last night, the navy and air force of Savient launched an unprovoked attack against our kingdom without any declaration of hostilities. Casualties in the Sixth Army have been reported near Esferian, men who even now bravely resist for the sake of our kingdom, and in obedience to His Majesty King Rahian ..."

My absolute shock is mirrored on the stricken Resyan pilots, and on Havis, who stares at me as I stare at him. "You understand the report?" he asks.

The radio still sputters in Resyan, exalting the noble resistance of the army in the north, and I don't care if Havis now knows the secret I've held from him for so long. I don't care about anything except these impossible, terrible words. "This can't be true, Havis. Not so soon. How could it happen this *fast*?"

That is the only fact which registers for me. Because I was just with the Captain, mere hours ago, and the Landorians.

How could *no one* have seen this coming?

"I don't know," he admits, and his hollow, defeated response terrifies me further.

I'm not sure why I thought Havis should have anticipated this betrayal.

But he's as human as anyone.

"... King Rahian wishes all to remain calm and fearless. We have done nothing to warrant such hostility, and our honour will *shine in light of this betrayal. We will fight with a clear conscience. We will defend what is ours. . . ."*

"The League will condemn this," I say desperately. "They'll involve themselves and put pressure on the Safire to stop. They must!"

"It's too late," Havis says.

I spin in my seat, overwhelmed. "Too late for what?"

"To intervene and choose either side. Instead of claiming innocence, Rahian has raised a weapon. He's fighting back. Now he looks like he has something to hide from the world."

"He's *defending* himself."

"Perhaps—or perhaps not. The League won't involve themselves so long as the truth remains unclear."

"That's not fair!"

"No. But then, what in politics is?"

I'm angry now. Truly furious. *This* is why the Captain said Resya wasn't safe. A warning of sorts, perhaps born of kindness, but not good enough. He knew his brother was plotting an imminent invasion even as we sat around those glittering tables, discussing peace. I thought we had a few precious weeks or months. Time for the Commander to fully rouse his war machine and find fresh evidence and make a new case for action. But he didn't wait for that. He just launched this hell, breaking all the rules, and the Captain's interest in our parley was nothing more than a sham, buying them the hours they needed for this surprise attack.

". . . Resist, beloved Resya, and we will be rewarded with victory. . . ."

"I'm the real fool here," Havis admits. "My mother will kill me. And then your mother after that. I'll be dead twice over."

His weak smile tries for humour, but it's a waste. I feel numb, touching my amber stone, as if it might undo reality, take me far, far from here.

There's a loud knock on the aeroplane door.

Outside the window, a small truck idles beneath the pinkening sky, a girl about my age leaning against it casually.

"Don't say a word," Havis orders me as we rise.

There's no time to ask why. A woman appears before us in the cramped aeroplane, anger on her brow, grey hair braided, the deep lines on her skin unable to steal from her beauty. She glowers at Havis, then at me, then Havis again.

"You *fasiri* of a son!" she hurls in Resyan. "You knew! Surely you did! And still you brought her here?"

"I didn't," he protests, but it lacks his usual confidence.

"He can't know she's come," the woman barges ahead, limping towards us, favouring her right knee. "No one can. It's foolishly dangerous."

Havis gestures at me. "Mother, she—"

"No, I don't care about any mad ideas you have! She should never have—"

"She speaks Resyan."

That silences the woman. She looks at me, recognition dawning. "Ah, Your Highness," she says, backtracking quickly, as if formality might undo her harried entrance. "It's an honour. I've longed to meet Sinora's daughter!"

She kisses me on both cheeks, rather aggressively, and since I'm still not sure what's going on, I wield civility as well. "Thank you, Lady Havis. You're feeling well these days?"

"Why wouldn't I be?"

"I know you were ill last spring . . ."

Her eyes run over me briskly, an offended frown on her lips. "Never better. Do I look ill?"

I shake my head, realizing at once that this was another of Havis's invented lies to get away from our palace, to do whatever it is he does for his own self-serving agenda. It's hardly a surprise, but I still pin him with a disparaging glance.

He shrugs guiltily.

"You look faint, Sarriyan," his mother announces. Like *fasiri*, it's another local word that my mother never taught me.

"There's a war on," I reply pointedly.

Dark humour warms her face, a familiar shade of her son.

"There's always a war on somewhere, dear. Eventually everyone gets a turn. Come, let's find you breakfast. You must be famished."

She picks up my trunk with ease and limps for the aeroplane door.

Havis waves. "You heard the woman. Best do exactly as she says if you value your life."

With a scowl at him for good measure, I follow his mother out onto the lamplit tarmac, into the mild morning air.

For a breath, I simply stand there, letting this one fact settle—I'm truly in the South. It isn't as monumental as I'd anticipated. Simply a standard aerodrome with sun-bleached hangars and colourful gardens. But apprehension creeps across my skin as I watch the fleeing throng of urgent faces, the panicked shouts and shoves. Everything in me begs to turn back. To get into that awful winged contraption and go home. These people are escaping before the worst hits, while I'm marching right into the crosshairs.

This is why I came, I remind myself. *I'm here to make a difference.*

The very idea now seems profoundly preposterous, in light of that radio address.

As Lady Havis packs my trunk in the idling truck, I tug her son's arm back towards the aeroplane. "Please take me to the palace," I beg Havis. "It's our only chance at peace and I need to at least try."

His strained, distracted gaze finds mine. "And how do you factor that?"

"My mother. She'll intervene on Resya's behalf and stop the General from advancing. He's her ally, isn't he? He might listen to her, and now is her time to be the bridge of reason."

"There's no way in hell that will happen," Havis declares shortly. "Clearly the parley was a disaster."

"The General wasn't at the parley," I point out, then raise my chin. "And besides, I won't leave until she does. I'll be a guest at

King Rahian's court, in the gunsight of the Safire Army, until she goes to the General and does whatever she must to make him stop and listen."

Yes, this is a risk, and goes against everything she's worked towards with her image—striving to erase any loyalty to the South—but it's the only thing that might save Resya. This invasion is not the way to solve the lingering tension, and she needs to act—fast.

But Havis looks down at me, a bit pityingly now, the look I've come to dread from him. The promise of half truths and unspoken devils. "She can't intervene. It's not possible."

"Why not?"

"Because your mother isn't who she says she is, and if anyone finds out where she actually came from, it will mean a disaster for her, for you, for your brother."

I step back, stunned. "How dare you suggest—"

"Remember we're not alone on this tarmac," Havis interrupts, lowering his voice and ushering us deeper into the aeroplane's shadow. "It might be difficult to hear, Aurelia, but your mother wasn't highborn. My family bought her a title and noble pedigree. We know how to create an illusion. How to pay off the right people. Your father thought she was the daughter of a count, and so did the rest of the nobility in Resya. Believe it or not, it isn't difficult to lie at the very top. Not when you have money."

I stare at him. "My mother was a *commoner*?"

"I suppose that's one word for it."

The revelation is utterly stupefying, provoking a thousand questions. But I'm also still reeling from the prospect of war—immediate, tangible, filling this tarmac with sweaty panic—and it overwhelms my sense of personal regret. It strikes the flame of fear, of desperation. There's no time for the baffling past, only the demanding present. "Then I'm still going to the palace," I declare. "My mother's lineage aside, *I'm* still a princess, the daughter of a king, and I will do what I can to stop this war." I meet Havis's annoyed gaze. "Lark and I had a mission to expose the truth, Ambassador, and I intend on doing just that. With or without your help."

"You're not going to the palace, *Your Royal Highness*. I'm keeping you safe, and we're heading for Thurn."

"Thurn?" I repeat. "But that's a war zone!"

Havis glances at his watch. "Yes, and as of a few hours ago, so is Resya. Except here we actually have eight divisions of Safire steel pounding towards us at this very moment, while in Thurn, if you find the right corner, the right city, you can exist quite removed from everything. We'll wait the nightmare out, then fly north when it's time." His eyes crease, a flicker of concern there. "I know Lark wanted you to find his secrets. I understand that. The two of you spent too much time together, and perhaps I should have stopped it. Or perhaps I wanted you to find his secrets, too. But not like this. Not with a war that will endanger you, bring your mother down entirely. Lark is dead, Aurelia. Make a better move."

I'm about to reply, but a cough sends Havis and me stepping away from each other. It's the girl from the truck, watching us curiously. I'm not sure how much she's heard, but I pray not the part about my mother's false title.

She reveals nothing. "Her ladyship's impatient to go," she informs Havis politely, gaze quickly occupied with the tarmac at her boots.

He pins her with a pointed glare, then marches past, headed for his mother. When the girl's gaze pulls upwards again, I'm greeted by deep amber eyes, the shade of the necklace I wear, and the flash of a thin, cautious smile. The barest edge of a welcome, given the nightmare we've arrived to find.

I can't return it. I'm staring up at the mountains now brushed with brightening sun, feeling suddenly very alone.

What now, Lark?

With three minutes of the radio address—and one unfortunate twist in our family history—our mission has been completely upended. Lark's words echo in my head, telling me his father, my mother's brother, wasn't so grand as her, his humility suggesting a reality I never thought to imagine. A Southern woman who not only took the crown of a Northern king, but who doesn't even have the expected lineage to justify her inherited title. Half of my life is built on a precarious lie.

And only the Havis family knows?

It's a disaster. An utter disaster, with war already upon us, no speeches or declarations to announce it. Hellfire simply unleashed in the dead of night. Lark said the Safire would destroy the world and rebuild it again as they saw fit. Perhaps he's right. Perhaps there isn't anyone in Savient with a heart for negotiation.

I touch my necklace.

No.

There is one—and I'm suddenly sick with the idea of him flying into those deadly mountains, even at this very moment, somewhere north of me. Is he already in the air? Is he as frightened as me? He doesn't belong in a sky like that. He's too alive, the way Lark was, and I have to keep him that way. Somehow. I have to believe the General and the Royal League and all of these men who claim to desire peace, deep down, might yet listen to reason and give King Rahian a chance to explain himself.

And since my mother can no longer intervene, it will have to be me.

14

Black Sea, Coast of Resya

Our first sortie is to escort the second wave of bombers.

I've spent three hours pacing in the *Intrepid*, trapped and helpless behind locked doors, and my claustrophobia and anger have reached their exhausted zenith. All I want is to fly. To get out there and *do* something.

When the all clear's given, it's early morning. We storm out with a frenzy which must mirror Army Group North, now storming the coast. In the distance, the *Victory* can be seen unleashing her fighters in rapid succession—Thorn Malek and his fellow pilots, swooping down low over the waves, following the ground troops as amphibious vehicles hit the boiling beachhead, too close to the gun-infested earth for comfort. The entire coastline is smoking. A deadly riot of thunderous shells and flak firing on every side. The battleships still pummel enemy fortifications farther inland, their giant batteries shooting streams of fire high into the sky, and on the shore, the poor kids of the infantry struggle to disembark beneath a barrage of bullets.

The naval guns are so loud, I can hardly hear Filton as he stands above me on my plane's wing root, offering a sunburned hand to help me up. Kif's skinny arms feed the machine-gun belts, his freckled face riddled by pale nerves. It's a familiar echo from Thurn. Both of them graver this time, more focused. I realize I wouldn't want their job. Entrusted with the weighty task of keeping their General's youngest son alive.

But once I'm in the cockpit, a fatherly smile crooks Filton's lips. "They won't even have a chance at you, sir."

I expect to smile in return, but I don't. Or I can't. My eyes are on Garrick, his red hair smothered by his flight cap, and I wonder how much he actually loves that girl in Etania. As much as I love Ali? And does Ollie regret taking the fall for drunk Garrick? Reputation now shot? And what about Sailor? He's done this a dozen times, even though his brother was killed in Karkev and his mother ordered him to stay home. He's still here. He loves to fly. Farther down the flight line, Captain Lilay adjusts her headset, iron confidence in her habit. A woman who's been flying into battle since the glory days of Savient's birth. Trigg fixates solely on his ground crew. Maybe scared. He's never done this before. And next to my fighter, Cyar salutes me, something meant only for us.

They're all suddenly too real.

Routine. I need to focus on routine. And anger. I plug in the radio cord and oxygen tube, adjusting the rear-vision mirror. My hand flicks the starter pump, my plane shuddering to life with a jolt. It's always so abrupt—almost a surprise, though it shouldn't be—rattling my bones and stomach. I became good in Thurn about not dwelling on my fear. I forced myself to focus on the moment. On Captain Efan Merlant and his steady strategy, the honourable pilot named for a long-dead king. But now I know the truth—those battles around Havenspur weren't a real war. Not like this one, with its incendiaries and white phosphorous. Bones to dust.

What if honour can't survive here?

"Lightstorm, form up," Lilay orders her squadron over the radio.

With engines snarling, Lightstorm surges off the *Intrepid*, then Eastwind.

Moonstrike follows last. I quickly have Cyar on one side, Trigg on my other, as we eat up the air, pushing for 10,000 feet.

We spot our mission above the haze of smoke.

Fifty Safire twin-engine bombers have already left their distant island runway, their wings alone spanning twice the length of our fighters, giant propellers growling on either side. A transparent nose serves as window for the navigator and bombardier, while gunners man positions along the flanks and tail. They're deadly and vulnerable at once, too heavy to maneuver sharply, easy prey for enemy fighters, yet able to press farther into Resyan territory than any battleship gun can reach. A relentless softening of resistance far behind enemy lines, hitting bunkers, roads, railroads, supply lines, anything to clear a path for the Safire divisions on their way.

We pull up alongside the gently swaying herd. Too many of these didn't return last night. They're probably as angry and scared as us right now.

"Charm, do you copy?" Garrick's voice crackles over the radio.

"Copy," I reply.

"You too, Fox. And Avilov."

Great. A parting message for the three rookies.

Cyar's wing drifts closer to mine.

Trigg drifts downwards.

"It's time to forget those games from Thurn," Garrick says calmly. "No straggling here. Stay high and don't let the enemy pilots lure you down low. And when things get wild, take care of your own ass. That's it."

We each affirm, Moonstrike now above the bombers, flying top cover. Lightstorm and Eastwind are on either side. Flashes of flak already explode into the sky ahead, Resyan anti-aircraft guns trying to peg our position, and it's a safe bet their fighter squadrons are coming to greet us. Far below, the beachhead is pure chaos, soldiers struggling to hold it, to press inland, the tiny shapes of Thorn Malek's squadron darting here and there above them. Past that, the coastal hills are charred with giant swathes of scorched forest and crater shells. Remains of Safire bombers still smoke, spread out like grotesque butter among the trees.

I try not to look down.

Up.

Always up, to the horizon.

"Lightstorm under fire. Two o'clock low," a scratchy voice says.

I think it's Ollie. I'm too busy scouring the sky to confirm. Black dots like stars materialize on the horizon, and my finger slips to the trigger as I ground myself into the cockpit, ignoring the gut-kick of fear. Stick between my hands, feet on the rudder, trigger ready. Time to remember Merlant's strategy.

Height. Sun. Wingman.

"Fox, keep close," I say.

"Copy that, Charm," Cyar replies.

"Avilov—you still there?"

It takes a long minute. "Uh, yeah, Captain. Where else would I be?"

"Could you answer a little quicker?"

"Just enjoying this cup of tea back here. I've got an idea, let's—*shit*, Captain, one o'clock high!"

That's all the time I get for Trigg's warning. Tracers pummel us from above, red hissing past our wings. Two shadows drop like hawks. No time to plan. No time to think. I throw my plane down and away, Cyar scrambles out to the right, and Trigg disappears behind me.

Alone.

Just like that.

As I hang on to my shaking stick, my plane shudders between my fists, gloriously ready, and for the first time a flicker of thrill returns. It feels wrong, but it's there. Adrenaline. Here. Now. My chest aching with the brilliant dive into nothing. One of the attacking Resyan planes hangs on to me, visible in my mirror as I level out. Tracers hurtle past. He's overshooting, since I'm shifting around too much, but damn, he's good.

Every move I make, he matches.

I'm so busy looking behind me that when grey fog suddenly

overwhelms my cockpit, I nearly jump out of my skin. It eats my plane right up. Visibility at zero. But then I realize it's cloud cover. Just cloud cover. This could be to my advantage. Let him lose me in here, the lonely grey. For a moment, the tracers stop and I feel a smug surge of victory.

Then red shoots past me again, too close, and I forfeit that celebration. I throw myself into another dive instead, getting the hell out of the clouds, the sky opening up below again.

I'm plunging right towards the bombers.

Shit!

It's Trigg's voice I hear in my head, but I can't stop. Every Safire bomber is covered in deadly corners—side gunners, tail gunner, all trying to keep the enemy at bay. All ready to shoot at any fighter hurtling towards them, friendly or not. The only ones who should be pressing into this onslaught are the Resyans who made it their mission.

Not me.

But I push my stick down and go anyway, passing under a bomber close enough to see the white-skinned surprise on the left gunner's face. A thunderous roar pounds behind me—heavy machine-gun fire. He's after the Resyan on my tail. Thank God for that unexpected ally. He tries to make work of my pursuer, but does little damage, and the enemy pilot is still after me. I spin between the bombers carelessly, the worst place to be.

They're firing.

We're firing.

I'm really terrible at choosing my direction. Ear-piercing flak reverberates off my wings, jolting me, far too close, and another Resyan fighter hurtles straight at me from ahead. I have no choice. Trapped, one enemy behind me and one right in front of me, I offer a wordless apology to the bomber I'm flying parallel to and haul myself right over it, skimming straight across the front of its glass cockpit. I've probably just given both pilots a near stroke. They think we're show-offs, and I'm solidifying that reputation today as I hurtle my small fighter before them and out into Lightstorm territory.

I've cut clear across the convoy and emerged on the other side. The Resyan's still on me, and I squint into the noon sun, praying all my counting of stars has helped. I make out a Lightstorm fighter not far off, the flanking details singing to me, close enough to reach, to get some help.

"Moonstrike approaching from east, bandit at my six," I say into the chaos of the radio, trying to be calm, to catch his attention.

"See you, kid," the welcoming voice says. Older, wiser. "Break right in five seconds and climb your ass up as fast as you can."

"Understood."

Time to charge ahead and hope for the best. Jamming my throttle wide open, I gain speed and prepare for a steep climbing turn. This Resyan pilot may be good, but he still isn't flying a Safire plane, and soon I'll be hurtling upwards faster than he can hope to keep chase with. And before he realizes it, he'll have a Lightstorm pilot on his tail. A veteran pilot with years of deadly practice.

With eagle eyes above.

I feel that tendril of thrill licking again.

Here.

Now.

I blow past the Lightstorm fighter and the Resyan struggles to follow me, lagging behind slightly.

The Lightstorm pilot pounces.

He explodes.

A flash of fire and smoke as another Resyan . . . Another Resyan fighter shoots between us and downwards in a reckless arc. I stare in my rear mirror, the Lightstorm plane falling in pure flame, years of glory gone in an instant. I don't know who he was. Only a voice. A faceless voice who tried to help me— and failed.

I abort my climb and opt for desperate airspeed from a dive. Panic nudges my heart rate higher as I flip over, and I'm beginning to feel a helpless kinship with this Resyan pilot behind me, who's still keeping up, still blasting at me whenever he can.

I hate him, but he's all I have.

Frustration builds like a steep pressure beneath my sweaty skin and I throw myself into another barrel roll, then weave rapidly through the seething convoy and merciless flak. Before me, a bomber falls end over end, a giant beast collapsing with broken wings. The crew bails out the sides. One of them gets his parachute tangled on the left propeller, dragged down with the plane. Another's chute doesn't open. Right when it can't get any worse, a burning Resyan fighter collides into the dead bomber's tail, breaking the fuselage in half. The entire thing explodes, bodies plummeting alongside the fiery metal carcass.

You see how cheap we are, Ali? You believe I'm special, something precious, but I'll go down just like that, like nothing, and no one watching will even care.

Rapid cannon fire explodes behind me and I instinctively brace for a dive. But Cyar's victorious voice fills my earphone. "Got him, Charm!"

My eyes dart to the mirror and I watch as my Resyan enemy falls away trailing slick black oil. I can see him scrambling to open his canopy, racing to eject, but the flames catch, his cockpit disappearing into smoke. My strange friend is as cheap as anyone else once in the crosshairs of Cyar's gun.

"Thanks, Fox."

Giant clouds have begun to billow below us, popping brightly, one after another, like fireworks the wrong way around.

"Bombs away, return for home," someone orders.

Lilay?

Garrick?

Doesn't matter, and our three fighter squadrons—what's left of them—follow the bombers as they swing in a wide arc back for the coast. The spotless formations from earlier are shattered. Wounded aircraft struggle all across the sky, some sinking into their final death plunge, pulled lower and lower by an invisible hand. Wings on fire. Bombers shot-up to the point that I'm convinced only the pilots must be alive. Everyone in the fuselage? No chance.

And as we hobble back like that, something fierce and furious growls inside me.

Something angry.

My gaze darts down, scoping out the earth. *"Don't let them lure you low,"* Garrick said, but damn that. He also said *"Don't think so much,"* and he's right. I won't let them lure me low.

I'm going down on my own.

"Stay with me, Fox," I order. "Bandits at 5,000 feet."

I can see the black stars hurrying along below us, certainly on their way to intercept the Safire squadrons fighting above the beachhead.

"But they said we're—"

"Follow me," I say, my foot going to the rudder.

"Wait, Athan, we—"

I ignore him. Stick forward, my plane moves into a savage, delightful dive, altimeter whirring at me in horror.

10,000 feet.

9,000 feet.

6,000 feet.

The bombers are abandoned behind and distantly I hear Cyar over the radio—"I've lost my wingman, Captain!"—and Garrick hollering at me to get back in formation. They're too far. I'm only aware of the sky dropping away, the straps digging into my chest, my gloved hands on the stick, the black stars growing in size and shape, becoming planes.

Enemy planes.

They don't see me, blinded by sun, and I cut the throttle, lower my flaps, slowing and thrusting right into the middle of their little convoy. My machine guns open up and the one in front of me smokes in seconds, a cloud of glycol bursting, the pilot probably wondering what the hell just happened. My cockpit stinks with the familiar odor of burnt gunpowder. The scent of victory, of not running away.

Don't think.

I swing out of the way and the enemy pilot behind me—no doubt stunned—fires too late, overshooting. He hurtles above me as I drop away. No time to correct himself. I throw my throttle open again, my plane snarling with urgency, regaining the lost altitude. Forget hanging back. They always tell us to wait until we can make our shots and protect our own skin. But there's only one way to be sure you're going to make a kill—and that's to get in too close to miss.

"Sorry, girl," I tell my plane, pushing her into the frothy wake of the Resyan. Caught in the slipstream, her wings shudder murderously, but I don't stop until we're right behind him. Behind is a pilot's worst nightmare. A terrifying blind spot.

I give him two bursts of cannon fire and think of the disappeared *Fury*, the mutilated bombers, my own cheap bones—angry as hell—as the entire enemy plane explodes right in front of me, debris pelting my fighter, cracking glass and pounding metal. Oil splatters. Everything shudders again, heaving me right along with it, and my head smacks the metal frame of my cockpit hard.

Pure darkness.

Pain.

Coppery blood on my tongue.

Then we're beyond the smoke, into the blue, and fractured veins spider across my windshield. Something wet drips from my forehead. I shake away the thick blur in my vision and focus on a third enemy plane now fleeing right, aiming ahead of him, finding the place he will be, moments from now. My guns fire. In a breath, before he can even understand what's hit him, he's falling for the earth too.

"Goddamn it, Athan—*stop*!"

The furious, panicked voice catches me.

Cyar.

Has he been talking this whole time? How many has he taken down? I've lost track of the scattered enemy formation.

"Three's enough!" Cyar hurls at me, his plane spinning too close above mine, like he's going to try and cut me off next. But that would be suicide.

"Not yet," I hurl back, tracking an enemy plane now diving even lower.

To the invasion.

It's far too near the deck to be remotely safe, but I flick over into a steep dive and follow.

800 feet.

400 feet.

Raging like a meteor accelerating with every foot of air, I glance down, seeing the ravine of the lines growing in size— soldiers crouched, tanks thundering forward. It's all a mess of smoke and sparks of light. I have no idea what's what, but I hope seeing a Safire plane chase a terrified Resyan is a welcome sight for the advance divisions of Army Group North battling their way inland.

The enemy fighter can't outrun me after my dive and I hurtle towards him, my cannons firing. He implodes. There's no time for thought or parachute. In seconds, he's smoking on the earth.

"Get the hell back up here, Dakar!"

Garrick's voice is ragged in my ear. Angry enough to use my real name as flak explodes off my starboard side, too close. I fling my plane up, having a sudden terrifying vision of death. Of my ashes left forever on an alien hillside. Forgotten. Alone.

"Copy," I say, but it sounds more like a gasp.

My head throbs.

Blood drips.

"You idiot," Garrick snaps.

"I know."

My fighter limps back onto the *Intrepid* with broken legs.

The prop sputters to a weary stop, something hissing and clicking deep inside her, in her mechanical core. A defeated sigh. I climb out, and Filton's horrified eyes rake over us.

"What did you *do*, sir?"

"Shot four planes down," I reply.

"And your own!"

I jump off the wing and turn to see for myself. Good God. He's right. She's battered like an old tin can, torn to pieces in the wings, canopy covered in deep scars from the rain of debris. An entire chunk is missing from the nose.

Goodbye to her, I guess.

Garrick marches over. I expect him to be furious, but his expression is as startled as mine, slightly mad looking. "What the *hell* were you thinking?"

"I wasn't," I say, his face a bit blurry. I squint, trying to see clearer. "You told me not to."

"No." He raises his hand to hit my head, then sees the blood. He stops. "I said don't think *so much*. I didn't say stop thinking altogether."

I glance around him, at the others. Cyar's face is set with an awful glare. Trigg's is slightly in awe. The rest of Moonstrike gapes, along with a few sailors, while my plane sits stranded like a corpse, a thing I shouldn't have jumped out of alive. I walk closer and stare at her. No longer gleaming, no longer fierce.

Ruined.

"I'm sorry," I say, and I'm not sure if it's more to her or to Filton.

15

Madelan

As it turns out, the Havis estate—my new prison—is far love-
lier than I ever imagined.

Settled just outside Madelan's limits, it's nestled like a tiny
gem of grandeur in the sloping hills, filled with pastures of
beautiful horses and shimmering blue-water pools of colourful
tile. Lady Havis drives the truck, expertly adjusting the stick,
rumbling us along at a steady marching pace. The hot wind
snatches my hair, and I'm jealous.

If I knew how to drive, perhaps I could escape.

We pull up to a grand house of long verandas and tall pillars,
the swaying palms deceptively peaceful, and I refuse to speak
more than a few words to either of the Havis pair as we enter
their home. They're clearly planning to hold me hostage in this
luxurious realm of claw-footed tubs and rose-scented rooms,
the warm, humid morning slithering in between billowing curtains, a copper kettle whistling somewhere. As soon as they
deposit me in my guest room, I change quickly into one of the
simple dresses Violet packed for me, annoyed I didn't bring any
pants, or even a pair of riding boots.

When my stomach begins protesting too bitterly to ignore, I
break my self-imposed isolation and head downstairs, investi-
gating every corner along the way—searching for a secret way
out. Lady Havis attempts to be a kind warden, offering me a
spread of dates and fruit and bread, and I play obedient as we

eat on the sunny terrace. She refuses to turn on the radio. Instead, she tours me through the extensive gardens, where peacocks peck at pathways lined with ferns, blossoming orchids, jasmine, and colourful bulbs I can't place.

"I'd like to meet with King Rahian," I inform her formally as we walk, determined to assert my royal bearing. "There might be a way to stop this war and—"

"I'm sorry, Sarriyan," Lady Havis interrupts. "I think that chance has passed."

"You can't be sure, though. A negotiation might still halt this."

She raises an elegant brow. "But what if war isn't the exception? What if *peace* is the exception, the temporary reprieve from a struggle that began long before you or I came on the stage—and one that will continue long after we're gone, too?"

"That's a dismal theory," I reply flatly. "You'll just stand back and let it carry on, then?"

"Yes. Very far back, in fact, Sarriyan."

"Why do you keep calling me that?"

I'm annoyed by her unhelpful cynicism, and I'm beginning to think it's a Havis trait—retreating from danger and watching the world go up in smoke.

"You know the word for star?" she presses.

"*Sari.*"

"And north?"

"*Iyah.*"

"Very good. Now you can certainly put the two together?"

Aware I'm being quizzed, I venture with, "Star . . . of the north?"

"Exactly. The one you call Northern Star. *Sari* was once the address for our princesses. Our little stars in the sky of history." She makes a face, halting for a large peacock crossing our path. "I find that rather deprecating, don't you? I prefer something stronger. So for you, *Sarriyan.*"

I refuse to take any pleasure in that favourable nickname.

When we round the garden path, however, I find something truly perfect. A stable yard of cerulean tile opens before us, a groom leading a gleaming chestnut towards a row of stalls beneath an arching roof. No dusty alley or hot tack room. Everything sunlit and welcoming, iron shoes ringing, and I can't resist the large bay head which emerges from the stall on my left, greeting me with ears perked. The soft muzzle pushes at my hand, the handsome face so much like Liberty's back home. Gently, I blow into his curious nostrils, saying hello in the way Father once showed me.

Lady Havis chuckles. "Ah, I recognize that heart. My granddaughter was just like you. This was her favourite horse."

"Oh." I step away, as though I've touched something that isn't mine.

"No, no, enjoy him," Lady Havis assures, reaching out to scratch the large neck with affection. As she glances at me, a question hovers in her gaze. Something secret, indistinct. "This was my late husband's stallion. He's an ancient fellow and quite happily retired now. But I'm certain he's glad to see you. He misses my granddaughter."

"She's no longer here?"

Lady Havis doesn't appear offended by my bold question. I'm beginning to think she might prefer things this way, the Resyan style. "Not any longer. But she was my heart. We used to drive to the aerodrome and watch the planes take off together—only biplanes back then. She wanted to be a pilot, and truthfully, I thought it was possible. I'd have given her that."

"What happened to her?"

"The Nahir."

The grief in the older woman's voice is unmistakable, and I glance away. I'm not in the mood to feel sorry for someone who bears the name Havis, but I have to ask. "Are there many here?"

I don't want to imagine the Nahir in Resya—perhaps several,

far beyond just Lark, further confirming the Safire's suspicions about this kingdom. But I came here to learn the truth, so I must hear the answer.

Lady Havis pauses. "They're everywhere. They're an idea, you see, and ideas are never stopped by borders. Are there some in Resya sympathetic to Nahir resistance of Northern control?" She shrugs. "There's one in every family, I'm sure. Youth will always carry on the fight. Youth is where change begins, and I respect that, though I may not always respect the means."

I've never heard anyone talk of the Nahir like this. Neither approving nor disapproving, simply offering an objective interpretation that feels . . . unbiased. There is both good and bad to these young revolutionaries, hiding in their dark corners and smoke-filled basements, plotting illegal operations in neighbouring Thurn. Willing to pay any price for freedom. Willing to consider this woman's granddaughter worth the cost when caught in the crossfire.

It frustrates me.

How can something be so simple and yet so complicated at once?

"Does the rest of your family still live here?" I ask, prying from a different angle. "I heard you have seven sons."

"Had," she corrects. "I lost one to sickness as a child, and another to murder. The rest are elsewhere, in business, wealthy, no longer interested in me."

As if on cue, Havis himself appears round the stable corner, sweating and flustered and waving impatiently for his mother.

Lady Havis pats my shoulder. "My pride and joy summons."

The trace of sarcasm on her tongue is nearly another point in her favour.

Nearly.

Left alone, then, with the stallion, I savour his inquisitive expression—the sort of stare a horse can give that feels both divinely eternal and cheekily mischievous at once—and I breathe in his familiar scent, letting it soothe my heart in a way nothing else here can.

"I think I'll call you Oraluk," I inform him.

It means *liberty* in Resyan.

"Unfortunately, he already has a name," another voice says behind me, the Landori words accented. "Savas."

Startled, I turn to find the maid girl watching me, the one who brought us from the aerodrome.

"Captain?" I translate.

The girl nods, brightening at my quick understanding. She switches to Resyan. "He's been to war, you know. During the troubles with Myar years ago. A lot of men went to the southern border and died. A lot of horses too. Savas went with the late master of this estate, and I think he's quite earned his rank of captain, don't you?"

I nod, kissing the stallion's nose, as if that might take away whatever darkness he's lived through. I can't imagine this beautiful creature on the frontlines.

The girl comes to my side. Up close, she's younger looking— at least my age, but with narrow shoulders, nearly bone-thin beneath tan pants and a smudged blouse. Her curly, raven hair is tugged backwards into a hasty knot that's barely contained.

"I'm Tirza," she offers shyly.

"Aurelia," I share in return, relieved to have found someone who might be an ally. "Do you work here?"

"Yes. My brother and I both."

"With the horses?"

"Whatever Gref wants at the moment," she replies with a laugh, but I don't echo her amusement. She's just called Havis by his first name, and that fact immediately undoes the hope of a newfound friend. She rushes on, apparently sensing my distaste. "I'm also a writer," she reveals. "A journalist of sorts, actually. It's my most important work."

"You write for a newspaper?" I ask, surprised that someone so young is involved with such an influential task.

"Well, newspaper might be a bit generous, Princess." She smiles sheepishly. "My brother and I run a small press out of our basement, and our circulation remains rather . . . limited. But we do our best to record what's happening."

"That's good," I say, nodding. "We need people to document."

"Yes." She pauses. "And I really loved what you said to Gref this morning, about wanting to expose the truth. That's our hope too. Especially now."

We share a smile—a real one this time—and my attention drifts down to the colourful bracelets encircling her delicate wrists.

"They're from Havenspur," she says, offering one for closer inspection. "My cousin lives there."

"Ah, I have a friend who's toured Thurn," I reply. I don't mention his "tour" was as a pilot of the Savien Air Force. "He said Havenspur was very pretty, with the sea and the promenades."

Her smile fades. "Yes. The lovely promenades. Havenspur's most noted feature."

I've clearly offended her, catching the bitterness in her tone, and I realize I must sound terribly foreign and uninformed. I wish I could share all that Lark taught me last summer—how I truly do understand that there's more to Thurn than fierce revolution and sunny walks by the sea, all of the in-between space, the history simmering up between cracked stones, the forgotten kings and queens and conquests. But my knowledge feels suddenly very tiny and insignificant next to hers.

"I'm sorry," I say. "I know how that sounded." I struggle for a way back to the pleasant common ground we had before. "Perhaps I could visit your press? I'd love to see what you do."

"We don't really allow visitors. My brother's rules. To protect the integrity of his work."

"Oh."

I've touched on something sensitive again, but I don't understand exactly why, and I have no idea how to redeem myself. But to my surprise, Tirza tugs a violet bracelet from her wrist and offers it to me. "Here. I have many."

I stare at the unexpected gift, the colourful threads woven with false gemstones, and her gaze reflects her own hesitation—watching me like she's equally hopeful and apprehensive all at once. Perhaps she thinks that a princess won't be friends with a girl like her. Perhaps she thinks our connection will begin and end here in this stable, because I have a crown and she exists in another world entirely. Some world that has clearly been unkind to her, judging by the gaunt shades of her skin.

But I take the gift and slip it on. "Thank you, Tirza."

She gestures at my necklace. "That one's special too."

"Special?"

"Yes. The boy who sells those in Havenspur is famous. He and his father make them from the ancient rocks on the shore. You have to climb down the pier when the tide is out, crawl into the caves, and the Landorians don't like it. But these stones have been there for centuries." She reaches out and turns the amber stone over, her hand against my neck. "Perfectly cut. This could be thousands of years old."

I swallow, feeling the warmth from her skin, remembering every time I've dismissed this creation as crude, precious only because it came from Athan. But it has its own story. Another gentle imprint glimmering on its surface.

Deeper.

Farther.

Stronger.

"Do you want to go for a ride?" Tirza asks, tickling Savas's nose. "I can take you."

Shadows from palm leaves speckle her cheeks, a note of true desire slipping through her voice, and I long to accept her perfect offer, desperate for a connection that feels familiar and true—the shared love of rhythmic hooves and breathless winds and reins against raw palms.

And yet . . .

"I'd rather go to the palace," I suggest softly. "Perhaps you could take me there instead?"

Her hand stops against Savas. "Why?"

"To find the truth of this war."

I hope this works, an appeal to our other shared passion, a reason to break the rules for me, and something flickers on her face. Surprise, and then respect, like I've chosen the more noble option. "Gref already made me swear not to do it."

"Of course he did," I mutter.

"But it's you, Princess, and I'd do anything for you. We can steal one of the motorbikes!"

Her smile emerges, brighter than I've yet seen, and her words hold the weight of something else, some devotion which makes me uncomfortable. It's like being offered something I haven't yet earned. I may be a princess, but that shouldn't mean I can do anything I want. I'm the one who has killed. I'm the one who squandered valuable evidence to save my own family.

But I still feel some smirking satisfaction when I think of poor Havis, anticipating my gambit. Unfortunately for him, he's underestimated the bond of two girls who love horses—and who share a mission.

"We'll need to lull them to sleep first," Tirza cautions. "My cousin always says that's the first rule of revolt."

"I might also need some pants," I confess. "And boots."

Tirza's sudden laughter is a sweet sound. Genuine and unaffected. "Don't worry. I'll lend you a pair." She puts her foot against mine. "See? We're the exact same size."

I don't know why, but seeing our shoes touching, a perfect match, sparks hope I haven't felt since landing here.

Escape.

16

North of Esferian

Army Group North marches hard. As Arrin's divisions push inland from the sea, Evertal's army strikes the eastern border from Thurn, opening up a two-pronged front to stretch the Resyan forces thin. Our squadrons fight to keep ahead of the advance—Arrin issued that order at me personally. Power lines, railways, bunkers. Wherever we can hit, we hit, and on the third day of war, we're sent to a captured enemy airfield for our next base of operations, hoping the field gunners haven't torn up the entire tarmac in an overly enthusiastic siege.

But I fly with a sickening fear. All thanks to a rumour I heard right before we left the *Intrepid* for the last time. It doesn't matter that Cyar is sitting off my portside, still fuming about the first engagement. It doesn't even matter when black stars materialize from the beautiful evening haze. Resyan planes? Or is my throbbing head playing tricks again? My finger drops to the trigger, instinctual, almost disappointed when the distant enemy formation disperses quickly, perhaps hesitant to provoke death this late in the day.

We lower, leaving the orange sun behind.

2,000 feet.

800 feet.

Hell.

That's where we land. Wheels jostle down onto an uneven runway, shrouded by thick trees and a half-destroyed building that was apparently an airbase this morning. I stop my plane and stand in the cockpit, my fear growing exponentially. Wounded men sprawl at the edge of the tarmac. Limbs spill out of makeshift medical tents seething with groans, canvas sides dripping in the dank heat. The smell is assaulting. Dried blood, days-old sweat. Vomit and urine and every imaginable piece of insides. Everywhere, skin razed open in the humidity.

And the sounds . . .

I'm suddenly very aware of my clean olive-green jacket and mudless boots. I shove past Cyar's anger and Trigg's startled face, both of them marooned by the sights around us, and sprint for the place I need to go. One soldier with a half-burnt face still manages to spit at my winged uniform as I pass, his condemnation like a fist to the gut.

We weren't there to save him.

Sun and skies.

Up.

Halting in the doorway of the medical tent, I face the nightmare. It's every horror I witnessed in glimpses as a child of revolution—the stiff limbs, the charred bodies—now spread before me on a banqueting table of repulsively epic proportions. I'd managed to suppress the memories I only remembered in fragments, enough to know I didn't want this life.

But now, here I am—and it might have finally stolen something real from me.

"What the hell do you think this is, kid? A holiday at the damn sea?"

I shake myself as a glaring medic stalks towards me, his white sleeves sprayed dark red. I realize I look like the worst voyeur standing here in the doorway. "No, I'm just trying to find my—"

"Follow your captain and get to the ops room!"

He hurries by, not a clue who I am—or just not caring. I remain there, frozen, unsure what to do next, when a familiar voice asks, "Hey, Charm, you okay?"

I turn. Ollie's behind me, his black hair still askew from the runway. He and Sailor have taken to smearing oil on themselves, some weird ritual from Karkev, and now he's got cavalier black smudges on his sloping cheeks. But his dark eyes are concerned.

I give up. I have to tell someone. "No," I say bluntly. "I heard a rumour this morning that my idiot brother went in with the first wave." Supposedly his left flank was stuck on the beachhead, and he decided to go fix it himself. I yank at my hair, trying to stop the fresh throbbing in my head. "I just need to know that someone's seen him since then, but apparently it's like the hand talking to the foot with the army and air force, and no one has any damn clue. I have no idea if I should be worried or not. Someone would tell me if he was dead, right? Or would they not tell me? Would they keep it a secret? Maybe they'd keep it a secret from all of us, for morale reasons, but I have to know. I *have* to know. He's my brother!"

I sound like I'm panicking. I probably am. But Ollie's voice is calm. "I hear you, Charm. One of my good friends is in army intelligence, right over there." He points across the airfield. "I got him a date with my cousin once, so he kind of owes me. My cousin is amazing. A pilot, too, actually. I'll make sure we find something."

His words—steady and ordinary—steady me as well.

"Thank you, Ollie. Really."

He nods. "He's fine, Athan. I guarantee it."

Ollie can't guarantee that, not at all, because if anyone thinks it's impossible to kill a Dakar son, that's a damn myth. And Arrin's only going to increase that likelihood if he runs into the fire to rescue his own divisions.

I saw the way those soldiers looked coming off the beach.

There's too much that needs to be stuffed back inside.

But Ollie jogs over to intelligence, and the sun's now behind the trees, gas lamps blinking to life. Sounds still spill from the tent behind me, crawling against my wet skin. Haunted howls of bodies in a death spiral. They're all dosed up on painkillers but what good does that do when you wake and see your liver glistening?

I'd be screaming, too.

I'm still watching the place where Ollie disappeared when I sense Cyar at my shoulder. There doesn't seem to be any anger now, only exhausted disbelief at the hell we've stumbled into.

I don't face him. "I sent Ollie to find out if my brother is alive. Do I want to know?"

"Yes. You do want to know."

I let out a breath.

I trust him.

"Thank God Kalt isn't here," I continue as a truck barrels in carrying fresh injuries from the frontlines. "I keep seeing the *Fury* going over. I swear it was down in under ten seconds. Ten damn seconds. There's no time to . . ." I turn, finally. Cyar's expression is wounded. "I'm sorry. I shouldn't have left you behind."

"What the hell were you doing, Athan?"

I shrug, confused by my own logic. "Trying not to think so much? I wanted to see what would happen if I did nothing but follow my instinct."

His dark eyes narrow. "Well, that's a stupid thing to do. You can't just run off and do what you like."

"I'm a Dakar," I reply bitterly, the pain in my head intensifying. "What do you expect?"

He steps into my face. "Yeah, you *are*, and your brother didn't go in with the first wave because he decided to stop thinking. Because he felt like doing his own thing. He went *with* them, because he knows what it means to lead." Cyar pauses pointedly, well aware that praise for Arrin is the last thing I've ever wanted to hear from him. "I know you hate it, Athan, but he's good. He's really damn good and there's a reason he wins. And now that you're here with me and Trigg, you sure as hell at least better give this thing a proper try. You'd better push yourself or else I might regret ever letting you take first place in Top Flight."

I stop rubbing my forehead. "Wait," I say, "you let me—"

"I'm kidding." He rolls his eyes. A wry smile twists his lips. "Look, you don't have to be him. In fact, please don't be. You're *better* than him and I've always believed that. But now you have to prove it to everyone else too. You have to use your Dakar brain for good." He stops, glancing down. "Not to mention . . . you're my only brother, the only one I worry about. So no, I won't let you mess this up. I need you here."

Oh, God.

I feel like utter shit now as I look at him, his shoulders still tense from the flight in, something strangely older in his strained gaze. Like I'm seeing a version of him from the future, how I imagined him looking years from now, back in the Academy days. But the future has already caught up to us. It came all at once, in three hellish days of invasion.

"Then let's do this together," I say quietly. "Always."

"That's the only thing I've ever asked for," he replies.

He's right, and across the runway, Ollie gives me a thumbs-up, grinning beneath the oil streaks.

Relief floods me, my stupid brother alive for another day at least, and Cyar eyes the wound on my forehead. His smile switches to concern. "Now go get someone to look at your head, you idiot. You're bleeding again—and we're strafing a bridge at dawn."

17

Madelan

Tirza and I make our break for the palace at dawn.

For two days, I've bided my time as Tirza advised, pretending I'm as impervious as the Havis family and content to ignore the daily radio addresses spewing horror and death. I've learned how to wield both a snarling motorbike and a wide range of Southern curse words, the most popular invocation being *"fasiri,"* a local specialty which can mean coward or fool, or whatever you want it to mean really.

Lady Havis also teaches me about the best rifles, made with Haroshi steel.

"They don't stick in the rain or mud," she says affectionately. "Loyal as a lover!"

I hide my disgust and fake interest as she instructs me on the tricks of firing a bull's-eye, how to aim so it can't miss. I pull the trigger when she commands. The rifle kicks into my shoulder and the ear-piercing cracks sing my guilt. I'd desperately hoped the bullet I fired at Lark was a fluke of sheer luck, that I hadn't meant to aim so true. That it was all fate.

But now the board in front of me says otherwise.

Flawless shots.

"Brilliant, Sarriyan!" Lady Havis says. "Such instinct!"

Her praise stabs my heart. The cool steel feels too easy beneath my fingers. The same dark creature that killed Lark, that killed the boys before the wall. A creature who can begin wars and end wars and change worlds forever.

"You know what I can do," it seems to say with a smirk. *"You know my power is greater than the truth."*

Not if I can damn well help it.

I've had two days to plot what I'll say to Rahian, to compel him to choose negotiation and end this war, and I'm ready to act. Wearing a blouse and pants from Tirza, along with a pair of her leather boots—a perfect fit, as she promised—I look like I'm her sister. Our dark hair tucked back and wrists graced with matching bracelets.

She steals one of the motorbikes, which makes me feel a bit guilty about compelling this girl to betray her employers, and thieve no less.

But who am I to complain? The bike belongs to Havis, after all, and I quickly climb on behind her, the machine beneath us jolting to life. Then we're off, sprinting out the gates and down the mountainside for Madelan's city limits. I breathe in the fragrant dawn air, closing my eyes to revel in the joy of escape. It's like riding Ivory with abandon. The rattling horse growling between my legs, the hot fuel tank near my calves, the thick rubber wheels jolting and sparking when metal strikes pavement.

We reach a curve in the road, and Tirza swings us to a dusty halt beneath a twisting throng of juniper trees. The ridge overlooks Madelan, the entire city seeming to grow out from the mountain forest. It's built in elegant tiers, the spires and colourful roofs illuminated by sun, giant bridges crossing a wide river that cuts through the valley. My breath catches at the sight. A place far from the cold grey stones of Hathene, full of lush and vibrant beauty.

This is the home of half my heart, I think, waiting for the tingle, begging my blood to sing in response.

But there's nothing.

Northeast of us, aeroplanes dot the skies, and Tirza squints her eyes. "Fighters," she identifies. "It must be getting worse."

"Worse?"

"Fighters are defensive. Bombers offensive. I don't see any of our bombers, which means they must be desperate to defend the northern cities, no time for anything else."

I raise a brow. "Do girls in Resya always study military strategy?"

Tirza laughs. "Some of us journalists do. And my cousin Kaziah, the one in Havenspur, she's a sniper. She's taught me plenty."

"The Landorians allow women to *serve*?"

It seems impossible, especially from a kingdom which adores tradition, but Tirza shrugs. "When you're surrounded on every side, the first thing to go is pointless custom. Who says a girl can't fire a bullet as well as any man? Look at what you did yesterday."

Yesterday's target practice is the last thing I want to be proud of, but we're already off again, no time for my rebuttal.

We race down the hill and I shut my eyes, indulging in momentary fantasy. Imagining it's Athan on this bike, his warmth for me to press against, the scent of sky and kerosene, firm beneath my hands, alive, alive, alive. He and I exploring this new kingdom together, only us, chasing the highest mountain peaks and learning each other's thoughts and patterns, getting into fights and debates and breathless fits of laughter, because even when he's rotten and I'm stubborn, we're still the most wonderful to each other.

Is it wrong that I want this war to end not only because it's horrible, but also because I don't want us to die before we have a chance to repeat that hurried first kiss? Am I made entirely of selfish fears and dreams and—?

Tirza hits the brakes, the bike screeching, and my eyes fly open, fantasy shattered. Our roadway has become a sea of automobiles and trucks and marching people. It's congested as far as I can see. A staggering group of perspiring women, bewildered children, and leathery-faced men with muddied boots and sunburnt arms. Everywhere, threadbare coats and dresses caked in dust.

I holler into Tirza's ear over the noise. "Where are they going!"

"Probably here! They must be coming from the north, from the villages."

Stars, how long have they been marching this road? Since the first bombs fell? And where will they stay once they've arrived?

Horns honk as we go against the crowd, pushing north, towards the downtown, but everyone else fights to go the opposite direction, south, away from the capital.

Tirza shifts in frustration, putting us onto another road altogether. We scoot through rolling neighbourhoods, past shuttered stores and marble pavilions and city parks, and I struggle to read the signposts at the intersections, to gain my bearings and scour for any clues about Lark's address. *Rayir d'ezen Cala*—Flower of the Sun Street. While my spoken Resyan is strong, my ability to read and write it is less so.

But there's little time for that. Tirza crosses another intersection and we're forced to slow again, hitting a river of olive surging the same direction as us. Young men in Resyan uniform and officers hollering orders. A giant beast with a metal turret snarls out from the street running perpendicular to ours, rolling right in front of us, snorting black smoke while men atop motion for space with their rifles. Everyone below covers their ears frantically, civilians scattering into the grass.

I stare in shock. I've never seen an armoured tank before, only on newsreels. We have none in Etania. There's no need. But here it comes, forcing its way along, another close behind.

They're uglier than on film. Harsh and angled and loud. A bit dirty. They squeak and hiss on clicking tracks, and the soldiers fall into line behind them, marching as before down the wide road. Officers thread through on horseback, their elegant caps bearing the red and gold kestrel of Resya. Heeled boots kick into gleaming flanks and the horses don't hesitate. They surpass the tanks, trotting onward at a trusting pace.

"They're not using those horses in battle, are they?" I exclaim.

Tirza stares, true regret on her face. "These mountain roads aren't easy for vehicles, not after a heavy rain. There's only one way to navigate them quickly. Just like Savas once did."

My heart throbs. Tanks and horses. How can they go to war side by side? At least the men have a choice! They're choosing to follow an order while those poor horses won't understand the truth until it's upon them.

We swerve onto a narrow, cobbled road, the rising sun bright in my eyes, and I desperately rehearse my lines to Rahian, my appeal to reason.

The clock ticks.

18

North of Esferian

The sun's a sharp glare on my fighter's canopy as Sailor and I drop low. Sweat trickles down my spine, my cockpit cramped, my parachute harness hot and constricting in the heat. Grabbing at me.

"Got anything yet?" Sailor enquires over the earphone.

"Nothing," I reply.

We're clipping along at around a thousand feet, enacting the role I devised for us in that faraway strategy room. It's still more terrifying than any dogfight, coming this close to the ground. Danger hidden in every green crevice. But I have a bomb today—five hundred pounds of ordnance strapped to my fighter—so I scour the earth, eager to just drop it and peel upwards again. Sailor's right behind me, carrying his own load.

Back at base, Cyar's sick as a damn dog. Whatever the medics poked him with on the ship failed miserably, and he woke up slick with fever sweat, nearly heaving all over my boots when he forced himself up and tried to dress.

"You sure as hell aren't flying," I informed him.

"I could," he protested weakly. "Someone might just need to clean the cockpit after."

Then he threw up again.

I ordered him back into bed and once on the flight line, managed to maneuver myself amongst the Moonstrike pilots, passing Trigg off on someone else and taking Sailor as wingman.

We were all nearly sick by that point, though, because one of our nearby barracks was visited by Resyan bombers in the night, and the stench from the incinerated bodies—sour and sharp and putrid—was amplified by the morning heat, filling the airfield.

My fingers dance on the trigger as I look down. I couldn't do much for the sorry bunch in the barracks. But I can do something now.

And there it is.

"Tank, four o'clock."

"Good eye, Charm! Theirs?"

It sure doesn't look Safire. Lighter metal, smaller turret. A machine able to strip flesh clean off the bone.

I throw my stick forward.

I want this over with. Only seconds away from knocking it out of the game for good. The tank grows larger, and as always, for a fraction of a heartbeat, I pause. Finger on the trigger. Not pressing. Because there are people down there. Real people inside that machine, sharing a weary smile, trying to survive this, and I want to give them one more second. One more breath. One more chance to remember home.

Then, time's up, because they've chosen to be here, same as me. That's as much as I can afford to give, and I release the bomb clinging to my plane's belly, over them so fast their turret can't even begin to train on me—not that it would do them much good at this steep angle.

The tank explodes to a smouldering cloud of black.

They never even saw it coming.

Better that way.

"Your turn, Sailor."

Wide blue sky fills my windshield again.

"Got it, Charm, let's—wait, *Charm*! Six o'clock on your—"

Sailor doesn't finish the thought. We both missed a second Resyan tank, camouflaged by trees and modified with our worst enemy—anti-aircraft guns. In my rear mirror, Sailor's fighter disappears in a flash of white-blue brilliance, pieces of him and his plane raining across the earth. I haul backwards on my stick, hurtling upwards, out of range.

My shaky breaths echo in the stark silence of the radio.

"That was damn fast," I hear myself say.

I don't know why.

I'm talking to no one.

Sailor's dead. And if not for a medic's faulty injection, it would have been Cyar.

19

∋ AURELIA ∈

Madelan

We find King Rahian's palace perched high above the downtown, nestled behind imposing walls and manned by a pack of agitated army officers. As we approach the iron gates, I search my memory, grasping for everything I know of him—a widower with a young son and a drinking habit, the only royal left in a land of revolt and overthrown monarchies.

"Now what?" Tirza asks, eyeing the armed guards apprehensively.

"Now I announce myself," I reply, sounding a lot braver than I feel.

I swing off the bike and approach, shoulders back, chin high. Perhaps I should have come in a gown, but there's nothing I can do about it now—I simply have to be the dusty-haired princess with grit caked onto her skin.

With as much formality as I can muster, I introduce myself as Princess Aurelia Isendare of Etania, daughter of Sinora Lehzar and betrothed of Ambassador Gref Havis. That last bit tastes like pure poison in my mouth, but I throw it in for good measure, praying fervently that my mother's purchased title still means something here. That her name wields the respect I always assumed.

Someone goes back to mutter over the radio, and I raise my chin higher, to be sure they see I mean every word.

Like magic, the iron gates open.

Behind me, Tirza appears stunned, the power of my crown at work. I get on the bike again and we grumble forward, entering the peaceful realm of Rahian. Gone is the clatter and chaos of the streets. A new world opens up with gardens of magnolias and roses, trees of passion fruit alongside trimmed shrubs in precise plots. The merging of North and South. All of it overlooks the valley beyond, the colourful tapestry of Madelan spreading out in a wash of red-roofed buildings, blue spires, and mountains. Ever-elegant palms sway in a lazy rhythm above the paved drive, and when we round the bend we discover a courtyard bursting with military vehicles and anti-aircraft guns and armed soldiers. The white-walled palace looks uncomfortably out of place next to them.

We sputter to a halt as the uniformed crowd stares at us. Servants weave between the soldiers, pinched with nerves, the way our footmen looked the night of the coup. At the top of the marble stairs, an ornate wooden door opens and a tall woman emerges from the shadowy entrance, dressed in a fitted cream dress that accentuates strong hips and belly, wearing dark sunglasses, her raven hair puffed into a knot and a cigarette smoking in her dainty hand.

All of the men straighten as her head tilts down at me.

"Aurelia Isendare?" she asks, rather tonelessly.

I stare up at her in confusion. Has Rahian remarried and no one bothered to mention it? This woman is clearly in command, the atmosphere in the courtyard transformed to rigid expectation at the sight of her, and I slide awkwardly from the bike in my mud-splattered pants, suddenly very aware that before this gleaming jewel of a person, I hardly look worthy of representing my mother's interests.

I truly should have thought to bring a gown.

"Did you come from Etania by way of motorbike?" she continues, the barest wry edge to the question, and I can feel her eyes—hidden by the shades—travelling over my pathetic state.

"I've been held hostage by Ambassador Havis," I reply quickly, which might be a step too far, but I need to ensure no one sends me back to him. Not yet. "I wish to speak with His Majesty immediately. Is your husband here to—"

"Husband?" the woman interrupts. She laughs as tonelessly as she spoke. "You wish to speak with my brother-in-law, I believe. Perhaps about this war he's waltzed us right into?"

Her bitterness cuts through the sudden smile on her faultless fawn-coloured skin, marring her attempt to make light of the situation. She clicks down the marble steps, teetering on heels, and the sunglasses are finally removed, revealing hazel eyes. She kisses me on each cheek, wafting the scent of lemon and tobacco. "I am Jali Furswana, Princess of Masrah, and I welcome you to Resya. I'll not let that fiend Havis steal you away any longer."

My brows rise. A princess? From *Masrah*? I think there's a sparkle of jealousy in her gaze at the mention of Havis, and as she drags on her cigarette, my brain scrambles to remember first where Masrah is located—across Thurn, far in the east—and second, how there can be a member of the Masrahi royal family here when Lark told me in his history lessons that all of the Southern royals, save King Rahian, were gone and it was better that way. He never shared much else, too focused on the present, on his Nahir principles of independence and reform. But if Jali is truly a princess, then I'm fairly certain she doesn't have a kingdom. Not anymore.

"Please," I say, "take me to your brother. It's pressing."

"My brother-*in-law* has been trapped in meetings with the military all morning, Aurelia, but I suspect for you he might make an allowance." She peers down at me, some meaning in her gaze I can't interpret. "I do hope you've brought us good news."

"I hope so as well," I reply honestly.

She smiles then—a glasslike thing—and takes my arm, ushering me inside the palace. Tirza follows, appearing both stunned and ecstatic to be swept along in my wake. Indoors, more men in military caps stamp through the alabaster foyer, their beige uniforms drab against pale walls and vibrant tapestries, officers resting on a bronze fountain while a parrot squawks nearby. A little boy is also waiting, a mop of curly dark hair above moon-wide eyes.

"His Highness, Prince Teo," Jali informs me proudly. "My nephew."

The boy draws immediately to her side, and when I try a friendly wave, he ducks his head behind her knees.

"He's scared," Jali explains, gesturing at the soldiers. "How truly awful for a child, isn't it?"

I think of the children fleeing down the roads at this moment, right past snarling tanks, through mountain roads for days on end, and I think little Teo should count his blessings.

But before I can say this, another voice beats me to it.

"Ah yes, God watch over the children with only *three* pools to choose from," Havis announces, pushing through the doors behind us and perspiring profusely. He looks like he nearly ran here.

Jali's false smile brightens a fraction, which only piques my suspicion further. "Ambassador, you were supposed to bring us peace from that parley. Instead, we get this?" She sweeps a manicured hand at the herd of uniforms. "Also, Aurelia says you held her hostage."

Havis gapes at Jali, then at me.

"I'm sorry," I tell him. "Though it's somewhat true."

"I was keeping you safe," he retorts.

Jali's laughter echoes. "Stars, Havis. Is that how you treat your betrothed?"

My introduction at the gate has evidently caught up with me, and Havis appears vexed—perhaps even a fraction embarrassed. Perhaps there's something else between these two. Something from before I entered the picture. And clearly, he hasn't yet informed the court here of his yearlong quest to woo the Princess of Etania. Convenient.

Well, they can have each other then, because I have more important business.

"Where will I find Rahian?" I ask Jali formally. "I think we all understand the timeliness of this."

"Indeed," she agrees, toneless again. "Come along."

"I'll do all the talking," Havis whispers at me as we march up the stairs, trailing in Jali's lemony scent. I don't confirm or deny that directive.

At a pair of tall doors, footmen bow slightly, allowing us to enter a parlour with a ceiling canopy of painted leaves, ornate gold lattices across the windows glittering with sunlight. Behind a grand desk sits a man about my mother's age, his black hair curling and flecked with grey. His eyes widen on the three of us.

"This is Sinora Lehzar's daughter," Jali informs him grandly. "Come all the way from Etania to visit!"

Rahian stands, waving his remaining officers and footmen from the room, then he's round his desk and striding for me. "Aurelia," he says in disbelief, pulling me into an unexpected embrace—tight, earnest, like I'm a long-lost child returned home. Flustered by his lack of formality, and the whiff of liquor on his breath, I push back and try to compose myself. "Your Majesty," I say, "I'm truly honoured to be here and see my mother's beloved homeland at last. Though it appears I've stumbled into a war?"

He shrinks back, expression caught. "I've made a mess of this, haven't I?" he admits, rubbing at his weary face, one that's handsome in a simple, uncluttered way—green eyes, elegant nose, and a slightly too-big chin. Somewhere in his veins is the faint reflection of his great-grandmother, a Northern princess of Elsandra, the girl who merged Prince Efan's blood with the Resyan throne. "I should have suspected the damn Safire wouldn't be cowed by the League's ruling," he continues, glancing to Havis, "but I won't stand for this. Surely the North will see I've been provoked and rule I have a right to defend myself?"

"Your Majesty, I think it's quite evident the League's rulings no longer matter," Havis replies hesitantly. "Not to the Safire."

"Then all the more reason to resist their vain expansionism. To prove their folly."

"But is that worth the cost of your own life?" Havis presses, stepping closer. "Your Majesty, I didn't wish to bring you this news, but truly, you'd serve Resya better by leaving now and saving yourself, your son. I fear if you stay for this reckoning, you'll only lose everything that—"

"*Enough*," Rahian interrupts sharply. "I will not abandon my people, Ambassador. What king would I be then?"

Havis and Jali say nothing, and I suspect their responses to that statement are both equally cowardly. Havis always advocates running, saving his own skin. I saw him do that very thing at our coup in the summer. And Jali? I've known her fully ten minutes, and I already suspect what bone she's made of. They're a matching pair.

"Your Majesty, might we speak in private?" I ask, and I can practically feel Havis's eyes narrow at my back. "I have a message from my mother, for your ears alone."

The lie comes easily off my tongue, and it works. Something hopeful edges into Rahian's gaze. "Of course, Aurelia. Anything you wish."

He gives Havis and Jali a swift, royal nod, and they retreat resentfully for the twin doors, a suspicious, mutual question in their eyes. Once alone, Rahian walks to his desk and fills a diamond-patterned glass with brandy. "There's something you wish to say," he acknowledges. "Speak freely, please."

There is indeed something I wish to say, the lines I rehearsed on the bike ride here, and I switch to Landori so Rahian will see I mean to be a diplomat, not simply a friend. "Your Majesty," I begin, "my mother wishes you to negotiate. That's been her hope all summer, to arrange a meeting of North and South, to prove that Resya has no reason to invite suspicion about supporting the Nahir. If you agreed to this, immediately, you might yet save face and the lives of your people. She would help you. We could create a lasting peace for all."

Rahian gazes at me like he senses the false fabrication of my story. "It is hardly so simple, and she knows that as well as I."

His tone makes it clear I've just stepped into an adult's realm, offering foolish advice, and it frustrates me—especially since I know I'm lying, creating something my mother would never agree to, yet desperate enough to try. But then he smiles sadly. "Oh, Aurelia. I have no choice but to fight. There are those in my own kingdom who despise me, who believe I am aiding the Nahir in their revolt. They are welcoming the Safire even now. Rejoicing in my downfall."

He speaks in Resyan again, a tired sound that's trying to be brighter, for my sake, but can't manage it, and his words startle me. The realization that some here in Resya might not be against this war. That some even welcome this intervention— no matter how drastic.

"No," he continues, "to repel this unlawful invasion and expose the Safire on their own aggressive agenda is my only hope. Negotiation no longer stands. I will lose everything if they arrive in this city. If they press me into their ruthless tribunal." His wounded eyes meet mine again. "Besides, what would your uncle say?"

I frown. "My uncle?"

"Yes."

We look at each other a long moment, my expression confused, Rahian's slipping to stark discomfort. "But your mother sent you here. I thought . . ."

No, no one sent me, because I came here on my own, and beyond the window, a bird sings—one I've never heard before.

"Oh, child," Rahian says after a moment. "You don't know."

"Don't know what?"

He steps closer, an offer of comfort, as if I'm the one with a kingdom being overwhelmed by bitter steel, but I'm too busy trying to figure out what Uncle Tanek has to do with any of this. "Understand one thing, then," he says. "This isn't about me and my own fate, and to think of it in such small terms will only make it worse. What Seath and the Nahir dream of . . . It's far greater than Resya, than this one war. It's an idea that can scarcely be believed. And I fear he might succeed at last." Wind tickles the silk tassels and skitters the drapes, a warm breath of faint smoke and orange blossoms. "Can you not see it happening already, Aurelia? You're from the North."

The blurry picture slides into focus at last. The thing I should have recognized right away. Last summer, Lark suggested that perhaps Rahian could be pressured, or even threatened, by Seath into helping the Nahir in exchange for a peaceful, untouched kingdom. Rahian is the sole royal left in a land of ruined monarchies. Has he made a deal to save his throne—lend arms for the Nahir insurrection in Thurn, and spare Resya itself from their violent anti-monarchical revolt?

Perhaps he's as guilty as the Safire claimed before the League.

An immense sadness wells inside me for this man, unexpected, because what an unenvious decision to be forced to make, one no leader would want to face. Whatever I once believed was wrong, because this situation is far too tangled for mere negotiation. Not with the League now rendered powerless, and a nation like Savient on the march, and a man like Seath of the Nahir plotting invisible games which condemn entire kingdoms.

Rahian gives me a mustering smile. Brave, not yet defeated. This king who has been coerced into the darkest of corners. This father trapped between the swell of Nahir revolt and spreading Safire ambition. This man choosing to stay and fight, to defend his people, to accept the consequences he invited.

And to my surprise, I find I want to help him.

I'm confined to palace grounds after that. A well-meaning order, since everyone's convinced enemy aeroplanes might materialize from oblivion at any moment, but for me, it's another prison sentence. I pace the garden walkway—all of the vibrant flowers far too cheerful for this miserable reality—and I run the facts over and over in my head. Everything at hand.

"There's always a way forward, Cousin."

There is. I still believe Lark's words, and I just have to find it, somehow. The world needs to know this entire situation is far more complex than they imagine. The world needs to know that the Safire can't simply march in here with guns blazing, refusing to listen to reason, defying the League's clear ruling.

The world needs someone to explain.

"Princess?"

I spin, finding Tirza following a few feet behind me, and her presence is a welcome relief. Her warm amber eyes.

I'm not sure where to begin, so I simply launch right into it. "Last summer," I say, "an idea nearly destroyed my home. A thousand men marched for my palace, compelled by a lie about my mother, determined to seek justice. They hung by their necks for that belief. But my brother, he wielded another idea, one of innocence, and he brought neighbouring kingdoms to our aid, because they believed him with an equal conviction. Enough to save us." I pause, struggling to gather all my racing thoughts, hammer them into a shape that makes sense. "I see now how powerful ideas are, Tirza, and so I believe we need to share the right ones about this war. We need to prove its wrongness and force the Safire to answer for what they're doing here. But I can't do that on my own. I need your help . . . reporting." I take her hands. "We can record this awful war together. We can make sure it ends better than it began."

True surprise fills Tirza's face, but it quickly shifts to understanding—relief, as well. The unexpected realization that a Northern princess is going to work in Resya's defense. "You're right, Aurelia," she says earnestly. "War is simply a story. And we have the means to tell it properly."

My name spoken by her, like a friend, is enough. I may not be able to stop generals and kings and commanders, but we can still fight—all of us. We can use our words, not weapons, and perhaps, together, we can open eyes and write a better ending.

I'm here, Lark.

Dear Ali,

I'm not sure how long this letter will take to reach you, or if it even will, but I want to at least write it so if you ever ask me someday—did you think of me? Did you remember us when you were at war? I'll say yes, because I am. And I do. This is my proof. You're all around me here in Resya. Your mother's kingdom is beautiful from every angle, and I'd give anything to explore these mountains. From my plane, they look like green castles, with pillars and ramparts and tumbling cliffs. A place we could hike for days and never grow bored. Trails twisting to the horizon.

But I'll admit, it's always a shock when I do walk on the earth. The sky above is wide and empty. If someone dies up there, they're gone in an instant. Nothing left behind. But down below? You see the waste. It doesn't matter how careful you vow to be with a shell, somehow the wreckage always goes farther than you think. I try to feel glad I'm not in the army. I don't have to march through the ruined towns, talk with the stunned people, be confronted by my own guilt. But maybe that's delusional? Do you think I'm as bad as them? I should mention that some of the Resyans are glad about us being here. I swear to you, they're grateful, selling us coffee and fresh fruit, encouraging us onwards . . .

Alright, I think this is a conversation we'd have better in person. But the truth is, a lot of people in this world don't like kings, whether from the North or the South. I know you've got a good heart, Ali. You care. But others with crowns? I think they're a bit selfish, and I'm not even sure they know their own people.

I'm sorry. I'll save this debate for a day when you can challenge me right back and tell me kings are noble and good and God-ordained, and where would this world be without them? And isn't it hard to command an entire kingdom and ensure every last person is perfectly satisfied? And how is ruling with a gun any better? (Am I guessing your lines right?) I'll stop there, and tell you instead that I saw a farm horse the other day that looked exactly like yours. I think it had good withers or frame or something like that. I even fed it wild clover. Kept my hand flat just like you taught me—and only lost two fingers in the end!

God, has it only been eleven days? It feels like longer. I wish you could see it here, once everything's beautiful again. You don't want to see it like this.

Yours always,
Athan

Dear Ali,

Twenty days and somehow I'm still alive. I guess my training is actually paying off! Every dusk, I count stars to sharpen my vision, and every morning, I do a hundred sit-ups to strengthen my core, to resist blackout while flying. All of these little tricks to stay alive, but do you want to know something funny? (It's not really funny, but it feels a bit funny as I'm sitting here in my cockpit.) I think the soldiers on the ground have it better than me. If we do well, and provide cover, they love us. But if we're late to the game, caught up in our own battles at 12,000 feet, they hate us. They spit on us, like it's our fault we couldn't get there in time to save them. They envy the freedom of the sky.

But think about it. As horrible as they feel their lot is, at least they have each other in the end. They die side by side. It's bloody and awful, but they get a friend with them, a real voice. The earth is final and tangible. You can touch it as you leave it. But when I die, I'm going to die completely alone, in some empty expanse of sky. Just the fuzzy static on the earphone and searing metal. I hate the smell of smoke now. Whatever happens, I'm not going to burn. I keep my pistol close, right below the throttle.

Quick.

See, this isn't really funny at all. I don't know why I used that word. Maybe I mean this is ironic? They think the sky's *better, but it's actually worse? You're the one attending university, so I'll trust you on the proper word choice. I only know numbers and angles. I'm the worst with words. Are you even reading these? Can you send me a little sign in the stars or something? You believe in that kind of thing—and I'm counting them every day, waiting.*

I miss you.

Athan

Dear Ali,

I don't think I'm as good as I once thought. Will you still like me if I'm a terrible pilot? Because I think I'm becoming terrible. I'm still getting planes down, of course, and everyone says I'm doing well, that I'm certainly on my way to earning my squadron. But that's because they don't know my secret. They don't see how much I struggle to stay out of enemy gunsights before I get those planes down. How much effort it's taking just to stay alive, to stay fastest. That's terrifying, Ali. Sometimes I feel a panic growing in my chest. Suffocating me. I'd describe it for you—what it's like to watch those tracers skim your wings, inches away from your own death—but I won't. Not right now. I see it in my head every night, which is too much as it is.

I must not be that good. Someone recall my Top Flight status.

(I don't know why I'm telling you this, because I'd rather have you think I'm the best pilot in the world, and a hero. Stupidly brave all the time, like my brother. But I don't want to lie to you, so here's the truth. Just the shameful damn truth. Don't tell my father.)

Missing you always,
Athan

Ali,

A month of war.

An entire month, and I need to finally admit something: My name is Athan Dakar. And I should have told you long ago.

If you hate me now, I'd understand. I'm sorry. I'll be sorry for what I did every day of my life, however long or short that is. If you haven't stopped reading this or thrown it into the trash, please know I want to go back in time and do the summer again. I want to go back to that moment in the garden when I was stupid enough to try and ask you for directions. I want to give you another bad luck flower. I want to dance another waltz and hike another mountain and instead of being the stupid ass I was, I'd tell you my whole name, right there with that beautiful view, and you'd be surprised for a moment, and then you'd shake your head and tell me, truly, I don't look important enough to be the General's son—that easy way you diminish whatever I've said when you're annoyed or playing difficult to get. (I actually love it when you do that.)

I'm sorry, Ali. I'll explain everything the next time I see you. I swear. If you let me, I'll kiss you and prove to you how much I care. Forget my words. Just let me show you. But that means I need to see you again, I need to stay alive, and I will—for you.

Yours always, always, I swear,
Not a farm boy, but please forgive me

Lieutenant Athan,

I hope you are good. Your sister says I will write to you and practice my Savien. We can make my Savien good, together. She also says I will write to her, when she is in Thurn.

I am sorry I was the bad news with you, but you are not all terrible Lieutenant Athan. Fight like you are good. See more than your gun. See the chest.

Is the drink from Karkev good?

Thank you.
K. Illiany

Leannya,

   What the hell are you doing in Thurn?!

   Whatever you're thinking—stop where you are and don't do it. This letter had better be forwarded to you quick, because Father is going to kill you when he finds out. And in the event these happen to be the last words you ever receive from me, I hope my efforts aren't wasted and you turn around and go back to Valon. Do you hear me? My dying wish is that you stay the hell away from all of this.

   Dying.

   Wish.

                         Your loving and possibly soon-to-be-dead brother,
                                                          Athan

Dear Athan,

I know I can't send you this letter. I can't even write my own mother, since the cables are down and used for encrypted military communication only now. But I still think of you always, still wonder where you are, if perhaps you've been stationed in Thurn again. Surely you haven't been called up to this campaign. You're too young. Too inexperienced. You're being trained somewhere, and I'm going to pretend that's true. It's the only way I can wake each morning and carry on.

Since I can't send this to you—at least not now—I'm going to tell you the truth of what I'm doing here in Resya, because I believe you'll understand why. Someday I'll explain it better in person, when I can properly ask your forgiveness, but for now let this attempt at a testament suffice. You see, I'm exposing the unjust nature of Savient's invasion in this kingdom . . . and before you react, let me explain that it's not because I wish any harm to you or Cyar or any of the kindhearted soldiers I believe exist in your ranks (never, never, never, I swear). But unfortunately, it seems the course of this war is not being recorded properly. In the North, your General is trying to make them believe that Resya is guilty of terrible things, and therefore everyone in this kingdom deserves to suffer for the crimes of a few. That they deserve this horrific invasion because, in the end, it will lead to a better state for the world as we know it. But Athan, why should these innocent people endure such a war? How is that right? I feel obligated to ensure their side is also revealed before the world, to keep things fair. And surely you agree with that?

Let me paint you a picture of what I'm trying to say. There's a woman I've met here, Jali Furswana, and she's a princess like me, though her kingdom (Masrah) was overthrown in a Nahir-inspired revolt many years ago. She never talks about what happened to her, or how she eventually arrived in Resya, her sister marrying Rahian, but I must confess that I see in her some frightening version of myself. What if our coup in Etania had been successful? Would I now be living on another court's charity like this, in denial of my fate? What if you hadn't managed to get me to the throne room in time? Where would my mother be today—convicted of a false crime and blamed for my father's murder?

It seems all too possible now that I know the stretch of this earth. The sheer brutality and injustice of these political games. And yet do you know how this princess spends her days? She floats about the pool like a listing swan, a wine glass in hand, oblivious to the increasingly dire developments on every side. She cares little for her adopted kingdom, convinced that she, at least, will survive to the end, safe behind palace walls. The other evening, a lieutenant with his arm lost below the elbow showed up to one of our dinners, his stub freshly bandaged from the front, and she had the nerve to ask if he could perhaps be a dear and keep it hidden below the lace tablecloth while she ate. And she's not the only one. Oh no, there are other wealthy nobles in this kingdom who don't yet understand the consequence of this war, who even hope for a Safire victory. Anything is better than violent Nahir revolt, they think. Anything is better so long as they get to keep their titles and their prestige, even as thousands march into those mountains to be sacrificed for their right to exist in luxury. So you see, this is why I have to care, Athan. Because too many people, who have the chance to make things better, re-

fuse to look and see—both in the North and in the South, it
seems.

I'm sorry. I feel I'm lecturing at you here, and this must
sound like some university essay, but truly, it's easier to sim-
ply write about these events as if they're far away, to not feel
them too deeply. Our newsreels always show young soldiers
smiling, lifting victorious rifles like they aren't stumbling
backwards with every day that passes, and I think that part
is fine—the necessary façade. They have to pretend they're
winning, that victory is on its way. But it's the proof of their
fantasy that fractures my heart. Resyan tradition forbids
them to show any dead bodies, even the enemy, so it's always
your aeroplanes they film in defeat, smoking like an ember
shot to the earth. A little puff, a little flame, then someone
smiling again, because see? You can be killed. You can be
beaten. You're only human, like us.

Athan, they don't know how human. It's you. You're in
those planes, and Cyar. They celebrate it, because they don't
know the stories behind each little puff of smoke. The secret
histories. They don't know how you held my hand as we
climbed our mountain, the way you jumped along the rocks
for the fun of it. They don't know how every night I dream of
pressing myself to your chest, feeling the expanse of you which
is sacred to me, every heartbeat like my own, every touch
made of stars, because I remember exactly the way your
breath—so alive, so gentle—felt against my neck, your lips
following in soft exploration . . .

I need to stop. Thinking like this always breaks my resolve
not to cry. But please, Athan, when you watch your reels,
imagine the stories too. Each Resyan plane is also a heart.
They're your enemy, but they're still alive, and I pray you
remember that and act with honour. The things I've seen from
the front, from your soldiers . . . No. This isn't what you need
to hear, not even if I could send you this letter. Of course
you're doing the right thing, even in war. You care too deeply,

like me—and you always will. And in fact, you're not even in this war. You're in Thurn, far away, and someday when I tell you all of this in person, it will make such perfect sense, because you and I, we're the same.

Holding your heart forever,
Ali

IV

THE CAULDRON

20

Adena

For a month we fly dawn to dusk, following the steady advance. There's no rest. Arrin won't let anyone stop, not with the pincers of our two fronts so close to snapping together, pushing the Resyan army into retreat. From the sky, the war looks simple and clean—we see the mushrooms of black as Army Group North fights its way through the tangled terrain, the trail of supply lines spreading out behind. A patchwork hell. A chess match of smoking squares.

I do my part, the only thing I can do, even as it gets harder and harder for me. I obliterate enemy trains and tanks as they rattle for the front. I pound my guns into them, little shapes that scatter in flame. But mostly, I wound enemy fighters. Cyar shadows me into the blue and we duel them at 10,000 feet. The dark marks multiply along my plane's flank, and Kif has to repaint them at least once a week since I keep managing to knock my fighters out of commission, getting in too close to my kills, crash-landing when a brake line's shot.

Filton begins to look wistful every time he waves my planes goodbye.

"I've never ruined a *single* fighter," Ollie informs me before a sortie. "Two wars. Dozens of missions. And no scratches! I knew you weren't that good, Charm."

But it's not really about being good, and he knows it. It's about luck. I can count all the stars I want, do sit-ups until I feel sick to my stomach, but in the end some lucky hit from a rookie Resyan pilot might pierce my fuselage at its weakest point—and then I'm butter.

Just like that.

Just like Sailor and three other pilots from Moonstrike.

On the fortieth day since we lit up the mountains, we finally come within one hundred miles of Irspen, the royal city where Rahian spends his summers. The place Arrin once thought he could take in two weeks. It's nearly laughable now. Irspen's the industrial hub of the north—factories and steel mills built along the Lirak river, railways running to Madelan and every other large city. A strategic point, though they'd be idiots to do anything but surrender with Evertal driving from the east and Arrin driving from the north.

They're about to be caught between two anvils.

We're gearing up to fly near the recently captured city of Adena as Garrick briefs us for another day, the Moonstrike pilots circled together on the patch of sun-dried grass where our planes wait, and it's too damn bright. I throw on sunglasses, rubbing at my always aching head, half listening, half watching two of our soldiers yank around a horse. They've latched their packs onto its back, but it refuses to stand still, swinging in terror.

"Thief, why don't you shadow Charm today?" Garrick suggests to Trigg.

That pulls me back. Trigg, too. A few weeks ago, Trigg showed up to the flight line tossing an anti-tank grenade back and forth in his hands. He refused to admit where he got it, and just like that, the call sign for our new wingman was decided. *Thief.* He grinned when we bestowed it on him—as is tradition—and cheerfully said, "It's a goddamn honour, gentlemen."

He still has no idea it wasn't a compliment, and now he looks at me as I look at him. Garrick's order is a meaningful one since Trigg hasn't gotten anything down, and I suspect Garrick would like me to monitor him for once. I should have done that long ago, since he's supposed to be in my future squadron, but I honestly don't give a damn about Trigg Avilov. Not right now.

My headache works itself into a pulse.

Nearby, the horse whinnies.

Cyar can't take it anymore. Muttering about "army idiots," he marches over and grabs the rope from the nearest soldier, a Rahmeti boy. Cyar scolds him in Rahmi, saying you can't treat a horse like a dog, they don't work like that, and for God's sake how do you think yelling is going to make anything better? With a gentle hand, Cyar does his scratching-the-neck thing, calming the horse in a way Ali would like.

Ali.

I shake the thought of her away quickly. Every time her name finds its way into my head, I feel the instinct to squash it. I don't want her to be a part of this—the downed planes, the scorched mountains. I want her in the evenings, when the stars come out, a secret escape just for us. Her warm kisses brushing my neck in some faraway throne room. But not here. Not in this place where I'm plagued by an emptiness that's growing inside me every day. A hollowed-out space where all my guilt should be, twisted and raw and shameful.

Instead, it's just nothing.

Nothing except this damn headache.

Sweat pools beneath neckerchiefs as we ready to fly, running through our personal rituals and superstitions. We all have them, little things that feel like luck. But Trigg's are more obvious. He runs his hands along each wing—right and left—then the tail, and finally the nose. He holds one hand high like a prayer. I realize, as I tighten my parachute, he actually *is* praying.

"I don't think God appreciates thieves," I remark on my way by.

"Says who?" Trigg grins, the dirty kind. "God keeps the best alive, you know."

"Guess you'd better watch your back then."

His smirk disappears.

I'm not sure when I got so mean.

There's a sudden commotion across the airfield, and we both forget our mutual suspicion. A truck screeches to a squelching stop, prompting a flurry of activity and salutes. It takes a very long moment for me to recognize Arrin. He has no cap or badge. Nothing to distinguish himself as Commander. He's thinner and in a dirty uniform that's seen much better days.

Followed by his officers, he hustles across the field towards a camouflaged transport plane. No one notices us pilots standing there waiting to go up.

"They'll burn the bridges," a colonel worries at Arrin's heels.

"They won't," he replies. "It's their only way back to the capital. They'd be goddamned fools to burn them now."

"We're stretched thin already, sir, and they're mobilizing the base at Erzel."

"Won't matter once we're across the river."

They sweep past us, and I hear myself speak before I can stop myself. "Arrin!"

He halts in his tracks. Turning, surprise brightens his tired face as he peers between all the pilots, finding me. "Little brother!"

I wave.

"Some idiot show-off came right down to 200 feet above my lines and shot up a Resyan bastard." He grins. "There's a rumour it was you."

They all look at me—Trigg, Garrick, Ollie. I might have chased another to the deck yesterday. But with Cyar, of course.

I shrug. "My brakes weren't working."

Arrin doesn't get the joke. He knows nothing about airplanes. "Do it again," he orders me, already moving for his transport. "That was brilliant! Exactly what they needed to see."

Then he's gone. Flying south for some other part of the line.

Like clockwork, we're in the air again too, clipping through the sky. Trigg's locked on my wing. He flies with good pitch, his plane hardly wavering in the strong wind. He's solid, I can admit that. Steady. But he says nothing over the earphone. He's just there, a wing's span from me, brooding.

Engagement comes quickly. A handful of Resyans fleeing below us. They're trying to get somewhere—and fast—and don't even notice us until we're on top of them. Guns and cannons fire. I let the others take the lead on this one, since I want to watch Trigg. Two Resyans are trying to slip off to the east. An officer with his red-tipped wings, another shadowing him. We've learned the higher-ranking pilots always distinguish their planes from the rest. And this one must be someone important if he's trying to get the hell out without even firing a shot.

"Thief, you're on the officer. I'll take the wingman."

He doesn't move.

"Do you understand, Thief?"

"Understood, sir."

Sir? Something's definitely up.

The two Resyans open their throttles, putting desperate space between us.

"Thief, get on that officer. Engage him."

"Yes, I—"

"Stop talking and do it!"

Bullets spray from Trigg's plane. Right into the Resyan *wingman*. Fuselage damaged, the enemy fighter's belly before it explodes into a charred skeleton of a plane, careening for the forest below. A deadly shot executed with easy precision, and the Resyan officer flees wildly for the horizon.

I'm so angry I could shoot Trigg myself.

I swing back for our group and he dutifully follows. As soon as we land again, I jump from my cockpit and march past Filton—who's thanking me for being nice to the plane—ripping the goggles and headset from myself as I go. I'm dripping with sweat. Everything soaked. I'm hot and furious, unable to

comprehend how someone could be this damn obstinate. Defying a direct order. He sure as hell won't be anywhere near my
squadron.

If I get one, of course.

If we all live that long.

"Be respectful about it," Garrick warns, striding alongside
me. "You're the leader here."

"He's deliberately pushing!"

"Yes, it's not very pleasant having someone under your leadership who doesn't want to be there, is it? Someone who doesn't
want to listen, who does the things you order but everything in
their attitude says, 'I don't care what you think and I'm doing
this only because I choose to.'" A grin tugs at his lips.

"I wasn't this bad," I huff.

"I'm sure Thief doesn't think he's that bad either."

With that, Garrick falls away, leaving me on my own marching for Trigg's perfect, untouched plane. Not a dent. Not a
scratch. Disappearing in dogfights does have its perks.

"What was that, Avilov?" I demand.

He faces me with arms crossed. "Sir?"

"I said go after the officer and you did nothing. You just sat
there. Then you take out the *wingman*? What's going on in your
idiot head?"

It feels good to lay into him finally, and we glare at each
other. His jaw ticks, like he wants to say more, to snarl back at
me, but he knows better than that. The one shred of sense he
has left. Then he backs up a step, arms uncrossing in what
might be surrender. He looks at the plane, at the ground, his
boots, anywhere but my eyes. "I didn't know which one it was,
Lieutenant."

"The one with the damn red-tipped wings! How much more
clarification do you need?"

"I know," he says, voice a few inches tall. "I couldn't see it."

"It was right in front—" I stare, confused. And then it clicks.
All at once. "Are you—?"

Colour blind.

I don't say it out loud.

The utter shame on his face says it for me.

"How did you get into the squadrons?" I exclaim, dumb-founded now.

"Well . . ." He looks even more like a worm in the sun. "You see, my uncle who contracts with the navy. He . . . well . . ."

"Yes?"

"He's not really my uncle. He's my mother's lover. He's been trying for years to get her to leave my father, but she won't do it, and he does whatever she asks, and I wanted to be a pilot, right? It's all I've ever wanted. And he's always trying to sweet-talk her or me, anything to win favour, and he said he'd get me here. And he did."

"He snuck you into the air force?"

"They might have removed a few bits of the vision test for me. Among other things."

I have no words. The very idea that there are people shuf-fling favours, sneaking in colour-blind pilots, and all beneath my father's nose . . . It's confounding. I never thought anyone could get away with it. I sure as hell can't get away with any-thing.

How did they manage this?

"You've been hanging back because you don't know which plane to hit?" Saying it out loud, this sounds like a disaster.

"Only at first," he corrects quickly. "It's when they're far away. But once we're in the thick of it, it's easier."

Oh, God.

My expression must be conveying this sentiment, because he rushes on. "I study the shapes of the models. Memorize details, theirs and ours. I can usually figure it out fast, but I've been nervous here. Being wingman to pilots who don't know the truth? I'm just waiting to be found out. To be court-martialed for lying." His eyes beg me. "I know I'm a liability, Lieutenant, but I can do a good job for you. Once I'm on it, I give everything

I have. I can bring those planes down. I just need a bit of extra help." He meets my gaze again, pitiful. "I *love* flying. It's the only thing I'm good at."

I don't know why, but I feel bad for him. I really do. I don't know what I'd do if I couldn't fly because of my eyes. And I remember what he said about his family needing him to do this, as a Safire officer. If he went home now . . . Well, maybe he'd be in about the same position I'd be in. Never able to live it down.

I glance around the sad state of our makeshift airfield. It's already nothing like the proper squadron I imagined. "Fine. Fly with Cyar for now. He'll point you in the right direction."

Trigg looks startled. "You're going to let me fly with *him*?"

I almost laugh. "Cyar isn't my personal property, and he's the only one here who will actually pity you enough to do it."

"But you won't tell anyone?"

"Not *yet*."

Trigg nods. "I trust you."

It's a bit uncomfortable, the fact that I'm suddenly bound to Trigg in a real way, hiding his secret. "You'd better get this right," I remind him. "If you're not bringing down planes . . ."

"Oh, I will, Captain!"

I don't want to make this any more dramatic than it is, so I offer my hand, the one thing I can think of to convey respect. That's what Garrick told me.

Trigg grins, restored.

We shake and that's that.

At dawn, there are shouts across the field, someone hollering for all pilots to the flight line. The base dissolves into chaos and palpable panic. Mechanics sprinting for the planes, tent flaps thrown open.

Groggy and already sweating, we sit in front of Torhan, bracing for the worst.

It's worse than the worst.

"The Resyan army corps from Erzel broke through southwest of here," he says, disbelief in his voice. "They've cut right below us and slashed our advance in two. We've lost contact with the advancing Fourth Division."

Rain drizzles on the tent, slapping at the canvas in mocking applause.

"Then we should swing the Fourth farther east?" Ollie suggests. "Surely we can outflank their move?"

"It's too late. Both bridges over the Lirak have been blown," Torhan replies bluntly. "An entire Resyan division has been caught on our side of the river. They can't get back to Irspen. So if ours go east, we run right into them. There's no way out. Trapped on either side."

We each stare at the map, reality wobbling together in our exhaustion. Three divisions of soldiers—at least twenty thousand in each—are now surrounded on all sides. One Resyan division is trapped between our 4th and Evertal's advance from the east. Our 4th is trapped between the river and the freshly mobilized Resyan corps marching up from Erzel. And the Resyans from Erzel will soon be running headlong into us, coming from the north. A disaster of conflicting lines.

Why the hell would the Resyans blow their own escape route?

"Where are the engineers?" I ask. "We can fly them into the circle. Get bridges up, get ours over the river."

It's the least we can do until we figure out what's happening with Evertal to the northeast.

But Torhan shakes his head. "The nearest engineer battalion is with the Seventh Armoured."

"And where's the Seventh?"

Torhan swallows. "A hundred miles behind us."

It's a nightmare, then. The initial thrust was history in the making. The tanks piercing through, a giant wave of military might sending the Resyans into a frantic retreat. But the tanks can't keep up with us. Not in these mountains, with the engineers forced to blast out fortifications at every turn.

Arrin does have blind spots after all.

And when Torhan tries to reach Arrin for the official report, the next move to make—they realize he's with the 4th.

Encircled.

My damn brilliant brother has walked himself right into a trap.

21

❧ AURELIA ❧

Madelan

This is how a month of war crawls by for me—quietly, lit by chandeliers, my pen scrawling away as I draft dozens of press releases which Tirza helps me edit and translate into polished Resyan with her journalist's eye. I'm grateful for all the essays Heathwyn had me compose last summer. It was practice for the University exams, but now I'm discovering a far better use for this skill of persuasion.

Together, we share the photographs the official papers refuse to publish—the dead, the mutilated—to drive home the true cost of Savient's willful disregard for the League's ruling, both to Resya and to the world. I keep a copy of everything we write, knowing it will be necessary evidence once the inevitable end to the conflict arrives and the war for culpability begins.

I also try to bring Jali Furswana into friendship, since I believe she could be a powerful voice to represent Resya's interests should Rahian be found guilty and left out of the equation. She's someone who understands that violence is hardly the answer, whether it comes from the North or South, who could speak to both the danger of national insurrection and the arrogance of foreign interference. Masrah has weathered both over the decades.

Unfortunately, Jali holds little interest in my political questions, refusing to speak about her tumultuous past in Masrah or how she wound up in Resya. She simply pens endless poetry while she suns herself beneath the palms, forcing me to listen to her compositions.

> *This is the land of a hundred generations,*
> *the land of my heart,*
> *and here I stand, a mountain you cannot pass.*
> *O my enemy, my beloved.*
> *My own brother!*
> *I offer myself on this sword.*

I have to admit they're rather beautiful, inspired by Masrah's classic heroes, but what good are ancient knights in this modern war? With Rahian endlessly distracted by changing battle lines, often touring his battalions, his home is left in the hands of Jali—an opulent realm of fantasy—where no one notices what Tirza and I are typing away in the shadows, Havis occasionally plotting an elaborate escape to Thurn in between rounds of increasingly disillusioned liquor shots.

While they feast and smoke and flirt, we write.

At the beginning of the sixth week of war, I discover a photograph to change it all. It's early morning, the usual Resyan officers disappeared in a flurry, which alerts me to something afoot. Someone mutters eagerly about an encirclement, a surge of victory in the air, and I hurry past the banqueting hall now serving as army intelligence, searching for my new friend Officer Walez.

Walez won me over immediately because he's the perfect reflection of Reni. Dark haired, hazel eyed, wielding a serene pride that's nearly weightless. I miss Reni and Mother so terribly—not able to receive or send communication with the cables down—and being with the young Walez makes me feel I'm closer to them somehow. When Walez caught me rustling through reports in the briefing room after his superiors had left, he didn't scold me or turn me over. He simply smiled, bowed from the neck, and said he'd be happy to pass along whatever information I desired. Perhaps it was the power of my crown at work again, but he's been so faithful in his mission that I truly believe he does wish the truth of this war to be revealed for all. He never asks why I want to know these things.

He simply helps, an unspoken understanding between us.

Today, thanks to Walez, I possess photographs captured straight from enemy lines, and I know they're a true prize.

Tirza's wide-eyed delight proves it.

"Stars, Ali! These are perfect!"

I try not to look too closely at the grainy shots. They might be perfect for our pamphlets, but they're a terrible glory to behold. Perhaps I'd hoped the Safire would prove us wrong. Perhaps I'd hoped that the outright brazenness of this invasion would be their greatest crime. But now I know that's not true, because in my hands is an image of lumpen figures sprawled on the earth who were once Resyan prisoners—all shot in the back. Safire soldiers idle nearby, some with guns still raised, complicit in this callous tactic, ruthlessly ignoring the rules of war. The fact that this photo even exists is the greatest insult they could do to a Resyan soul. Lifeless bodies desecrated before the cameras, captured forever in a disturbing mockery of their final moments. We've seen terrible images over the past weeks—individual cases of brutality, trickling back from the front—but this is the first that feels indicative of a larger Safire policy towards prisoners which holds no mercy.

"The official reports will never show these," I say softly. "They'll be locked up for the duration of the war, hidden away."

Tirza nods with a sigh. "Why the stars should the evidence disappear simply because we don't have the heart to look at it?"

It won't. Not if we can help it. But then, what should we do with them? It has to be the right move. Evil used for good. On a nearby table, I catch a glimpse of the morning's paper,

180   JOANNA HATHAWAY

abandoned by Havis after his late breakfast. The front page, as usual, features a Safire plane caught in a fiery nosedive. I've forced my heart to keep beating when I see them.

Not him.

Not like that.

But it sparks an idea, gaining clarity. "We should write something in Savien," I suggest. "Safire soldiers might be picking up our pamphlets too, and they need to know we aren't afraid to share these with the world."

"But neither of us speaks the language," Tirza points out.

I smile, a bit sheepishly, pulling out the Savien textbook Reni gifted me.

Tirza's mouth drops open. I've been studying it in secret, trying to remember what Athan taught me in the summer, the pronunciation, the inflection, the sound of *his* voice saying these strange words. And while I still don't know much, I'm fairly certain I can patch together a compelling sentence or two.

I grab my pen.

"Call them all arrogant swine," Tirza prompts. "Say their days are numbered and Resya stands to defeat their vile attempts at imperialism!"

My pen hovers as I think. "No, we have to actually get through to them, Tirza. Not with insults, but with the facts, like we do with everyone else. We have to make them *listen*."

Tirza appears skeptical, but I hurry down the words that seem best. When I've finished, pleased with it, I discover she's still watching me, an expression on her face I can't read.

"They're encircled," she states. "A noose around the Safire forces."

Some inner apprehension lurches within me, though I'm not quite sure why. I haven't even read the entire front page yet, too focused on my writing. "A noose?" I repeat, and I can't hide my fear at how much death that might mean—for both the Safire and the Resyan armies. An attrition of horrors.

"They deserve this, Aurelia. You know they do."

"The Commander deserves this," I reply sharply, standing from my desk. "Not the thousands who were forced into this war, bound to an order. Can I not grieve death wherever it happens?"

There's no way for me to explain my conflicted heart to someone who doesn't have friends who wear the fox and crossed swords badge, and it's a long moment before she says, "I think it's time you saw our press."

The unexpected shift catches me off guard. I haven't been allowed to visit yet. Tirza simply takes the words we write and claims her brother has means to distribute them beyond Madelan, though it must be done discreetly, to avoid any lurking Safire sympathizers from suspecting our involvement. That would only reflect even worse on Rahian, since we're right in the palace. And truthfully, sometimes I wonder if Tirza is suspicious of me, too, since I do often come to the Safire's defense in a roundabout way. But I'm eager to prove myself to both of them.

I'm on their side.

I am.

Our photographs tucked away, she leads me through the palace maze she's devised for her stealthy escapes to visit the press, to avoid running into Havis, who would certainly find a way to force me back inside. We dart through the kitchens only for staff and out the back gardens, to a gap in the fencing hidden behind a thick shrub—in use by some maid and footman for a clandestine affair—and burst off of palace grounds.

The cobbled streets open up to a pleasant breeze, sunshine bright, and I breathe in the pristine taste of freedom. Neighbours huddle together in quiet, sober conversation, mothers dragging stubborn children along from store to store. As Tirza leads me onward, I wonder how many of these people have read our pamphlets. How many are in mourning even now, having lost someone beloved in those hellish mountains? Are they glad the ugly truth is being shared and remembered?

When Tirza eventually halts me, we're before a small row house, its walls a patchwork of coral paint and leafy green. The faithful late-morning rains have begun to descend, splattering us both, and Tirza rushes down a set of stairs to the basement, banging on the door.

The boy who opens it is about Reni's age, dressed in a brown leather coat, his black hair shaved and a cigarette hanging off his lips. His green eyes widen.

"Hurry up, it's raining!" Tirza orders without introduction.

He swings the door open as Tirza pushes inside, urging me to follow, and the boy steps back quickly. I shake out my wet braid, stepping into the cramped, cool space with desks pushed into corners and papers fluttering everywhere, a press at the very center.

Tirza waves at the boy. "My brother, Damir." She turns to him. "And this is Aurelia, the princess."

Damir nods a nervous greeting and steps backwards, away from me, his boots creaking on the scuffed wood floor.

I allow him the respectful distance and turn my own circle, taking in the room while Tirza lectures victoriously at her brother about the day's discovery. As rain stammers against two tiny windows, I inspect the small iron press, curious about how it all works, the stamping pieces currently suspended and evidently in need of someone to feed the next leaflet. Then I come to a sudden stop at a board against the back wall, pinned with dozens of black-and-white photographs.

Tirza's determined monologue fades from my ears. Everything disappears except for what's before me. There, printed far too large, is a young man with a bullet hole in the middle of his forehead. Unlike the distant photograph of the executed Resyan prisoners, his stunned eyes still stare upwards beneath the mess of blood, every detail of his expression captured by the camera. On the paper next to his, a dead woman curls round the stiff figure of her infant, clutching the child to her breast. And then, an entire field of bodies—hands and feet and gaping faces—scattered and abandoned in some lonely expanse.

I want to retch on the floor.

"It's terrible, isn't it?" Tirza says quietly, appearing at my shoulder. "Pictures leave a stronger impression than words."

I can scarcely stand to look. This is far more overwhelming than our solitary photographs from Walez. These aren't even soldiers. These are *civilians*.

"Where the stars are these from?" I whisper.

"Thurn. We've been writing about it, to let Resya know the truth of what's happening next door, when the people there attempt to resist Northern power. Our underground contacts send these, but even here . . ." She shrugs. "It's like Resyans don't want to know. They don't want to see this, or imagine it could happen to them. And the Landorians always concoct some explanation in their official papers. They'll claim they've 'accidentally' mistaken farmers for Nahir, or an entire family walking the hills for a rebel unit. They have their noble excuses, anything to not feel guilty while they're playing on the coast in their gambling halls and seaside spas."

As I look at the board, I realize that Lark's photographs from Beraya reflected only one crime of many, and suddenly I wish I knew why he brought me that particular atrocity and not any of these dozen others in Thurn.

What were you trying to say, Lark? Why did you pick Beraya?

But he can't answer me—not anymore—and my helpless gaze roams higher, to a single pamphlet pinned at the top of the grotesque display. It has no photograph, but it's large, commanding attention. A cartoon. In the right-hand corner, a little sketched cat prowls, facing off against a giant, snarling lion, the sun large above them both. But the cat's shadow on the wall behind doesn't reveal itself. Instead, it casts a large dog, frothing at the jaws and dark furred.

"The lion needs its match," I say, reading the caption aloud.

"I drew that," Damir shares, the first time he's spoken. Cautious pride warms his voice as he points to the cat in the corner. "It's a *si'yah* leopard. There aren't many around here, but in Thurn, there are countless."

"And the lion?" I ask.

He pauses. "That's war. Death. Every dark nightmare in this world we have to stand up against. It's so large, it seems unbeatable, and the *si'yah* feels small. But we have to summon the lion's match. The cat has to bring out its inner dog."

I feel another little flutter of unease, and again, I'm not sure why. "Who pays for your press?" I ask, turning to face the siblings. "You charge nothing for your pamphlets."

"Lady Havis," Tirza replies quickly.

"And how do you gather all of this evidence? You don't even live in Thurn."

Damir glances at Tirza, as if confused by my lack of knowledge.

She waves him off. "I didn't tell her. It didn't feel like the right time."

Her abrupt tone stirs an unexpected hurt in my chest. The scent of a secret I've been kept apart from, despite everything we've been working for together. "Tell me what?"

Tirza doesn't answer right away, only stares at me like she did in the palace, measuring me silently, something strangely aloof in her gaze. But she makes her decision, offering me her hand. I take it and grasp tight, too afraid of ruining the tender thing that's grown between us these weeks.

I can't bear to lose my only friend here.

We head outside again and the rains have moved westward. Tirza pushes us northeast at a rapid pace, the houses on either side of us dimming, becoming smaller and more tumbling, cats stretched on still-damp pavement, children playing on front stoops. When we eventually crest a high hill, I realize exactly where we are. Below is the large airfield we watched from the motorbike over a month ago, wire fences surrounding hangars and runways, a rash of military vehicles zipping about. Three aeroplanes head north at an urgent pace—heavier-looking bombers.

Offense.

I almost laugh darkly, because I can identify them now. Wouldn't Athan be proud? But my wry thoughts are swiftly pulled from this tactical development, centering instead on a strange village of tents and cobbled shelters at the outskirts of the base, huddled along a thin river. Children roam the desolate paths, women laying out laundry to dry in the fresh sun and cooking over small fires, smoke drifting upwards.

"Those Northern soldiers you mourn," Tirza says. "They made this camp. They forced these people to flee over the border, for safety, after they turned Thurn into a nightmare."

Her expression holds something older, greyer, as we stare down at this pathetic specter of a village, flung far from the city center and right beside an airfield at battle readiness.

"But why are these people . . . out here?" I ask, confused. "Aren't there proper homes for them to stay in?"

"Who's going to let someone from Thurn stay in their home?"

"But these are children."

"*Nahir* children," Tirza corrects bitterly. "Hardly children at all, to some."

I have no answer to that. I can see the tiny figures—skinny arms and legs, like Teo who's safely sheltered in the palace. And they're left out here? It's too astounding. It makes no sense that anyone could allow such a thing when Madelan's glittering with wealth. How could a child be Nahir? How could anyone believe that? Everyone wants to know the secrets in Resya—the truth of Rahian's allegiance—but perhaps *this*, this is the secret that should be shared.

This feels desperately cold and heartless.

"When the Northern soldiers punish the resistance in Thurn," Tirza continues, "they make sure everyone pays for the actions of a few. There's a town, not far from the border here, and the things that happened there are unspeakable."

My heart trembles, because I'm afraid I already know. This town that feels like my own curse. "Beraya?"

Tirza turns to me, stunned. "I didn't think anyone in the North knew."

They don't. Because of me. Because I hid the only evidence

and used it to save my own family. Guilt grabs my throat, a re-
morse I'll never escape. "I saw photographs, Tirza. The ones
executed before the wall. Some of them were too young."

She looks at me, a ghost of emotion on her face. "They were."

Staring at her here, at the top of this deserted road, over-
looking the camp, I finally recognize her expression for what it
is. Not anger, or disgust. Not judgment. It's simply grief, turned
to stone so that nothing can get down deep. So that it can't hurt
again. I saw that in my own reflection after Lark's death. I saw
it in Athan's eyes, on our mountain, when he talked of losing
his mother.

I see it now in her.

"What happened?" I ask hesitantly. I have no idea if she'll
want to share, but she's brought me here for a reason, and I
want to give her the opportunity.

Her delicate hands play with a silver button on her blouse.
After a moment she says, "It was like any other day. The usual
Landorian tanks on the streets, the usual panic before a
roundup. They always do it the same. Arrests, interrogations,
firing squad. But on that day, they didn't make their usual accusations. They simply went from house to house in our neigh-
bourhood, grabbing every man or boy old enough to hold a gun.
They took three of my brothers, Aurelia. I tried to stop them.
Said I'd write them up, get them court-martialed. But they just
laughed. They were Safire. The outsiders, untouchable and
ready to show the Landorians how it's done, and when they
grabbed my youngest brother, crying, straight from my mother's
arms—" She draws a single breath. Slowly. Deeply. "He was
only twelve," she whispers. "I couldn't watch them do it. I
couldn't bear it, and for that I'll never forgive myself. My
brothers should have seen me, with them right to the end. But
instead my mother made me hide. I'd already begun writing
against the occupation, and we were so scared they'd arrest me
next. I've heard what they do to their prisoners. I had to run."
She gazes down at her shoes now, her grief aglow in the sun.

"Damir was already here in Resya, working on the Havis estate and trying to make a place for the rest of us, so I went to him. I survived. We both did. But you see how hard it is for Damir to speak. He's the only brother left, the oldest, and he feels he should have been there. What the hell could he have done, though? Gotten himself shot, too? No, there's nothing you can do. You just get up the next day and keep fighting back, in every way you know how. You don't disappear."

She turns to me, eyes lifting again. "My mother was a teacher and she taught us everything, Ali. Three languages. A love of books and writing. She wanted us safe, but the trouble is, the more you read, the less you want to be quiet. What's the point in learning about the world if you can't do a thing about it?"

Faint laughter rises from the distant camp, two little girls squealing as they race along the river far below. I realize I'm crying. I try to wipe the wet from my eyes, since Tirza is the one exposing her most personal grief, and what do my tears matter? But she doesn't notice. Perhaps she has no tears left.

"Was it the Commander?" I ask, needing something useful. The way forward from this horror, towards justice. "The General's son?"

Tirza gives a short laugh. "Yes, he was there that day. And the Safire have been starving the city ever since I fled. No one goes in. No one goes out. No food, no weapons, no escape. But this is what Northerners do. This is how they are. They kill us by a thousand cuts, then have the nerve to condemn us for defending our own."

I grip my arms to myself, feeling sick. I don't want to imagine that any person could be this heartless, this indifferent to suffering. It doesn't seem possible. Athan promised me that no matter what the Commander has done, the rest are trying to do the right thing. Athan would never use his gentle hands to kill like this. But soldiers wearing his uniform have dragged a boy straight from a mother's arms, and in my bag is a photograph of prisoners executed by Safire guns.

It's all too possible.

"They'll pay for it," Tirza continues firmly. "The Commander will pay for it, beginning with this encirclement. I hope he bleeds out slow with a shot to the neck."

The fierce certainty in her voice frightens me. What frightens me more is that I think, in theory, I want the same. He deserves it. The soldiers fighting for him might not all deserve it, but he does—because he has power in his hands. And he has done something unforgivable. He's allowed arrogance to turn to cruelty.

Words burn inside me, all of these things I want to write down and send North, to the ones who let truth disappear across a vast expanse of dark sea. Who don't care to look closer, to listen to the stories worth sharing. They're silencing an entire world here. They're making judgments and proclamations in their League, debating who to side with, who to condemn, safe in their distant realm, so far from these warm days and fragrant mountains now witness to shameful disgrace.

"I'm embarrassed that I ran," Tirza says suddenly, softly. "I left my mother behind. But I was scared. I didn't want to be arrested, that's all." Her voice is too young. "Not like that, Ali. Not by them."

I don't think. I grasp her hand, our fingers slipping together, familiar, and I squeeze. "You haven't disappeared. You're still here, fighting, and we're not going to let them get away with this."

She squeezes in return, and we stare at the camp a moment longer, both waiting, searching for something that cannot come. The past will never be undone. The dead can't give voice to their pain. Yet everything feels connected now, the shadow of the Commander hovering across every injustice—always the Commander—manipulating Safire honour into something wrong and terrifying, spreading across the South with laughing indifference.

But I will hold him to account.

And I pray he finds my next pamphlet—because it will be written in perfect Landori, a message just for him.

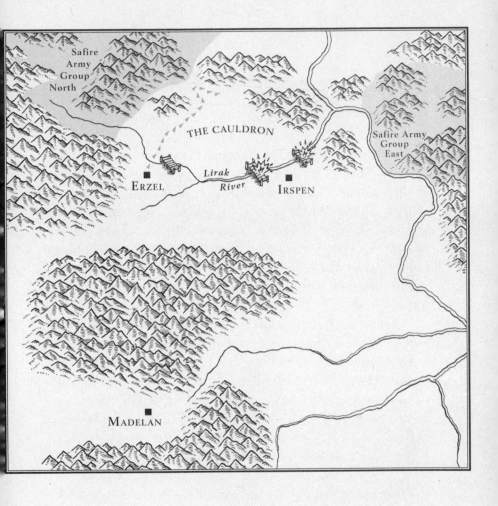

Safire
Army
Group
North

THE CAULDRON

Safire Army
Group
East

ERZEL

*Lirak
River*

IRSPEN

MADELAN

22

Adena

Three days lurch by and our trapped division is a ghost on the horizon. Their radio lines rarely work, cables torn apart by incessant shrapnel. Communication is crude at best. We can see the explosions and shells, the flashes at night, both trapped armies—Resyan and Safire—determined to cut each other's throats. A few transports try to fly in ammunition and supplies, but half don't come back and the rest have no idea if they've just accidentally blessed Resyan soldiers with a gift of Safire bullets.

Commander Vent ambles in with his 7th Armoured Division on the fourth day, an impressive show of tanks and loud engines, but it's too late. They should have been here five days earlier. The tank commanders and engineers look like hell. About as exhausted as anyone else, pushed through these steep, bumpy roads in stifling metal furnaces, blasting away at every obstacle.

"I couldn't get here in time," Vent says to everyone he sees. "It was impossible."

I'm not sure who he's trying to convince. No one looks confident on his behalf, since there's only one person who matters, and that person shows up without announcement in an unmarked plane, ready to interrogate the ones who saw Arrin the day he jogged across our airfield and disappeared into disaster.

Father descends on the small base.

Pistol in hand.

"Why the *goddamned hell* is he out there with them!"

His voice is dangerous, the question one we're all asking. Arrin, trapped with his division. But the truth is, this was bound to happen eventually, since clearly Arrin isn't afraid to take matters into his own fists when things get hot. He proved that the day he went in with the first wave and shouted those soldiers up the beachhead himself.

"He was trying to beat Evertal to Irspen," Vent explains. "We couldn't reach him in time."

"Couldn't?" Father repeats. "Or wouldn't?"

"I tried, General. The bridge was—"

"I know what you did to my son."

The pistol fires.

I think Vent was doomed to this fate the moment he provoked Arrin in the meeting room. He proved himself to be too questioning for my father's tastes. But that fact doesn't stop every officer in the vicinity from sweating a little harder, presented with this searing new punishment for tardiness. I avoid looking at Vent's blood pooling on the earth, but there's still a breath lodged in my chest when Father marches by me, everyone else clearing the hell out of the way.

"Evertal should have had the east," he growls. "She's too goddamned slow!"

No one answers that. She's not even here to defend herself, busy capturing Irspen on her own now. Those still alive and in Father's favour follow him into the tent, to plan whatever's next, and I'm ignored by him. I'm doing what I'm supposed to be doing and therefore unworthy of any special attention. The best place to be, in Father's world.

But I'm impatient. Itching to make a move. If I brought Arrin back, maybe Father would finally forgive me for Etania. Loyalty proved in blood. It's incredibly deluded, and I'm not even sure what I could do for a trapped army, but it's better than nothing. They must think we've abandoned them, offering no air support.

They have to know we at least tried.

"Time to make our move?" I ask Garrick, who's been as impatient as I have to get into the sky again. "It's now or never."

He looks more hesitant, Father still yelling at everyone in leadership, but he nods. "Let's talk to Torhan."

Another secret ally. Thank God he's as guilty as us. I think everyone feels the wrongness of this. Doing nothing. "I knew your brother was going too far," Torhan confesses to me, "but how could I stop him? I can get you the coordinates. They're stretched thin, but they have a small HQ far from the perimeter. Don't expect much." He pauses. "And let's load up those planes."

Maybe I should be alarmed at all the willingness to subvert orders right under my father's nose—the one who just shot a man in the head for being too slow, and now Torhan's the one sticking his neck out for me—but I'm already flying with a colour-blind pilot who bought his way into the air force.

Father doesn't know everything—and maybe that's fine.

It's barely dawn when we make our break. Filton and Kif are the least impressed by the whole plot. They don't like the idea of me flying off with only one plane and no way to fix it. But they pack me up with a few tools, a canister of fuel, and give advice on what to do if the guns get out of alignment.

I wave them off. "I know how to care for her."

Filton's frown silently disagrees with me.

Every other inch of empty space is filled with bullets and weapons for the trapped soldiers. Twelve fighters silently loaded to their limit. We all start our engines at once, a roar that overpowers the airfield. In minutes, we're airborne, hurtling for Torhan's smuggled coordinates, ops shouting at us over the radio to get the planes back on the ground.

We don't listen. Garrick might be ruining himself, but I guess he's ruining himself with me—and for Arrin. It's either brilliant bravery or brilliant stupidity, and it's not our place to worry about that right now.

We just fly.

The brightening sky doesn't stay quiet for long as we cross into the cauldron. The flak's immediate, erupting on every side. As always, the sharp sounds make me wince. Little knives all along my aching head. We stay low to avoid tipping off the Resyan fighters, weaving constantly, making it hard for whoever's shooting below. I catch glimpses of hell between the trees. Burnt-out tanks, dead horses, smoking bunker ruins. Mangled bodies left behind. Luckily, none of ours take a hit and we arrive to a rough field that's been strafed. No runway at all. Cyar nearly overturns his fighter on a massive crater hole as he lands.

I think we're all breathing heavy when we cut our engines and survey the new surroundings. It's a strange mess of ranks and service branches. A busted-up transport plane is beached under the trees, a nose-crumpled bomber across the clearing from it. Wounded soldiers sleep in the shade, most with superficial injuries. Arms in slings and legs wrapped. A few medical trucks idle with pilfered boxes from our disastrous supply plane effort. I have no idea who's left to protect this bit of ground, I only know that Arrin will be here.

I don't let myself think otherwise as I jump out. The soldiers on guard are stunned, gaping at the sudden presence of twelve aircraft, and one runs for what looks to be a dilapidated dispersal hut.

With a shrug at me, Garrick strides after them and I follow. The rest of Moonstrike waits outside. We enter a broken-down building that was certainly once a home, its walls hit by shellfire, a yawning hole in the roof, but memories of a former life are still littered behind—a dining room, photographs, children's games. Damp, dusty lace curtains fluttering.

A young ops soldier sits at the table with his headset, listening carefully, then spots us entering and his eyes widen. He stands, pale skin dripping sweat.

"The Commander?" Garrick asks bluntly.

"On the line," the boy replies.

Of course. Arrin's surrounded, his perimeter poised to shatter at any moment, and instead of holing up in here—like a strategist should—he's out inviting a bullet to his chest. Then what? The division collapses entirely?

The boy fills us in further, saying the more seriously wounded are a mile down the road, the few medics there going mad with lack of supplies. Everyone else capable of wielding a weapon is on the line. Even the two transport pilots who crash-landed here decided to make themselves useful.

Garrick shakes his head and creaks back out the way he came.

I stand there, aware of the ops boy's gaze flickering on me as he redials his headset, listening to troop movement and passing directives. His wiry fingers tap awkwardly.

"What's your name?" I ask.

He glances up at me. "Karruth."

"You know the Commander well?"

"Since Karkev, sir," he replies.

He's older than me, then. I leave him to his job and sit in the destroyed parlour, wondering who might have lounged on this tattered couch before me. It's sweltering inside, but other pilots filter in after a while, eager to avoid the direct sun.

Shells rumble in the near distance, the steady stammer of bullets. When Arrin finally returns, he stomps through the door a disheveled mess, and he's already furious. He saw the planes. He saw Garrick.

And then he sees me. "What the *hell* are you doing here?"

"Don't worry, I brought a gun," I reply from the couch.

"You're not supposed to come help me dig a grave!"

"You're digging it fine on your own," I observe, looking pointedly at the vehicle he just hopped out of. The one that brought him like a welcoming target to Resyan snipers.

He growls something unintelligible and motions me after him. We pass Karruth with his perplexed, wide-eyed expression, entering the little room that was once a study.

"You have to get out of here," I tell him once the door is closed. "This isn't worth you staying. It's a lost cause."

Arrin looks at me like I'm the idiot. "And give up our position? They'll push right through, rout Evertal!"

"Then regroup. Try again."

"That's your strategy?" He snorts, sitting down in a squeaking chair. "This is exactly why you're not as smart as me—and never will be."

I ignore the insult. "Vent's dead."

"Dead?"

"Yes. Do you want to be next?"

He sits silently, looking at me like he thinks I've made this up, but why would I? He can mock me all he wants, but the fact still remains the same—he's surrounded. He's put himself into a trap. Even Arrin Dakar can be outflanked.

He seems to sense my thoughts, expression twisting. "If that bridge to Erzel had actually been blown like it was supposed to be, I wouldn't be in this nightmare."

"Vent couldn't get there in time. It was impossible."

"Not Vent. Damn it, listen to me. This has nothing to do with him. Or the Resyans."

I raise a brow, because it sure seems like it does.

"There were two bridges to Irspen, Athan. The Resyans needed them to make their retreat, and I needed them to get across, and both are gone. *Both.* Trapping them here with me. And that bridge to Erzel? Untouched. Ready for the fresh corps to cross it and surround me like a noose."

I look at him, his bitter expression.

"Think about it, Lieutenant. Why would they blow their own escape route?"

"They wouldn't," I reply.

"No, they wouldn't."

My neck goes clammy. He's right. The Resyans didn't blow their own bridges. It was a suicide move. But if they didn't do it, then someone else did, and that someone couldn't be in Safire or Resyan uniform.

Irregular fighters.

Arrin cracks his knuckles, frustrated. "I've had Nahir tailing me since we got here. They're supposed to be helping us, stirring trouble behind Resyan lines. Kalt got those plans from Havis. Exactly where and when they were going to be, and that damn bridge to Erzel was supposed to be blown by them, not the other two. That fresh Resyan corps should never have been an issue for us."

"Arrin . . ."

"Listen," he ploughs on, bordering defensive. "I can handle loss. I'll sacrifice a hundred soldiers to save a thousand. That's just the way it is sometimes. But this was on me because that bridge wasn't supposed to be there. I walked them into this. And now I sure as hell am not going to leave them behind until Evertal comes through. Do you understand?"

I stare at him and just say the truth. "Seath betrayed us?"

It's the only way to explain this. The gaping reality.

Arrin shrugs. "He's supposed to make this look real."

"Arrin."

"Maybe one of his factions went rogue."

"Arrin."

When my brother looks at me, I can see in his eyes he believes it about as much as I do. It finally releases inside me. Anger. Revulsion. Disbelief. This is the absolute worst way to be shot in the back! Seath's taking out thousands of lives to renege on his alliance with us. Soldiers, civilians. Everyone trapped in this cauldron of hell. And all for what? To make a point? To suddenly throw away everything we've been working for together? And everyone in my family was too stupidly arrogant to even see it coming?

So damn much for my short war.

I discover there's an interesting side effect to six weeks of bad food, battle exhaustion, and constant headaches—the anger can't survive. It flashes and goes to smoke. A single burst of flak. There's nothing left but the hollow space inside of me taunting.

I hit my head a few times.

The little knives stay.

When night comes, I don't breathe a word of the betrayal to Cyar or Trigg, just listen as they bicker, oblivious, finding comfortable spots to sleep beneath a giant fig tree outside. We're all attempting to ignore the fact that anyone could be creeping through the underbrush. Sentries rotate their posts every hour, but we're still surrounded. It's only a matter of time.

"Let's take turns for our own unofficial watch," Trigg suggests, munching on fig fruit.

"I second that," Cyar says.

"Third," I say.

They grant me the first shift—a gift, since there's nothing worse than being woken up after midnight and handed a gun. Of course, that presumes one is actually sleeping. Which might be questionable for me. Dog-tired, I lean against the gnarled trunk, legs outstretched, ready to stare up at the stars and think about Ali's lips—and hopefully nothing lower. It's getting harder and harder to be a gentleman about it. Now that I'm a qualified killer.

I prolong the inevitable by watching Trigg and Cyar, who are on their backs, fascinated by the breathing shadow-shape of them. A few thousand soldiers were like this only a day ago. Now they're husks left behind with no life in them. One moment pulsing, the next moment nothing. It doesn't make any sense that God would make us so fragile and thin. Like paper ready to catch flame with a spark.

Just worthless paper.

"Hey Fox, want to play a game?" Trigg asks after a while.

"Not really," Cyar replies moodily, though it's not like he's sleeping either.

"It's an easy one. It's called 'move your smelly boots away from my head.'"

Cyar shifts with a grunt.

A moment passes. "Either of you ever been with a girl? Not kissing. That doesn't count."

Silence.

"Figured. You got a cigarette, Fox?"

"You know I don't smoke."

"All right, so how about another game?"

"No."

"Tell me about your girlfriend."

"No."

"Can't I see a picture?"

"No."

"She must be ugly," Trigg says, and I kick him in the shin. It's close to my boot. "Come on, Hajari," Trigg tries again, more pleading now. "Just a hint."

I know this is one query that won't get anything. I've been waiting six years for the answer. Nothing's worked.

Cyar breaks the rules though. "Her name's Minah."

The unexpected name makes both Trigg and me startle, squinting at his shadow.

"Anything else to add?" Trigg asks, hopeful.

"No."

"Then she's definitely not real," he says to me.

I can't help but laugh.

"I told you her name," Cyar counters defensively. "Isn't that enough?"

"Nah."

"Why would I make her up?"

"I don't know. Lots of reasons. I saw the way you were look-ing at me earlier. Don't deny it, Haj—"

"All right! Here."

Cyar pulls something out of his pocket and shoves it at Trigg. Trigg flicks his lighter, and for a half second, I'm sure he's going to put the photograph to flame. He doesn't. He just holds it carefully, studying. "Wow." He sounds intrigued.

"Hang on," I say, realizing what's just happened. "Why did you never show *me* her picture?"

Cyar's expression is caught. I can see it even in the dark. "Because I didn't think it would last, Athan. I only see her a month each summer. Every time I go home I think she'll be gone. Why would she wait? She's older. Funny and smart. I'm just . . . me."

I don't buy it.

"If I were a girl, Fox, I'd wait for you," Trigg offers, which might be the nicest thing he's ever said. Then he adds, "But not you, Captain. No way. That would be a mistake."

I kick him with the edge of my heel this time.

Cyar snorts, and I snatch the picture from Trigg. Trigg offers his lighter flame, illuminating the mysterious Minah, and there she is—laughing eyes and a smile that's made of fireworks. Part mischievous, part pure seduction. A good match for the little tyrant Cyar used to be as a kid.

"I can't believe you showed Trigg before me," I say, feeling moody now too.

Cyar tucks it away. "I just wanted to keep one thing for my-self. You had . . . everything else."

I stare at him. "What's that supposed to mean?"

"It means he's jealous," Trigg offers. "Happens in long-term relationships." His grin is loud in the dark.

"Oh, don't worry," Cyar snaps. "The Captain's got himself a princess. He doesn't need me."

I glare at Cyar. "You're calling me that now too?"

"A princess?" Trigg asks, intrigued again.

"She thinks he's a farmer," Cyar continues, the damn traitor.

"A farmer!" There's a pause, then Trigg's laughing so loud he's going to wake the entire Resyan sector. "That's *rich*! You! A farmer!" He guffaws. "Tell me, Captain. When is corn harvested? Wheat? How do you—" He stops abruptly, laughter gone. "Wait."

He stares into the forest, and all three of us stop breathing.

"I see something," he whispers, gun up.

We drop to our stomachs in rapid succession, trying to hug the sweet earth, terrified.

"How can you see anything in the dark?" I whisper hoarsely.

"Aren't you partly blind?" Cyar adds.

"*Colour* blind," Trigg hisses. "I can see shapes in camouflage real well."

We wait. And then—a distinctive crunch. All three of us spring up, raising our pistols at once, and fresh laughter breaks the excruciating silence.

"Hoo, look at these pilots go!" Ollie announces, walking out of the brush. He zips his pants. "Ready to charge into battle!"

Two audible sighs exhale on either side of me.

"Battle?" Garrick replies, materializing as well. "I don't think they'd know what to do with a bayonet."

"Stab it in your eye?" Trigg suggests.

"Judging by the exceptional number of planes you've shot down, I don't think you have that kind of aim." Trigg pretends to thrust the blade at Garrick's back as he passes, but Garrick doesn't flinch. "Just get some sleep, bootlickers. Let the soldiers do their job."

"There are two transport pilots out there somewhere," I remind him.

"Yes," Garrick replies, "and they're damn terrible. They've been requisitioned to ferrying injured on the trucks."

He and Ollie laugh again, and for some reason, it's oddly

contagious. The thought of two hapless pilots trying to do their part on the frontlines, and failing . . . I give in to the strange laughter. Let it come in waves, sucking the last of my energy in a wonderful moment of easy, welcome delusion.

Soon it's quiet again, only Trigg munching on his fig fruit.

Still alive.

Still breathing.

Clutching my head, I close my eyes and start tracing Ali's lips in my mind.

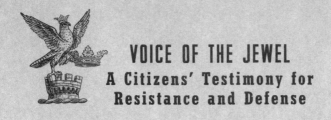

BELOVED FRIENDS OF
RESYA:

We know our kingdom was birthed from negotiation—a royal Southern throne which wedded itself to the Northern line of Prince Efan. That is our legacy. We are two worlds at once. We survived while those around us refused to surrender to the Northern fist at their necks, resisting and fighting even as their farmers were worked to the bone, the riches of their earth plundered, their nobility forced to pay Northern hands for the right to exist. Have we looked away too long? Have we forgotten the truth? We are Resyan, but we are also Southern—a shared history bright with our own heroes, our own honour, and we appeal to that history today, certain that no Northern steel will cut it away.

Now the fist is at Resya's neck. Safire boots thunder through our mountains at this very moment, and perhaps you think they come with honour, with a new way of looking at the world. Perhaps you think they will save us from Nahir insurrection and a weak king.

But even with all of their alluring words, their glorious promises, the Safire spirit cannot make amends for the darkness they've perpetrated in these weeks of war. It cannot undo the crimes they've committed in the besieged land to our east, the cities there strangled to death, the innocents left without home or voice. Their General's own son has wielded this cruelty—vain, wicked, merciless—and if you pretend he comes to save us, then you will only offer up Resya as willing sacrifice to a hungry creature who craves our cobalt and copper and gold, who will weave a deceptive tale against ours and write a history that is not true, to craft their illegal victory.

But we will show the world our honour, united and standing against this foreign aggression with a courageous spirit. We will see the Safire tried for their monstrous crimes before the Royal League, starting with the General's own son. We will make this his final war. We will see him humiliated and his arrogance put in chains.

RESYA UNDIVIDED!
RESYA ETERNAL!

Here we stand—a mountain they will not pass.

23

Madelan

With the tide of war seeming to turn in Resya's favour, a jubilant Rahian ventures off to visit his army, struggling to maintain their unexpected foothold. And with Tirza's personal history now out in the open, our hearts feel quietly closer, the uncertainty of new friendship replaced by understanding that I have heard her most raw secret and refuse to judge her for fleeing to safety. That I still consider her one of the bravest girls I've ever met.

In return, I've decided to share my own secret.

"This was from my cousin," I say one morning, showing her the letter from Lark. It's always with me, like the turquoise earrings from his sister which dangle against my neck. "He died this summer, but he gave me an address here in Madelan, and I believe there's something he wanted me to find."

I can't yet tell her the full story—the dreamed-of negotiation, Seath wearying of this fight, Lark's Nahir allegiance and hope for peace—but this has to be enough for now. Enough to intrigue her.

And it works.

Eagerly, she joins me on the hunt as we head out into Madelan to find Lark's home, which is buried somewhere among these buildings of ginger and scarlet, among the citadels and wide avenues of trolley cars and automobiles. We pass all of the people carrying on beneath the weight of war—elderly men

playing card games, boys chasing one another with toy aeroplanes, women dressed in the black of mourning. We buy cups
of lemonade from a little barefoot girl in a dirty dress. She's
clearly been swept along by the relentless tide, deposited here
in a city far from her home in the northern mountains, and the
sweet upturned face beams when Tirza offers one of cousin Kaziah's many colourful bracelets. She tugs her cart along, staring
happily at the woven bracelet like it's gold on her wrist.

We even pass a little private aerodrome with a few ancient
planes, and the strong smell of petrol immediately rouses memories of Athan. It's so potent, it's as if he's suddenly beside me,
close enough to touch.

As if he never left.

I breathe it in, savouring the sensation, and an elderly mechanic waves at us. "Hello, wandering girls! Lost on this sunny
day?"

We've got our map open, and we've passed the aerodrome
twice in the space of an hour, after making a wrong turn and
doubling back.

"She's from the North," Tirza volunteers with a grin. "I made
the mistake of following her."

"Ah, but she's come to the right place. The Jewel of the
South!"

His pride in this kingdom is evident—even with a war tear-
ing it to pieces all round us—and it's nice to feel I belong in this
place, blending into the crowd with my faded floral-print dress
and dusty riding boots.

And then, at last, we find it.

Rayir d'ezen Cala. Flower of the Sun Street.

It's up a hill in the old eastern parts, announced only by a
faded sign half-covered in vines. Small homes sit buried under
palms and junipers and crawling honeysuckle, the road strangely
quiet, forgotten.

Cautiously, Tirza and I walk forward, as though disturbing
old phantoms, and when we reach the house I've come across

the sea for, I find only a peach-coloured shell sitting in evident decay. The wood veranda is peeled and sagged, lattices torn back from the tall windows, the door barred shut with nailed wood. When we climb the rotting stairs—each with a warning croak—we find smudged windows and drawn curtains.

"Can I help you ladies?" a voice calls from the street, and we both spin.

A well-dressed woman stands at the gate, a suspicious question in her eyes, and I offer a quick hello, hoping she won't assume the worst of us. A pair of intruders.

"I'm looking for the owner of this home," I share, creaking back down the steps. "Someone from abroad had a delivery?"

I hope this sounds vague enough—and not really connected to me personally.

"The owner?" she asks, her face shadowed by a wide sun hat. She turns her brown eyes on the decrepit home. "I doubt they'll be returning."

"But I had an address. I thought someone lived here now?"

"Name?"

Unsure what to say, I show her the letter. "Lark Gazirem and his family?"

The woman frowns. "No, they don't live here. Not anymore."

"How do you know?"

"Because that, my dear, isn't a Resyan name, and their kind left years ago."

Now I frown at her. "Not Resyan?"

She gestures impatiently. "You see the *Irem*? That's Rummayan, and they're all gone from this city now. Perhaps you got the wrong address?"

I force a smile and try not to look devastated. "Perhaps. It wasn't my delivery anyway. I'm only the messenger."

She nods, giving a last apprehensive glance behind me, then continues on down the empty street.

I stand there, staring at Lark's home—or whatever it is, whomever it belongs to—and I'm mad at him, suddenly, for never sharing more about himself. He always had a hundred thoughts on my history books and the moves he thought I should make. A hundred thoughts on Thurn and the South and the Landorians and the Safire. But he rarely talked about his own personal history, and then he had the nerve to just leave me with a damn letter and a damn address and expect me to figure it out. I'm not going to find his sister. She isn't here. Perhaps she never was.

Stars, I'm the fool! Lark's *dead*.

He won't be waiting for me anywhere except in a lonely grave, and the sense of being too late nearly overwhelms me. This Safire invasion. The camp at the edge of Madelan. The crimes continuing unhindered in Thurn. Perhaps this abandoned home represents the truth—a world already gone. We missed our chance. Lark brought his last reckless hope for peace with Seath and I ruined it when I put a bullet in his neck.

But I still stand there, like something might happen.

I *need* there to be more.

Determined, I march back to where Tirza waits on the veranda, and I hold up a rock from the front drive. "We're going inside."

Tirza stares at me. *"What?"*

"There's something here my cousin wanted me to find and I'm going to find it."

Before she can stop me, I face the dirty window, the curtains drawn tight on the other side, willing myself to just do it. No thinking. The rock flies through the glass, shattering it, Tirza wincing with alarm, but no one comes to stop us.

We're utterly alone.

I shrug at her and ease myself through the cracked glass, taking care with the jagged edges. My shoes drop onto a beautiful red carpet sprinkled with window shards, stitched with intricate designs. Couches sit covered in sheets. A piano rests in the corner, elegant and sad looking, left to silence.

Walking softly across the carpet, I'm unsure where to begin.

Tirza stays put by the window. "If anyone asks, I had nothing to do with this," she declares firmly.

"It's all on me," I assure her, tiptoeing for the shelves. Countless books line them, with names like *Anatomy of the Body* and *Principles of Medicine*, and it makes sense. Lark's mother was a nurse, and she tried to save all—Resyan, Nahir, Landorian—before she was killed herself. These volumes of life and healing feel like a vestige of a time long gone, back when the world might still have been healed. Before all of this.

My heart throbs as I pick up a framed photograph of what must be Lark and his mother. He's tiny and knobby-kneed, and she's in a white nursing coat, her unglamorous face decidedly gentle and resolute at once. I long to speak to her. I long to apologize for what I did.

I can't.

My fingers keep trailing the textbooks, the embossed spines, until I find a more hopeful one. It has no lettering on it. No words. It's a faded blue, crumbling at the edges, like it's been through rain and cold, rotted with age. But I know what it is at once.

A photo album.

For a moment, I don't want to open it. I don't want to know the memories it holds. Whatever's there will be far more painful than the framed photograph I just touched. I'll have to look at Lark's life and know what's to come, all of the smiles and love leading to one moment in time, one single night of fire and fear. My trigger.

But I ease the cover open, the aged book vulnerable between my hands. The first page holds the portrait of a young girl. It's old—even older than the one of Lark, with faded spots and water marks. She's not smiling, a sad-eyed girl, and the bottom simply says, *"Lia Lehzar, remembered forever."*

She has my uncle Tanek's face—a bit narrow and birdlike, faintly nervous—and I feel a smile grow on my lips. This is my family. My aunt, a sister my mother left behind long ago. I study her solemn expression, recognizing a part of myself there at once, the tug of familiar hearts.

Mine.

Gently, I turn the frail page and find a large photograph glued haphazardly. Three people sit on a leather couch, two young men and a young woman.

My skin goes cold.

"Ali?" Tirza asks behind me.

I ignore her, the delight of discovery displaced entirely by disbelief. The woman in the middle is my mother. It's her— younger, beautiful, raven haired.

And yet . . . she's a stranger.

I search the photograph madly, trying to find the part of her that I love, the part that I've known for seventeen years, but it isn't there. There's only bitterness in her familiar gaze. A somber, hollow bitterness that pierces me even across the expanse of years. Uncle Tanek sits on her right, skinny and bespectacled, a bit awkward with the gun on his lap. And on her other side lounges a rugged man with long dark hair pulled back, a handsome beard on his face, a cigar between his grinning lips. A rifle in his easy hands.

They all have weapons, I realize.

Even Mother.

I turn the page, heart pounding, but I don't face Tirza. I can't let her see the truth. The truth of my family, rifles slung over their shoulders, standing near the crumpled forms of dead Landorian soldiers. I flip desperately, finding on each page a stranger who wears my mother's face—smiling in a way that feels false. It's her, but it's also not her. She laughs in one, and even in that soundless sepia capture, it's not the laugh I know, warm as sun on skin. It's rough. Mocking.

Empty.

"Ali?" Tirza asks again, sounding worried now.

I realize I'm flipping too fast, not wanting to see these people—my mother, my uncles—whom I should love entirely.

These are versions of them I never wanted to know. My mother is a *queen*. She's not . . . this.

She can't be!

"Ali, we should leave," Tirza begs. "Please. There's nothing here."

I don't understand her fear. She has no reason to be scared. But I do. *Everything* is here. Every kind of danger—evidence that would condemn my mother completely. I don't have to know the specifics. That Southern rifle in her hands says enough. It will say enough to the Royal League and anyone else in the North who sees dead soldiers in the same photograph as her.

Fear claws at me as I scour my memory, trying to make sense of this, trying to imagine what Lark would tell me if he were here, what he was trying to say all along.

I sink to my knees.

"Why did that woman say my cousin's name wasn't Resyan?" I ask Tirza numbly.

I don't know how to explain it, but at once, this seems like something I should have seen long ago. The reason I've felt so removed from this kingdom.

Tirza doesn't speak, and I wonder if she'll simply drag me out of here, compelled by her irrational fear. But then I hear her step towards me. Feel her warmth as she kneels down behind me. "Because your cousin's name is Rummayan," she says softly. "That's the Resyan word for their kind, but in his language, they're Rummhazi, and they have no home left. It was once southeast of here, but it's been erased from the map. I have a pamphlet on it, actually, and . . ." She stops, seeming to realize that her black-and-white reports are not what I need right now. Not by any fraction of the imagination. "What happened is this," she begins again. "Their home was annexed by the Landorians long ago, offered to Myar in a land agreement, and many fled over the border into Resya. They wanted their land back, of course, and thought the whole thing was temporary, but no one would help them. No one wanted to stand up to Landore, or Myar. As the Rummhazi grew discontent, many forced into camps, their frustration was met with rejection and violence. And that only made things worse. Eventually, they were forced from Resya entirely, and they've been scattered to cities across the South." Her hand touches my shoulder. "It's Resya's greatest shame, one no one talks about. But people were afraid, and when people are afraid, they don't think about others. Perhaps they'll protect their own families—but no one else's."

Raw bitterness tugs at me. I don't know where it's directed, where my anger and sorrow should fall, but it burns inside viciously, searching for foundation. Resya has always been my other home. A faraway one, a bit faded and foreign, but still mine. I've been speaking Resyan since I was a child, listening to the music with Mother, eating the food on sunny afternoons in Hathene Palace. Yet has our extended family ever once visited us? And have we ever visited them? Never. Resya was always kept at a distance, Mother and Uncle Tanek rarely discussing the specifics of their life here. Lark was the first to show up. A boy fighting for freedom. I never understood his obsession with the Nahir cause, because I thought he was Resyan, like me.

But he never was.

Nor am I.

I shut my eyes. I've lost my own history. I have to start over, but I'm frightened of what's there. Smothered secrets and stories from a world that came before—a world that will never be again. A world that clearly *wants* to be known.

"The people of Beraya . . ." I turn to face Tirza finally. "Are many of them Rummhazi, left there with nowhere else to go?"

The second part of my question remains unspoken—*"Are you?"*—since how else could she know this history so intimately? But her grief is my answer, honest on her heart-shaped face, and I close my eyes to the immense pain rising up. A shared sorrow. A shared history. This is it, then. Lark picked the one crime committed against a people who don't even have a home. The most innocent, the most vulnerable, who were already at everyone else's mercy. A people uprooted and abandoned by the North.

Our people.

Tirza's.

Mine.

I want to cry. I want to shout it from the rooftop. I want everyone to know. But I can't even tell my friend what's inside this album, my own mother fighting like a Nahir revolutionary— dangerous, duplicitous.

Overwhelmed, I let Tirza lead me back across the empty living room, clutching the photo album close to my chest, this evidence which would condemn my mother to a Northern noose a thousand times over. It's going with me. It's going to be hidden away, and no one will ever see it again.

No one.

And for the first time, I realize the irony of this moment. This desperate compulsion which too many others have known before me.

I want a truth buried—and I want it buried forever.

24

The Cauldron

It turns out we're not the only ones stuck in hell.

The road near our encampment streams with local people, farmers and women and children from nearby towns, all pushing for some unknown destination—perhaps anywhere but here—like they sense something terrible gathering, about to unleash.

Our soldiers struggle to keep everyone moving quickly. We watch warily from the roadside, scouring for the flash of hatred in passing faces, someone who might like to add another Safire casualty to their list.

But nothing happens.

They just walk, staring at us like we're a mirage that will simply disappear in time, adrift in their own tragedy, and Trigg's busy eating some fruit he's rustled up when the first act of violence occurs. Someone launches something at his head. It bounces off harmlessly and he looks annoyed a moment, then bends down to open whatever it is.

He gives a low whistle.

Cyar and I walk over. The crumpled paper is a pamphlet, a grainy image of a Resyan pilot tied to a tree and mutilated nearly beyond recognition. No eyes left, face blood-soaked. We can't read the words. It's all in Resyan.

"Don't suppose they're cheering us on?" Cyar asks uncomfortably.

Another crumpled paper is thrown, bouncing off Trigg's arm this time.

He scowls. "Hey, come on. Why are you all aiming at *me*? He's the General's son."

Cyar slaps his pointed finger—at me—down, and I open the second pamphlet. It's another photo, this time a pile of dead soldiers. But that's not what gets me.

What gets me is that I can read it.

"It's in Savien," I announce, stunned.

Trigg comes to my shoulder eagerly. "What's it say?"

"Stop and look at your crimes," I read aloud. "Is this truly what you stand for, honourable soldiers of Savient?"

"Ouch," Cyar says. "Straight for the heart."

He's right, and I snatch the first paper from Trigg's hands. As I head back for the makeshift headquarters with both pamphlets, my weary anger rallies to pounce now that I have a target. Arrin never shares anything. Not about if the lines are shrinking or growing, and certainly not about mutilated prisoners of war. Karruth was ordered to silence, following Arrin around as dutifully as I'm sure he did in Karkev—right up until a stray piece of shell sliced his jugular and he bled out in six minutes.

The new adjutant—Karruth's unlucky successor—lets me wait in Arrin's little office. His nose wrinkles at me, since I've been cleaning out of a bucket for far too long. But I ignore it and wait. Arrin's desk boasts just a map and a gun.

When he finally shows up, he's half-naked with wet hair.

"Is there a shower here no one told me about?" I enquire.

"There's a pump. Ranking army officers only. But I suppose I could make an exception for you—you need it."

"No thanks. I have a bucket."

He ignores my pointed glare and throws his own vexed scowl at the New Karruth—for whatever reason, he doesn't like this kid nearly as much—then shuts the door. He hangs out his shirt to dry, and it's the first time I've ever seen his back in broad daylight. I stare. It's not the tattoo covering his right shoulder, the flourished name of some long-ago girl—*Rozmarin*. It's the sinewy burnt flesh that begins halfway down his back, disappearing over a hip, ugly as hell.

I don't ask.

"What do you think?" I demand instead, dropping the pamphlets on his desk. The tortured Resyan pilot with his eyes brutally gouged out. The massacred prisoners. "Is this *truly* what you stand for, honourable Commander?"

"I really don't have time for your noble speeches right now," he replies sourly, then deigns to look closer at the images. "And I thought there was a 'no dead body' rule here?"

"Apparently not always."

"We're supposed to be the damn liberators. Who the hell is publishing this?"

"At this point it doesn't matter. Because it looks rather real."

"What can I do?" he retaliates, exasperated. "Our soldiers are angry. Strafed day in and out by enemy planes. They *hate* these pilots. And where are we going to put prisoners? We can barely take care of ourselves." He sweeps a hand at the pamphlets. "Besides, we don't even know where these actually came from. It says we did the torturing, but what if it's the Nahir? Those traitors sure aren't doing us any favours here."

I sink into a chair, massaging my head.

He's making sense. If ours are doing it, then who can blame them? They're exhausted. Out for blood. And if it's the Nahir? Well, they're the ones who trapped thirty thousand human lives in a cauldron and left it to boil. They're not exactly beacons of nobility. Mutilating soldiers and pinning it on us would suit their new narrative just fine.

But I point at the tortured pilot. "I get it, Arrin. I do. But if I'm ever shot down, I'd rather not be captured by his friends . . . I doubt they'll be feeling very charitable. This affects *me*," I press. "This affects us all."

My brother slaps the image of the shot prisoners, our soldiers lingering with guns nearby. "That's not even one of my divisions, Athan. Look at the uniforms. It's Group East. Evertal's tough as hell when it comes to—"

"It might not be yours," I interrupt, "but you have to at least say something. Anything's better than silence and you know it."

He huffs.

Me telling him what to do is a first, and he's well aware I'm right this time.

"Fine," he finally says. "Then will you stop thinking about it? Because I need you ready to fly. We have a chance to put your fighters to use, after I get some reconnaissance tomorrow."

I perk up. This sounds like progress.

"I'll go scout."

"No. Not you. Garrick and Ollie have done this before, and there can't be mistakes. I'm losing my best here every day." He frowns at the door, where New Karruth sits. "Left with idiots."

Swatted down from action yet again, I go back to massaging my head furiously and Arrin fiddles with his watch, muttering that the one I goddamn stole from him probably works better. I snatch it from his hands eventually, clicking it open for him, then shove it back.

"Why did you separate Kalt and Folco? That was a bastard move and you know it."

He raises a brow. "Damn, you're testy after a month of war. Just think how you'll be after a year."

I'd be doing a hell of a lot better right now if I could actually sleep.

He fiddles inside the watch now, winding it. "Don't bother worrying yourself over our dear brother. I was trying to do Kalt a favour, since I think it's dangerous to serve on the same ship as your lover, but I have it on good authority that Folco Carr has been miraculously promoted to the *Warspite* as well. A comfortable officer's position, one deck below Kalt." He shakes his head. "Can't underestimate anyone in this damn family. You're all snakes. And you thought it was revenge."

Annoyed that he's right, I ask, "Vent's assignment was all about revenge, wasn't it?"

"No, that was a long time coming."

"Father shot him. Right in the head."

Arrin looks up.

"In under five seconds. Said 'I know what you did to my son' and bang."

For a moment, I don't think Arrin's going to enlighten me any further. But then he says, "You remember that lovely time Father broke my nose? Apparently, I was a lot of trouble when I was younger." He makes a face, like it's all a fabricated conspiracy against him. "But after that night, it seems he realized he'd never hit me again. Didn't have it in him. So, he sent me to the army school and had someone else do it for him."

I shift uncomfortably. "Vent?"

"He's always been a bastard. Had too much fun using his fists on me."

We sit in silence, and I don't know what to make of that. I remember how Arrin used to come home from the school with fading bruises. Always assumed that was why I never wanted to be in the army. Too much physicality. But this doesn't sound like Father at all. He believes in doing things himself. He doesn't send others to do his dirty work . . . or does he?

"Whatever happened," I say, "I think Father only learned the full extent of it now. Because Vent just got his final sentence with a bullet."

That observation works, and Arrin appears a fraction hopeful—the realization that Father might actually be making up for this past oversight—but before he can respond, a knock on the door interrupts us.

Arrin grunts, "Come in," and it creaks open, slightly lopsided from when the house took a direct shell hit. A young woman stands there—braided dark hair, pretty face, a wrinkled dress.

I look back at Arrin, freshly clean, and then I know.

He shrugs at me.

"I'm sorry," she says, her Landori words accented. "You said two o'clock, Commander?"

"It's fine," he replies. "The Lieutenant is leaving."

I'm still staring at him. Either furious or horrified, I can't decide.

"It's not what you think," he says to me in Savien, so she won't understand.

"Really?" I ask. "What is it then?"

It's wrong in too many ways. He has no right to be with a Resyan girl, not when he's sending airplanes over her cities and armies through her mountains. Not when we're doing whatever terrible things have shown up in these pamphlets. It's dangerous for him, too. Just about as bad as parading himself along the perimeter.

Who knows who the hell she is?

He slaps the watch back on his wrist, standing. "You're dismissed, Lieutenant."

I don't move, and he looks down at me with a silent threat. One that says he'll haul me out of here himself if he has to. "This girl has been across the lines every day for us," he hisses in Savien, eyes narrowed. "Without a gun or a plane. She's braver than you. Braver than me. So just get out and quit with that noble judgment. It's hilarious coming from you."

"What's that supposed to mean?" I ask.

He gestures at the girl standing, confused, in the doorway. "I'm not lying to her."

It's the jugular. Right for the kill. I feel momentarily disoriented, sitting in this chair, in this shattered house, two sets of eyes staring at me and waiting for me to move.

I stand finally, hating where I am. Hating what's happening around me. "What would Rozmarin think?" I ask, the only weapon I have, this girl he once loved enough to ink on his own skin. "She's the one you got pregnant, isn't she? When Father tried to marry you off? You don't even care. You just move from one to the next and don't give a hell about what it means!"

He shoves me roughly for the door. "You're *wrong*."

"One day," I snap on the way out, "you're going to get yourself killed and it'll be entirely your own fault."

"Believe me," he snaps back. "I know."

And he slams the door in my face.

25

❧ AURELIA ❧

Madelan

The days after my discovery at Lark's address are a strange blur. I feel entirely alone with the truth of my family, no safe place to turn for answers, and my sleepless nights are spent sifting through every conversation from this summer, struggling to explain Lark's final bid in Etania. To explain how my mother could ever rise from revolutionary to queen. The photograph album is hidden away in my room, and I can't bring myself to look through it again.

I'm a fraud, I think. *I'm avoiding the truth, just like everyone else.*

But I'm also terribly afraid, and my tangled thoughts are often pulled back to the camp by the airbase—ignored, left to the wayside—and I feel a deeper kinship with them now, some memory of shared blood. What will happen when the frontlines reach Madelan? Who will make sure they're safe? We need to move them into proper homes, the protests of the locals here be damned.

Somehow, this feels within my reach, a place to direct my miserable, restless energy, and I'm on my way to appeal to the one royal here who might understand their situation when Officer Walez catches me, joy on his face.

"We decoded a recent directive from the Safire Commander," he tells me under his breath. "Any soldier caught shooting prisoners is under immediate court-martial." He smiles with relief. "Congratulations, Princess. I think your words found the right ears!"

I can scarcely believe it. My Savien pamphlets actually *worked*? It's a small shared victory in the face of darkness, a reminder that reason can still exist.

On impulse, I embrace Walez, desperately grateful.

By the time Jali Furswana appears for her daily ritual in the pool—wrapped in her usual cream robe and dark sunglasses, black hair pinned high with gold clips—I'm waiting for her. I sit at the edge of the water, dipping my toes in, and her smile dies at the sight of me. No doubt anticipating another round of prying into her personal history. With a half-hearted wave, she removes her robe, limbs luminous in the sun, then settles herself into a lounging chair near me, helping herself to a platter of fresh fruit meticulously cut into star shapes.

I don't waste her time, or mine. "There's a camp in the city," I inform her, taking the chair beside hers, "and it's filled with people from across the border. They have no home, no proper shelters. Rahian is afraid to help them, but perhaps you can convince him otherwise?"

She doesn't answer, flicking her lighter to a cigarette first, a peacock etched onto the bronze metal. "He refuses to act," she says finally, "because he's being *wise*. People like that only bring trouble."

Her tone is so pragmatic, I find I have no patience for it.

"But they're not Na—"

"Oh yes they are," Jali barges onwards, "and Landore's the one stirring them up to the point they feel frantic enough to leave Thurn. If you'd like to blame someone, blame the North. Blame yourself. All of you were content to draw up borders and lines and scatter people to the wind, taking the wealth for yourself. Now *we* have to suffer the consequences of your foolish arrogance? It's preposterous!"

I fume, knowing she's right, but also knowing she's being as absurdly selfish as anyone.

"How can it be a burden to help *children*?" I ask, pushing one of Tirza's leaflets at Jali. The dead woman and her infant.

"Look at this and tell me you don't understand why they're running."

Jali raises her sunglasses, studying the mother. For the first time, I see something soften in her eyes. Something almost sympathetic. But then she shakes her head. "I was ten years old when the rebels came for my family, Aurelia. My parents always said it would be fine, that the Nahir's revolutionary influence could never spread to Masrah. But they were wrong. Their propaganda roused dissent, made our people rise up, and the day they came into our palace, even our own guards turned on us. I watched as they shot my brothers and father like criminals. I never saw what they did to my mother, and perhaps that's for the best. They put my sister Callia and I in a little room with no windows, said we were next. Everything after that is mostly gone from my memory. I remember a lot of darkness and endless running. Somehow, Callia got us both out. She was only sixteen, but she took us west, to the one royal left in all of the South. When we finally showed up in Madelan, we scarcely looked better than those people in the camp."

"Then you understand," I press, sensing a victory. "You know what it's like to run and be afraid."

"Understand?" Jali grips my arm, her long pearly nails biting into my skin. "What I *understand* is the moment our own guards turned on us. Those young men—they played with me every day. They worshipped us, and I don't think they ever wanted to overthrow us. But they did. Because in that moment, when the guns were firing and things seemed very hopeless, they forgot about what was right. They saved themselves." She flings a hand towards the iron fence surrounding the pool, towards Madelan. "*That's* what common people are like. They save themselves when the monsters come."

Her hazel eyes are pained, her heart finally exposed from beneath the sunglasses, and I want to tell her I understand. I want to say yes, I know the fear, I remember it from that night when I almost lost everything as well, our own coup.

But the pity doesn't hold.

I pull from Jali's grip. "I'm sorry for your family. I truly am. But why should we be so afraid? Why should we tremble? We have guards and palaces. An entire *army* ready to fight at our command. We have everything, and those people in the camp . . ."

I gesture at the pamphlet, the mother and child.

Slain in the crossfire of a game they certainly never asked to be part of.

But Jali only laughs shortly. "Don't you dare make me out to be the callous one, Aurelia. As I said earlier, your Northern imperialist friends are the true fiends here. These massacres are their bloody work. Power-hungry fools who have no right to even an acre of this Southern earth. And the Nahir? They have no right to it, either. They're mobsters happy to profit from chaos. To upset the natural balance. But while Resya, Myar, and the kingdoms of Thurn endured their time beneath Northern rule, my beloved Masrah alone stood for a *thousand* years without a single day under foreign influence. Not one day!"

"But did you even try?" I demand, unable to curb my own anger.

She blinks. "Try what?"

"To defend those other kingdoms that fell! Or did you simply watch them being devoured while you were safe, feasting in Masrah."

"Stars, Aurelia. I will *not* feel sympathy for some Nahir propaganda." She crumples the pamphlet. "They stole our home right out from under us, and I refuse to fan the flames of their resistance in Resya now, too."

"*Nahir* propaganda?" I repeat.

"Of course! They think they speak for justice, for freedom. But Seath and his rebels? They only want *power*. They want to destroy the order of things and be the only ones with an answer. And this is how they do it."

She shoves the destroyed leaflet back at me.

I'm still struggling to register this one accusation—Nahir propaganda—when a noise across the pool makes me turn. Tirza stands there, frozen. "I was looking for Aurelia, Your Highness," she says to Jali. "I apologize for interrupting."

That's all she says, but her gaze catches mine—anger and guilt and fear there. And it reveals enough. All at once, like a snap of fingers, I see it. It's not as shocking as when Lark's revelation came. This time it feels like an inevitable conclusion. A place that, somehow, someway, makes perfect sense given the patterns of this world I now know.

"Where did you get these pamphlets?" Jali demands, ignoring Tirza altogether.

I make a split-second decision. "Someone was passing them out in the square," I lie.

"Ah, you see?" Jali's eyes spark with satisfaction. "The Nahir have infiltrated this kingdom already! Isn't that the irony? The Safire condemned us for this, and everyone ran to say it was a lie. But soon enough, there will be a reckoning."

I don't like the dark pleasure in her voice.

It's her own brother-in-law who stands to take the fall.

Tirza has escaped back inside the palace, and I move to follow, desperate to reassure her that I won't reveal her secrets— never—but Jali clutches my arm again, the cigarette still smoking in her right hand, sour stench making my eyes water. "Did you know one of my favourite officers found a leaflet in the streets the other day? Some passionate drivel against the Safire, and it quoted my poetry, which is rather absurd since I've never published before. Where, then, would these propagandists get my poems from?"

I keep my mask calm, unrattled.

Why the stars didn't I think of this before I borrowed her line?

Her fingers tighten. "Listen closely, Aurelia. When this is over—and it will be over quicker than we think—you don't want to be found sympathizing with the wrong cause. Justice comes for us all. Choose your side now, before your *family* chooses for you."

It's a clear warning, from one princess to another, a threat and a promise, and her pointed emphasis on my family only stirs greater alarm. She couldn't possibly know the truth about where my mother came from, what my mother has done with a rifle . . . And yet the fear is there, reminding me that something still lurks out of sight, something dangerous.

The dark thread tightening all of this together.

The thing I can't quite reach.

But I give her one more chance. One final question.

"There are children in that camp," I say. "Little girls. *Sisters*. The same as you and Callia, and if we don't move them to shelter soon, they'll be offered up to Safire guns."

Jali looks at me a long moment, then sighs. "It was their decision to come here. Why should Resya be burdened with their safety?"

I don't know if it's the helpless regret in her voice—like she's simply being practical, reasonable—or the fact that I now stand before her as only half a princess, but I find my tolerance for her sapped completely, and my view of the world recast forever into something I never imagined, a strange new certainty finding foothold.

"All my life I've believed we were born to rule," I say, pulling from her manicured grasp. "But truly, I think Masrah might be *far* better off without you."

And then I leave.

I catch up to Tirza in the Queen's gardens. It's her favourite place on palace grounds, the place she always goes to be alone, because it's filled with sweet-smelling orange trees—the favourite fruit of both the late Queen Callia and Tirza's little brother who died in Beraya. Distant city noise drifts over the walls, butterflies spinning lazy circles, and far in the distance, out of sight, two armies stagger to death between the mountains.

She's silent for a long while, offering me a slice of orange she's stolen from a nearby tree, neither of us yet acknowledging the place we must go. The word hovering between us.

Nahir.

"I hate them," Tirza eventually says, voice tight with anger. "These rich swans who have never known a hungry belly. Who have never gone a winter without bread or been forced to kneel at a checkpoint before foreign guns. I hate them all—Northern and Southern alike. We suffer, and they never even glance out the window. They have no need. A thousand years of pure delusion."

I say nothing, simply let her speak.

"They despise Seath and turn him into a villain," she continues. "Claim he only speaks in violence. But that's hardly all of him, and they'll never understand what he's given us *common* people. He's given us the strength to challenge and break and make new. The means to heal and protect. To seek justice and revenge. He's sacrificed everything for our right to independence—and I'm not ashamed of who I am. Or of him."

Her eyes meet mine, glittering in the sun, and I see only determination there, the reflection of Lark. Didn't Havis once warn me not to underestimate my cousin? And in the end, he was right. Lark was a real person—full of far more depths and wounds than I imagined. Determined enough to turn his gun on Athan, to use me as a hostage even though I'm certain he never would have hurt me. He had a hidden tempest, a desperate courage that wasn't afraid to sacrifice, to demand what was owed, and perhaps he wasn't the only one.

Perhaps, I do too. My mother's fierce heart beating inside me.

She tried it her way—a way that must be buried forever—but I'm here now, compelling the Commander to wage a better war, scaring Jali Furswana with my words.

I have a strange power, a blood of two worlds coursing through my veins.

A girl who is both princess and Rummhazi.

I put my hand on Tirza's. "I believe you, Tirza, and I can go where you cannot. And I *will* go. I will make sure your story gets to those who need to hear it."

She peers up at me, fragile hope in her gaze. "Where will you go?"

"To the Royal League itself," I say. "And they will look their shame in the face."

26

The Cauldron

We hear Garrick and Ollie before we see them.

They left fifteen minutes ago, sent on the reconnaissance mission Arrin devised for them, discovering an entire enemy regiment camped in a town just to the northwest of us. That regiment is the only remaining barricade between Arrin's trapped force and the Safire frontlines at Adena we left behind a week ago. Breaking through them will reunite us with the southern march of Army Group North.

Huddled around the radio, we've been listening as Garrick reports numbers of artillery and tanks. He and Ollie are supposed to keep high enough to avoid trouble, but low enough to see what stands between us and breaking through. It sounds like a lot. Possibly an entire armoured battalion alongside the regiment.

Nothing happens, though. No one fires at them, not a single puff of flak, and they circle back, bickering the entire way about who did more work and gets the medal.

"Don't touch my victory cigar, Charm," Ollie's voice crackles over the radio. "I'll know if you sneak a drag."

It's the last one he has, entrusted to me for safekeeping.

"He won't know," Trigg whispers at me.

"And you too, Thief," Ollie's staticky voice adds, and everyone grins.

"That's that," Arrin says as their engines echo in the distance. "You pilots have an enemy regiment to strafe tomorrow evening before we make our push through. Make sure you bleed them out well."

Both Cyar and Trigg look a little apprehensive at that. I'm sure I do, too. But there's only one way back to our lines and it's through that regiment.

An explosion erupts north of the airfield.

"Damn it," Garrick's voice says over the radio. "Flak."

"Who the hell's shooting at us?" Ollie demands.

We all turn to Arrin.

Arrin frowns. "Everyone's been ordered to hold their fire. They know our planes."

There's another shattering blast, and it can't be from our lines. Everyone stands there, confused about how Resyan soldiers managed to crawl this close to our camp undetected, but I look at Arrin. The faint alarm in his gaze says enough.

They're not Resyan.

"Shit, that was near my engine," Ollie says. "How's my fuel line?"

"Not good," Garrick's muffled voice responds.

"Left aileron's hit too."

"Hold up—come to the right. You've—"

The radio goes fuzzy again, but we don't need to listen anymore, because there they are, flying in just beyond the runway. Two fighters side by side, one oozing black smoke as it weaves sporadically. A hit aileron means steering is a nightmare, and alarm grazes my spine.

"Get the extinguisher," Arrin orders a soldier nearby. "He's going to crash."

"Hydraulics fading," Ollie's voice says, slightly panicked now.

"Get some height and bail," Garrick orders.

"I'm not bailing here."

"Then turn off the engine. Cut the—"

"I'm not dead-dropping onto this runway either!"

"You've got fuel draining all over your ass! Cut the damn engine!"

I want to shake Ollie. He has no choice but to bail or crash. But then I realize why he isn't bailing. He's hurtling towards this runway, where everyone in Safire uniform stands in shock, and his fighter's spitting flammable fuel. There's no room for error in this packed clearing and he can barely steer. And if he bails, this fighter goes wherever it wants. It will explode on impact. Right into us or into the wounded soldiers lying helpless beneath the trees.

"Clear the field!" Arrin shouts at the same time Garrick says the same over the radio.

Now we all recognize the danger, and some scramble in vain to move the fighters sitting on the ground, others running to evacuate the wounded. Garrick struggles to slow his plane down, to stay with Ollie's rapidly dropping height. We watch in mute disbelief as the pilots in the sky lower. No time to react.

500 feet.

400 feet.

"Hang on to it!" Garrick yells. "Land straight!"

"I can't even—"

The leaking fuel line finally explodes. A billow of flame. Ollie's entire fighter disappears, choking, veering sharply somewhere just beyond the runway as Garrick's fighter bounces down onto the grass, jolting to the wildest stop I've ever seen, nearly spinning over with the force of its left turn.

"Extinguisher!" Arrin shouts again.

No one moves.

But Garrick's moving, like a bat out of hell, leaping from the cockpit and sprinting for the trees.

"No," Arrin says, staring after him. "No! Stop him. Lieutenant!" He shoves me forward, in Garrick's direction. "I'll get the medic!"

I don't understand at first, but I run. I run hard, chasing Garrick past the giant fig tree, following the black tombstone of smoke. Somewhere as we're sprinting, I finally understand my order, and I try to overtake Garrick, almost tripping on a huge root.

I'm too late. He's already there when I stagger to a stop beside him, both of us heaving in the oppressive heat. There's no acknowledgment of my arrival. Ollie's fighter sits blistering in a little clearing, flames licking from every side. The nose and propeller are smashed up, but the wings are intact because, somehow, he managed to land it in a near perfect line between the trees. A hopeless attempt at salvaging what was left. Veering away from the clearing to save us all.

Through the shattered cockpit glass, his hands are on fire, still reaching for the canopy in his last attempt to get out.

I touch Garrick's shaking arm.

He doesn't move.

He won't stop staring at the damn cockpit, fixated on the blackened, roasted flesh, and I want to hit him over and over until he moves. The smell. The heat.

"He was scared of heights," Garrick says suddenly.

The fire crackles, and I take the risk of pulling on his shoulder. It finally works.

He steps away.

Enough.

27

Madelan

Dusk falls, and in the quiet of my room, I dare to open the photo album for the first time since I hid it away. If I'm going to the League, if I'm going to force them to see the truth, then I have to do the same. I have to know who I am when I stand before them.

Sitting on my bed, I search the photographed faces again. Slowly. Deliberately. I don't look away. I let myself imagine the fire that might have brought my family to this point of sharp fury. I let myself see the world through their eyes—forced into exile, abandoned and vulnerable before a storm of steel.

Lia Lehzar, remembered forever.

How did she die? Why? Her forgotten gaze haunt me, and anger fevers my grief as I keep turning pages until I'm far past the point I looked the first time. My mother and Uncle Tanek standing on a cliff's edge. My mother and the rugged dark-haired man—another uncle? A lover? I can't tell, and I force myself not to feel distaste. To not judge. To simply look and see.

To learn.

And when I turn the last page, a lone photograph hangs there in sad abandon, no longer fully stuck to the page, as if someone started to remove it, then left it alone instead. I nudge it horizontal again. It's a picture of Mother resting in a metal chair near a bleached home covered in sun-withered vines. Her boots are kicked up on the table. Across from her is a lanky man stretched in his own chair, both of them young, tired, smiling like the desolate world round them is a paradise. His angled features are too familiar. Tattoos on his arms, a happy dog at his feet.

General Dakar.

General *Dakar*.

I sit there, my heart pounding, struggling through this final twist, struggling to bring all the pieces together—my mother holding a Southern rifle, sitting with the General. The reason my mother has stayed far from this riotous mess. The reason Lark came to us, wanting her to intervene and redeem herself before Seath, the lingering debt that was owed.

And all at once, I realize there *is* a traitor to the Nahir cause.

It's the Queen of Etania, a Southerner ruling in Northern splendour, and allied with Seath's two greatest enemies—Landore and Savient.

V

INHERITANCE

Dear Athan,

I'm sitting here on this balcony, the highest one in the palace, and I'm thinking of you. You once said you thought of me when you looked at the night sky—the stars and the velvet and all of that—and in return, I'd like to give the early evening to you. With the sun setting, and the afternoon rains over, the city's colours seem brighter and stronger, stirred to new heights. Leafy terraces pooled and shimmering. Ginger and caramel tiles gleaming.

You are that brightness, Athan. You can reflect the sun or the cloud, depending on the day, but in your heart, you're all of these colours glittering before me.

You're the dusk—beautiful and warm and layered.

A light I could capture in my palm.

As I sit here, facing the mountains to the north, I listen for the heartbeat in my veins. I'm listening for you, crossing those distant ridges and asking you to come to me, drawing you to me like a line in the currents, always finding you even though we share no bond of blood, nothing to hold tight except the beat of your breath from when we last danced—wonderful, alive.

Come to me.

Come to me.

I say it over and over and I hope you'll hear it, that you'll know I want you here and whole and with me again. I will *always want you, Athan, but you have to promise that you will always want me too. I might not be easy to love, but I promise I will get better. I will fight to gather the pieces of myself together, to become who I am meant to be, because you and I, we're stronger than any war. I know we are. I can sit here on this balcony and ask you to come to me and you will. Even without this letter, you'll hear me.*

I'm calling you now.

Can you feel it? Can you sense it in the beat of your breath? You're going to come over those mountains soon, and I'm waiting.

I'll always be waiting for you.

Ali

28

The Cauldron

The night of our gamble, Garrick's still sequestered in the hut with Arrin. The entire day has ticked away, our looming mission hanging over us, but there's no captain to actually deliver the logistics.

We've lost pilots over the past month and a half. Some injured, some dead. But never a first officer. Disbelief bruises every face in Moonstrike, even the new replacements. Most of them have had Garrick and Ollie since Karkev. Over two years of flying together. Hundreds of sorties. Of course they're taking it hard. For me, it still feels strange and detached, not yet real. Ollie was always good to me. Garrick's lackey, sure, but unafraid to talk to me and treat me like a real person. Like I was more than just my last name.

But there's a strafing run planned for tonight, and it still has to happen.

Even without Ollie.

Arrin eventually waves for me to join them in his office. I try to rehearse my lines, the pathetic attempt at consolation that feels obligatory, but I'm not prepared for what I find inside. Garrick sits alone at the desk, nursing a contraband drink—from Arrin, no doubt. He's a mess. Red-eyed.

Once we're alone, he just shrugs at me forlornly. "You know I don't drink?"

I stare at him. It's looking quite the opposite at the moment.

"I don't," he persists, wobbling a bit on the words. "My father always did enough of it for me, and I swore I'd never be like him. But on the *Intrepid* . . ."

He concentrates on the bottle again, and I think we're both remembering him sick all over the deck on the way over here. Was that his *first* drink? Has he only ever been holding wine glasses all these years, trying to fit in? I don't know what to do with the confession. It has nothing to do with the lines I rehearsed. And as bad as I feel for him, now simply isn't the time.

I try to take his bottle away, but he makes a noise, gripping it tight. "No, listen, Athan. My brother's always walking himself right into our father's gunsight. He wants to quit the damn navy. Told me that right before we shipped out. God, I can't protect him from everything. That's why I worked so damn hard to make Top Flight, to be the best and distract our father from Folco's harebrained ideas. I was never smart like you." He looks up. "I made that score out of pure sweat and pride—and it killed me to see you overtake it without trying."

I realize what this is finally.

It's an apology.

"It's fine, Garrick. Here, I'll get you water and—"

"You could just die tomorrow, you know. I should say it."

I don't allow myself to be irritated by that, and he sits there, red hair plastered to his forehead, black smoke still coating his face in patches. "I miss him already."

"I know."

"No. You don't." He looks at me, empty. "But one day you will."

Now I am angry at him for saying that. Like a threat. But I'm also determined to pull him back into himself, anything to get him ready to fly in an hour. "Look, I've got your plane armed. Everyone's ready for the briefing and Arrin says we can take that regiment." It sounds simplistic, even to my own ears, but I hit the table for extra emphasis, to encourage him. "We're ready to go."

"I'm not going."

My mouth drops open and he gives a short, self-effacing laugh. "Your brother knows I can't do it. Not like this. I've never sat one out, but I won't be a liability."

"But—"

"I can't fly, Charm. And there's only one pilot here in line for a squadron, so I think he's going to have to lead this one."

I shake my head. "The Moonstrike pilots won't fly under me, Garrick."

I also don't want to tell him how hard it's been in the air for me lately. Like it's all slipping away, barely able to take care of myself. But Garrick's gaze is firm.

"They've seen what you're capable of, Athan. They'll follow."

I have nothing to say to that.

Maybe it's true.

"I'll do it then," I concede reluctantly. "For you." I stand, glancing at his slumped, sad self. "And by the way, I heard Folco just got promoted. My brother's watching out for him, so you can give yourself a break on that front."

Garrick sits back. There's a sliver of relief in his grief, like I've offered something worthwhile at last. "That's good. Real good." Then a tiny warning frown crosses his lips. "But, Lieutenant—don't you dare leave any of my squadron behind tonight."

That's how I end up taking over the briefing. I don't think Arrin ever expected to be in this position, delivering his plan to me of all people. But here we are, sitting across the table from each other, his voice all business, perhaps to mask the pure absurdity of his next objective resting entirely on his littlest brother's shoulders.

There are three heavy batteries hidden and waiting to fire on his division, he says, gesturing at the map between us. Unless those guns are eliminated, his soldiers will have a nightmare when they push to link up with the main line again. Evertal's got an opportunity to finally pierce through to him in the east, and he's going to use us to pierce the opposite side, back to Torhan and the rest of Army Group North. A double-edged sword. No more exposed flanks.

"How did you get the coordinates on those hidden guns?" I ask.

"Army intelligence," he replies, too quick.

The coordinates definitely came from his local girl. A valuable source of information that no one else here could have scrounged up in the middle of an encirclement.

I have no idea if she can actually be trusted.

"There you have it," Arrin announces. "Hidden batteries and a regiment. I need both softened up if I'm going to get my divisions out of this trap tonight. Got it?"

He's all done, and now it's my turn. He doesn't know how I'm supposed to accomplish this mission with only ten planes—and he doesn't care.

I just need to do it.

I nod, but forego any salute. He won't squeeze that one out of me.

"Got it."

When I reach the door, though, I stop.

He's still staring at the map, unmoved.

"What's wrong?" I ask, because honestly, I suspected a few more subtle insults thrown into this historic brotherly briefing.

Arrin hesitates before pulling a paper from the desk. It's crumpled beyond recognition, like it's been intimately acquainted with his angry fist. "Apparently," he says, "our little pamphlet-writing friend thinks I'm a criminal and this should be my last war. And do you want to know the truth?"

I wait.

His tired face looks up. "I hope to God they're right."

It suddenly dawns on me what we're about to do. All of these soldiers he's about to march into either victory or death. There's no easy way out of this cauldron. Even if we win tonight, people are going to die. Soldiers, pilots, civilians. They're going to be churned up like cheap bones because of a decision he's making here in this lonely room.

There's a cost.

What if this is the last time I ever see my own brother?

Arrin's expression changes. He gives me a crooked smile. "Don't look at me like that. I'm not a ghost yet."

And then he's up and out the door, the mission underway.

The airfield's nearly on fire with the setting sun as I deliver my strategy to Cyar, Trigg, and the remaining Moonstrike pilots. All the replacements look about as skittish as Cyar and I did last summer. Ten planes. Ten pilots. It's not nearly enough, but since no Resyan fighters came after Garrick and Ollie, it's possible the Resyan Air Force is conserving their power for a better battle. I order the Moonstrike pilots to take the regiment, then volunteer myself, Cyar, and Trigg for the hidden guns. It's the more dangerous piece of the mission, but it requires fewer pilots. One bomb on each of our planes. One for each heavy battery. And if we don't eliminate those guns, then it will be an absolute slaughterhouse when Arrin marches his division north.

They *have* to be knocked out.

I can tell the older Moonstrike pilots are a bit wary as I talk, but appreciation hovers in their grudging nods when I don't force the battery run on any of them. It's on my shoulders. If it goes wrong, I'm the one who gets blamed—or ends up dead.

At least there are no headaches in graves.

We start our engines as shadows curve across the field, and Trigg shouts at me from his cockpit, over the roar of the prop. "Congratulations, Captain. This is getting more official!"

For once, his wild grin has the right effect on me. A bit mad. A bit cocky. I return it, letting it fill the emptiness in me with something concrete, then check my watch, determined to get this over with before nightfall. Arrin will be marching his soldiers in the dark, and we need to destroy those guns and as much of the Resyan encampment as we can before they venture out.

We can do this.

I can do this.

I think.

As we fly upwards I'm sure we're all imagining Ollie's plane peppered and smoking. Everyone hurtles for height with impressive speed. It's a strange thing once we're up to 8,000 feet, because there's not actually much room in the cauldron. The sky feels small here, only fifteen minutes' flying away from the frontlines of Army Group North and yet they might as well be on the other end of the horizon.

"Charm, ten o'clock," Cyar calls.

It's the first disaster in my strategy. The Resyan Air Force hasn't given up. Perhaps we've surprised a few scouting crews, but either way they wheel out of the gathering dusk, machine guns blazing. I order the rest to keep on for the regiment, and Cyar and Trigg follow me, engaging our attackers and trying to draw them away.

The Resyans are relentless. There's too many of them, and I fling myself around, struggling to shake two off my wings without abandoning Moonstrike.

Garrick's only order.

It's a hell of a lot harder to fly for yourself and also nine other pilots. Cyar and Trigg keep up, putting a few down in smoke, but we're still overwhelmed. The Resyans have our battered squadron hopelessly outnumbered. It's a jumble of voices over the radio. No one down, but everyone fighting hard. I realize they won't make it for that regiment and I won't make it for those batteries. The enemy will be fresh and waiting when Arrin storms out to break their line. He's relying on me.

And I'm failing.

I slam the throttle and get in close to a Resyan fighter. Spray the fuselage with a burst, shattering his tail, then haul back before I can get lured into a chase.

"Uh, Captain?" Trigg says suddenly. "I think we have company."

"Company?" I'm overwhelmed enough I feel furious rather than afraid.

"Five o'clock!"

I spin my head to the right, trying to peer into the hazy light. A swarm of black dots materializes below, charging upwards. Right for us.

"Thief, what make are those fighters?"

Trigg pauses for a long moment. "Round wing tips . . . Landorian, I think?"

"Landorian?" both Cyar and I say in unison.

"Did they just declare war on us?" Trigg's shaky question can't hide his panic.

I'm feeling the same. Have the Landorians finally decided to come rescue their losing ally, King Rahian? We're the ones who broke their royal verdict and invaded Resya. This might be the moment where we pay the price.

There's only one way to find out. I adjust my radio, trying to pick up on another channel. "You at vector one-ten. 4,000 feet. Speak fast or we will open fire."

I try a bunch of frequencies and get only static and jumbled conversation.

My finger flicks to the trigger.

They rise higher, faster.

"Prepare to engage," I tell Cyar and Trigg, and we're all ready to pounce, the beginning of a new war.

Against *Landore.*

But then an elegant voice fills my ear, slightly muffled. "This is the Royal Air Force, Lion's Paw squadron. Looks like you lot need a hand. Copy?"

Ecstatic relief floods me. *"Knight!"*

"How now, Lieutenant?" Captain Merlant responds, sounding far too calm for the chaos on every side. "You didn't think you could go after the Nahir without us, did you?"

"You're already halfway across Resya," Greycap's familiar voice chimes in. "Took us a bit to catch up!"

An entire Landorian squadron of twelve planes approaches, and the familiar voices from Havenspur are the miraculous fuel we need to keep going.

"No time," I say quickly. "Cover my second flight, would you? They're getting pummeled."

"On it, Charm," Merlant says, and the Landorian planes swing past us, lions blazing on their flanks, olive-green wings murky in the shadows. They plunge into the maelstrom, calling out strategy to the struggling Moonstrike pilots, and I check my watch desperately.

Battling these enemy planes has cost us too much time. The regiment is probably already mobilizing, aware of our strike. We've lost any element of surprise.

"Fox, Thief, we're getting the guns," I say, "and then we'll come back and grab whoever else we can for the regiment."

I expect a protest. A logical one from Cyar, and a stubborn one from Trigg. But instead they both affirm quickly over the radio, willing to follow me into this hell, and something inside me, somewhere in the hollow space, feels almost good again.

I don't deserve their loyalty.

But I love it.

Throttles opened, we careen ahead for the battery coordinates. They're camouflaged from the air, but if Arrin's girl is right, then we should be on top of them within a few minutes. Dropping low, it's Trigg who spots them first. They're exactly where they should be. Giant square shadows. One by one, we drop our bombs and the shadows explode to brilliant flaming torches in the darkness, a sign to Arrin's divisions that we made it.

They can push out.

Finally.

My breaths come rapid from both exhaustion and thrill. In the distance, Moonstrike and Lion's Paw pilots still battle, and we pick up a few of our Safire fighters, heading for the regiment. A Landorian chases off a Resyan trying to tail us as we locate three roads below, all funneling into one town—a town which now has tanks and anti-aircraft guns infesting it. It looms beneath our wings, hiding lethal power. One well-placed hit and any one of us could be flaming down like Ollie.

I won't think about it. Not with Cyar and Trigg on either side of me.

Not when we've already come this far.

I throttle back, my gunsight aimed, cannons ready, bracing for the rattling assault on my senses. All of my leftover arsenal spent at once, wherever I can aim. Tanks. Trucks. Artillery. We have one chance to make this count and do damage, and I'm going to make it count like hell.

"When I start hammering," I order, "you follow."

There's quick affirmation over the radio.

We're flying right at the town now. The shapes of soldiers appear in the growing darkness. Flares lit. Exhaust from vehicles and idling armoured carriers. The air's quiet around our three planes though. No whistling. No flak. Below, no tank turrets spin, training on us. It's silent. The calm of dusk.

300 feet.

200 feet.

I open fire, my cannons bursting to life. Red trails strike the sea of metal below. They light up a tank. A truck after that, then two anti-aircraft guns. One after another in a ferocious spree of fragmenting shells and bullets. The tiny soldiers stagger, fall. They're running everywhere, artillery bursting apart around them. Cyar and Trigg sweep to the left and right of me, the other Moonstrike pilots farther afield. The earth hurtles by and all I can do is press the trigger.

Don't think.

It's glorious. Pure victory, all of it licking through my veins, the acrid gunpowder like a sweet scent of revenge. Payback for days of hell, all those souls extinguished like cigarettes. It's the rattling bite of justice.

Here.

Now.

Alive and raging and powerful.

Then it's back up into the sky. Cyar and Trigg follow, the silence over the radio a testament to our adrenaline. Only rattling metal and propellers. We're far from the other flight and Lion's Paw, and it's pitch-black out now. No landmarks to spot.

I glance down at my map.

I was never good at this part.

"Hey Charm." It's Cyar. "Looks like we might make it back to Army Group North after all." When I don't answer immediately, he says, "Remember you showed me the Fifth Army's lines, where Lightstorm is stationed? Northeast past the regiment? You were right. We could make a run for it."

He's lying. I never checked the map beforehand—he did. But he's too good for me, back there fiddling with his compass and finding the coordinates. He's giving me a gift. A chance to look even better in front of Trigg and the Moonstrike pilots.

"Right," I say. "Hang on." I turn the radio, pushing it to its greatest limit. "Control, do you read? This is Moonstrike, heading vector one-three-zero at 4,000 feet. Do you have a runway for us?"

No one answers.

I try again. "Control, this is Moonstrike. Do you have a runway for us?"

It's a long shot, but then—"Understood, Squadron Leader. Airfield will be cleared for you."

A flare shoots up in the darkness, illuminating the sky about ten miles ahead.

We've done it. We've broken out of the encirclement and run right across the Resyan lines. Behind us, flashes of artillery brighten the sky like ghostly lightning. Arrin's division. No heavy batteries are left to disintegrate their lines, their march made infinitely easier, and the torched Resyan guns still glow luminously in the darkness. Our victory.

Ahead, the runway is a real one, a flare path waiting. Our fighters descend, greedy for earth, for safety, and it's not until I've rolled to a stop that my heart finally begins to slow its relentless gallop.

And when I step out of my cockpit, it isn't the usual bone-weary silence that greets me. Cheers erupt on every side, from the mechanics and soldiers and officers. They're clapping Cyar on the shoulder, Trigg, the other pilots. They're cheering for *us*, because we just led the impossible charge that will save our entire advance.

We did it.

And for the first time in weeks, my headache surrenders to elation.

29

Madelan

The numbers from the tragedy to the north of us trickle back in defeat. Gone is the flurry of excitement when the encirclement was first announced in the papers. Gone are the bustling uniforms waving communiqués as if they're already Savient's white flags of surrender.

It's the death of Rahian's army. The heart of his best divisions sucked dry. And then the true blow arrives—the Landorians have joined the fight against Resya. They've betrayed their fellow king, their squadrons linking with the Safire's, their army pushing inland from Thurn.

It's a shock to all in the palace. A final crushing blow to morale. This entire Safire invasion was in pure defiance of the League's ruling, and now the Landorians have taken their side? Given the necessary support for Safire victory?

I want to shatter something. In particular, this impossible Savien-Landorian alliance which has betrayed Resya entirely. But as I stand on the highest palace floor, watching the little specks of aeroplanes above the farthest mountain range, some plummeting in smoke, I'm faced with the imminent arrival of my own personal reckoning.

I have to get back to Lark's house. If there's incriminating evidence left there, I need to find it before the Safire—or anyone else—beats me to it. Up until now, it was a quietly abandoned home. Forgotten. Now it has a suspicious smashed window and there's a very real possibility that someone else might know of its existence—and relish the idea of ruining my mother in one fell swoop.

Havis was right.

The consequences of these Resyan secrets would destroy us all.

Tirza joins me as I head out into the frantic city, and I plan to press her once we're there. She's Nahir, and her earlier alarm said enough, the thing centering her fear on Lark's house. I'm suddenly determined to hear if there's a version of Mother's story she has heard. Perhaps only in snippets. Perhaps more myth than fact. The fighter who became a queen. But I need to know, before I go to the League and make my case.

On all sides, people scramble to ready for the inevitable assault on Madelan, shouts echoing, distant heavy guns growling like endless thunder in the noon sun.

I count thirteen aeroplanes breaking north.

Tirza's hand grips my arm, cautious, but I don't stop, determined to get to the house. We've entered the congested thoroughfare and the sight that greets us is truly overwhelming, even for beleaguered Madelan. Four tanks grind up the hill as civilians dodge out of the way. Uniformed men litter the road, collapsed and wounded on the cement in crumpled defeat.

"Stars," Tirza breathes. "The front has finally reached us!"

It's not her words that stir my pulse. It's the whisper of terror in her voice. We hurry down the sidewalk, the road at a complete standstill as the tattered army retreats in from the mountains. Parents shriek at children to stay close. Anti-aircraft guns lurch through market squares. Iron shoes echo as officers ride past, their exhausted horses lathered in sweat and bleeding from the bit. They're shouting at everyone to make way, while the men on the ground holler at them to get back to the front and defend Madelan. Tempers simmer and roil. Someone's crying, saying it's all over, that the city will burn like the ones in the reels. No one seems to know if the war is over or if the worst is yet to come.

I try to ask a passing soldier, one who seems young enough he might consider me a friend. I say I'm from the radio program, but he only hobbles forward, his left boot blood-soaked. "I know nothing," he says, over and over as I persist. "I have to get home. Please. Go away!"

It's an expression of shame.

Of defeat.

"At least tell me this," I beg urgently, "did you *see* atrocities at the front? We have photographs, sir. But we also need a witness statement."

The boy stops abruptly. He looks at me fully now, and I see how young he truly is. Perhaps only a year or two older than me. Lips chapped from sun. Haunted brown eyes ringed by sleepless shadows. "What do you mean?"

"Prisoners shot in the back, tortured. Anything that would be considered illegal."

Beside me, Tirza has her notebook and pen out, ready to record. A journalist's quick instinct. Even my words sound too calm to my own ears. Our endless writings have removed the stomach-lurching sting of them.

The soldier swallows nervously, and at once, I realize why he's hesitant. His side won't be winning this war. The Safire will, and he doesn't want to make an accusation that might easily be called a lie—and make him worthy of a noose.

"Your word will bring good," I assure him, because it will. When I present all of this darkness before the League. Proof of what their alliance with Savient has yielded. Photographs of the faces they dismiss as mere numbers, personal stories to offset the clinical reports they view from their realm of luxurious dinner parties and peaceful, unbroken sleep.

It's the end for the Commander. The last campaign he'll lead. Perhaps the last Safire campaign entirely.

I'll make sure of it.

The boy hobbles nearer, away from the tide of the city street. "The Safire had no place to hold prisoners," he explains. "Their advance divisions were moving too fast. Easier to shoot prisoners." He pauses, eyes darting to the road. "But they weren't the only ones."

Tirza's pen halts against the paper.

"Go on," I encourage.

"We exchanged fire with Nahir insurgents twice," he admits under his breath. "So did my brother's unit, in the east."

I stare at him, confused. "Were they targeting you or the Safire?"

Tirza still isn't writing.

I don't dare turn to look at her.

"At first we weren't sure," the boy replies. "They belong to no kingdom. But then I heard . . . I heard they blew out the bridges. The ones that stopped the entire damn Safire advance in our favour."

My blood turns cold. The *Nahir* made this decisive move to trap the Safire? That will only look worse for Rahian, defended by the revolutionaries he claims he has nothing to do with. I want to interrogate Tirza on what she knows, but first I also need to assure this boy—who looks as if Resya has fallen down at his feet, as if he's the one to be blamed—that he's given me something that will matter.

"Thank you," I tell him firmly. "You've been brave and—"

A sudden roar cuts me off. A building far down the hill explodes, disappearing into dust. When the smoke clears, an entire corner has disintegrated away, retching its contents onto the street below—furniture, glass . . . bodies.

I stare in horror, sirens wailing forlornly across the city.

"Artillery," Tirza hisses, and her steel hand grabs my arm. I have no time to say goodbye to my soldier, or even get his name, because she's dragging me down the nearest alley, circling back for the palace. There's no choice. She understands this danger far better than me.

We race round a bend and sprint ourselves right into an over-flowing hospital. The courtyard out front—what was once a plaza and trickling fountain—is filled with cots of injured men, the rest left stranded on the cobblestone. Bodies torn in differ-ent ways. Missing limbs, missing faces. Their raw pleas are ago-nized, trapped outside the building, exposed and vulnerable as a wall of shellfire nears.

One soldier kneels over an injured body. "Doctor!" he shouts, his hand on a neck wound, but the doctor doesn't appear.

Safely indoors.

Twisting on his knees, the soldier spins, searches, lands on me. "Please! Hold this!"

His distraught expression is too much. The distant propel-lers are a drumbeat of what's to come, but I won't stand by and do nothing, and this is the least I can do.

I can offer my hands.

Harnessing my fear, I drop down beside the soldier. The wounded man gasps the way Lark did, blood sputtering from his neck, forcing me to stare at my shame. He looks like my father—brown beard, refined face. I decide he *is* a father. It doesn't matter if it's true or not. It's true to me and I let my hand be guided to the wet bandage, feel my fingers touch the mush of skin and warmth.

I don't allow myself to be sick.

"Hold this tight," the soldier orders, then he's bolting for the hospital as anti-aircraft guns stammer overhead. A few streets away, inky smoke rises.

I hold on to the bandage, terrified to even breathe, not want-ing to kill another person. The man stares at the sky, not at me, and I'm glad. I don't want him to see me, in case this doesn't work, and I do it wrong, his blood escaping my fingers like the sea finding shore.

When the soldier appears again, he has a young nurse who's risked venturing outside. She stabs a needle into the injured one's arm. "What happened to him?" she asks, removing my hands from the wound, bandaging it up herself.

"Strafed by a damn Safire plane," the soldier replies hoarsely. "We were trying to get into the city, didn't fire a thing at them, but they still shot us up . . ." He turns to me. "Get to safety, miss. They have no heart!"

The nurse hits her fist against the bloody concrete—her bitter frustration a mirror of my own—then she gently gathers up the wounded man by his chest, the soldier grabbing his legs, and they rush inside. I find myself kneeling alone, sticky red on my hands, reality pulsing in my palms.

Strafed by a Safire plane.

Shot while in retreat.

Tirza hauls me to my feet, and her anxious face is level with mine. "You've done what you can, Ali. We need to *go.*"

I shrug from her touch. "It's not enough."

Someone weeps nearby, blinded by thick bandages across his eyes. He's trying his best to crawl for the door, no one there to help him. And what of the camp? When artillery comes for the airfield, how can it ever avoid the people there? The overwhelming sorrow in me ignites to a flame of pure temper, wicked and dark and consuming. Fury at this war the Commander began for his nation's greed. This war Rahian prolonged for his stubborn pride, and this war the North has now condoned. I gaze up at the wide sky, and it's like a realm I've never seen before—too big, too treacherous—and I hate it at once. Hate its giant power.

No one ever told me this secret thing, that to be small is not to be helpless.

It's to be *angry.*

Recognition alights in Tirza's gaze and she grips my shoulders. "Ali, I know how you feel, but we can't do anything here. Those Safire planes won't care who you are when they're above our heads. They won't care that you're a princess." She winces at the *pop* of flak, closer yet. "You have so much more to do, with the power you hold, and your uncle would kill me if I let you waste your life for a few Resyan soldiers. Not here. Not like this."

I stare at her, confused. "Why does Uncle Tanek care?"

"Tanek?"

"My uncle."

Tirza stares back a moment, guilt suddenly suffusing her expression. The *pop-pop-pop* is more insistent now, the whine of sirens spiraling across the city, everyone running for shelter. Swiftly, she hauls me onwards, down a narrow alley, the cracked walls blotting sun, our boots heavy on the stone.

Something appears in my head through the nauseating fog. The invisible strand I've been following, the one that's pulled me across the sea and down these winding streets, to an abandoned home with a photograph of my mother and her two brothers. Two uncles, both holding guns. A world she refuses to talk about—ever.

I take it all in my hands, really seeing it for once, searching the colours there.

The boots stop.

We've both halted, standing in the alley, and I'm staring at my hands.

My hands.

"Tirza," I whisper. "What's in my blood?"

It's too strange a question, but the only one I can manage, and Tirza understands. Her eternal honesty has finally betrayed her. "The desire to fight," she says softly. "For revenge. For justice."

A sob crawls into my throat.

"To challenge and break and make new."

Your uncle.

"The desire to heal and protect."

"You should worry more about your uncle."

That's what Lark said last summer. He said it and I ignored

it. Lark, Havis, even Rahian. They've each tried to tell me without telling me, and I stand here now, trembling, the proof of it sitting before me. The fact that Tirza won't say his name aloud even now, in this tiny alley. She's speaking in circles. Words that no one listening could ever understand—but I do.

This is why Lark spoke the language of resistance. Why my mother herself could look me in the face and tell me our debt to Seath was nothing at all, that everything would be well with the one man in the world the North fears, the man she betrayed.

Of course she wasn't afraid.

He's her *brother*.

"Please," Tirza says, "don't be ashamed. He's a—"

I pull from her comforting touch, tears stinging hot. I don't want her excuses. It doesn't matter if they're right to resist, to fight for something better. Look what Seath has done! Look at this hell! He's not wearied at all. He's threatened Rahian into something dangerous, paved the way for the Commander's claims and unleashed the Safire upon this innocent kingdom. And now there are too many gone. Too many still yet to die before this can end. Thousands upon thousands, and it's partly because of my skin and my blood.

My hands.

My family.

A Resyan fighter plane hurtles overhead at a reckless speed. He's low enough he nearly skims the roof, spent shell casings clattering down. It doesn't take long to see why he's running so fast. The shells are from two Safire fighters on his tail, their deafening engines snarling, hunting in the sky above, guns firing with ruthless fury.

Tirza and I flee like the Resyan planes.

30

North of Madelan

With the encirclement broken, Army Group North and Army Group East join forces for the first time since war began. Evertal took Irspen all on her own—which, rumour has it, caused a little love lost for her beloved Arrin, the one who ran himself right into a trap and abandoned her. But it was still an astonishing victory, only made possible after our codebreakers in Thurn cracked the Resyan cipher, allowing Evertal to discover an enemy feint on her left flank. She exploited the maneuver. Crushed them and pierced through.

And when Arrin himself broke through the Resyan lines and arrived in the dawn light, standing on a halftrack, victorious, I saw the thing I knew I would see, but somehow still didn't expect. My father waiting for him—relieved.

Relieved.

The expression is barely detectable on Father, but it was there, and it said enough. Never mind his drunk words to me last spring. Never mind the promises. I was never the favourite.

It's always been Arrin.

And I don't know why I care.

As I wait for Moonstrike's next orders, sitting on a discarded box of ammo at the side of our latest runway, the celebration of our sortie has already dissolved into more hammering against my skull. I try to recapture the elation. The pride. But every weary soldier from the encirclement that passes me—haggard, smoking, completely oblivious to the truth of Seath's betrayal—guts me with guilt. Safire blood now soaks the Resyan earth, thousands of lives snuffed out in a matter of days, and they don't even know that we gave the Nahir those weapons. Funds swapped, guns delivered under the cloak of secrecy. It wasn't supposed to be like this. My father might be ruthless, but he always has a sharp purpose. Nothing's gained without a very precise sacrifice.

This . . .

What kind of man can throw everyone into the same furnace? Northern and Southern alike? Seath has just betrayed the only person in the entire world who might have spoken for him—my father—and ruined two armies at once.

For what?

"Hey, there's the lucky charm!" someone calls behind me. "Practically a captain now!"

Thorn Malek's hand is gripping my shoulder before I can turn. He grins down at me, still wearing his flight suit and goggles, dust baked to his face. Must have walked right off the tarmac.

I shrug. "Lead one op. Nothing official."

I'd like to muster more for Thorn, the kind of grin Trigg always has on hand, but nothing comes. The emptiness returns. The nothingness.

"Yeah, one op right out of a damn encirclement! And three batteries ruined for life."

"Lion's Paw helped out," I admit, then pause. "We lost Ollie Helsun."

Thorn's grin fades. "That's a shame. He was good. I'm up to six gone in my squadron. Trying to keep track of the replacements now." He blocks the sun with a hand. "Been to Madelan yet? I just took a little spin over the prize and it's a nice way to get a few more marks on the plane. No resistance left. Like cherry-picking those Resyan fighters. They're saying we could have it by tomorrow night."

"They also said the Nahir were on our side."

Thorn gives me a thin, warning smile to keep my mouth shut. "Hard to say right now. But I need water. Want to get water? It's damn hot."

He's deviating around the accusation, but he's right. We can't talk about it. Not here. We walk for the nearest pump, and Thorn splashes his face and neck, rubbing. I feed the pump for him, but my gaze drifts across the road to a fresh group entering from the north. Marching boots and hacking coughs. Probably more of our battered divisions, finally free of the cauldron.

"Hey, a bit more water?" Thorn asks.

I stare at the columns of soldiers. No, not ours. Resyan prisoners. Their hands are held high, bandages wrapped around heads and arms and legs. All dazed and shell-shocked.

Thorn rubs at his wet face. "Must be part of the regiment we captured. Heard they turned themselves over right as your brother arrived."

I glance back at him. "The regiment surrendered?"

"The entire group. Lucky stroke. Apparently they had the terms already drawn up."

Something queasy hits my empty stomach.

"Terms?"

"To offer the surrender."

"Did we know they were surrendering?"

Thorn looks at me. He knows *we* means Arrin. "Encirclement is confusing," he says quickly. "It might have been a ruse. You can never know for sure if they're going to honour that kind of thing."

A ruse?

I was there. That artillery never even fired on us when we dropped on the town. The tanks never spit out shells and the soldiers never raised guns. It was all one giant surprise, something they weren't expecting, because they had terms already written. Because they were surrendering. They didn't want to fight us. They didn't want to be there any longer.

And I tore them to pieces.

I shove past Thorn.

"Charm, what's—"

I don't stop. The hollowness inside me fills with something at last, a rage that's high on injustice and self-loathing, the realization that perhaps every single one of those pamphlets was completely true. The massacred prisoners. The tortured pilots. We did it all—both Evertal and Arrin well aware—and as I march through the wooden doorway of HQ and into a briefing room, I reel with the fact I'm now as guilty as anyone else. They're all hovering around a map. Most of Army Group North leadership. No sign of Father, but I only need my brother, who's hunched over the table, saying, "I want this entire city brought to its knees tonight. When we enter, I don't want to lose a single soldier. God knows we've lost enough already."

"*You,*" I snarl.

Arrin straightens, cocking a brow. "Excuse me," he says to the rest. "I need a moment with the Lieutenant alone. He can be—"

I push Arrin in the chest, catching him off guard and throwing him back a step. "Did you know they were going to surrender? Goddamn it, did you!"

I've gone too far.

He knows it.

I know it.

His hands seize me and he drags me into the adjacent room, slamming the door closed behind us and me right onto the sharp edge of a desk. Pain stabs my lower back. But I'm going to keep up to him. I won't leave here until I have my answer, until I know exactly what sort of filth lives in his soul.

I stand defiantly. "Tell me the truth. Did you send me on

that run knowing they wanted to surrender? What did your girl tell you?"

He stares at me, jaw clenched.

He won't deny it.

"Athan, this is noth—"

"No, don't tell me this is *nothing*! I did it. I did your dirty work and now it's on *me*!"

"Don't be—"

My fist is in his face before I can stop it. I feel the satisfying thud, the crack, a savage hit of rage and jealousy that I've waited too many years to execute.

His revenge is faster.

Excruciating pain explodes on my nose, sudden darkness, my entire head splitting apart in agony and then I'm on the floor. I stare at my hand, blood dripping onto it. Warmth on my lips.

I look up.

Arrin towers above me. "I've got two of these," he says, holding up his fist. "Be goddamn grateful I'm going easy."

Blood streams now, and I tilt my head back, trying to staunch it with my hand. When I move to stand, everything sways. My skull feels like it's entered a flak field. Fireworks the wrong way around, and I can't walk out of here. Everyone in that room will see how small I really am. The realization is an ache as unwieldy as a plane with no rudder. Fatal. Everything Arrin once told me in Rahmet is true. That being valuable is the only thing Father will accept, and he's right. That's what Arrin is. He can get himself out of cauldrons and win wars, and no matter how hateful that is, no matter how dark and gnarled on the inside— he survives.

I realize I'm tired of being small.

He shakes his head. "Look at you. Mother thought you were the good one. The perfect one. But you see how easy it is now? One minute you're the hero, the next you're *this*."

That hurts more than his fist. The idea that this strafing run was intentional, the sick chance he needed to ruin me. To make me like him.

Too late I realize Father's in the doorway.

I struggle to rise again on shaky legs, my face feeling numb and sharp at once. My headache at war with my nose. I don't know how much he's heard of our fight. But his glare isn't on Arrin.

It's on me.

He grabs my shoulder and we're swiftly out through the ops room and into the sun, the sudden brightness accelerating my pain further. I try to shut my eyes. Try to block out the torturous light. We march across the tarmac and I blink through the sting. Straining to see properly, to see where he's hauled me.

A pale horse stands there. Its rear leg hanging at an awkward angle.

Father hands me his pistol. "Shoot it."

I don't move.

"Shoot it," Father repeats. "It's finished."

Blood still drips from my nose as I take the pistol and hold it to the white furred temple. It looks like Ali's horse. Gentle eyes, long whiskers, but it's mangled. It wheezes in the heat, nostrils bleeding. There are other injured horses nearby. All broken, waiting for a bullet. Did they belong to the enemy? Were they in the town I strafed? This one's back leg is torn wide open, the sort of damage a twenty-millimeter shell could do. It was my plane. It had to be. Why else would I be standing here now, forced to make this choice?

My hand—the pistol—hovers.

But what if it could be saved? Cyar would know what to do. He healed that horse in Etania, and maybe he could heal this one too, with the right plant or food or . . . something. It doesn't have to die just because it's ruined. It can be fixed.

Cyar could heal it.

He'll heal it.

I know, then, that I can't shoot this horse. In the sky, I can pretend to be the version of Athan Dakar that needs to survive, where the emptiness takes away all the regret and makes it into dark steel. Father's ruined the one place in the world I loved best. He's stolen the sky from me. But he can't steal this. This is my power. My line drawn. I have a fighter plane sitting twenty feet away with sixteen black marks on the flank, and he can't diminish that.

He can't diminish me.

I lower the pistol, facing him again. There's nothing in his expression. No crack or fissure, no hint of my fate, only a stare that would have ground me to the mud months ago, back when I needed him. But I don't need anything here. Not in this hell. I don't need his love or his trust or his brand of "favourite."

Sixteen black marks.

An ace.

I'm the thing *he* needs.

Disgust glowers in his gaze now, the beginning of a threat— or ridicule—but before he can say anything, the gun is yanked away. I look down in surprise, a drop of blood falling onto my now empty hand, where the metal was.

Arrin pushes the barrel to the drooped head of the horse and fires.

For a moment, it's like a parody of death. The horse sways, then falls to its knees, red spurting, collapsing onto the withered grass. The nostrils flare with one last breath, suffering ended.

Arrin throws the pistol at Father's boots. *"Enough."*

31

Madelan

The palace is panicked at last. I arrive on a fit of rage and grief, sweat-soaked, desperate to escape the truth Tirza has just enlightened me to, the one that's hovered over my life, one I've never even noticed.

Tirza tries to reassure me, but her words are meaningless right now, and I wheel down the palace halls, straight into the fleeing Lady Havis. "Aurelia, we're flying for my home in Sanseri," she orders briskly. "Last chance before this entire city becomes a battlefield."

I glare at her, well aware the Havis family is evermore intricately tied to this conspiracy. They gave my mother the title, the nobility. They had to know—that she's sister to this dark man, their wealth and prestige building up her fiction, and I'm fairly sure they've been richly rewarded for it.

Lady Havis steps back at my cold greeting. "Or not."

"I'm going nowhere," I announce. "As it turns out, my family is very *necessary* to all of this."

She flinches slightly at my sharp implication, seeing right through it, to the thing I can't speak aloud. But I also wield new power, and it's both revolting and emboldening. "Very well, Sarriyan," she relents, leaning over to kiss my cheek. "But whatever happens, always fly south if you're in trouble. Come to Sanseri."

I don't nod, or promise anything, and she gives a grim sigh. Her face is sad. Whatever else she hides, this part of her feels true. Then she's gone, escaping the worst like a Havis does, while I march onwards for Rahian's private study.

The war is lost. The palace knows it now, completely, reduced to an echo of panicked boots and dying hope. I find Rahian pacing before his oak desk, surrounded by his usual circle of officers. His strained expression says it all, his own fate now sealed. Whatever he's been hiding is about to be brought into the Safire sun.

"Please, Your Majesty, offer the surrender before they bomb Madelan," a harried army commander begs.

"They won't target the city," another responds stoically. "Let them march in here and find us on our feet, refusing to grovel!"

The first gives a bitter laugh. "You place too much faith in Safire honour."

Rahian appears torn, sending everyone in uniform from the room, leaving Havis, Jali, and me alone with him. His tormented gaze finds us.

"When they arrive," he says, "I can't surrender to them. They'll shoot me on the spot."

"That's doubtful," Havis replies, his voice the smooth one I recognize from countless court dinners. The voice that could promise anything while hiding everything. "They'll bring you before the League to make their case. They want to make an example of you."

Rahian sinks into the chair at his desk. "No, not this time, Ambassador. I'm dead already, and Teo . . ." His hands cradle his head. Brandy in a nearby glass.

I stride forward.

"*I'll* negotiate your surrender," I say, the words out of my mouth before I can stop them. This entire disaster is now tied to my family, but I can do better than them. "I'll secure a promise for your fair trial."

All three stare at me. I'm standing before them with wild hair and a frantic gleam in my eye, I'm sure.

"You'd offer the surrender?" Rahian repeats incredulously.

"I would, as the neutral royal party here."

It's such a lie. I'm hardly neutral, not any longer, no matter what I want to believe, but I refuse to walk away from this. Not when I can do good.

"You most certainly are not offering the *surrender* to the Safire army," Havis intervenes. "How is this even an idea in your head?"

"I've dealt with them before," I reply. "It's possible."

"Look around you! This is *war*. This city's going to burn. If an exhausted, trigger-happy soldier finds you in their way, they won't stop to ask questions. You'll have a Safire bullet in your head before the truth ever crosses your lips."

"No, she should do this," Jali proclaims suddenly, and we all turn to her. "Let Aurelia be the one to offer our white flag. Brother, please," she says to Rahian, an edge to her impossibly calm tone. "You must end this. At last."

His face relents, and he looks at me. "Very well."

Havis's mouth drops open, nearly comical in this room of strange royals—a frightened king facing his defeat, a spoiled princess in exile, and a seventeen-year-old girl whose uncle coerced the cowering king's allegiance and began this whole thing.

I'd laugh if I wasn't so scared of everything about to happen.

His jaw snapping shut, Havis announces he'd like to speak with me in private. We stride for his quarters side by side, the palace now approaching hysteria. Soldiers, maids, footmen. It's all falling apart, aeroplanes snarling in deathly duels high above.

Once alone, Havis turns on me. "This is madness, Aurelia! Do you want to announce yourself to the Safire as a friend of Rahian? The man who's about to be convicted of aiding the Nahir and committing near treason against Landore?"

But my anger is too ruthless, matching his. Anger at everyone who lied to me about who I truly am, who let this nightmare get to this point—especially Havis.

"I'm not afraid of them," I snap back. "Not the General or
the Commander or even *Seath*." I spit the name, as if it could be
hurled from my veins. "Or should I fear my own uncle, Havis?
What haven't you told me?"

Boots stomp faintly in the hall beyond, and Havis doesn't
deny it.

I know I've won.

He has no words.

"You knew," I hiss. "As long as I've known you, you knew my
blood connection, and you said *nothing*." I want to strike him
with every ounce of my strength, but he's also the only one
with answers. "Who else knows?"

"Only Rahian," he replies swiftly. "Possibly Jali because she
gets her nose into everything."

That explains her warning to me—which was certainly also
a threat. If she knows Seath is my mother's brother, there's no
reason to believe she wouldn't use that information to her own
advantage if the opportunity arose. She sees no one but herself.

But then I remember the words from the soldier on the
street, and another question follows hot behind. "What was in
that briefcase you gave to Captain Dakar? You had it on you
the whole time at the parley, brought from Rahian with your
peace proposal. Then you gave it to the General's son before he
left Norvenne, and clearly it didn't bring peace, so what was in
there?"

His mouth flattens. "A ruse."

"And how much did Rahian pay you to do *that*?"

"No. Not Rahian."

Which means Seath, and he hurries on in his own defense.
"The Safire need a dose of reality, Aurelia. To let them march
unmatched would be foolish for the entire world. To let them
think they're invincible."

Stars, it's all a game! The Nahir really were the ones who blew out the bridges. And somehow, Havis facilitated it.

"Why would you do this?" I ask, emotion beginning to strangle my voice.

"Powerful people pay well to have someone enact their dirtiest deeds in the shadows."

I laugh at him harshly. "Ah, so you don't trade in arms, but you still trade in death? You're a damn hypocrite!"

"They're all going to tear each other apart in war anyway," he retaliates. "Somewhere, somehow. Why not hurry it along and gain something for myself in the process?"

My fist flies at him.

But he catches my wrist, gripping firmly. "Whether I intervene or not, there's far more at stake here than what's visible, and you need to recognize that, Princess. I'm going to tell you a story no one knows, from before Savient was born, and you'd better listen well. It was an attack on the General's hidden base. Took out half of his burgeoning air force and killed his second child. A little girl." His grip tightens. "That attack shouldn't have been possible, Aurelia. No one knew of the base. Which means the one who made it happen was an old ally, a former comrade who betrayed him and nearly destroyed everything he'd bled for."

"What are you saying?"

"I'm saying this war is about *vengeance*, and you should be very careful about stepping into the middle of that. There's no such thing as justice in revenge. Not the way these men play. And they will bring down anyone who gets in the way."

My heart is so overwhelmed—by the past, by the future—and I can only tremble with one furious certainty. "I don't care about you men and your games. Burn yourselves up. Destroy yourselves for gain! But I do care that my mother let her own brother create this deadly storm . . . and then she turned her back on it."

"What if she did it for *you*?" Havis asks. "For love? Will you spit on her for that?"

"Well, if that's true, then love is an unfortunate distraction, because she damn well should have done more! And if she won't, then I will."

"This isn't on you, Aurelia. It's not your responsibility."

I yank away from him.

"No, it is. It *is* my responsibility! It's my family. My mother. My uncle. Last summer, I betrayed the innocent to save myself, and I'll never do it again. The Lieutenant put my cause before his own when he helped me. He knew it was the right thing to do, even if it ruined him. *That's* what it takes to make a difference. It takes sacrifice. And I refuse to stand here and do nothing. Not while the rest of you think only of yourselves!"

I suck in a breath, my lungs spent on this one raging speech, the anger a brilliant heat inside my chest, and Havis stares, the hard edges of his angled face finally surrendering. Guilt. Regret. And then—defeat.

"I won't stop you, Princess," he says. "But promise me two things."

Flatter me all you want, I think, *and I'll still hate you for the rest of my life.*

"Never forget that your mother's a deadly shot, even from a distance." His eyes burn with certainty. "And don't you *dare* compare yourself to the Lieutenant. You're far better."

VI

SURRENDER

32

Rahian's Palace

The windows begin to rattle just before midnight.

It's very faint, a beelike tremor, quickly swallowed by perfect silence. Then the tremor again. A hum beneath my fingertips, emanating from some distant place. For a while, I don't move from the table where Tirza and I sit, both of us silent and tense. I can see her haunting fear of what's to come, the reality of Safire boots surrounding her again, ready to arrest and interrogate and wound. But she refuses to leave me. No matter how I order her, she's decided to stay. She knows I'm scared, and since she's been scared, too, we are now scared together.

So we wait, wordless, as if speaking aloud will only shatter some possibility of another reality. The tremors will pass. They'll move on. They won't touch us.

Then the chandelier wobbles overhead. Its tiny gems shift, a wind-catcher for war, and I rise from the table, tiptoeing for the dark parlour with its wide windows. A faint glow tickles the marble mantel.

I peer between the drapes.

The edge of Madelan is in flames. Red plumes rise, a sinister memory from last summer, from the masquerade, but this isn't even close to the same. This is an entire city under fire. An inferno.

"They'll say they aimed for the factories and military posts and airfields," Tirza explains behind me. "That's how they'll justify it."

"But those factories are among homes. And the camp . . ."

Tirza says nothing. Her silence says everything.

High above the smoke, aeroplanes float in their distant formation. They're too small to see distinctly, shadows moving gently, releasing death. From that height, it must seem only a patchwork of black and orange and little else. How do they know what they've hit? Even if they were aiming for their chosen targets, how could they ever be sure?

An explosion lights up the world very close, and the whole room shakes. I step back from the window, terror kicking in. Death from high above my head. An unseen creature that doesn't know my name, doesn't even have me on its list—yet it falls, whistling, prepared to consume my flesh in a furnace of flame.

Tirza touches my arm. "They won't hit the palace."

"Why?"

"They only target people with no names."

The unfairness of it scalds my heart.

"This is *wrong*," I whisper.

She looks at me, her face luminous in the orange glow. "It is. But there will be justice."

I scarcely sleep. Tirza shares my bed, her warmth beside me— she says she and Kaziah used to do this, to keep the panic at bay, sheltered by the breath of another living person nearby— but I still tremble, tangled up in moments of darkness and strange dreams. I'm not sure what's real and what's my fear twisting fragments into some in-between place. I see smouldering palms, featherless burned birds, and a glass of lemonade in my hand bursting in flame. My hand throbs, and Lark kneels down, trying to hold the wound, trying to poke at it with something sharp, and then Athan's before me. Skin charred, his face half-destroyed.

I wake with a scream.

Grey light touches the window, smoke in the hazy sky. Shells reverberate on faraway streets. Rumbling ever closer, towards the palace.

Jali appears at my door. "Come, Aurelia," she says quietly, and for the first time, she looks free of her manicured act—a bit unsettled, hollowed out. Perhaps the approaching thunder reminds her of another palace, from her youth, in Masrah.

In her room, Jali dresses me in the royal gown her sister Callia once wore. "Today you'll be like our brave hero, Sedoraha," she says, fastening the buttons. "You offer yourself for our sake, as she did centuries ago."

"I'm not trying to be a sacrifice," I reply, in no mood for her ancient tales. "I'm simply the only option right now."

Which is the truth, undecorated by any romanticism.

But Jali doesn't listen. "She was our greatest knight, not much older than you when she died."

"Is this meant to be reassuring?"

She kisses my right cheek, softer. "She fought her traitorous brother in battle and after being captured, she refused to kill him when she had the chance. Rather than betray Masrah, or him, she fell upon her sword and took her secrets with her, because the enemy was also beloved."

Again, I feel frightened of Jali. A story that could be about my own mother and her brother, a veiled threat in the form of myth. But I realize she's not telling the tale for my sake. She's telling it to herself. "That's the courage my family was made of," she says quietly. "We ruled a thousand-year-old dynasty. We never faltered. We never begged or made false promises or fell at the feet of Northern kings. We've always endured. Now, isn't that the only way to survive? With iron pride?"

I finally see, in that question, why she can't bring herself to truly love Rahian. His kingdom surrendered to the North, and hers didn't. Masrah refused to bow.

A mountain you cannot pass.

And in the end, it was eaten from the inside out.

With that, we walk for the King's council, and I feel an utter sham as I go, a dim imitation of the queen who once wore this dress. All of my years, I've felt like a princess. I've known it. Understood it. But not in this moment, when it matters.

I feel false.

At his desk, Rahian's downing wine already. The dull roars are closer now, nearing the palace gates. I can't see outside, since the heavy drapes are closed, but the chandelier jingles mockingly above our heads.

"Are you ready?" Havis asks me. He asks it as more of an expectation.

I nod, glancing at the door and wondering how we're to know when it's time. I think Havis is about to say something to this effect, when there's a violent shudder below us. The entire palace trembles. Goblets roll along the table, spilling drink. Then it's silent again. An overwhelming and pristine silence. Rahian's soldiers have been ordered not to resist.

Havis hands me the Resyan flag.

"Bring us peace," he says.

I despise the very word on his rotten lips, but I take the limp cloth. Everyone watches me, perhaps regretting this decision to send me into hot Safire guns, but I don't linger. Their concern will only make this worse. Make me hesitate.

Bring us peace.

I can do that.

Both today and to come.

With chin up, head higher than I feel, I stride for the alabaster stairway. I half expect to find Safire uniforms already there, hiding in corners, waiting to grab me. But there's nothing. That same empty silence. I take the steps slowly, heels clicking, a lonely sound while aeroplanes rumble overhead. At the bottom of the stairs, the abandoned foyer is littered with debris. It's a dry bed of activity, remnants of palace life scattered in its wake—dropped trays, frayed maps, the broad oak doors blasted open.

The Commander stands there.

He's a lone figure in the ruin of the doorway, a gun in his hand, his leg bent and head tilted, like he's looking up and up and can't find whatever it is he's looking for, somewhere high in the vaulted ceiling.

He hears me to his left and turns. His guarded face changes to shock. But it isn't his expression that catches me—it's the gaunt shadow of his entire being. He's not the same person who stood beside me at the air show last summer. The glamorous confidence is gone, leaving behind a bruised sort-of rock that reflects nothing.

"What the hell are you doing here?"

His question echoes, flat and startled.

I feel suddenly too gleaming, too exposed. I'm certain he can see the truth written on my face, on my blood and in my bones. My shame and guilt.

Seath, Seath, Seath.

Swallowing fear, I extend the flag. Outside, voices shout in Savien. "His Majesty King Rahian offers his formal surrender. The army is in the garden waiting for you. All weapons have been laid down."

He stares at me a long moment, his leg still crooked. "He sent *you?*"

I nod.

The Commander's eyes narrow, striding forward at last. "No. No, he can do it *himself*, not send a little girl on his behalf. Get his goddamned royal ass down here!"

"Commander, please, he's nervous to see you and—"

"He sure as hell should be nervous!"

He tries to step round me, but I block him. It's a miracle it works. He's still so very tall. "Please, Commander! Promise me he won't be harmed. He has a son. A young child. Let them be spared and he'll give you whatever you ask for. This isn't—"

"Are you trying to negotiate?" he asks, bewildered now. "This is a *surrender*. There's no negotiation. You get whatever I give you."

"This isn't His Majesty's fault," I lie. "The Nahir stirred up this kingdom, not him."

The Commander laughs. A harsh, unpleasant sound, and I notice, now, the wound on his forehead, poorly patched and red as fire. I notice also the dirt on his face, the ruin of his dusty uniform. The gem of his beauty is gone. The anger is ugly.

"Tell me then, Princess," he says, "why I just spent weeks slogging through these mountains and wasting lives? Why did I even come?"

His bitter rage lights mine.

The hellish night I've just witnessed.

"That's a very good question," I snap back. "You brought this war and he had to fight. He had no choice!"

"No choice?"

"This is a sovereign kingdom which *you* invaded."

"Liberated," he corrects. "From a drunk king who encourages violent unrest."

"You did no such thing! You've destroyed it!"

Again, the Commander looks like he might laugh. A savage amusement. His eyes swing up the stairway, sharpening. His hand on his gun. "Then is he going to deal with me himself, or am I to have these political debates with you, as ever?"

I realize how very alone I am. Last time we battled, it was before a throne room of witnesses. Now it's only us and an entire Safire army outside these doors. He could tell them my body was found in the rubble of a shattered doorway. An unfortunate casualty.

I take a step back.

"I already told you," I say, trying to hide my panic, "the army is in the garden, waiting for you. And Rahian will come to the table. I'll make certain of it. Please don't hold all of Resya to account for one man's weakness."

The Commander still stares.

I hold out the flag again, a bit desperately, and an aeroplane passes close enough overhead that the windows rattle. I wish suddenly for Athan, for his face. The only Safire uniform I trust. But I don't even know where he is, or if that could be his aeroplane above, or if he's miles from the capital still in some newly conquered airbase.

Or if he's in a grave.

"Please," I say, "let Rahian speak for himself. Give him a chance."

The Commander doesn't move. He's as giant as he was in the throne room, an indomitable force I must look up to, made of sweat and filth and dried blood, of raw violence, and I resist the urge to run. But he does nothing. The anger between us fades, quite suddenly. A flash of emotion that can't be sustained, not with what's outside these doors.

He takes the flag, then straightens and steps back, shouldering his rifle. I realize how very mad it is that he's come in here all alone. Only him. A solitary, exhausted figure in the echoing silence.

"Which way to the garden?" he asks tonelessly.

I gesture towards the east doors.

He bows, mostly insincere, and heads that way, disappearing round the corner. I let out a terrified breath. It's been captured in my chest too long. Walking forward cautiously, I step through the golden rubble of the grand façade, through the silt and debris and broken glass.

At the top of the front palace steps, I falter.

Tanks and armoured carriers swarm the courtyard, the kestrel badges gone. A new uniform fills it, tired faces staring at me from above rumpled collars, from beneath tilted caps.

Dozens stand beneath the palms, wielding weapons, gazing at the sky where two aeroplanes fly low. And from the gates, the Resyan flag is lowered.

The fox and crossed swords are raised.

Indistinct fury rises in me, billowing like the smoke still staining the blue sky. I fumble for the jewels at my neck, rip Callia's necklace from my skin, then pull off her bangles of glory and the gems from my ears.

In the face of war, I will not gleam.

The first official negotiation is held over a dignified dinner of wine and spiced meat, the table covered in lace and satin—the strangest meal that's ever been shared. Ripe with mistrust. Rahian, Jali, Havis, and the Resyan generals are already present. Rahian sits at the head, appearing about ready to jump out of his skin. Havis sits across from me, slight agitation to his gaze. He *should* be nervous. He's as guilty as any, and if the Safire discover the ruse he gave them in that briefcase . . .

Commander Dakar enters at precisely noon, cleaned up and impressive once more. His uniform is no longer stained with mud and blood. It's the glorious one with medals, and I try to reconcile the fact that while Madelan still burned, someone was charged with the task of flying in a fresh costume for this conquering warrior.

His gaze fixes on Rahian at the far end of the table. A deathly, brutal stare, and Rahian gestures to the only open seat.

We've made sure to put ten feet of fine dining between them.

The Commander sits and takes a bottle of wine. A servant rushes to help, to pour the glass, but the General's son is already drinking straight from the decanter itself, and the room stares at the spectacle. When he's finished, his gaze falls on Rahian. "You have something to say to me, Your Majesty?"

"Please, help yourself," Rahian replies, an edge to his voice.

"To what? This?" The Commander waves at the rich spread before him. "To your kingdom?"

"You've rescued us. You've rescued me from Seath."

"Goddamned lies!" The Commander's voice snaps, his hand still gripping the wine. "You could have surrendered the first day, but you didn't. Your guilt condemns you."

No one speaks, and I feel obligated to intervene. "This is a *sovereign kingdom*," I remind the Commander, "and the League forbade your war. Of course he'd fight if invaded. It has nothing to do with guilt."

The blue eyes dart to me, seated on his right. "Honour may demand a fight, Princess, but not for this long. The innocent would have welcomed our investigation. But this man"—he jabs a finger at Rahian—"chose to take the hard way. The League was wrong, and I've proven it."

Again, no one speaks.

Havis stares at his hands.

"It's not that simple," I say, forging on. I feel like the only one still trying.

"Not that simple?" the Commander repeats. "The Nahir have been after us every step of the way to Madelan. They were already in this kingdom, as I said long ago. It's a shame it took all of *this* to make the world see it."

"They were never on my order," Rahian interjects.

Everyone turns, Jali's brow arching sharply as she does.

The Commander cocks his head. "Then you were aware of them?"

"You know that's not what I meant."

"Do I?"

"Commander, I—"

"Then there are no Nahir revolutionaries within your borders? You blew out your own bridges over the river Lirak? That was you destroying your own infrastructure? Two five-hundred-year-old bridges, priceless relics of Resya's history? Trapping your own army in a cauldron of slaughter?"

"Do not mock me, boy!" Rahian growls. His sudden passion is riled and fierce, with the elegance of a monarch. "I've already lost too much these past months. Look at my city! Look at the waste! You think I would invite this? This kingdom is buried. You've buried it, child!"

The Commander hurls the decanter to the floor.

Crystal shatters, blood-red bursting, and he stands to his full frame. "How much it has cost *you*? Sitting here? Eating all this?" A platter of meat joins the glass shards and wine, ringing on tile as everyone sits rigid, on a razor. "Do you know what that one bridge from Erzel cost me? That one bridge? *Three thousand lives,* Your Majesty. Never mind the hundreds I lost every day we were trapped. And you sit here and tell me what you've lost? You don't even know what you've lost! You don't know the ones who fought for you or where they've been or what they've seen. You know nothing!"

It's very slight, but his eyes glimmer with rage—and possibly grief. And looking at him, standing there, everything destroyed on the floor at his boots, something sharp tightens in my stomach. Something painful.

Three thousand.

Because of one bridge!

I feel my chest constricting again. Too many numbers that have no end. I was naive to believe Athan was alive, somewhere. He isn't. He's only one of the hundreds lost every day, and I have to prepare my heart to live in a world without him—without so many others—and the truth is, I'll probably never learn his fate.

I'll wonder forever, in vain.

A story with no end.

"Are you all right?" Havis asks, the first thing he's said.

I realize he's looking at me, across the table.

But my grief doesn't matter. Rahian is standing now as well, his expression defiant. "I am a king," he declares. "Tell me, Commander, if leaders should be with their soldiers, then where is your father? He's a general. Why would he send you to do this? Why are his boots not as dirty as yours in this *wretched* business?"

Tension quivers in the silence, and the Commander stares at Rahian. "Save your excuses for the League, Majesty," he says, scathingly polite. "You're under arrest until my father arrives."

33

⇥ ATHAN ⇤

Airbase, Madelan

The third night in our newly occupied barracks, the nightmare comes again. It's like the one I had when I was drunk on the pier, fusing together with distant sounds outside our little hut. Drunken laughter rings with the metal wings in my dream. The creaking wind shudders like a cockpit and faint cigarette smoke becomes the scent of searing metal.

I cry out. I know it's me—my own voice loud in my head, too close—and someone shakes me awake. Blurry, out of focus. A shadow-shape I'm terrified of.

"Relax," Cyar says. "You're dreaming."

Terror recedes in the face of relief. He's towering over me, looking slightly afraid—an expression I see more and more when he finds me like this at night.

"What the hell goes on in your head, Athan?"

"A lot of headaches," I reply, trying to grin.

He doesn't return it. He doesn't understand that I'm too afraid to speak the dream out loud and somehow make it real again, even for a second. But he's still giving me his pitying look, and for some reason, it annoys me. "It's the same one we all have," I relent. "Got hit and couldn't get out. Couldn't shatter the canopy, even with my pistol. It didn't break."

"But you're fine," he says.

I sit up, strange frustration scrambling again. "No."

Cyar pushes me back. "You're *fine*."

"But you weren't. You were dead."

He stares at me. It's just a stupid dream. It's the fear we all have, every pilot in every air force—trapped in your own cockpit as you plunge to fiery death, and your wingman's gone. It's nothing special or unique, and I know it, but the feeling of helplessness is like a beast snarling inside me. It has to be how those Resyan soldiers felt when I killed them. Friends falling down on every side. The horror of it haunts me, and it feels good for Cyar to understand finally. To stop with his stupid words that mean nothing.

"I'm not going anywhere," Cyar says. "You'll never have to fly without me."

No.

Still the stupid words.

I glare at him in the darkness. "That's a damn lie and you know it. We're not invincible. We're not deathless. I'm the General's son and I'll die up there like anyone else. At least they'll remember me. But you? You're just—"

I almost say, *"just a kid from Rahmet,"* and Cyar's looking less sympathetic now, more like he might hit me.

"I'm going to pretend you didn't say that," he replies after a moment. He ducks back into his bunk below mine. "Good night, Athan."

There's literally nothing good about it, and I jump down from the bed, heading outside, banging the door behind me. In the compound, a few tipsy pilots are staggering back from an evening of leave. Greycap and Spider and Garrick. Lion's Paw and Moonstrike, reunited again. They've found the nearest drinking hole, a place with rooms to rent for an hour, and the last person I want to see is Captain Merlant—the one who taught me to be honourable. A pilot made of an ageless nobility. I've been avoiding him, petrified he'll look at me and read the truth. That I slaughtered surrendering men.

And, of course, he's the one I smack right into.

"Headache," he greets brightly, his old nickname for me.

He's nobly escorting one of his stumbling pilots to their barracks. "Can't sleep?"

That's an understatement—and I never thought the nickname would prove fortuitous.

"Thirsty," I lie.

Relinquishing his pilot to another, he stays with me beneath the lamps, seeming to sense my guardedness. Perhaps he knows I've been avoiding him. Perhaps he knows what happened with the regiment we took out.

I can't tell, and his smile lessens slightly. "I was hoping to catch you, but you've been scarce."

"You've caught me now."

"Good, Lieutenant," he says, voice lowering, "because I'm going to tell you something as a favour, since you know I admire you." He looks at me, clearly probing for our lost connection. I nod reluctantly. "You lot are damn lucky General Windom took enough pity he mobilized us to come to your rescue. Or rather, his daughter pitied you and pressed him to intervene with our king. But you should know His Majesty Gawain isn't pleased with this mess your brother got himself into. The sheer bloody scope of this campaign."

My brother didn't make the mess, I want to snap back.

There was a plan.

A solid plan.

The *Nahir* made the mess when they betrayed us.

But I can't say that, so I nod again.

"What I'm trying to say," he continues, "is that I'm not sure your family should be expecting favours of this magnitude every time. You might pass that along?"

"I appreciate the warning, Captain."

"Please, take it with my respect. I don't mean to offend."

"Of course not."

We stare at each other, me mustering the closest thing to a smile I've got right now, then he pats my shoulder, a sad expression on his face, and wanders back towards the Lion's Paw barracks. Maybe it's good if I start keeping him at a distance. The Landorians are friends, but they're also not. They've got their own agenda. We have ours. And maybe it's even good if Cyar and I start fighting more. I need to begin cutting him away. Need to learn to live without him.

I hit my head, hard.

What the *hell's* wrong with my brain? These thoughts have built like a sickness. I've somehow destroyed the shred of decency I once clung to, the thing that made me believe I wasn't like my family. But as it turns out, I'm exactly like them. Because when my guns fired into that Resyan regiment, I felt nothing but thrill. Victory. Desire for the power in my deadly wings. That's my dark secret, and none of this will go away, never, not even in my dreams.

Dying was supposed to be the worst fate in war.

But it isn't.

The worst fate is surviving and learning to live all over again—like *this*.

VII

WINGS

34

Rahian's Palace

Rahian's house arrest saps the palace of whatever remaining nobility it had left. At the enemy's mercy, the remaining officials and staff operate under an uneasy truce as whispers trickle in about the eastern parts of the city that suffered the worst of the bombs. Homes destroyed, bodies buried, limbs turned black.

Two thousand.

Five hundred.

An entire family.

The numbers start large, overwhelming, then shrink down into individual names who will never be remembered beyond Madelan. The ashes of war. The Commander refuses to answer my questioning, but the one named Evertal, a powerful woman in Safire uniform, stoops to address me. It was a mistake, she explains. Bad winds. Stray shells. They could never have deliberately done such a thing, she assures—and since she won the war, everyone nods and pretends to agree.

I silently add the numbers to a notebook I'm keeping of evidence.

I'm terrified to ask anyone about the camp. No one mentions it, and perhaps to them it never existed, but to me it holds every piece of my sorrow and regret, the forgotten symbol of all this horrific conflict represents.

The void where hope disappears.

"I can't take this any longer," Havis finally announces a week after the surrender. He looms in the doorway of my room as I sit on the sofa alone, trying to decide what message I'll cable my mother, now that the wires are up again. "We need to get you away from here. An escape."

I let my pointed silence answer him. My page is still blank, because I have no words for my mother. None that I can send like this. A thousand questions demanding answers.

"The General won't be arriving for another few days," Havis persists. "It's a long journey from Savient."

I find it incredible how many excuses people will concoct for a powerful man. He should have been here days ago. But Havis doesn't give up, sitting beside me, his weight crushing the cushion. "I know you swore never to forgive me," he remarks, "but what if I offered you the one thing your heart desires most?"

"Peace throughout the world with not a single lying man left in existence?"

"All right. Perhaps the *second* greatest desire of your heart?"

I glance up finally. "I'm not leaving Madelan, Havis. I have to be here to mediate with the General."

"We won't go far," Havis assures, and if he thinks I'm mad for putting myself into the negotiations, he doesn't touch it. He's getting wiser. "Just our estate."

I sigh. The offer is tempting. A place filled with flowers and sunshine rather than cigar smoke and suspicion. Away from the unpredictable Commander hovering at my neck. The Commander who watches me every day, his suspicion coiling, like there's a secret message written beneath my skin, and someday, very soon, he'll read it and know who I am.

It's exhausting, being afraid.

"Why did you help Damir and Tirza?" I ask Havis instead, a question that's been weighing on my mind. "You gave them work here, support their press. You did a good thing, and I'm not sure what it offered you in return."

Havis laughs shortly. "Yes, imagine that. Me helping someone and getting nothing in exchange." He shakes his head. "I know you think I'm purely mercenary, Aurelia, but I do care. I do have a heart. And I did the only thing anyone can do—I helped a family. One brother, one sister. You can't save everyone. You simply can't."

"It didn't occur to you they might be Nahir?"

"Oh, I was fully aware. But here, that's part of life, and you don't judge people based on who they are. You judge them based on what they *do*." He pauses. "And that's an idea you might want to consider carefully in days to come."

I don't have to ask what he means.

He's talking about my mother, the angry blank page still sitting before me.

"All right, I'll go to your estate," I relent at last. "But only for one day."

He brightens. "Good—and you might want to put on something pretty."

I ignore that ridiculous request and lace up my leather boots, throw a few things in my traveling trunk, then head for the door.

I realize quickly that we're headed in the wrong direction. Our automobile rumbles down avenues which now hold Savien tanks and soldiers directing stunned residents through the shambled city, and it's not towards his estate. Though Havis steers us clear of the worst wreckage, the damage still lurks, and in my shame, I don't wish to look. Yes, Safire planes put this city to flame, but it was also the ghost of a man—a man who runs in my veins—who brought them here. A man who doesn't want to negotiate, who condemned this kingdom to war.

When the motorcar finally stops, I'm confronted by a wire fence, foreign soldiers posted on either side of a wide gate. Two aeroplanes swing down onto a runway shivering in the afternoon heat.

"An airbase?" I ask, confused.

"It's the only one that survived the bombing. And I think it might hold something of value for us."

"Why? What's in your briefcase this time?"

He chuckles, scratching at the shadow along his jaw. "Can you believe a year ago I found you wearisome? As it turns out, you're actually quite clever and interesting, and I've begun to wonder what you might accomplish if you had true cards in your hands."

"I don't follow," I say, suspicious of his sudden flattery.

"I'm telling you that you're someone I *like*, and there aren't many people I'd put in that category. For that reason, I'm going to give you a gift, trusting you'll use it wisely, with the good sense I know is in your head."

The trouble with Havis's compliments is they end up sounding a lot like pandering.

"I'll still never forgive you," I inform him. "I've seen what you *do* and my judgment is final."

He rolls his eyes. "Indulge me for a moment," he replies, sliding from the driver's side.

Annoyed, I follow him out into the heat, my sundress sticking to my sweaty knees. The air holds the wet warmth that precedes an afternoon rain, and the Landorian guards quickly make way for the papers Havis offers them. Two more aeroplanes patrol overhead. I shade my eyes to watch their rounded green wings and breathe in the smoky scent.

Like this, they're still beautiful. Peaceful and bright in the light.

"May I be of assistance?" a voice asks, refined in its Landori accent.

I peel my gaze from the sky and find a pilot with dark hair and blue eyes approaching. "No, it's fine," I say quickly, since I have no clue what valuable thing I'm supposed to be searching for. I hope it's more evidence to take before the League.

When I turn to Havis for help, he's busy showing off his

fancy automobile to a gaggle of pilots, Safire and Landorian alike.

"Captain Merlant," the pilot offers with a gracious smile, though it's a bit hesitant. Certainly he senses the awkwardness of this exchange. A young Resyan lady and a conquering officer—an officer from the kingdom which *should* have been on Resya's side in this business.

I scramble for an answer. "I'm Ali, the . . . future Lady Havis." I want him to know I'm nobility—even though I look half-rustic, my long hair loose and thick with humidity—but certainly not a Northern princess. Explanations feel like a waste of breath right now.

Merlant keeps discreetly glancing at my leather boots. I know they look nearly comical with my sundress. "Forgive the intrusion, Captain," I try. "We're here to—"

I stop.

My thoughts disappear.

"Yes?" he presses politely.

There, across the tarmac, standing by an aeroplane, is Athan Erelis. I'm sure it must be a dream. A thing that isn't real, another stretched mirage from my helpless sleep, but the sun is hot on my neck, and the air is damp in my mouth. I can smell kerosene. Petrol. I'm not floating, I'm here, and then he sees me.

His expression is stunned.

"Forgive me," Merlant says. "We haven't had many local guests yet and I—" He turns to see who I'm looking at. "Oh."

I brush past him, caught on a river, rushing for shore, everything inside me demanding to be known and recognized. Hope, relief, terror. It's too wonderful and too terrible at once, so many weights hanging on this one moment, threatening to push it one way or another. Athan walks over in the same trance. He's wearing a short-sleeved shirt, uniform pants rumpled and dusty. Leather boots like mine. Near enough, now, I can see the thinness to his beautiful face, the uneven shadows.

He's more bewildered than me.

"Ali," he says, voice hoarse. "You're *here*."

The frightened sound of my name on his lips, alive, is like someone being roused from the dead. He was dead to me. I tried to imagine it, to practice the feeling of a world without him. But he's not dead. He's a foot from me now, saying my name, an oil splotch marring his cheek, his nose bruised. An echo of the summer.

I want to laugh in wild relief.

I want to cry.

I can only stare. "I came with the Ambassador," I say, longing to throw my arms right round him, never let go. "I wanted to tour Resya, to see my mother's homeland. And then . . . I got rather stuck."

Now, he looks nearly terrified. "You've been here the whole time?"

I shake my head quickly. "No, not here," I lie, wanting to take his fear away. "I wasn't in the capital. I was in the south, where it was quiet." I wave at Havis, who's speaking with Merlant, keeping an eye on us. "And now, I'm waiting for the negotiations to begin, for Rahian's trial."

Athan says nothing.

His chest moves with a slow breath that's so very alive and yet so very distant.

I can't read him.

He's a familiar stranger, far across the ravine of war, my boy of the sky, and I try a grin, gesturing at his nose. "Did you run into a prince somewhere?"

It takes a moment, but finally the frail edge of a smile grazes his lips. I reach up, gently tracing the oil from his cheek, and I'm surprised by how deeply my skin has richened in the Resyan sun, next to his hue of pale gold.

He touches my hand, a touch that I feel all the way to my belly. "I *am* happy to see you," he says softly, seeming to sense my desire for this moment to be something more than it is. "I'm just scared for you," he admits, his voice as thin as his face.

I smile, desperate for him to return it. "I'm perfectly fine, Lieutenant. I promise. It's over now. Instead of worrying, why don't you run away with me? Havis has an estate outside the city. It's an escape, and you can come."

I see now exactly the bribe Havis wants to give me—and I intend to take it.

The gift of Athan Erelis is one I'll never refuse.

"Go with you?" Athan repeats, looking over my shoulder, certainly at Havis.

"Can't you take leave?"

There's another moment of silence between us, and apparently I'm now playing the role of Havis. Convincing Athan to escape when he's clearly still drowning in the reality of this horror. What a strange world this is.

But I'm determined to be something good for him. To give him something better.

"I do," Athan finally says, rubbing at his head.

"Do?"

His grey eyes find mine. "I mean, I do have leave. We all do, but no one takes more than a few hours of it. It's better to stay close to base."

I nod then, understanding. He isn't a boy here, but rather a Safire badge that holds too much bitterness still. I can wander these streets. He can't. He's in a place that despises him—a place that doesn't want to know him beyond this dirty uniform.

But I want him. And I'll take him away from these barbed-wire fences and memories of war.

I hold out my hand. "Please, come."

He hesitates, eyes darting to all of the curious faces surrounding us, and I realize he can't touch me. Not until he's begged for permission and packed his bags and shed this other identity, this one I've never known. Not like this, on a runway in the middle of a settling battlefield.

"I'll meet you at the motorcar?" I ask, unable to hide the hurt in my question.

He nods. "I'll request my pass."

Recognizing he won't give me anything else, not here, I turn and head back for Havis. I feel confused and happy and alone all at once. I've made it only a few steps when his fervent voice carries on the breeze.

"I'm glad to see you, Ali!"

The words are urgent, honest, and sorrow and hope fight for space in my chest. I'm already scared of what's happened. What will happen next. And yet, the sound of my name on his lips, a voice brought back to life from the grave . . . My heart picks up a rhythm that feels like a race. My skin is flushed, my hands tremble, and I face him again, grinning right as the first drops fall from the sky. The warm afternoon rain of Madelan, mixing with sun. Making the tarmac shimmer all round us.

His tired face is resplendent with desire, and he smiles back.

Hope wins.

35

⟩ ATHAN ⟨

I'm in a daze as I request an evening off base, telling Garrick it's going to be all three of us—me, Cyar, Trigg—venturing to the infamous bar with rooms by the hour. Everyone else has tried it out already. He nods, half-distracted, as I concoct my story, but he also looks a bit relieved to see us doing something other than sitting around being virtuous angels.

I also suspect he's seen me wandering in circles late at night.

"Twenty-four hours, Lieutenant," he says, writing the pass. "Don't stay out after dark."

"Yes, sir."

"And be safe."

"I've got my gun."

Garrick gives me a look like I'm twelve. He tosses something at me, and I find myself holding a bit of army-issued prophylactic. "Right," I say, as if I knew he meant that all along.

"Someone has to watch out for you. And it isn't going to be your brother."

I'm not sure if I should feel grateful for the intervention, but at least I can get the hell out of here, free of suspicion. In our barracks, I pack a bag, throwing all of Katalin's half-legible letters into the trash. I don't even know why I kept them. Stupid. Then I try to pull myself together, looking in the tilted mirror. I'm a mess. I need a haircut, need to be wearing something other than a sweaty uniform that's been washed in a bucket for weeks.

I need another name.

Another life.

But I'm not going to get either of those things in the next ten minutes, so I take this unexpected dream and run with it. She's here. It's entirely illogical, and part of me is still panicking at the realization. The thought of her anywhere near a frontline, anywhere near the opposite side of a gun—our guns. *My* gun. I'm sick with a worry that shouldn't exist. She's safe and it's over. But the thought of it . . .

"This is a bad idea," Cyar says from his bunk, watching me.

"Just do it, all right?" I tell him. "Say we rented a room somewhere and got drunk and forgot to come back."

"How many days can we buy with that lie?"

"Two would be enough."

"In *Madelan?*"

I turn to face him, shouldering my bag. He's still mad at me for the other night, and I'm still nurturing this idea of learning to resent him. At least a bit. It's good for both of us. "You know this is the only thing I want. Be a friend, all right?"

I don't wait for the answer. I'm already out the door, not wanting to give him a chance to speak his reasonable thoughts that don't know the truth. Ali isn't dangerous. She's the opposite of that—she'll give me life.

I jog for the waiting motorcar, and Havis gives me his subtly appraising look that says, *"I've just brought you a gift, now what will you give me?"*

I'll worry about being in his debt later.

For now, I have Ali brushing against me on this seat, a girl of soft skirts and softer skin. She glows in the sun, her dark eyes bright. Her hand creeps onto mine, holding—a rope, a connection—and I don't want her to ever let go. I'm on the earth and she's my gravity, holding me in place while my thoughts sprint ten steps ahead.

Havis's estate.

What the hell am I doing?

The drive is a wonderful blur because I'm mostly looking at her. She has a dozen stories to share, which means I get to stay quiet and just listen. By the time we pass through the gates into an elaborate complex of gardens, rolling pastures, I've heard all about the horses and the motorbikes. When we step out of the vehicle, it's perfectly quiet—just birds, sun, wind. Everything wet and glistening from leftover rain.

It's wonderful.

"Isn't it lovely?" Ali asks me as Havis gives orders to his attendants. "This must be much better than wherever your fellow pilots were going for their leave."

I give her a wry smile. "With our wage? Definitely."

Her humour fades. "That's not what I meant."

I shrug, since there's no way to really explain how the money I made these past two months for killing other human beings will maybe equal the cost of her latest palace banquet. I want to laugh, to be funnier. But I'm standing in the middle of this fancy estate wearing last week's undershirt and a bruising wound on my lower back from when Arrin dropped me onto the desk. Underneath, I'm all filth of war. A person who slaughtered men trying to surrender—and enjoyed it.

The realization that soon enough she'll begin to sense the ugly emptiness inside me, and the guilty name I bear, makes me sweat with impatience. There's a ticking clock on these pleasantries, these initial moments of glorious reunion. I'm dreading it. The moment she sees me as I am now.

Athan Dakar.

Wounded and filthy and deadly.

Inside the large home of shiny floors and cream walls, Havis allows us to tour on our own, wisely retreating—or else just hoping I'll take the hint and say the things I should.

I'm clearly not as noble as he expects.

Ali leads me along, showing off the terraces and helping

herself to the cats that sprawl leisurely in sunny spots. A pond is filled with colourful fish flitting through the water, some big and fat, hardly moving, and she dips a finger so they follow it, hoping for food. An orange cat hops up onto the ledge beside her. Ears perked, it tracks Ali's movements, fixated on the fish. The fish don't notice. Trapped, moving forever in tiny circles in the tiny pond. Easy to capture. Easy for a cat's paw. Waiting to be ripped apart like scraps, plucked from the air and—

"Athan?"

I realize Ali's looking at me, kneeling against the ledge. Her face is delicate concern.

"What?" I ask, hoping to God she wasn't talking and I missed it all.

She stares a moment, then says, "You look tired."

I'm exhausted, I want to say, resisting the urge to rub at my damn head. But then she'll tell me to go to sleep, and I don't want to go to sleep. I want to be with her. I want to be in this moment, entirely alive and electric and full. She looks older now, a new weight to her buoyant energy, and it's beautiful— sunlight made firm, something I can hold in my arms.

I want to hold her.

But I don't know how to ask for that, or offer it, since I can hardly construct a proper sentence right now. She simply takes my hand with a sad smile and leads me back inside.

We find a lunch prepared for us, the table set. Havis surprises us both when he says, "I'm off, then. A third person isn't necessary here."

"You don't have to go," I say, not wanting to seem too desperate. Too in his debt.

"No, no," he replies warmly. "You have two days? I'll leave you both to it. I'm sure you have much to discuss."

"We do," Ali agrees, clearly happy to have him disappear.

"Don't leave anything untouched, Lieutenant. War, aeroplanes, family history . . ."

"Suggestion noted, Ambassador."

"I'm simply trying to help," he replies, bumping my shoulder as he turns to leave.

I still can't stand him. But he's right. She *does* need the truth, and I won't let the moment slip from me, not this time. Clearly she didn't get my letters. Probably sitting back in Etania, un-opened. I'll do it, but first I need her to remember why she likes me. This precious thing between us feels thinner than last summer. Not because it isn't still there—I'm convinced it is—but distance and time have a way of bringing up nerves and strangeness again, like we're back at the beginning. We need time to restore our friendship. To feel honest again.

As we sip lemonade, she recounts the previous weeks—the city in turmoil, the men on horses, the bombs. The palace was burst open and then she herself offered the surrender to the Commander of the Safire forces.

Goddamn it.

"You said you were in the *south*," I remind her, unable to hide my accusation.

"Oh." She blinks, caught by her own fabricated story.

I'm horrified by all of these things I didn't know, beginning to fever as I listen, and I set to work picking the bones out of the half-eaten carp in front of me. It feels calming somehow. One, two, three, four. It takes a few tries, but they're in a pre-cisely neat square when I sense, more than see, Ali's frustra-tion.

"You're upset with me?" she asks pointedly.

"You put yourself in danger," I reply, nudging the last bone into a better place.

She's still staring, and I think I've made the first wrong move. "I had to do my part," she informs me. "You were in danger every day, for the same reason. Surely you understand that?"

No. I don't understand. I care about her. Doesn't she hear herself talking? Offering the damn surrender. To Arrin! Now she's convinced she can put herself into the negotiations, help

Rahian out, but it will only make it worse. This whole thing is far from over. In fact, it might only be beginning, thanks to Seath. And I just want Ali and me to be the same as we were, last summer, before all of this, but I don't know how to get there.

She crosses her arms. "We've talked a lot about me. Tell me what you've been doing."

The innocent question holds a challenge.

She knows it.

"Not much," I reply, scattering the bones with a finger, destroying perfection. "Just a lot of . . . flying. But I want to hear more about Jali and Callia. They really walked here from Masrah?"

"You're doing it again."

"Doing what?"

"Talking round my questions. I know you're good at that, but I really thought we'd have moved past it, especially by now."

Her veiled annoyance stings my frustration. "I don't know what you want to hear, Ali."

"Everything."

"You don't."

"I do. *Damn it*, I do!"

Her self-righteous fury is insulting. I glare at her down the table. She's trying to get closer; she senses the same distance I do, but it's all the wrong way. "You want to know about me? About what I've done? Fine. The truth is I haven't done a damn thing I'm proud of. There's your answer. They're all things I want to forget—or do I need to confess them each to you one by one by one?"

Bones, one by one by one.

We glower at each other, birds squawking outside the window. Her face is granite, so focused on me she might shatter my resolve with those perfect, dark eyes. "You stayed alive," she says finally, "and that's all I've asked of you. All I'll ever ask of you."

I'm sure she means it as reassurance, but the anger in me gives way to utter exhaustion again. There's nothing about that I want to hear. I've honoured her request—but still ended up worse.

"Staying alive is the easy part," I say quietly. "You need to expect more of me than that."

Those words break the spell.

Her resolute expression fades to sorrow, and she stands, coming to my side. She kneels down, her hand taking mine again, so very soft. "All right," she says. "Stay alive. Always stay alive. But you also have to find me on the other end of it, wherever you are. You always have to come for me. Do you promise?"

Her expression is too hopeful. I can't bear to see her disappointed in me. "Yes. But that promise involves you, you know."

She nods. "Then I'll do my part, too. It's the bad luck from the flower you picked last summer. We have to share it evenly— the good and the bad."

I feel a smile tugging at my face. A painful one. I can't believe we're basing our fate on a damn flower, that faraway garden in Etania, that moment when I should have just walked away or said the truth or abandoned my family forever. But I'll take it. I need it.

"It's a deal," I say.

"Never forget it," she replies, and she kisses me on the cheek, another kind of promise.

The first order of business, after food, is to get me clean clothes. I think I smell well enough, but I definitely look like I've come through seven weeks of campaign. Wrinkled and scuffed, my green uniform's had the colour sapped by the sun, practically back to the grey I'm usually in. Ali sends the estate servants on a mission to secure me something that might fit. They return with too many fancy suits.

Apparently, the Havis family has high taste in fashion while profiting off wars.

They eventually produce brown pants, a short-sleeved shirt, and a cast-off leather coat from Havis's brother. "Mountain wear," they call it, unimpressed.

Which is just perfect as far as I'm concerned.

As I hand over my uniform to be properly washed for once, beginning with the jacket, I realize Ali hasn't left the room. Her smile is teasing, and I'm honestly not afraid of stripping down in front of her—I'm more afraid of her getting her hands on the metal tags around my neck. They're still hidden by my undershirt. And they need to stay that way.

I try to stall, but her expression changes, the smirk transforming to a frown.

"You're rubbing your head again," she points out.

"Am I?"

I hadn't even noticed.

"Yes. You've hardly stopped since I first saw you."

"Just a headache."

She refuses to relent, as usual, reaching up to touch my forehead gently. "You also squint a lot in the light."

"Because it's sunny?"

"Please, Athan. You know it's not normal."

"Fine," I admit. "Maybe not."

"When did the headaches start?"

"I made a stupid move in my plane. Hit my head. They started after that."

She sucks in air, a sound that makes me a bit weak because it's so concerned on my behalf. Her hand is still touching me. Warmth across the steady thud of pain. "Headaches and light sensitivity," she muses. "Any other symptoms? Trouble sleeping?"

I snort. "What's sleep?"

"Irritability?"

"Ask Cyar."

She shakes her head, taking her touch away. I miss it already. "It sounds like a concussion."

"A concussion? I didn't know you decided to study medicine at your university."

Her smile is weak, lacking its usual luster. There's no pride in her voice. "My uncle was a doctor and my aunt was a nurse. My cousin taught me a lot about the body last summer, and clearly it's going to serve you well, because now I've diagnosed you. Why on earth didn't you see a medic?"

I shrug. I don't quite know how to tell her that medics hate being interrupted by headaches when they've got patients with gangrenous limbs and missing faces. Blinking a lot in the sun is rather low priority. "It wasn't that bad," I lie. "I didn't want to bother them."

She doesn't look convinced. "You don't have any medication for pain?"

"Used up the pills in my kit over a month ago."

Now she looks horrified. "What have you been doing since then?"

Not sleeping. Hitting my head. Generally waiting for it to disappear on its own.

"Fighting a war," I say honestly. "Is this ever going away, Doctor?"

"As long as you don't hurt yourself again," she instructs firmly. "You need to actually rest, let it heal. All of this stress likely exacerbated it."

For a split second, I feel relieved, because this means I might still be a great pilot. It wasn't me struggling in the sky. It was the concussion slowing me down.

Then I want to shoot myself for even thinking that.

Ali closes the few inches of distance between us, her face sad again. "I want you to smile," she whispers, her hands moving to my chest.

"I want to give that to you," I reply, losing my breath a bit.

"Perhaps you're ticklish?"

"Clever. But not at all."

"How else can I make you laugh?"

"Be yourself."

"Perhaps like this?"

She's impressively fast. She reaches to steal my metal tags and it's only instinctive reflex that gives me the advantage. I hold her by the wrist, the chain in her hands, and she grins up at me, eyes alight.

"Come on," she begs. "Let me try them on."

"These are air force property," I remind her, trying to grin, to not sound entirely panicked.

I shove them beneath my shirt again.

"So are you," she teases. "Am I not allowed to hold you?"

The scent of her, this close, is like every late-night fantasy brought to perfect life. Her lips—and her question—lure all kinds of thoughts, inviting me to act on them, demanding it even, but I can't, not until I've told her the truth. Not until she knows the person she's kissing.

I wish my headaches were the worst secret I held.

"Maybe after I'm wearing something clean?" I suggest.

She relents, stepping back and heading for the door. She tosses me a last smile. "As long as you promise, Athan Erelis."

"I swear it."

As soon as she's gone, I throw on the new clothes and tuck my stupid tags—and the name Dakar—back under my shirt.

Two days to convince her I'm a dream come true.

And now with a concussion!

36

Being with Athan again is the hardest and most wonderful thing at once.

Sorting through my bag, I find a few of my pamphlets tucked in a folder, the ones I've collected for this post-war period, and they taunt me cruelly. I glance out the window at Athan, waiting for me in the sun. I should tell him what I really did during this war. The incriminating leaflets I wrote against his own army—against *him*. I promised him, in the letter I never sent, that I would explain it all in person. But now that I have him right in front of me—wounded, tired, hollow—I find the words have disappeared.

They're simply not helpful right now.

That's what I tell myself, anyway, as I tuck them back into the folder, rejoining Athan outside. Together, the two of us wander the gardens, savouring each foot of earth that is ours to explore. I try to take him to visit the horses, but he refuses to go, even more apprehensive of them than he was last summer, so instead, we lie on the grass while he points out the Safire aeroplanes that fly overhead with droning regularity. I learn them all, the small details only he knows. Fighter. Reconnaissance. Light bomber. Transport. I have to ask questions, to fill the silence that he seems hesitant to disrupt, and I'm frightened of the truth surfacing before my eyes.

He isn't the same.

Before, he was full of sunlight, eager to lead the way and explore the world round us. Now, that only shows in cracks, in startled moments when it's almost an accident. A wry comment. A smile flickering to life when I tease him. He's tired and full of weight, an invisible thing that makes him move more slowly, consider his words more closely. Perhaps it's the lingering concussion. Lark said he fell off a horse once and earned himself the same injury—it kept him struggling to read for months afterwards.

On the second afternoon, after Athan's taken something for the pain and enjoyed a good night's sleep, he begins to shift slightly. His eyes are brighter. His words quicker. We swim together in the narrow stream that winds through the estate, diving for colourful rocks and whatever else we can discover below. It feels bolder in the wetness. His hand finds my ankle, dragging me along, and I push him from me, laughing, before I realize that I'm practically in his arms. The water feels safe, like we're not actually touching. But we are touching—his shirt off, his arms and chest against me, and I commit to memory the way his sun-golden skin looks this close, a few freckles along his shoulders to match the ones on his nose. All of him firm to touch, yet too gentle, like fine-spun flesh ready to be snuffed out with a tiny puff of smoke.

The memory of fear still makes me ill.

By evening, stories finally trickle from his lips. Stories I don't want to hear, but I must—for his sake. Planes burning up. Pilots on fire. A horse, shot in the head. His spirit is wounded in a place I can't reach, and I remember my mother's many lectures, that I don't want a man who can be ordered and broken. But what if we're all fractured? Every single one of us, struggling to hold the pieces in our hands? And perhaps the ones who can't be broken—perhaps *they're* the ones I want nothing to do with.

I want a heart that breaks. A soft heart.

"I just think too much," Athan admits at the end. "I shouldn't be telling you all this."

"No, you should," I assure him. "There's nothing you can say that will frighten me."

I wish I could say there's nothing he's done that would make me look at him differently, but I know that isn't true. Wickedness has happened, and my heart begs him not to tell me anything that will destroy the perfect vision I hold of him.

He's not like them.

He's good.

"Do you think this invasion was wrong?" I venture, wanting to hear him say it aloud. Needing him to say it, now that he's admitted these horrors. These things that clearly needle his sense of honour.

But he's silent, still studying the sky above us.

I think of the photograph I saw, of General Dakar with the dog at his feet, beside my mother. I've wondered in sleepless nights since if perhaps the General once believed in the Nahir's quest for independence. The theory isn't as entirely preposterous as I might have imagined. I've always believed that Lark and Athan would have had much in common, had they ever had the chance to sit down and talk. But whatever the long-ago truth is, it's doubtful Athan could imagine the possibility of an alliance with the ones who destroyed the bridges and trapped them. And that photograph would condemn Dakar as easily as it would my mother before the League.

"Perhaps what you told me last summer was right," I suggest carefully. "You said we can't force loyalty on others, that maybe the people of the South were right to resist, and now here we are yet again. Coming across the sea and thinking we know best. Perhaps all we do is make things worse." I pause. "In fact, I think if you really thought about it, you'd realize you Safire have more in common with the Nahir than you'd like to admit. Your fire for change and independence. Your resistance to the old ways of monarchy. Maybe you—"

"You think we're like *them*?" Athan interrupts sharply. He peers up at me as if I'm mad.

"Not entirely," I clarify. "But perhaps a bit."

He pulls himself to a sitting position, and gone is the shame and sorrow from his gaze. Now there is anger. "You don't know what you're talking about, Ali. The Nahir, they're . . . honestly, I don't even think *they* know what they want. They just create chaos. Destroy things. That's it."

I stare at him, piqued by the fact he's sounding like Jali Furswana. "But you haven't seen what goes on in Thurn," I rejoin. "There are photographs that—"

"Might be lies," he finishes.

"You think pictures of dead children are *lies*?"

"Maybe." He shrugs. "Maybe not. I haven't seen them."

We're both thoroughly annoyed now, refusing to surrender, and the certainty in his voice frustrates me. I'm sure I sound equally unyielding, my dark secret taunting.

Yes, the man you've been fighting, the one who designed this war, who's been burning up the whole world and spreading discord, is in fact my uncle, my own family, and my mother never even lifted a finger to stop him.

But I force a smile, a practiced smile from a lifetime of formal dinners, as if our disagreement doesn't matter at all. I won't let it sabotage our precious time together.

"Stay tomorrow?" I ask quietly instead. "One more day?"

He hesitates, then nods and leans closer.

"I believe in you, Ali. You alone are true." His hand moves to my cheek. "And I will always try to be good for you."

I find him doing sit-ups on the fourth morning—a wonderful sign, because it certainly means his head is feeling better. He's always awake before me, sketching on the terrace with tea, soaking up the quiet of the gardens, the early sun still creeping in at the corners. But this morning, he's shirtless on the lawn, and I watch for a long while, not wanting to disturb his rhythm.

Eventually, I can't resist.

I kneel down beside him with a grin. "So, Lieutenant, how many of these do you have to do?"

He pauses briefly, panting. "Can't stop . . . forty-one."

"Does this help with flying? You look miserable."

The teasing question works, and I'm beginning to enjoy how easily distractible he is, so quick to follow a shifting target. He sits up, sweat glistening on his bare chest only a foot from me. One simple breath of a foot away.

"I'm strengthening my core to avoid blackout while flying," he explains, as if he really does need to justify this to me. "I wrote you a letter about it actually. I guess it'll be waiting for you in Etania. One of our pilots went into a steep spin and blacked out, came out of it only a few hundred feet above ground. Lucky bastard. I'd rather not test my own luck."

"Makes sense," I say, shifting closer and copying his position on the grass. My arm brushes his. "Let's do our sit-ups, then, so we don't black out."

"Forty-three," he says, leaning back.

"Forty-three," I agree, doing the same.

He grins. "Cheater."

We do a few in quick succession and my stomach begins to burn like it's being torn in half. I give up after six, and Athan pretends he was going to finish at fifty anyway.

"Next is push-ups," he says cheerfully.

"Stars, no."

"Come on, Pilot. That stick gets heavy in a dive."

"Can't I just watch you?" I ask slyly, because he's on his hands now, his back exposed and glistening and I might as well simply state the truth. He has a lovely back. And lovely shoulders. The kind I can't help but imagine lying beneath, his chest above me, strong and—

"Watching won't save you from the enemy," he interrupts seriously, his arms holding him up, ready to begin.

"All right, fine," I say, and mimic him again.

Fantasies might help this go faster—and I can't ignore a subtle challenge.

We make it through only two before I fall into the grass.

He looks down at me, amused. "Do they not make you do push-ups in the palace?"

"Can't we at least eat breakfast first?"

"You might not even *get* breakfast on campaign."

I laugh, because it dawns on me suddenly that maybe I should have been swimming laps in the pool with Jali all this time, instead of sitting round writing pamphlets and studying my Savien book.

Savien!

I jolt upwards, and Athan does the same. He raises a brow at my sporadic shift, but little does he know what a surprise I have. On my knees in the grass, I take a deep breath, preparing myself to slaughter a language I barely know. "How are you, Lieutenant?" I ask in Savien, the words sticky in my mouth. "It is a perfect day and I love the sun."

The reaction is better than I could have dreamed. His eyes widen in astonishment, and then a smile stretches bright across his face—an entirely beautiful smile. "You . . . ?"

"I've been learning from a book," I admit, switching back to Landori. "But how do I sound?"

I test a few more silly phrases—basic words and greetings—and his smile grows even larger. "You sound amazing, Ali! Your accent. I love it!"

I feel myself blush, because I've never thought of myself as having an accent. He's the one with that pleasant feature. But I suppose I must, to his ears, and the idea is unexpectedly satisfying.

I assume my position for another triumphant push-up. "Let's try again?" I suggest, since I refuse to let him best me without a solid effort on my part. Surely, I can do at least ten. I place my hands back down and sharp pain stabs my left palm. "Ow!"

I snap back onto my knees. Red pricks my skin, and Athan immediately takes my hand in his own. "Ow," I say stupidly again, because it's all I can think of.

Athan stares at my palm. "Oh, God. A Resyan bramble."

"A Resyan what?"

"One of our soldiers got this in his foot during the encirclement."

"And?"

He looks up at me. "We had no choice. We had to get rid of it."

"The thorn?"

"The foot."

All of a sudden, my happiness dissipates. I don't even know what the stars a Resyan bramble is. This is my kingdom—or *was*, so I thought—and I've never heard of a poisonous weed with thorns this dastardly!

"Athan." I can't hide my panic. "We need to get this out! I've never—"

I realize his face is contorting with pleasure. It lurks at the edges, then blossoms into the loudest laugh I've heard since he arrived. Joy, like pure sun, and I swat him on the shoulder—hard. "You're truly awful!"

He smirks gleefully. "I couldn't resist." He reaches for his pack, pushing his charcoal pencil and paper aside. "I've got antiseptic and everything else—minus the painkillers, obviously," he explains, "but I'm not really a medic. If you trust the air force training I had, though, I think I can handle this."

I make a face. "I don't have much choice, do I? Otherwise I'll be losing a limb."

He's still grinning and takes my hand again. The angry red thorn looks terrible, but my face flushes slightly watching him hold me like this. It's so precise, so focused. His calloused hand, larger, supports mine from below, my palm exposed to him, and it feels like I'm entirely naked before him.

I want to kiss him.

"It might sting a little," he says instead, looking for approval from me.

"It's fine," I reply, thinking only about his mouth, too close, so close.

He dabs at the red mark, and it burns like an entire damn fire! I have no idea what the stars "sting" means to him, but I'm proud I don't flinch. I may not be able to do more than two push-ups, but brambles I can survive. I'm determined about this until he pulls out a pointy metal object and presses it to my skin. "Don't you dare dig anything out of me with those," I warn.

"How else are you going to remove this?"

"Wishful thinking."

He looks up at me, apologetic. "I promise I'll be gentle." And I know he means it, so I relinquish the right to him, and try to focus on the roof of the Havis home. Then I realize that's even worse—I need to see it happen. He pokes down, as careful as he promised, and I wince a bit, more at the sight than anything else.

"I got a lot of these during Academy training," he shares. "They made us crawl through the woods on our stomachs, which never made any sense to me because I sort of thought they meant to put us in the sky." He makes a deep poke and I wince again. "Sorry. Anyway, Cyar and I had to wrench a lot of things out of each other, and believe it or not, he's not as nice about it as me."

And it's done. The offending thorn is removed, the pain with it, and Athan dabs again with the antiseptic. His right hand is still under mine, and he places his thumb over my palm, softly rubbing the place that no longer hurts. It's as if it were never there. It's as if he's never touched me before. My face feels warm all over, desire fluttering in my stomach. It doesn't help that he's still not wearing a shirt.

His expression must be a mirror of mine—it quietly wants, and needs. I don't care if he can tell I'm looking at his mouth, the memory of a hurried kiss in the dark, the ache to try it again. To taste him alive and well. But it's also more than that, something deeper, and he seems to understand. Without speaking, he draws me towards him, and then I'm in his arms, against his chest and his heartbeat. He's holding me, and there's nowhere else I want to be. After the fear, the horror, I'm safe here, his chin resting on my head, and I hope he knows he's safe with me, too, far from whatever it is he's trying to escape—to forget.

"Thank you," I whisper in Savien, listening to his rapid heartbeat.

"You're welcome," he replies in Etanian, and the lilting familiar words make me smile.

37

❧ ATHAN ❧

Four days, and I've laid myself bare to her in everything but my name. That will come. For now, I want her to be my friend again, to see if she can take these things that are forever worse than bearing the name Dakar. The name I was born with—I had no choice. But this war . . .

It's on me.

My decisions.

My strategy.

I've spent too many days away, far beyond what I got my pass for. Garrick's probably furious. Maybe they all think I've been stuck with a Resyan knife. Dead somewhere in an alley, and they're trying to decide what story they'll tell my father.

I hope it's a good one.

On the fifth afternoon, we unearth two motorbikes from the garden sheds, twin machines that are equally ancient. The good one is gone, Ali says, because she and a maid girl stole it to go to the palace. I try not to grin. She's got some bizarre story for every day she's been here. But she's delighted by the prospect of riding one, and she thrusts it at me. "Get it working," she commands, a familiar gleam in her smile—the kind I can't get enough of. She's genuinely fun to be with, and the idea feels almost foreign.

Fun.

I try to explain to her that Filton does most of the mechanics on my plane, but it's little use when she's looking at me with such determination. Besides, I think she can tell I know more than I'm letting on. So I fill the bike up with fresh oil and gas, then check the spark plugs. A heel to the kick start turns the engine over, seeming healthy enough. A test-go around the lawn proves it. It's nice the shrill sound no longer plants knives in my head.

"I practiced a bit on one of these," Ali shares proudly.

"Are we going to race?" I reply. "Because I'll warn you, I do fly airplanes and I might be very good."

"Can't really race round here, can we?"

"No. It's rather small. Also, that other bike's front tire looks beyond hope."

"Perhaps we should go down to Madelan then?"

"Ali, we can't leave here."

"Yes, we can."

"We can't."

She's already behind me on the seat, all of her pressed against my back, which puts my stomach in my throat. "Let's go, Lieutenant," she orders into my ear.

I consider just staying parked there for a few minutes, or an hour, to simply enjoy the feel of her holding me, then maybe asking her to hold tighter. But that seems a bit selfish—and more like an Arrin move—so I give us another test run, zipping around the stone fountain at breakneck speed in the hopes she might reconsider going all the way into town.

She only grips my leather coat harder—victory!—and says, "I want you to drive it as you fly your aeroplane."

We're facing the gates now.

"Do you not value your life?" I reply wryly.

"Fly!" she says into my ear, above the engine.

I do. I open the throttle—and it's glorious. We hurtle down the road, back in Madelan far faster than it took Havis's vehicle to crawl through the hills. Ali directs me, keeping us in the "good" parts of the city, but there are still too many Safire tanks and soldiers around. I don't dare let anyone see me racing around here with a local girl, and it becomes a stupid, wild, wonderful game avoiding them. The old motorbike is hot and rattling beneath us, angry at all the excitement as we avoid the wrong eyes, skidding on the corners, weaving us down roads and alleys. Ali's arms grip me tight, and I realize I like this better than my plane. It's just a blur of green trees and bright colours sailing by. The hot air choked with smoke as I grab the clutch, shifting the old bike into its snarling version of a flick-roll, Ali laughing into my ear.

We're both laughing at the madness of it.

"You're good at this," she declares. "I'm impressed."

"I can't do poetry," I reply, revving the motor again, "but I can get you anywhere you need to go in half the time!"

When she finally makes me stop, it's at a small city square beneath an ancient Resyan fort, a cautious market in progress, everyone looking half-startled by its existence. But as I've discovered between the coast and Madelan, these people know how to carry on. They don't stop. They sell their fruits and vegetables, their flowers and desserts, and Ali flits from stand to stand, procuring a meal to eat back at the estate. I wander self-consciously, eyes on the ground. I'm not in my uniform, and I could simply be another fair-haired Resyan—they do exist here. But I feel eyes on me. I know they're staring, and I'm afraid they can see the truth of who I am. That they'll know what I've done to them. Their brothers. Their cousins.

A war criminal.

When I glance up again, I'm at the mouth of an alley. Another line of little stands stretches into the shaded area, and a familiar figure in Safire uniform is haggling with an elderly woman who looks beyond exasperated.

Trigg.

I have no clue how we got this close to the airbase, with all the flying around on the bike. I should have been paying attention. Not that directions are my strong suit.

I turn to leave too late.

"Oh, Captain," Trigg calls. "You're *here*!" He sprints over to me, a grin on his face and a jar in his hand.

The woman spits at the ground where he just left.

"What are you doing?" I ask him warily.

"Acquiring interesting things." He holds up the jar. There's something that looks suspiciously like an organ in there. "But I'd rather know what you're doing, Captain. Or *who*."

His smile is sly syrup.

"No one," I inform him. "Did you give up the ruse?"

"Not me. But Hajari did. He's not very happy with you right now," he says as an afterthought.

"Did he tell Garrick?"

"You know he doesn't lie. And I tried, but I sort of ran out of answers. There aren't many legitimate places to go here."

Great. Now Garrick knows I'm with Ali. Not a helpful secret to offer him, although Garrick had his own undercover fun with the singing girl in Etania. We have one on each other—except mine holds far higher stakes than Garrick could ever imagine.

Trigg shades his eyes. "You know, you should just enjoy yourself, Captain. No one gives a shit about you. Not really."

I'm feeling nicer now that I'm headache-free, and I resist throttling him. "Thanks."

"Yes, sir."

I turn, not waiting for his half-hearted salute.

"Oh! Captain!"

I stop walking.

"I almost forgot. Your papa's arriving at seven thirty tomorrow morning. You might want to be there."

That gets my attention. "You're sure?"

"It's the word on base."

This is it, then. This has to be my last day with Ali. No more dragging out the daydream. "I'll be there," I reply reluctantly.

Trigg looks concerned. "I'd lie to him for you, but I think he'd shoot me."

No, he'll only shoot me when he finds out where I've been.

I wave him off and head back in the direction of Ali—or where she should be. Turning a circle, I realize she's nowhere in sight. Our bike sits abandoned at the edge of the square, and there's no girl in boots and a sundress flitting around anymore. Panic hits my chest, and I turn to find Trigg, but he's gone too. My throat constricts, my aloneness suddenly petrifying. Everyone in the square stares. They're all glaring at me, and I'm sure they know what I am. They saw me talk to Trigg in Savien. They see my guilt. Their unspoken hatred suffocates me, spitting from every direction.

I can't breathe.

Then somewhere high above, my name shifts on the breeze. The top of the fort.

I run like hell for Ali.

⇥ AURELIA ⇤

The view is lovely and vast, rooftops shimmering below with heat. The citadel's sandstone steps were beckoning when I found them, curving round the grand tower and wide enough to carry knights of old. I rest my hand on the thick walls, wondering what stories linger in each crack and crevice, from long before the North ever arrived. I trace the rough stone, then the air above, gathering the sun in my palm, like a gift.

There's a sudden commotion behind me.

I turn and find a very upset Safire lieutenant. I didn't think it was possible with his tan, but he looks deathly pale.

I smile. "You found me."

He stares. "You left me."

I realize he might actually have been very afraid just now, and the breathtaking view suddenly loses a shade of its beauty.

It's hiding smoke and bones, the reality I've fought to ignore—

if only for these precious few days—and I motion Athan closer. He obliges, walking to the edge of the tower, looking out for a long time, shadows and sunshine on his strained face, gradually calming in tiny breaths.

I hold out my bag from the market. "Marzipan. My favourite dessert."

He still doesn't speak, but he does look inside the bag.

"Have one," I urge.

He shakes his head.

There's something else in him, something struggling, and I wish I could drag it out. Athan Erelis has become a very complex creature. Even though it isn't his fault, it still frustrates me. I remember when he held me at the masquerade, the trapped look in his eyes behind the dragon mask, trying to be brave, and yet even then I knew that no matter how he tried, how he pretended, he was too gentle for a life of war, and it broke my heart. Because I knew he was still going to march right into it. He was still going to choose it.

It's both baffling and pitiful at once.

"I can't enjoy this," he admits, gesturing at the marzipan, "when Cyar's still eating the shit on base."

I wince at his coarseness, though I suppose I shouldn't be surprised. Cyar is always his weak spot. "You can take some of it with you," I suggest, trying to sound more optimistic than we both feel. "Give the rest to him."

Athan shrugs, and I have no choice. I have to win him back.

"Did you know I whispered you to me?" I say. "Before the war ended."

Two aeroplanes growl high over the fort, and Athan looks at me, confused. "You did what?"

"I told you to find me," I explain. "I said it on the roof of the palace, watching those mountains right over there. I willed you to come to me. I knew you would. And you did. You found me."

Truthfully, it was more that I found him, but that isn't important right now. I need to twist the story to bring him into it. To remind him that even when all of this feels terribly grey and empty, there's still something else at work, something unseen that brought us together. That wants us together again—here and now.

He steps closer at last, his face softer. "You made me come here?" he asks, and he's finally playing along. He might not believe me. But he's playing. I reach out to rest my hand on his, and I suddenly picture a wild horse of the mountains, running, bleeding, refusing to give up. He has that proud, scared spirit. His eyes hold all the regret in the world.

"I did," I whisper.

"You spoke it out loud?"

"Like an order."

He faces me, so close I can count every freckle on his nose. "What else can you make me do?"

"Many things, I hope."

His hand touches my cheek, something beautifully desperate in his gaze. His other hand goes to my waist, as if we're about to dance, a dance he doesn't even know how to do. But his touch is honest. Certain. His eyes are only for me. "Did you know I adore you, Ali?"

I'm not sure why that word reaches so deeply into my heart. But it does. It doesn't matter what's in my blood. It doesn't matter who my family is. This person *adores* me, as I am, and perhaps he'd even adore me if I told him the truth. He knows my heart—and that's all that matters here. That's all that matters between us, his hands on me, overpowering the words we can't speak.

It's not who we are.

It's what we do.

And this time, I don't have to ask for what I want. This isn't a dark room in the middle of a coup. This place is all light, all freedom, and his hesitant kiss on my lips is as gentle as his thumb across my palm, feather light, as if I might push him away. Perhaps I got us off on the wrong foot at the masquerade. I'll never push him from me again, not like that, because I want him close—closer than anyone has ever been—and I move my hands to his chest, letting him know it's fine, that I want the same, feeling his galloping heartbeat. At last, his mouth becomes wonderfully firm and precise, exactly where it needs to be. The fantasies retreat in the wake of what's real, and the heat in me matches the sky, all radiant and perfectly good.

He draws my hips closer. He's growing insistent. I love it. No fear, no darkness, only the sun of our desire across every inch of skin, the taste of his mouth, the edge of his tongue. Let it last forever and ever, this moment. The saffron-drenched air and the colourful city and nothing but peace as far as the eye can see—both of us high above, free.

On fire.

"What the stars is this?" a rough voice demands.

Our kiss dies in a rush.

We spin, broken apart, and find an old man glaring. His hands rest on frail hips. "This is indecent. *Here* of all places. This testimony of our strength!"

"I'm so sorry," I apologize in Resyan, flushed. "Sorry."

The man scowls further.

Athan glances at me, questioning. He has no idea what conversation is taking place, only that it's certainly about him, and we're in trouble. "Apparently he doesn't like the two of us kissing on this tower," I explain.

"Did you apologize?" Athan asks.

"Twice."

"This city mourns," the man hurls at me in Resyan, "and you act like a spring vixen with the enemy!"

That harsh accusation stuns me. He knows. He knows Athan

is Safire, and my breathless smile vanishes swiftly. Humiliation replaces it. I shake my head at the man, afraid to explain myself, because I have no explanation that will satisfy, and grab Athan's hand. Quickly, I drag him after me for the stairs, for the earth, for reality—my lips still tasting of him.

38

Guilt rears its head in full force as we leave the city. Though we're settled back on the motorbike, retreating for home, the old man's ire chases my thoughts. It wasn't his anger that frightened me. It was the hurt lurking beneath the offense, as if I'd spit on someone's grave—and in truth, he's right. I'm acting as if no one has died, as if entire worlds haven't been ripped in two. I got my bright sun back. I have Athan. But too many others never did, and now they're lost in an eternal night that no one sees.

By the time we reach the grand gates of the Havis home, it's well past sunset, lights shining in the windows.

As I dismount from the bike, Athan stands and urges me nearer in the hushed darkness. "Can I tell you one thing?" he asks.

I nod, unsure where this is going.

"I want you to know that even though my family believes it's possible to live two lives at once, to be a soldier or a real person depending on the day, I know I can't do that. I can only be myself, and sometimes that's damn complicated. The fact that I'm here with you proves it. I swear I always do my best. But my best gets messy."

I sigh, looking up at him. "No," I say, unable to hide my sorrow, "I think you'll have to be this other person for a while. You won't survive any other way. You've chosen this." He begins to speak, but I don't let him. "One day, though, all this will end, a distant memory, and then I want you to be who you truly are. Because I love you. I always will."

It's the first time I've said those words aloud. And it's the truth.

I do love him.

"I love you," he replies, a simple fact, and he kisses me.

How I long for a repeat of the citadel—that certainty, that perfection, away from the truth. But this time it all feels heavier. I was lucky to get him back from war once. What if it's the last? What if he returns, and he's always less and less like the boy I adore, a frail mockery of the real spirit buried within? I'm terrified by the idea of this being all that we have. Last summer wouldn't have been enough, but I'd have lived with it. A youthful infatuation buried with the passage of time. But these few days . . . they've given me something real. They've given me hope—and hope is dangerous.

Perhaps that's why his kiss is sad.

He's also sick with hope.

Silently, we walk inside the large doors, leaving our words behind. Our feet slip softly down marble halls, and I feel his breaths beside me. Feel each one like they're my own. He's taken the guest room a hall over from mine, and every night I try to imagine him lying there, so far from the tents and flies he's been sleeping with for an entire campaign. A large bed. Silk sheets. He must be lonely.

He *is* lonely.

That's the regretful expression he wears now, as we say good night as we have the past five nights, like he's saying goodbye for good already. As if he's never going to see me again and he's trying to remember every sweep and colour of my face. I imagine myself sleeping beside him, keeping him warm tonight. The bright, good thing between us.

"Stay with me," I say, impressed by my own boldness.

"Where?" he asks.

I nod at my room. "Here."

I don't know how to ask for this thing I want, a thing I don't fully understand. Not to mention, it might also be wrong of me to even suggest it. Not only because my mother would be horrified at my brazenness, but because if Athan knew the truth, the family I come from, perhaps he'd never want to kiss me again. If I were braver, perhaps I'd tell him.

But I'm not, and right now, I only want him.

I try what I imagine is a tempting smile, and for a moment he looks intrigued. It quickly flickers out. "No. I should go to bed."

"We both should," I agree, trying to say it more meaningfully without being . . . too meaningful.

He doesn't see it. His crooked smile appears briefly. "Good night, Ali."

"Good night, Athan."

I sigh once the door is closed.

❧ ATHAN ❧

My room feels incredibly large and empty now. Even worse than it has the past few nights. The pills Ali gave me have worn off again, and my head splinters in their retreat, everything looking like dragons in the dark—the clock on the hearth, the gaudy picture frames, the velvet chair in the corner. They reflect yard lights, glinting teeth and eyes, and they're watching me. Judging me for not admitting the truth yet.

I hold up my pistol, hand shaking.

I didn't shoot that horse.

I relive the moment. Fire it into my thoughts, to know that I can face my fear. I'm not my father. I'm not my brother.

I'm me.

Ali loves *me*.

I lower the pistol and think instead of her intoxicating offer. I'm not going to pretend I don't know what she wanted. When Aurelia Isendare decides she's chasing something, there's no way she can hide it in her eyes. It's all there, like the night sky. A thousand glittering possibilities. Everything I want.

Tormented, I shower obsessively, getting rid of motorbike grime, washing myself over and over—as if I can scrub myself into something better, something worthy of her love.

"What would Cyar choose?" I ask afterwards, into the mirror. My reflection makes a face.

No, that won't work. I know what he'd do. He'd go to sleep and hope for the best. Wait for the war to be over, assure himself that someday soon everything will be sorted out, problems solved, offers of marriage made and—there! A perfectly honourable kiss after some perfectly honourable pledges. He'd never dream of asking the girl he loves to squander her innocence for him, not when he couldn't promise forever in return.

"And Arrin?" I ask the reflection, just because.

Even worse.

I know exactly what he'd do, and it's the thing I want. That's frightening. Tomorrow Father arrives at the base, and I need to be up in time. In fact, I should be smart and leave tonight. I shouldn't stay here again. But one more night even in the proximity of Ali's breath is life-giving. I can lie awake and imagine her nearby, sleeping in that other room, wearing only a nightdress. It's enough to be close. To feel the heat from the idea of it.

It's also not enough.

I pad back down the hall barefoot. Ali looked so disappointed, and I have to do this right. I'll kiss her again, like on the fort, and I'll tell her my name. There's little I can do after tonight—I see that now. I'm too small, too easily broken up by invisible dragons. What good am I outside of a cockpit? On the earth?

But I can be good for her.

Somehow.

I knock, and after a moment the door swings open. Ali

stands there in the nightdress I've imagined every night, revealing more skin than when we swam in the river—all of it sheer, liquid as sin. I try to think of the words I was going to say.

Nothing comes.

"Do you want to play cards?" I hear myself ask.

Her smile is amused. "Now?"

"I can't sleep."

"Me neither."

"Great," I say. "Not great. But, you know."

"I know."

She stands there, and I stand there, and neither of us moves. She looks beautiful.

"Never mind," I say instead. "You look tired."

"I'm not tired."

"I don't want to keep you up."

"It's fine, Athan."

"I have to be out of here early tomorrow."

"So we'd best not keep you up?" Her smile looks even more entertained now.

There's a noise at the end of the hall. A servant.

"Come in," she says.

"I shouldn't."

"Get in here," she hisses.

"Ali, I should—"

She hauls me through the door as the servant appears, shutting the door firmly behind us. I wasn't resisting very nobly. She moved me like nothing.

We stand there in her room, silent again, and then she says, "I don't want to play cards."

I swallow. "Me neither."

"Really," she says, "I want to kiss you again. I want to kiss you a hundred times. I don't know what I'm doing, but I do know that after tonight I might never see you again. And I always want to remember you like this. I want you to know you're beautiful to me. You always will be."

She looks at me, determination in her face, lit by the fire in the hearth.

I wish I'd prepared a speech like that.

"Ali . . ."

Where do I begin? How? I won't always be beautiful to her, not once she knows my name, discovers the sixteen black marks on my plane and the soldiers I strafed and the suffocating emptiness at my core. I don't even know where to start. I'm the opposite of what she needs—the worst person for her, her enemy—and I think of her on that citadel today, lost in the sun. Her hands reaching out, tracing the Southern world before us, entirely at peace and in a place I can't follow.

"Please promise to remember that you're better than me," I say. "And I know it."

Her expression wavers. She doesn't like that. She thinks she can make it untrue through sheer resolve, but this is one place where her determination won't work.

"It doesn't matter," she says.

"It does," I protest. "I have to—"

"Take off your shirt."

It's a soft command, one that terrifies me more than any harsh order I've ever been given. I should refuse. But since I'm good at doing, at obeying, I pull it up and over my head, and she stands before me—creamy lace against her sun-brown skin, as many curves and arcs as a plane in the sky, rising, falling, hiding layers and depths and blood-hot adrenaline.

I don't move.

I'm damn scared, not wanting to seem too much or too little.

She chooses for me and closes the distance between us, near enough I can feel her breath against my bare chest. She places her palm gently above my heart. "I wanted to feel this," she says, her voice quiet. She has no fear. Her touch is warm, thrilling, stirring in me a longing that's as desperate as it is deep. It aches. Being alone in this room, being allowed to feel this way when Ollie and Sailor and too many others . . .

I don't let myself see dragons.

Not here.

Her hand moves lower, her eyes following. Counting ribs, tracing angles. I don't think of bubbling flesh, scorched earth, the marrow inside out. I'm intact. I'm here for her. Here for this moment, her fingers teasing my skin. The attentiveness of her stare makes it almost unbearable.

I feel very awkward and plain.

On fire.

"Please," I beg, backing up an inch. I try to see her as she is. A princess, Sinora's daughter. A girl who isn't mine and never will be. I can't promise her forever. "This isn't right. I'm—"

"What?" she asks. "Afraid?"

"No."

She presses closer, conquering my inch of retreat. "You think this isn't my choice?"

Her hands are on me again and I try to stop the wonderful fog from taking over my brain. A losing battle, and I reach for her as well, touching her skin carefully, the place where her neck becomes shoulder, wondering if I can make her feel the same way she makes me feel. "You're everything I want, Ali. But I can't do this to you. Please. I'm not my brother. You're too—"

Perfect.

Her lips silence me with a kiss. It's the fall into oblivion, altimeter shattering. All these reasons for decency seeming suddenly useless here, mad rules from a mad world far beyond this room, a world that tries to keep us following orders and marching in line. But that line might lead straight to a grave.

Be good, they say.

If you're lucky, you'll die quick.

We're defying them all right now, and she steps back onto her heels, her eyes wide and beseeching. *"Please,"* she says mimicking my tone with another smile. "You always try to do what's right. For once, you should do what you want."

I don't know what I want anymore. But I do want this—her,

here, now. I've felt death on my shoulders and I much prefer her hands there, reminding me that there still might be a place of myself that's worth knowing. A secret thing that no one's ever seen.

I look at my feet again. I gather my racing breath. "Ali, there's something I have to say first. It's something I should have said long ago. I'm sorry I didn't." I look up helplessly. "Everything's—"

She lets the nightdress slide from her skin. It's clearly intentional, the way she pulls her shoulders out from under it, letting it fall with a half-hearted attempt to cover herself, like there was a moment she thought it might be a bad idea. But now she's standing there, radiant in the firelight, her head tilted, daring me to come closer. If there were words in my mouth, they're gone now, disappeared from my tongue and replaced by nothing but the awareness of her unveiled before me. Her voice saying, "You always talk too much," with such hidden joy, like she knows her power.

Then her hand is beckoning for me.

A heartbeat in my throat.

I really am on fire now, abandoned in the burning, and when my arms move around her, her mouth finding mine again, I discover she's an equal flame, rising to meet me, so very wonderful and so very alive.

The horizon in my very hands.

And they can't take this from us.

VIII

⚜

EARTH

39

The stretched night is a familiar depth of hazy shapes and warm moments as we lie together, neither fully awake nor fully dreaming. I curl up into it, into the lovely fragments, a safer place, away from the world. I reach only for Athan. His steady desire in the darkness. He held me, trying to be as gentle as he was with the thorn. It still hurt, but in the heat of the dying fire now, there's only softness, his hot body next to mine nearly giving me a fever as he leans down and kisses my lips, then my cheek, then my neck and I decide never to leave this deliriously wonderful moment.

"This is for us," he says, his forehead against mine, the same thing he whispered during the coup.

"It is," I reply, knowing I'll never doubt that.

I'll keep this forever.

I don't know if I sleep, flushed as I am beneath the blanket, beside him, distantly aware of the sound of his breathing, his thumb tracing the edge of my temple, the shell of my ear. I kiss the rise and fall of his chest. I want to venture further but feel at a loss. I don't know if I should say words, try more, and I'm too tired to explain, overwhelmed by the reality of his nakedness so near to mine. He fills in the silence for me, with his mouth on my skin, his adoration, and I surrender to the melting sensation of his hand moving down my arm, beneath the blanket and across my bare hip, searching, exploring, testing my body like a throttle . . .

I don't know if he's still touching me or if it's in my wishful dreams.

I wake slowly. At first, it's the cold on my exposed flesh. I peer down at myself in confusion, at my bare limbs, all less romantic in the blue light of dawn, no longer caught by the fire's glow. But then my bleary thoughts remember Athan, and he's not beside me anymore.

I sit up with a start.

It wasn't the cold air that woke me. It was the warm ember of his body jolting out of bed. He's already half-dressed, throwing on clothes at record speed, and I stare in wonder at his sporadic activity, the shirt pulled over his chest and leaving me disappointed. I wanted to feel him again. I wanted to rest my head there one more time.

I also wanted to at least talk.

"You're mad," I say with a drowsy smile, pulling the blanket round me, a little less bold now. "Sleep for a bit longer."

He makes a noise of disagreement, buttoning his pants.

"Stars, why are you even up this early?"

He stops what he's doing and stares at me. "Early?"

I glance at the clock. It's seven fifteen in the morning, which I think is an unseemly hour for mostly anything besides bed.

A thin laugh escapes his throat, then he flings open the closed drapes. The velvet curtains make way for brilliant sun, the early morning bright outside. "Why would you sleep with these closed?" he asks me frantically.

"Why would you sleep with them *open*?"

"Because I always wake with the—" He stops, gaze dodging to his watch, and shakes his head. "Never mind. I have to go," he says, nearly running for the door.

"Go?" I repeat, horrified.

Now this is feeling very wrong, far too abrupt, and he turns, his face apologetic. "I'll be back. I just—" He stops again, expression choked as he looks at me. There's something he wants to say, but won't.

I wait.

He disappears down the hall, leaving me staring at the place he just left, but mercifully he returns swiftly. He's wearing his clean uniform now, the one he's abandoned the past few days in favour of the Havis clothes, and it's almost astonishing to see it again. I replaced the pilot with a boy—a boy of skin and bone, a heart stammering beneath a firm chest. But he's not just a boy. He's this other person, hidden behind foxes and crossed swords, and the painful yearning in his eyes chases away my lingering annoyance.

He crosses the distance to the bed and leans down over me. I look up at him, entirely naked, entirely willing, and he kisses me—a perfect kiss that undoes the pain, the regret, my bare skin feeling the rough wool of his uniform. "I'll see you soon," he whispers, into my ear like a secret promise, and I hate it and I love it at once.

"Soon" might be tomorrow.

"Soon" might be a lifetime away.

He pushes the hair from my face, tender, and then he's gone, racing off to meet some order I don't know.

There's a happy drunken butterfly in my belly. I need so much more, at once, but there's nothing else to come, and I flop back onto my pillow in a weary knot of emotion, staring at the ceiling, counting his retreating footsteps—rapid, fading. A kiss lingers in the curve of my neck. Memories I want to keep as vibrant and alive as they are this very moment: the way he felt on top of me, the pleasant weight, his fire-lit hair falling across his forehead, sweet and tangled . . .

"I don't regret this," I tell the ceiling. "I don't."

Yet part of me still feels dangling in the wind. He isn't someone I can have, not even in the best of worlds. He's a farm boy, bound to be far away—and getting ever farther, ordered from me in a heartbeat—and I'll be left behind for some spoiled prince who will judge what I've done here, even if he sees only the reflection of it written in my eyes. Though perhaps if I married Havis he wouldn't care? Perhaps he'd even let me carry on the affair? Look at these few days he's already given me.

I slap my forehead.

I'm actually entertaining the idea of marriage to Gref Havis!

With a sigh, I slide out of bed, throwing on a robe and dragging a brush through my messy hair, then drinking from the water pitcher.

"You pretty fool," Havis's voice snaps suddenly, and I whirl, realizing Athan left the door wide open. "I didn't intend to find that boy fleeing here like a dog with its tail between its legs!"

Of all mornings, this is the one Havis chooses to return? I've wondered often enough where he's been, knowing all the possibilities are ones I'd like to ignore. The illustrious fantasy of my mind.

"You promised to use your good sense when I gave you this gift, Aurelia."

I tighten my robe. "I did."

He slams the door shut, and for the first time in a long while, I feel uneasy standing before him. "You know I don't give a *whip* what fun you have, but you're not just any girl. You're a *princess*, and I hope to God the two of you at least acted safely, because a child would truly heighten this drama to a matchless level!"

I raise my chin. "We did. Now leave me alone. I need to ready for the day."

"You need to ready for your damn mother! She's at Rahian's palace and will be furious to discover her only daughter was just deflowered by a Safire lieutenant under my roof. You'd better have an answer prepared, because I sure as hell won't be stepping into the middle of this."

I stare at him, stunned. "She's *here*?"

"Yes. Though she should have come a day sooner, evidently."

My palms begin to sweat, an apprehension I didn't expect. My mother has come at last. With no warning, not even a cable to me. Stars, perhaps *I'm* the one she'll arrest, to drag home. No care for Resya or my mission. She'll simply protect her own crown and her own standing in the North. Once, that made sense to me. Not anymore. It's no longer enough, not now that I've seen the extent of what unchecked violence can do. If Reni were responsible for even a fraction of what Seath has spurred, then nothing would keep me from confronting him—not a thing!

Reni isn't Seath, a logical voice reminds me.

But I don't want to imagine that right now. I don't want to imagine that Seath might be so dangerous even my mother would refuse to cross him.

I need to feel we have a chance at making things better.

"Where the stars have you been?" I ask Havis instead, to put him on the defense. "Did you see Seath? What does he—?"

"Stars, girl! You can't talk like this. No one can *ever* hear you breathe his name out loud. I've told you that before." He marches closer. "Every secret your family holds is one luckless step away from being thrown before the entire world, which means you need to keep your cards close for as long as you can. You have to play for everyone, because that's what your mother does, and it's why she's still alive. They all think she's on their side." He pins me with a pointed glare. "And *never* trust the General. Not one damn word."

"I've learned very well who can't be trusted here," I say sharply.

"Are you so sure about that?" Havis holds out his hand towards me. "The Lieutenant forgot these in his room, and I think you should be the one to return them."

They're Athan's metal tags, the ones he wouldn't let me wear. Hesitantly, I take them, seeing in them the chains of his life, these tiny things that want to keep him from me, the things he doesn't even want to wear. I feel their weight, rubbing my thumb over the smooth metal, the embossed name.

ATHAN DAKAR.

For a moment, I simply read. Over and over, a useless rhythm of words as my head tries to make sense of why on earth Athan would agree to bear the General's name in battle. What help would that be? Why would he be so special? It makes no sense. He wouldn't be given a tag like this unless he was—

"I told you last summer," Havis says, interrupting my pitiful rumination, "never trust a thing until you've inspected it closely."

But it can't be.

He never once . . .

He didn't . . .

Heat floods my face, and I shove them back at Havis. "This isn't true. This is a lie."

I'm caught between disbelief and anger, unable to reconcile the fact that the chest I kissed last night, the heat of his perfect body, could share anything at all with the ungodly Commander. I still feel his gentle lips ghosting across my skin. His soft voice in my neck, so careful and warm and earnest.

But Havis doesn't take the tags. "For once," he says wryly, "this isn't a lie at all."

"I don't understand," I reply, trembling now. "Why the stars wouldn't he tell me?"

"You have all the clues you need. Use that clever head of yours."

The shock is draining away rapidly, wrestled down by something else.

Hurt.

Tender and bruising. The tags are still in my left hand, and I clench them a bit harder, as if I might interrogate them into admitting an explanation. "For . . . safety?"

"Or?"

"To be undercover?"

"Better."

"But why?"

Havis says nothing, and as always, his silence is telling. My brain flashes through everything Athan has ever said to me—where and when and why, the warnings, the coup—and every tapestry tells the same story. It's suddenly all right there before me. I just never imagined to look.

Why should I have?

Last night, he tried to tell me something before the fire's glow. The secret haunting every kiss between us, caught behind his eyes, the deeper shame in him I couldn't reach.

This was it? He didn't want to tell me the truth of his name? It's incredibly infuriating, his lie, but it also makes no sense. Why did he think I'd care? Yes, I hate the Commander, but they're two different souls, and surely I know as well as any how important that distinction is. I'm angry that he didn't trust me. Angry because I hate the falseness of it, the fraud of our beginning, the power in his hands.

"*I'm sorry,*" he whispered during the coup.

He apologized.

He has always apologized, over and over and over.

Then what has he used his power for?

Sweat begins to dampen my neck. Perhaps I'm looking at this wrong. Perhaps it has nothing to do with Athan at all, and everything to do with *me*.

My family, hiding Nahir blood.

My uncle, Seath.

My mother, a person I don't even know anymore—sitting with the General in a time long ago.

All at once, I'm struggling for a shore I don't want to land on. The hurt becomes wild, panicked. "Havis, you said this war was about vengeance." I force myself to look at him. "Where is the person who betrayed the General?"

He smiles. I've found the right scent. "The North. And the South."

The world sways, my heart a wingbeat in my chest. "My mother."

"Yes. Which is why I hope you've never said anything to that boy you regret."

He apologized.

"I'm sorry."

The palace was on fire because those protesters discovered the secret that my father was murdered. I only ever told Athan. He's the only one. And not long after, Hathene burned with rage, the buried history no one else knew. My own rage now overwhelms my horror. It destroys my despair, my hurt, and I think of that rotten bad luck flower. The fact that a lowly officer could "find" me in the garden, become my friend, all the while knowing his father had designs for revenge.

I want to shatter something into a thousand pieces.

Anything.

Everything.

"How?" I demand.

Havis doesn't need to ask what I mean. How could any of this happen? It's the complexity of the entire game, a game that feels unfathomable, impossible, yet terribly personal. And now it's become my own. "That's never the important question," he replies firmly. "The only thing that matters is what you're going to do about it. And right now, you need to pretend you know nothing until we determine the better path forward."

"I can't do that!"

"You can, Aurelia. You *must*, because your mother does it every day. You can't simply go before the world and announce the General is your enemy. Nor can he do it to your mother. It's only a story. A private myth. No one will believe, or care. You need evidence—something the world's invested in." He draws a breath. "Look, I'd really hoped the Lieutenant would do the decent thing and tell you the truth these past days. I believe the two of you together could be a powerful match. A princess and a general's son who—"

I slap him.

Hard.

The sound echoes in the room, and there's a long stretch of disbelief, Havis staring at me, my hand still held in front of me, tingling with the bright pain of it, the most satisfying sensation I've ever felt.

"That wasn't without warrant," he admits finally.

Tears sting my eyes, but I don't let them fall. "You have lied to me at every turn, Havis. You've deceived me, kept your secrets, let me walk into this entirely unaware and hoped to gain some twisted reward from it. But from *you* I expected it. From him . . ." My voice chokes, strangled. The pain is so fresh I can't even begin to fathom how deep it runs yet, how bottomless it might be. "I hate you, Havis." I smother the tags between my fist. "Yet even you, rotten as you are, can be glad your name isn't Athan Dakar today."

Dakar.

I see this kingdom going up in smoke. The rotten Commander and his fatal smile. All of it so far from good—so far from guiltless—and the anger reaches beyond my personal pain, into an endless night of stolen joys, days that will never be recaptured, peace squandered by this family who puts their own victory before anything else.

I'm going to hold on to my anger like a hot trigger.

I'm going to hold him to account.

"Stars." Havis rubs his cheek. "I truly do like you."

"Get the hell out!"

He does.

40

Airbase

Cyar's face is the first indicator of my fate. It's furious.

He doesn't say anything, though—just points across the compound to the main base, directing me to where I need to be, and I offer him the desserts Ali found in the market. Somehow, I remembered to grab them on my way out. He looks down at the little cakes, and softens a fraction.

Good enough for now.

I run for the base, sprinting through the doors, down the hall, and a Safire officer pushes me in the right direction. It's a half-sympathetic, half-alarmed kind of shove. I'm late. Or am I? I'm not even sure as I hurtle through the private office door and slam it shut. I drop into an empty seat, out of breath, my hair matted with dust. I'm a mess from having stolen the Havis motorbike and raced back. But I'm here.

Seven thirty-six.

I'm *here*.

It's silent in the room. The worst kind of silence. All three faces stare at me from around the table—Kalt confused, Father annoyed, and Arrin slightly astonished.

"Were you in a whorehouse?" Arrin enquires after a moment.

"A *what*? No! I wasn't—"

"Nothing wrong with it," he says, astonishment switching to a smirk. "I just never expected this from you."

My hatred flares beneath his dark amusement. After five perfect days with Ali, being near his bleak energy feels worse than ever. He can make all the jokes he wants, sitting here and pretending he didn't rearrange my nose in that outpost headquarters, that he didn't put these dragons in my head, but I won't forget. I won't let him win.

He can't touch Ali.

"Enough," Father says sharply to Arrin. "You sure as hell aren't one to talk about abandonment of duty. Running ahead and losing those bridges is the worst tactical decision you've ever made—and it was nearly your last. God help the mothers in Savient weeping thanks to your stupidity."

Arrin's amusement snuffs out. At the other end of the table, Kalt taps a pen, conveniently uninvolved, and I'd like to know what the hell he's been doing all this time.

"Let's assess where we're at," Father continues, his pointed gaze still on Arrin. "*You've* managed to put yourself in a trap and lose eight thousand lives in the process."

"Also won a war," Arrin mutters.

Father moves to Kalt. "*You've* done mostly nothing." His eyes swing to me. "And *you've* been God knows where since the surrender. Right now, there's only one child I'm pleased with, and she's not even here to see it."

Kalt stops tapping.

Arrin and I freeze.

"Yes, that's right," Father says. "Leannya got herself to Thurn and joined the codebreaker team. Figured out the cipher that gave Evertal the victory she needed at Irspen. I wish I had a damn photograph right now. You three think you're so clever, but you'd better think again."

I glower at Arrin across the table. He put these ideas in Leannya's head. He groomed her into wanting to be like him. Now she's following in his footsteps, storming into the middle of this, seizing her own glory.

"And now," Father finishes, "we've got the capital, we've got

Rahian, but the war here isn't over until Seath is dead. That god-damn traitor will sabotage us any way he knows. Mark my word."

He doesn't need to mark anything. We each know it. This battle isn't over, not here in Resya or anywhere in the South. Father's phantom game has been toppled over, the pieces scattered, and he can't get them all back overnight. Seath is doing exactly what Father would do, which is why he terrifies me.

He's brilliantly dangerous.

"Yes," Arrin tries, "but the Ambassador just brought—"

"I don't give a damn about Havis," Father interrupts. "Havis is *finished*. He's as much a con as the rest of them. The next time I see him breathing in front of me, I'll be sure to rectify the situation immediately." He swats at the map on the table. "Any air engagements around Madelan?"

Havis betrayed us.

Havis betrayed us.

I'm busy processing that obvious fact, how stupid I was to wander into his house, lured along by Ali, when I realize Father's talking to me. "Oh. One, sir."

That I know of, of course. I've been gone five days at the traitor's estate.

"First one since the surrender?" he presses me.

"Yes, sir. Two unmarked planes scouting southeast of the city. Might have come in from Thurn."

"The first?" Arrin repeats.

"Yes."

"Did they seem experienced?"

"They were a bit nervous, staying out of range."

"Nervous? That's normal. And did you come from above or below?"

"Above."

"Above?"

"Yes." I glare at him, since I don't know why he cares about any of this.

"I'm just trying to understand the logistics," Arrin explains, "since this was the *first* time. Big cannons at least?"

Kalt makes a slight snort, pinching the bridge of his nose. I realize, in one very startling moment, the trap I've walked myself into. But it's too late. Arrin's laughing so loud it lights the earlier tension right on fire, and Father growls at him to get the hell out and stay out.

Kalt's hiding in vain behind his hand.

"You can get out too," Father snaps at him.

He doesn't hesitate. He's gone.

Silence again, my face feeling like someone's stuck a scalding iron to it. My goddamn brother. He's the master of turning his own failure into someone else's humiliation. Who cares about the cauldron or the crimes?

His war is over—and he's putting me back where I belong.

As the minute inches by, painfully slow, I feel Father's stare on me, silently judging. I pray he really does think I've spent five days in a brothel. I pray that Cyar and Garrick and the rest didn't rat me out.

He can't know it was Ali.

Ali, who I long to sleep with again—not only for the obvious reasons, but because I'm desperate to be known away from this. Away from this family. To be seen as a naked soul with only our touch between us.

I want to hide there forever.

"I'm very impressed," Father says at last, and I hear him set his pistol on the table.

My eyes stick to my boots. Here it is. The slow burn into Father's wrath. The inevitable path I've always been meant to tread—too much, not enough, destined for a bullet.

"I'm very impressed that you could do worse than losing me a coup. That you'd defy me on the frontlines, then disappear for days into the enemy's bed and forget your own mother's death."

I might actually die this time.

"You've finally conquered yourself, Athan. You found your true potential."

For a moment, I can't move. Then I hazard a glance up, convinced it's a sick game. He's going to make me shoot another horse. He's going to make me shoot *myself*.

But he's . . . pleased?

The gun sits untouched between us.

"Where do I begin?" he says, and I'm really not sure. "Captain Carr told me that Sinora's daughter showed up looking for you on base, thinking she could play you some more. He said you refused her and went elsewhere instead. I don't need to know where, but your fortitude is telling."

I stare at him.

Why the hell would Garrick lie for me? Cyar confessed the truth of where I was. That's what Trigg said. But Garrick still covered for me? Against *Father*?

He pauses, looking at me. Actually looking, something like pleasure at the edge of his granite expression. "Not only that, I've heard nothing but commendations for you this entire campaign. From Torhan. Carr. Malek. All of them praise your incredible performance in the air and amongst the squadron."

I can barely find my voice. "Thank you, sir."

"They're saying what I've believed all along, that you're not only an excellent pilot, but also an excellent leader, with unbound potential." He smiles then—tired and wan, but real. "We're going to have to see about getting you that squadron. Sooner than I might have thought, Captain."

Now I'm shocked. Five minutes ago, he said Leannya was the only one who wasn't a disappointment. This has to be a game somehow, the bullet about to come, but I can't see it, and the terror of that blindness makes me panic. I don't know what move to make next.

His gaze eases slightly, as if he senses my paralyzed bewilderment. "You don't need to be afraid of me, son. Simply do the right thing and you'll be fine. You're enough."

You're enough.

He thinks this is what I want—his earned respect, a squadron of my own—but I'm suddenly seeing Ali on that citadel tower again, free beneath the wild sky, so far from this exhausting game, and maybe what I want and what I need are two different things entirely. His respect is a sentence worse than death. It's the thing I've always fought for, willingly or unwillingly, and now that I have it, I'm only further from the place I actually need to be.

"It's his star, not yours, and with him you'll always be the dog."

Sinora's voice rings in my head, unexpected, as I look at my father.

"Tonight," he finishes, "you'll come to the victory gala at the palace. Sinora has arrived, and I wouldn't be surprised if a few old grudges come back to haunt her." Dark amusement tightens his voice. "The Nahir's favourite daughter. Returned at last. And you keep an eye on the girl. I want to know what they're planning."

"Will you be a dog?" Sinora's voice asks me again. *"Will you follow the whistle like your brother?"*

Now's the time to find out.

41

Rahian's Palace

Rahian's home has transformed to another world in my absence. It feels like a palace again, the affluent aristocracy with no appetite for war having returned at last. The corridors glitter and swirl, though it's certainly by demand, a royal court occupied by Safire uniforms. The stiff smiles of the footmen betray this truth, the way they speak too graciously to each foreign officer, the way the courtiers move as if by rote, forced to resume a rhythm that's lost its center—Rahian.

"He's fine," Havis tells me as we step through the tense halls, on our way to my mother. "Still under guard in his wing. The League won't allow him to be held for long."

We pass Tirza, and she looks relieved to see me, an urgent question in her eyes.

I nod at her, a silent message that we'll talk later.

Mother's waiting in the guest quarters that were previously mine. She gazes out the wide window at Madelan, not speaking as we enter—nor even turning to acknowledge our arrival. The room is filled with her. Jasmine and quiet strength. The coiling, waiting patience of a cat, and I sense her anger. Her disappointment.

Today, mine rivals hers.

"Your Majesty," Havis begins, "might I—?"

"Leave." Her low voice is a command. "Now."

He doesn't question it, a bit startled—perhaps even afraid—

and gives me a look which might be apologetic, might be warning, then retreats from the room.

I'm alone to face my sentencing.

A thousand questions.

A thousand lies.

Sunshine shifts on the floor with the palm leaves outside, scattered patterns, and then she turns. Her furious face is fractured by pain. She's holding one of my pamphlets, sharp disbelief in her gaze. "A mountain you cannot pass? Such pretty words for this nightmare! And now you've forced my hand, brought me here. Are you pleased with yourself?"

The light is luminous on her skin, the dark loops of her hair unbound. Her cheeks are stirred alive already, as if all of her has been longing for this hot sky and fragrant air. If Seath is the shadowed moon, then she's the bright sun, and I try to imagine them as children. I wonder if they played together, laughed together. Where did it all go from there? How did they end up in such opposite skies?

"Don't I deserve an answer?" she repeats.

Lies.

I want to lie, too, to make us even, but there's no time. "You betrayed your own heart," I tell her, emotion rising. "You left this world behind and never glanced back. Now look at it. Look at what *you* let happen."

Her eyes narrow. She stalks towards me. "How many ways must you defy me?" she demands, ignoring my words entirely. "Do you have any idea what you've done in coming here? Putting yourself in danger? You're asking me to ruin myself for you, and I will. Stars, my darling, I will. I'll fall on my own sword to see you safe. But fight to protect the greed of men? To destroy the innocent along with the guilty? No! I don't raise my gun any longer."

She's practically confessed her past to me now.

My gun.

I glare at her. "I'm not talking about the greed of kings, Mother. I'm talking about the Rummhazi people—your people.

All of the ones left to suffer beneath boots because you kept yourself safe in the North. Because you refused to stand up to your own *brother*."

There's nothing on her face now, no emotion.

She simply stares.

"You lied to me," I accuse, tears threatening. "To Reni. To Etania. Even to Father."

"And would you lie to me?" she rejoins.

"No."

"Then you didn't see that boy here? The Lieutenant?"

"I did," I reply defiantly. "And I know the damn truth. I know who he is, everything between you and the General, and still I shared my bed with him."

It didn't quite happen in that order, and I hardly know anything about her and Dakar. But I don't care. I simply want her to feel true betrayal, to know the depth of my rebellion, and her hand raises. It trembles, as if she'll slap the very words from my lips. But she pulls me into an embrace instead, speaking softly in a language I don't know, and I'm afraid of everything— afraid of who she is and who I am. Afraid of this darkness in me that I never asked for. Now I know why I killed Lark. Why no matter how badly I try to do good, I still end up feeling this fierce desire to wound her and Athan, to wound everyone deeper and further than they've wounded me.

This blood in me is wicked.

"How could you do this to me?" she asks into my hair.

"I'm not ashamed," I whisper in reply, because that alone is true. Her dark history is hers, not mine, never. "But I am *angry*, Mother. I'm so angry I think I might hate his very heartbeat. I hate him more than I've ever imagined hating anyone in this world."

The hurt gasps to life again, remembering his tender hands on me. His perfect kiss. I realize how easy it is to suddenly despise something so wonderful, how complicated hatred is after living only a few hours with it.

A wound left to sour.

Confusing and maddening.

"No," Mother says eventually, still holding me. "You have no bones of hatred in you. Not like I once did."

Her words make me cry. At last. Weeks of unshed grief and hot tears trail my cheeks, long buried inside, stifled by necessity. I want her to be a safe place. I want her to make sense of me. I don't want to be angry and fearful, wielding my scars like a weapon. I don't want to be like them. All I've ever wanted is to be better, to do better, and I thought Athan wanted the same.

I thought we were *more*.

"I've never wanted you to walk the same path as me," she says quietly. "I thought I could protect you from it. But now I see the truth—you'll never learn until you've been there yourself. Until you come out the other side, fighting for all you're worth, and yet people still die. Still the world spins on and no one cares that you've been utterly spent, that your heart is dead within you. You fight and you destroy and it gives you nothing but regret in return." She pushes back, facing me fully. Jewels hang from her ears and dangle round her neck and glimmer in her eyes—tears. "And then you'll see, my star, that all you have left is love. All you can do is fight for the precious ones closest to you. That's all that matters in the end. The only thing worth going to a grave for."

I almost nod, for her sake.

But I don't.

Because that's not the only thing that matters—it simply isn't.

"Where's Havis?" I ask instead, wiping the wet from my cheeks, because surely he'll know what to do. How to keep all the fists from flying at once, Seath and the Safire and everyone else, while we figure out what's supposed to come next.

But Mother's smile is an empty one. "Havis is gone, Aurelia. When I said leave, I meant *leave*, and he must disappear now or face the General's gun. It's only you and I here—and we are alone."

42

Rahian's Palace

The fancy palace is radiant in the muggy evening, laughter-infused, but it feels more like forcing someone to smile while your boot is on their neck. Officially, Father's calling the victory gala a "reconciliation reception." A chance to prove that with Rahian removed, peace and normalcy is indeed possible for Resya. The elite of Madelan have returned in the days since the truce, restoring some nobility to this city on its knees, and they appear relieved the worst is over. They like the profitable idea of reconciliation.

They have no clue what that will look like once my father starts rooting in every corner of this kingdom for Nahir sympathizers. They don't know what measures he'll take to purge this new realm he controls. Two months ago, our victory would have been good for the whole South—Seath and my father kicking out the last remnants of royalty, and all these nations one step closer to true independence.

But Seath has reneged.

And now my father is *angry*.

Resya will be the first to suffer that development, and I wrestle down the itching dread inside me, because I know exactly how dangerous General Dakar is when betrayed. Everyone had better cooperate—and keep it that way. And if the Nahir are wise, they'll have already gotten the hell out of Resya and run back for Thurn. The ones who are stupid enough to actually stay behind . . . Well, I can't say they won't have it coming.

"Looking for someone?" Cyar asks as we enter the ballroom, his voice far from impressed.

I'm already trying to scope out Ali. We're both in full uniform, embellished with badges, buttons. They even gave us caps this time, which is either a suggestion of imminent promotion or just to make sure we're all sufficiently intimidating to everyone present.

His tone annoys me. "So what if I am?"

"You need to stop, Athan. You're damn lucky Garrick covered for you, because if anyone finds out where you were, you're going to—"

"I don't need your lectures," I snap, feeling a headache coming on.

Garrick wouldn't have had to cover for me if Cyar hadn't told him the truth.

"No, you do need them," he pushes back. "You live in your head and barrel-roll through reality, just barely managing to hold the two in check. I'm not going to let you do this to yourself—or to her."

"We spent the night together."

It comes out the way my confessions with Cyar usually do. All at once, bracing for impact, and his face is at first shocked, then horrified beneath the glittering chandeliers.

"Damn it, Athan," he breathes.

"What?"

"She doesn't even know who you are!"

Trust Cyar to skip the interesting parts and get straight to the shame. "She knows me better than most people," I protest. "Excluding yourself, of course."

"Damn you," he repeats, sharper. "You're a selfish bastard. Just like your brother."

That wounds. And he knows it.

"You sound jealous, Hajari," I retaliate.

"You're going to make it about *that*?"

"Not like you've done it."

"Because I want something to look forward to when this is over."

"Really?" I laugh. "Then you'll *die* like this. Those are the odds, stacked quite firmly against you."

It's the quickest way to victory. A firing of both cannons, and his anger dies, raw hurt on his face. I immediately want to grab the words back. Did I actually just use his honour against him like a weapon? It's the way he wants to live, and he's never forced me to do the same. He's only pointing out the ugly can of worms that I'm too much of a selfish ass to deal with. Ali should have at least known who she was kissing.

I hate this.

We're saying things we'd never have said before this stupid war.

"Maybe I will die like this," he says eventually, "but I'll have no regrets. Minah and I have been friends since we were kids, and we know each other inside and out. All those summers at home. We have a life together. What do you have? I mean, really have? Two weeks in Etania? Five days here? Ali doesn't even know your name. Not even your *name*, Athan."

His speech breaches the grief inside me.

His own deadly salvo that disintegrates my resolve.

"And what would you do?" I beg. "If your father was trying to kill Minah's mother? What then? What the hell would you do?"

"I wouldn't let it get to this."

"Then tell me what you'd do! I'll do whatever you say. You know I would."

It's the best apology I can give him. It's the truth. But before he can reply, there's a fresh stir in the room, a hush settling and violins fading. At the top of the grand staircase, a queen of the North stands—draped in bronze and red, her pearls abandoned for ruby and sapphire, her black hair studded with gold.

A miniature stands beside her. The perfect reflection of Resyan resilience.

Sinora and Ali walk towards my father, side by side.

"I don't have an answer," Cyar admits finally.

I don't blame him. There aren't any good answers, not for this impossible knot of a thing that's my life. I simply have to do better. I have to make this right.

I begin angling closer to Ali, determined to figure out my next steps on the way, and Cyar retreats to the table of food, where Trigg's already shoving down cocktails. No one cares about me as I push through the crowd. I'm only another Safire uniform in this strange mix, and their eyes are on the Northern royalty who have come to speak on Resya's behalf. Unfortunately, the Northerners hardly *look* Northern, and Father smiles at the sight, like Sinora's dressed herself up in a white flag of surrender.

They exchange their charming, deceptive pleasantries, as if Sinora's happy to be here and Father's grateful to see her, circling barbed discussions of who will occupy Resya and how the balance of power will progress with the defeated Resyan forces.

"It's very well done, General," she finishes with a false smile. "You have yourself a base in Thurn, and now an entire Southern kingdom. Do the men of the North applaud your march? Are they well pleased with your remarkable rise?"

If she's suggesting they aren't, she's bolder than I expect.

"I'm changing the world," Father replies simply, offering his arm. She takes it. A wolf and *si'yah* cat courting for show. "Everyone will reap the rewards."

I don't know why, but I push myself right in front of them.

I need to make sure Ali sees me.

Father's glare is subtle, but Sinora's lips finally upturn. She takes in my full uniform. The new cap on my head. "Ah, a captain now, little fox?"

Before I can answer, an icier voice intervenes on my behalf. "No," Ali says, at Sinora's side. "Only a lieutenant."

Her words are a cold insult, then she looks away like I'm not worth anyone's time with that humble rank. Father's glance at me is an order to get the hell out of the way. I obey, and they move on, Ali following, forgetting me behind.

I don't know what to do.

I trail them, weaving through the guests, determined for this to end once and for all. I'm going to tell Ali the truth. I try to catch her eye again as Sinora speaks with the beaten Resyan generals, but Ali doesn't see. Or she pretends not to. The generals perk up at the attention, suddenly looking less like sun-withered grass. They speak in Resyan, a beautiful sound, and Ali's done up in a wonderful gown of clinging silk, an expanse of her back visible, precious skin because it's all *her*.

God, I want to try last night again.

I'd be better now.

Someone tugs at my arm, vanquishing those humiliating thoughts. I find a girl behind me with a curious smile and black curls. Her dress is simple, probably a maid, but her amber-eyed gaze seems oddly familiar—some distant memory of a memory.

From Thurn?

I try to place it as she nods her chin in Ali's direction. "You?" she asks me in thickly accented Landori. "Princess?"

The question is muddled. I'm not sure what she's suggesting, but she's connected my heartsick stares to Ali. "I need to speak with her," I say in slow Landori, hoping the girl can catch enough of the words to follow my meaning. "Can you get the Princess?"

I mime a few actions, and the girl studies me, trying to understand. Then something clicks through the gulf of language. She puts her hand on my arm, nodding solemnly.

"Thank you," I say.

She disappears into the crowd, the same way Sinora and Father went, and I can only wait, listening to the swells of conversation.

Eventually, the girl reappears with Ali in tow.

Ali immediately looks betrayed.

It was definitely a bad idea to send a maid who can't speak Landori. I'm torn by frustration and guilt, and Ali looks like she might slice me open with her clawlike gaze. She's clearly upset for some reason. How do I even begin this already miserable conversation?

The girl smiles at us. "The two of you have a seat," she says in polite, flawless Landori, gesturing at a nearby table. "I won't intrude."

I stare at her. "You speak—?"

But she's already gone again, smirking at me like I'm the best game she's played all night, and Ali's still glaring. Helpless and aware I've just been duped by a maid for no reason, I offer Ali the chair and she takes it with stiff formality. She won't meet my eye. She studies the flames dancing in the candelabras and I pull off my gloves, rubbing my fingers, then my head.

I'm coming apart at the seams.

"What's wrong?" I finally ask.

She doesn't answer.

"I know something's wrong, Ali."

"You left me this morning," she says hollowly.

I stop rubbing. "This is about this morning?"

"Yes." She looks at me. "You just *left*."

The depth of hurt in her shaky glare says enough. I should not have left. I should have stayed—but I couldn't. "I had to go," I admit, hoping she can hear the longing in my voice. "I had no choice. You know I can't always do what I want."

"Can't you?" There's a sting of hatred there that's alarming. "Well, I'm happy to hear your schedule's more important than what we shared," she continues. "It was hardly that exceptional for me either."

No, I'm not in a good position right now. Engine smoking, on the way down.

"I'm sorry, Ali. I really am. Please, tell me what I can do to make this right."

She glances at me, and for a moment I think she's softening. Very slightly.

She hands me the nearest napkin. "Make me an aeroplane."

I don't question the strange request. I get straight to work, folding the cloth carefully, one wing at a time, then pinching it tight to be sure it will hold. I pass it back to her.

She holds it, studying.

Then she stares at me, studying.

I swallow, terrified of her meticulous inspection, nowhere near as enjoyable as it was last night, then she drops the napkin into the nearest candle flame, the whole thing igniting to a tiny pile of nothing.

I stare at the ashes.

What do you do once you're on the ground? Wait to be captured?

"Oh no," Arrin's voice announces from across our table. "Do I sense trouble?" He looms over us, and there isn't a speck of true concern in his grin. He's watching Ali more than me. "Are you upset with the Lieutenant?" he asks her. "I can have him punished, you know. Court-martialed?"

"No," she replies.

"Demoted?"

"No."

"Shot at dawn? How terrible is this?"

"*No.*"

He raises his brow at her anger, and she stands abruptly. "I don't want to see any of you right now, Commander."

"Any of us?" Arrin repeats.

But she's already gone.

My airplane smoulders pathetically in a pool of candle wax.

"*That's* who you were with last night?" Arrin asks in Savien, thoroughly unimpressed. "Wish it had been a whorehouse, little brother."

I glare at him, waiting for the rest of the lecture.

The reminder that I'm a goddamn traitor.

Instead, he says, "I know you don't like to take advice from me, but I'm somewhat of an expert with women, and you might consider following her."

Half of me thinks Arrin is definitely not an expert and this is terrible advice. The other half of me wants to find out for sure. But then his expression tightens, and he leans down. "Don't let anything happen to her, Athan. She's a valuable prize, and this party is a target. Keep a close eye on her. Can you handle that? Though maybe not as close as you'd like. You know what I'm say—"

I bolt across the room. His warning is enough. If Seath is on the move, looking to sabotage this situation further, then the last thing I want is for our misstep with the Nahir to endanger Ali. I'm an idiot about many things, but I won't let that happen. Not now. I race to keep up to her, because she's moving at a good pace, darting between the dancing and conversation, and I follow her out into a hall littered with anxious footmen. One tries to offer me brandy. I ignore it.

When I catch up, she's stopped on a balcony currently occupied by a wealthy Resyan couple. They both look startled by her sudden presence—and frightened of mine. They disappear quickly.

We're left alone.

She faces the shadows, away from the radiant palace, and the stars are wild above. I have the sudden feeling of being in a circular sky. Nothing beyond. Stuck in this infinite sphere of empty depths, around and around and around, a flame at the very center that can't actually be reached.

"Ali, please tell me what—"

"I hate this," she hurls, whirling on me. "*All* of this. It's wrong. Has everyone already forgotten what's been lost? I watched this city burn. Burn right up in flames! And all of the people here—" She flicks a hand at the bright doorway. "They saw none of it. They returned in time for peace."

I consider my next words carefully. Whatever I say has to be right, because she's liable to take flight again—possibly right over this balcony and out of sight. "The world justifies war too easily," I agree.

She glowers at me, fury in her eyes. "*Your* world, at least."

I don't know what that means. I've never admired these rich cowards, from the North or the South. Their only courage is in testing new wines and passing profound verdicts. Perhaps if I'd said this before, she would have laughed.

I don't think she will now.

Her chin rises. "Do you think what you did in this kingdom is right, Lieutenant?"

The question is a death sentence. *Lieutenant.* Not my name. I feel it like a weight on my wrists, metal against my skin. I've confessed nearly all of my sins to her, and maybe I shouldn't have, but now she's put that to smoke—leaving only one bone of a question behind.

"It was for the greater good," I say, hating the words, yet needing them to be true. Somehow. "It's not always pleasant, but that's life. That's how you get something better."

"Is that a line from your brother's speech last summer?"

"No, my brother never—"

I stop. The trap was sprung too easily. I was distracted by my own shame, and she pounced. Her expression's unreadable in the dark. Far across a sea of betrayal.

She flings something at me.

I catch metal tags against my chest, suddenly realizing they were even lost. That's how far gone my head is these days. It's all murky and knotted in there, a smog of thoughts and pain. "Ali, please listen. I'll tell you everything. It will make sense, I promise. Erelis was my mother's name. After she was murdered, we—"

"I don't care!"

Her words slap me. They're empty and cold, and they poke a hot coal of my own anger. She won't listen. She doesn't even *know* me.

Dark laughter throbs in my head.

Naked in all but your name, then?

"Don't you think I deserved the truth when we met?" she demands. "Before last night at least?"

"Yes," I say honestly. "I was going to tell you. I tried in a letter. I tried—"

She shakes her head. "Try isn't good enough, Lieutenant. Try is meaningless." I move towards her and she swings a hand, holding me back. "No! You think I'm angry at you? I am. I'm furious at you. But I'm even angrier with myself, because I was a fool. A *fool*. To think a junior officer could take me straight to the General in the middle of a coup. To think that made any sense at all! How could I have bought such a perfect lie?"

Because you were scared, I want to say. *Because it was the only way.*

"And when I faced him," she says, "you did *nothing*. You stood there and listened like a nothing officer who didn't matter at all. You let me face him alone. Tell me—did your father ask you to get to know me? Is that why you gave me the flower in the garden?"

I have no answer.

There's an entire story built in my head, but it's lost in the confusing mess of shadows and memories. It made sense at the time. It all makes sense—until it suddenly doesn't.

"I love you," I whisper. "I swear it on my soul."

"Stop lying to me!" She backs away farther, horrified, like I'm a rabid dog getting too close. "Your father is a monster who wants war. He wants revenge in the only way he knows, and his target is my mother. You thought I wouldn't figure that out eventually? What the hell is wrong with you?"

She knows.

She knows it all, and I can only stare at her while she snarls in my face. "You took my most painful secret and turned it into profit for your family. *You* did that, Lieutenant. No one else. So don't tell me you love me, because your version of it is something

I can't even fathom. Stars, I thought it was only your brother causing trouble. It's not him—it's all of you! You're all the damn *same*."

Wrong words.

Something breaks inside me. Something bruised and vicious. "I am *not* the same as them," I hurl back, "and you of all people should know that! Before you start pointing fingers, you'd better ask your mother for her story first. You think she's innocent? You think I'm the only one guilty here?"

"How dare you," she hisses.

But I don't stop. I pull out Mother's photograph from my uniform, the one I always have with me, that's followed me through both war and love, and hold it out to her like a gun. She stares, her rigid face stunned. "My mother bled out in my goddamn arms, Ali. Do you know what that's like? Can you even imagine it? You stand here, judging everyone else as if you wouldn't do the same thing. As if you're somehow stronger and braver, but you're *not*. You just haven't had to make the choice yet. And if I can do this, so can you—and that's the truth." My accusation hangs, dangerous in the silence. "Go ask your mother what she did to my family. Ask her why she's a killer. Then judge me all the hell you want."

Ali looks like she might hit me—for real.

Then she's gone.

43

I don't glance back. At last, I've let my anger unleash as it longs to, this inferno I've held tight between my hands all day. I've purged it from within, flung it at him, and he's only made it worse.

How dare he have the nerve to look *wounded*?

I charge down an empty hall, despising his pain, his manipulation of the fight, desperate to get away. Here, the reality of Rahian's palace becomes achingly apparent. A hollow shell in frightened subservience. The "life" in the reception is kept by a flame of necessity. Every other floor reveals a grief-stricken world still in defeat—memories of men in uniform now buried, the awareness of a king in chains, and a grand doorway in shambles from a short-range mortar.

"You think she's innocent?"

Athan's question mocks me as I flee. I'd wanted to slap him for that, and perhaps I would have, had I dared to get closer to his beautiful, wretched face. But the reality is, I know, now, she isn't innocent. Not at all. And when he showed me the photograph of his own mother, I knew, at once, the woman there. That same faraway smile from my mother's drawer, the one I found as I searched for Havis's letter last spring. The same sea-grey eyes as Athan.

Sapphie elski'han.

Those were the words scrawled in ink. A silent threat I

couldn't translate, and now it all makes too much terrible sense. A never-ending war of vengeance, as Havis said.

I stumble into my room, my untethered thoughts summoning a sudden picture of the little girl, the General's second child, burned alive when an old ally betrayed him. As blameless and tiny as the ones buried in this ruined kingdom. Athan's own sister. For some reason, that makes it more real. A child with an identity, one my mother considered worth the cost of revenge. Even if Dakar deserved it, how could she have exhaled the same cruelty as him? How?

I hit the wooden vanity before me again and again. I savour the ache in my bones, my reflection in the mirror taunting—a panicked-looking girl, decorated like a Resyan jewel. Stars, I promised myself I wouldn't gleam in the face of war. I rip away the necklace and earrings and bracelets. I yank down my hair from its gold pins.

My heart, at last, steadies slightly.

There I am.

The girl who wears leather boots and walks with Tirza. The girl who hopes, and rages. I take a few more shaky breaths, then grab a bottle of wine. I'm going to see Rahian first, then Tirza, and if I'm lucky, I'll make my escape tonight.

I'm not staying here.

I'm finishing this mission to stop my rotten uncle—even if my mother refuses to help.

I march upstairs for the wing where Rahian's being held hostage. Safire soldiers are posted by the doors, wearing guarded expressions, but I'm still the princess of an allied kingdom—for now—and they don't protest. When I find Rahian, he's sitting at his desk, scribbling hurriedly. He doesn't look up until he's finished. When his gaze meets mine, I find a broken man. Haggard and puffy eyed.

"I brought you something to drink," I offer, extending the wine. Perhaps not great for his habit, but there are far worse things to worry about now.

He ignores it. He simply smiles sadly and says, "I'm sorry, Aurelia."

He's teetering on the edge of an abyss, his pride ruined, defeated—and yet it's more than that. And I need to know what it is before I escape this place. I need to know before I look Seath in the face and gamble everything on our shared name.

Eyeing the Safire sentries, he motions me nearer his desk, and I relent. His expression is strained. "No one understands, Aurelia, and I fear my moment of testimony will be stolen from me. I'll never get the chance to write my own history. But let me at least tell you. Won't you listen?"

"Of course."

"You are kind."

"Not always," I say, thinking about how I just abandoned Athan, unwilling to listen or learn from his story, despising him for blood in his veins he has no control over. Blood like the kind in my own veins—ambitious and monstrous and frightened.

No, I'm not kind.

Not right now.

"Remember this, please. No matter what others may say about me someday. Remember that he only said I had to fight. I had to let the war happen. Give the lion its match. That was it. He never said he'd trap my people." Rahian's voice breaks completely. "Dear God, twenty thousand of them died when those bridges collapsed! *Twenty thousand.* I curse his mother's memory! I curse his breath!"

He doesn't say the name, but it shivers between us.

Seath.

This is Rahian's confession. The true depth of his guilt, and my heart aches. For him. For this kingdom. "I can't accept your apology," I whisper. "I can't accept it on behalf of the twenty thousand who died. Not for any of the ones who will never come back."

"Oh, but Aurelia, you at least—"

The floor shudders beneath our feet, the chandelier's jewels rattling, and I reach for the desk, bracing myself. Silence envelops the room. Then the walls shake again. Somewhere, beyond the open window, screams echo.

For a moment, I don't move. Nor does Rahian. Perhaps we don't want to know the truth. We want to stay here, hidden from it. But then I force myself to the window and glance outside. Smoke rises from the far edge of the palace, flames dancing orange. In the courtyard, the Safire tanks are on fire, one after another in a glowing line, a clatter of bullets and guns stammering too close.

I stare, fixated on the burning tanks. Safire men holler at one another, running about blindly in the courtyard, tiny shadows, and for some reason, some reason that makes no sense—I begin to laugh. A terrified, overwhelmed laugh as Rahian stares at me, stunned. But it's funny. Can't he see? Those Safire tanks came all the way through the treacherous mountains, weeks of painstaking journey, on bloody campaign, only to be destroyed along this beautiful palm-lined avenue. I laugh, because it's not metal burning up—it's everything this invasion represents. Pride. Arrogance. Conceit. The Commander isn't so genius after all. His little toys are bursting to flames right in front of us!

This feels deserved.

This feels like justice.

And then from somewhere far below, a raging voice shouts, "Resya undivided! Resya eternal!"

I freeze.

Bullets clatter, more shouts, and again I hear the words.

Resya undivided!

Resya eternal!

"Your uncle can't do this to me," Rahian whispers, truly terrified now. "Not like this!"

But this wasn't my uncle. This was me—my writing, my words—and at once, my strange humour entirely disintegrates.

The people are rising up. They're becoming a mountain, refusing to let the Safire pass unscathed, and I know what happens next. Aeroplanes, guns, a nightmare. There are too many possibilities of where this will lead, and they all have a bad end. For us. For Mother.

Mother!

There's no other thought in my head now. I abandon Rahian behind, bursting out into the empty hall, past the Safire guards with their guns raised, racing back downstairs. I nearly fall taking the stairs three at a time. Guns hammer, echoing up the marble stairwell, a familiar rhythmic, piercing sound, and I sprint for the reception. My courage is madness, but no one will touch my mother—no matter how much I despise her right now. To touch her is to touch me. To touch Reni.

I fly round a corner, right into Tirza.

I don't think. I grip her shoulders, hold her alarmed gaze. "Get out of here," I order. *"Now!"*

"Ali, I'm not leaving you to—"

"No, whatever power I have, I'm using it to send you *away*."

She can't be here. She can't get taken by the Safire, her worst fear come to life. My protectiveness aches, reaching for her as another explosion rattles in the distance, machine guns ricocheting from the courtyard.

"Ali," she says, "we did this. We gave this kingdom something to believe in—itself."

It's all happening too fast, and the words stick in my throat, the words I might say if I had more time. I want to tell her she doesn't need to feel alone any longer. Because I'm here. I care, even if the rest of her family has disappeared forever. I'll care no matter what happens, this love I bear for her birthed the night we held each other as bombs fell.

But now she needs to run.

And fast.

"Please go," I beg. "Disappear and keep yourself safe."

She finally listens, her lips kissing my right cheek, then my left. "They can't touch me," she whispers. "Not even in death."

And then she's gone.

My sweet friend.

I turn on my heel and race down the hall, running as if I could escape it all—my fear for Tirza, my fury at Athan, the realization that my words have done more than I ever imagined and that seeing those Safire tanks burn was a wonderful, beautiful, desolate delight.

Nothing is how I want it to be.

At the grand doorway of the gala, panicked disaster greets me. People bleed out on the ground—Landorian and Savien and Resyan—and Jali cowers in the far corner, her mouth caught in a scream, yet somehow also victorious, like the madness round her is some cataclysmic validation for her entire life, for everything she believes. The "commoners" rising up to steal from the rightful heirs.

"You see," she seems to say with her arms up in surrender, *"the Nahir are everywhere!"*

But I don't see any fighters. And this is far bigger than just the Nahir—I've roused an entire defeated kingdom. Who knows how many are now in revolt?

Hundreds?

Thousands?

Everyone important has fled the room, leaving the wounded behind, and I run through the trail of carnage, passing a footman with a hand across his gut, blood leaking between his fingers. Mother is nowhere, and my panic grows. I race for the patio to the main gardens, then stumble to a heart-stammering halt at the shattered glass doors. Spotlights flare. Voices shout roughly. The Commander is there, Safire soldiers shoving men against a wall, their backs to me. The ones lined against the wall face my direction and I recognize Officer Walez.

My Resyan officer.

He's placed defiantly before Safire guns, and I realize, at once, that this entire night is stretching much too far. Even the defeated army officers have joined the stand. A furious force rushing up from the ruins of surrender, to drown the victorious invaders.

Walez waits for the bullet, his chin raised.

I can't let them do this—he *helped* me—and I'm ready to run forward, to throw myself at the Commander in a fit of wild rage, but someone grabs me from behind, dragging me backwards into the shadowed gardens.

"Think," Athan orders into my ear. "Just think for a moment!"

I struggle against his iron grip. I don't care. I'm going to save Walez, somehow. This night is on me. My words. But then the report of guns echoes out of sight, too late, and I want to scream into the cold sky.

This is all wrong, no rules of honour or nobility.

War has none of it.

"We have to get out of here," Athan hisses again into my ear, still holding me against his chest, refusing to let go.

I'm struggling in vain when a fresh shot pierces the air—far too close—and he pushes us both down onto the grass behind a stone fountain. I gasp in pain. My side throbs, shoved against cement, and Athan Dakar's nearly on top of me as I peer up into his terrified face. His expression is the greatest and worst thing to see at once. It's too pure. Entirely honest in its fear. For me. Proof of his love—however twisted and mangled.

I glance backwards.

A Safire officer slumps beside a nearby rosebush, his pale temple blossoming red. A sniper's flawless shot. Was that the shot we just heard? The dead man's eyes gaze up, still open, and Athan finally loosens his grip on me. Cyar and another Safire boy are crouched behind him. I despise him—and them—but I also don't want us all to die.

Not like this.

There's no time to think, and I leap to my feet, the Safire trio looking petrified in the palace lights. "Get up," I order at them. "I have a way out."

They don't move, still cowering while I stand above. Who knows which window the bullet came from, but given the fast progression of this battle, I don't think they'll be lingering in any one place for long. I wouldn't.

"Get *up*," I repeat sharply. "You can follow me or face the Nahir yourself."

"Where?" Cyar asks.

"Your airbase. Then south."

When in danger, go south. That's what Lady Havis said.

But Athan shakes his head. "It's gone. Those were the first explosions."

"How do you know?"

"Him." Athan points at the dead officer in the rosebushes.

The corpse still bleeds, bubbling in little spurts. Feeling suddenly vulnerable, I reach down and take the pistol from the fallen man. Athan looks apprehensive, but I click it in defiance. "We both know I can use this. And I'm not leaving without one. Where's my mother?"

"With my father."

My heart staggers, and he must see it, because he shrugs desperately. "This whole thing happened too fast and we're all in danger! Not much choice how we get to safety."

I want to laugh. Clearly. No one here is safe, certainly not if my mother has been forced to escape with his father. At least I know now she's capable enough of dealing with him. A woman who can surely protect herself.

"Well, I'm leaving too," I announce. "And I have an aeroplane."

Athan still doesn't move and I realize, right then, he doesn't trust me any more than I trust him. How quickly our tender certainty has evaporated. One moment true, the next, only a myth. A memory.

But the third boy scrambles to my side out of nowhere, a half-terrified grin on his tanned face. "An airplane? I'm in!"

Cyar looks briefly annoyed, glancing at Athan, but hurries up as well. "Me too."

Athan is the last one.

He's deeply suspicious, but there's a battle beginning in this city and he has no choice. We count to three, then burst full tilt through the gardens. It's the way Tirza and I always went, through the rear garden wall.

"Where are the rest of your aeroplanes?" I ask Athan over my shoulder as we hurry out into the darkened streets of Madelan. The warm night pulses with energy, the sky alarmingly silent.

"Our nearest base is thirty miles north, but they'll be on their way." His meaning is clear. When the bombers arrive, perhaps little in the city will be spared this time. Targeting an unseen enemy who could be anywhere. "If we can't fly, then we need to take shelter and hide, Ali. We need to wait until—"

"*No*. I'm taking you south."

"With what airplane?" Athan demands, stopping us abruptly, his hand yanking on my arm. "There's nothing left at that base and no Resyan is going to give me their plane!"

"One might."

Athan looks like he's not going to move another foot until I can prove it, so I grab Cyar and pull him after me. A willing hostage and Athan surrenders, following. We run down the steep streets of the city, ones I know well now, taking us away from the main avenues. Terrified faces peer from windows. Smoke drifts through the sky. Soon enough, Safire bombers will arrive. The rain of death once more. Panic struggles inside my chest, the awareness that down here, in these alleys, we mean nothing to those beasts of the air. We'll be consumed. The Safire boys seem to realize the same thing, and their sprinting becomes more insistent.

When my destination appears, I'm not even sure if anyone will be here at this hour, but I bang on the metal hangar door of the civilian airfield. My thumps echo. I'm about to tell Cyar to just shove it open—we'll figure out how to get the aeroplane once inside—when it swings wide, the old mechanic peering at me nervously, a wrench for a weapon in hand.

"Wandering Girl!" he exclaims.

Thank the stars he recognizes me, even in the weak light of the lamps hissing above. A partially eviscerated engine sits behind him.

"I need one of your aeroplanes," I plead in Resyan, hoping to woo him, to remind him we're the same.

He gapes. "You can't fly! The radio said to stay inside and—" He stops, seeing the three Safire uniforms behind me, a twitch of anger surfacing. Hatred. But then his eyes are on my face again, and I'm sure he sees the genuine fear in all of us.

"Please, we have no time, sir. Let us fly one of your planes and I'll give you any reward you ask."

"I can't just—"

I pull out my Safire pistol. It glints, pointed at the man's chest, and finally he sees reason. Swift and true. I don't dare look over my shoulder to catch the reaction from Athan or Cyar. I don't care what they think of me right now—they'd do the same.

Sometimes, you need a gun to make a point.

And fast.

Surrendering, the old man waves us into the hangar. It's tiny and filled with uninspiring planes. No wonder it was spared any attention by the Safire when they arrived to occupy the city. The one he gives us is the largest and most impressive of his small supply. Propellers on either wing with a lumbering body that looks decent enough.

The Safire pilots don't share my optimism.

"We're supposed to fly *that*?" Athan asks.

"It looks like an ugly hippo," the third boy offers.

"If it has wings, I'll take it," Cyar counters. "Ours should be here in about five minutes?"

That's the observation we need, and we all break for the hippo.

Athan and Cyar swing up into the nose to fly it, and the third boy tugs me into the side door. He pulls out a map for coordinating with me and we sit behind the cockpit, in the empty space that's dirty and sparse.

"I'm Trigg," he greets, far too cheerful for the situation. "Where are we going, Princess?"

I point out Sanseri, where Lady Havis fled to, but truthfully I have no clue what we'll find there. I only want to get us away. Anywhere but here.

"We'll figure it out," Trigg assures me in Landori as the aeroplane comes to a complaining start. Everything rattling round us. "So, I heard you had a thing with the Lieutenant? Hajari says you like him but not the whole 'son of the General' bit, which is understandable. If you still hold any admiration for we Safire pilots and our skill, I'm pleased to say that I actually *did* grow up on a farm. A real farm, I mean. I'm not making it up. Do you like cows?"

It takes me a moment to realize what he's saying.

Right now.

In the middle of our escape.

Athan growls at him in Savien—something I suspect isn't nice—and Trigg obeys, slithering into the narrow cockpit to show them where we're headed. Cyar pulls back on a lever, the wing flaps creaking sadly.

He tries it again.

More creaking.

Athan draws a breath and glances over his shoulder at me. "Is this because of that damn flower? Because you can have your bad luck back. I don't want it."

I hate him for mentioning the orchid, for reminding me of our life before all of this. But it still pulls a tiny, nervous smile from my lips, because he's right.

I don't want it either.

We lurch forward, Cyar and Athan arguing away in Savien. The snippets I catch don't inspire confidence. Trigg motions for me to grab on to whatever's nearby, and I quickly oblige, gripping stiff leather straps hanging from the metal wall. With a shudder, the old transport plane springs down the runway, surprisingly perky for all its griping. We soar up into an uncertain night sky, a thousand stars beyond the cockpit window. This isn't the smooth aeroplane Havis brought me in on. This one clatters and reverberates, the propellers a thudding roar against my head. The empty space amplifies the sound.

We've only been airborne a moment when Trigg peers out the side window. "Shit."

It's in Savien, but I know that word now thanks to five days with Athan.

Athan and Cyar don't hear with the racket.

"What is it?" I demand, hoping the answer isn't a disastrous one.

"I think we've got friends arriving at ten o'clock high."

"Friends?"

I don't dare ask who, or how he can even see anything in this darkness. Nahir. Landorian. Safire. None are ones I want to meet in this grumbling hippo.

"Oh, *shit*," he repeats.

"What?"

"Twin cannons!" He turns from the window and flings himself at the cockpit. "Get moving, Captain!"

He changes to Savien abruptly and a very unpromising debate ignites, an unintelligible raucous in the eternal roar of the propellers. It's all panic. Shouting. Angry things that sound mostly like *"I told you so,"* and I holler at them to speak in Landori, so at least I can know my own fate, then grip the leather straps and resign myself to death in the air.

Truly, I'd hoped for any other way than this.

At least it might be quick.

I'm about to demand more information when Athan yelps at me in Landori—"Get down!" Trigg dives and pulls me to the metal floor with him. I have only a moment to register the grit poking at my cheeks, the smell of sharp fuel in my nostrils, before fireworks explode above my head. Flashes of colour and light. Obliterating sound. There and gone, and I feel myself beginning to laugh in rebellion of this whole mad death of mine.

Who would have thought?

After a moment of only propellers again, Trigg and I sit up, both of us trembling. Three-inch holes stagger across the far wall of the plane.

"What the hell was that!" I exclaim.

"Nightfoxes, if I had to guess," Trigg replies. It means nothing to me. "Those shithead bootlickers clearly have terrible aim."

I almost remind him that it's pitch-dark out, and it must be difficult to fire anything accurately, but then I don't know why I'm defending the ones trying to kill us. Athan yells something in Savien over the radio in his hand, Cyar desperately searching different airwaves, but Athan gives up and throws the thing down.

"Hang on!" he shouts in Landori.

"Please remember this isn't a fighter!" Cyar shouts back at him. "We can't—"

I have only a brief second to seize the straps again before my stomach flies up into nothing, the floor falling away beneath me. The sensation sifts through my limbs, a growing weightlessness. My head throbs and grey edges into the picture of Trigg across from me, also hanging on for dear life. The propellers hit a high-pitch whine of protest.

Then the dive stops, and the whole thing flings another direction.

I start to slip—up or down, backwards or forwards. I have no clue. I only know that I'm escaping myself, plunging through a place I don't belong, and something warm and firm grabs my hand. Trigg. He reaches across the little space, trying to say something to me, our hands connected in shared terror, but none of it makes any sense. He might be speaking Savien.

The fireworks hit somewhere behind for a second time. The tail?

We're going up again. Things slide backwards, including our map, which Trigg manages to save with an impressive dive and catch. I dare a glance out the cockpit window. All stars. Higher and higher at a mad rate.

This poor aeroplane.

"That was a nice move, wasn't it?" Trigg calls breathlessly, mustering a brave grin as we level out. "Didn't think this thing would get up the speed. But look at us go!"

"Where are those foxes now?" I ask, terrified of a repeat.

"Foxes." He laughs, then stops. "That's funny, Princess. I don't know. Might be following us. Might not be." He squints out one of the three-inch holes. "Hopefully they have more important things to do than tail an unmarked freight train. Hey, Captain? Can you write them up for this?"

Whether Athan does or not, I now have a firsthand report for my notebook. *Yes, I was in fact chased by a Safire squadron while in a civilian aeroplane without a drop of armament on it.*

I try to steady my panicky fury as we fly straight, the smooth darkness an overwhelming relief. The numb respite before the bruise begins.

Minutes slip past, on and on, when Athan finally says, "Twenty miles out from Sanseri."

Cyar adjusts the headset, fiddling with the radio. "Hello, hello, can you read? We're coming in from Madelan, in a . . . a . . ."

"A hippo," Trigg supplies, kneeling between them in the cockpit.

Cyar makes a face at him, and pretends instead the radio is hitting static, obscuring whatever it is we're flying. "We need to put down immediately," he says in Landori. "Losing fuel at 3,000 feet."

I'm glad I didn't know that part before.

"Damn stupid thing," Athan mutters.

One of the engines sputters pathetically in retaliation.

A propeller slows.

"Talk nicer to it," Trigg scolds. "You're being mean."

He begins to stroke the metal sides, murmuring, and I'm truly not sure what to make of him.

"Oh, I've got someone!" Cyar says, excitement renewed. He listens. His smile fades. "And they're not letting anyone land."

"But we're local," Athan protests.

Cyar looks at him pointedly.

"At least we are until we land," Athan amends.

"Now they're jabbering at me in Resyan." Cyar drops the mouthpiece. "What the hell do we do?"

"Give it to me," I order, crawling forward on my knees. I push Trigg out of the way and take his spot between them, trying to reach for the headset.

Cyar glances at me skeptically.

"Give it to her," Athan tells him.

He relents and I quickly have the earphones over my head. I shout rather aggressively in Resyan for someone to listen to me. I have no patience left.

There's a lengthy pause, then a hesitant voice. "I copy you. Resyan plane?"

"Yes," I say, curbing my frantic frustration. "We're mostly Resyan on board and we've escaped the attack in Madelan. Please. We're low on fuel and need to put down."

"Losing fuel?"

"One propeller has almost stopped. I'm sure things are worse than that, but I don't know what to tell you. I never fly. I *hate* flying," I add, hoping a distressed girl on a doomed aeroplane is enough to move them to sympathy. "I'm friends with Lady Havis?"

It's a last-ditch effort. Maybe someone in Sanseri knows her.

"What's he saying?" Athan questions, beginning to struggle now at the controls.

The whole aeroplane seems heavier, like a sinking stone.

I try to cover the mouthpiece, so the Resyans can't hear me speaking in Landori. "They want to know where we are."

"Vector zero-two-four from Sanseri at 800 feet," Trigg says.

"What's a vector?" I ask.

"Just say it!" all three pilots snap at once.

I glare at them and repeat the words, waiting for an affirmation. It comes right as the propeller growls to a halt altogether. The failing plane really does feel as though it might be half falling as we roar down onto the narrow runway, engine coughing. Trigg and I throw ourselves back into the rear, the aerodrome lamps flashing past, and I see that it's armed with flak guns and even a tank—thank the stars we didn't need to land without permission! We thump against the tarmac, the entire plane shuddering to a tight halt at the end of a short runway. My head hits the wall as we fling left. Little lights spark in my vision. I wasn't holding the leather tight enough, and I close my eyes to the pain, let it roll through me sharply, fading with the gathering realization that we've stopped.

We've stopped.

I open my eyes and I can see only trees beyond the cockpit window. Our nose is nearly into the forest, the farthest edge of the tarmac, and Athan's hands are white against the controls as the plane sputters to death.

Cyar lets out a shaky breath, loud enough it speaks for us all.

Night forest sounds filter in from beyond. Distant voices shout in Resyan. The back of my head aches dully, tender to the touch, and Trigg gives me a concerned look. He stands, a bit shaky himself. His offered hand brings me to my feet. The air swirls. I must be swaying, and Trigg grips my arm, leading me for the little door out of the aeroplane. Athan still sits in the front, staring at the trees.

"I think you'll need to do the talking first," Cyar suggests to me.

I nod, still looking at Athan, at his hands slowly releasing the plane, and I find my anger loosening its own fist. In its recess is something I can't quite place. I remember the way he told me about his fears, about the terror of life in the air, and I've tasted it now. I've felt a small, horrible fraction of it.

How could any father will their child into that world? One who has the power to make the opposite true?

I think of the Commander entering Rahian's palace, entirely alone. The Captain with his silence and sea-distant gaze on the balcony in Norvenne. It's not pity I feel. I could never feel sorry for them—certainly not for the Commander. But it's a sudden awareness that while my family is far from innocent, there's something even more wrong at the center of their world, and I want nothing to do with it.

Nothing at all.

I ignore Trigg's extended hand and jump down onto the tarmac. A lamplight swings into my face, blinding me, and Trigg and Cyar immediately put their hands up. I peer over at them, confused. The light moves on and I can see again.

Guns.

A lot of them.

"*Mostly* Resyan?" a sarcastic voice calls at us.

"Don't fire!" I say, fighting to sound more annoyed than terrified. "I'm Her Royal Highness Aurelia Isendare of Etania. These pilots rescued me from Madelan. I'm here to see the Lady Havis."

It's silent a moment. Crickets singing at the edge of the runway. This is as frightening as our dive in the hippo, because if vast portions of Resya are now in revolt against the Safire and the nobility who welcomed them—thanks to me, my pamphlets—then I've walked Athan and Cyar and Trigg straight into a deadly trap.

"Lady Havis?" one finally asks, right as another says, "A *princess*?"

"Yes," I answer both. "Now let us inside. We've had a miserable flight here."

The guns lower slightly and the soldiers glance at each of us in confusion—a princess who looks hardly like a princess, two Safire boys with their hands up, and another stumbling out of the cockpit in a half daze.

I pray Lady Havis can devise some story for us.

As the soldiers motion for us to follow them to the aerodrome, guns still at the ready, I glance back at Athan. In the yellow light, his expression is pale and guarded.

"There are two unfortunate truths here," I say to him hollowly.

He waits.

"One is that I'll never look at you the same, no matter how I try."

He drops his eyes.

"And the other, Lieutenant, is that I find I hate your beloved planes."

44

The woman called Lady Havis shows up right when I think the Resyan soldiers are going to forget waiting and start using us as target practice. Their immense hatred is palpable in the tiny airfield hut, and if they find out my brother's already gone ahead and executed the Resyan officers who helped organize the revolt, I'm sure they'll put a gun straight into my damn mouth.

Ali, however, they afford every courtesy. They bring her hot tea and offer her a chair with cushions. In fact, they manage to scrounge up so many cushions, she's practically burrowed in a ridiculous nest.

We're given the cement floor. As close to the drafty door as they can put us.

It's well past midnight, exhaustion kicking in, but we sit with tailbones smarting while Ali waits on her chair stoically. She has no idea how close to disaster we actually came. Three Nightfox fighters and not one of them managed the killing shot? It's a miracle. I have no idea what's going on back in Madelan, or where Father and Sinora escaped to. The radio's playing, but it's all in Resyan, and the announcer jabbers away furiously. Doesn't sound hopeful.

My eyes ache, and I let them close briefly.

One moment.

"Stars, what have we here?"

The piqued Landori words rouse me from momentary sleep. An old woman stands in the doorway, eyes skipping from Ali to the Resyan soldiers to us with increasing disbelief. She looks about as furious as how I'd imagine that man on the radio looking. Ali's out of her nest with terrific speed. They talk emphatically in Resyan, then to the soldiers. They each take turns, sometimes waving at us discarded on the floor, and everyone looks very passionate about their position. I hope it's in our favour.

"I never wanted to be a prisoner of war," Trigg mutters.

"We're not at war anymore," Cyar reminds him.

I'm not so sure about that.

There's a climactic rush of words before us, the soldiers and the old woman facing off against Ali, then Ali turns on a heel and marches back for her nest. She sits down on it, chin raised.

The woman shakes her head and waves in assent. She disappears out the door, and the soldiers hover near the radio awkwardly. Ali strides for us, kneeling down to be level with our faces.

"I'm sorry," she says. "They think you should stay here until they know what to do with you."

She apologizes to Cyar and Trigg. She doesn't even look at me, and I feel it like a kick to the ribs.

"Makes sense," Trigg replies. "That's what you do with prisoners."

Cyar elbows him.

Ali looks upset. "But I'm staying with you. I don't trust them."

That explains the defiant march back to her cushions. I can't help but wonder if all of this is for Cyar. Not me. Separating the innocent from the guilty.

"Please rest," Cyar says to her. "They won't hurt us. They have no reason to."

He lies pleasantly, but she sees right through it.

"I'm staying," she replies firmly.

"As a prisoner," Trigg intervenes, "am I entitled to some water? Possibly?"

It's a good mission to give her. She marches off again to face the Resyans, who now look supremely annoyed by our presence—and the fact that a Northern royal is providing us unearned protection. She fights with them a moment, but of course they give in. Soon she has water for all of us. Then she brings one of her cushions closer, settling on it. Even when she sits on the floor, she sits straight and delicate, like a princess.

"Sleep," she tells us. "I won't move from here."

I watch her through half-shut eyes, full of things I can't speak out loud, wanting one more sliver of a chance to set things right and give her what she deserves.

But I'm grasping at air.

She looks at me now and she sees only one thing. This uniform. This thing that has never felt like me. We're only a foot away from each other and it might as well be the entire Black Sea between us. A cold void of buried secrets and shipwrecked wounds.

I surrender to the exhaustion.

Dawn comes and I think my tailbone is about worn right off. Beside me, Cyar and Trigg were smart enough to sprawl out on their backs. Ali's still there, hunched over, sketching something on a piece of paper.

"Keeping yourself awake?" I ask, a bit bleary eyed.

It works. Surprised, she glances up with a weary gaze, forgetting to ignore me, to hate me. She hesitates, then reveals the paper. It's an impossibly intricate design, a maze of spirals and angles and flowers. No doubt it took hours. She began in one corner and is now halfway across the page.

"Thank you," I say, the only honest thing she might accept.

She stayed awake—for us.

She nods, face etched with defeat, studying me apprehensively. But her stare's a fraction softer now. Less impassive. In the panic of our escape, I think we both let our true colours show. It replaced the hot anger, if only briefly. I know now I'd die for her if she asked it, if she said it might make things right. I also know she'd run herself into danger for my sake, when it's a matter of life and death. Somehow, despite everything, she doesn't want me dead—and I almost feel hope. Because I'm an idiot.

Not wanting me dead is not the same thing as wanting me near.

Lady Havis returns as the sun charges higher, armed with a basket of food. She might not approve of us, nor Ali's decision to stay, but at least she won't allow us all to starve in a tiny airfield hut in southern Resya. She says Madelan's under Safire command again. The brief revolt was only a flash of rebellion, now contained, and we're to wait here. Someone will come for us. Soon.

The Resyan soldiers hate us even more now.

Fingers itching on triggers.

They turn on the radio again and fill the room with fuzzy, strange voices. There's a hush then, the kind of hush that's all wrong. Expressions turn gaunt. Hatred becomes shock. A rifle drops to the floor, and one of the men moans.

An impending sense of dread tightens my limbs. I begin to check the windows, the doors. An escape. I need an escape. Anything.

Frantic voices argue in Resyan.

One boy even begins to cry.

The window closest to Trigg might work. It's propped open with a fan. We could push that out, run for the nearest plane, try to—

"How *dare* he!" Ali's voice demands.

She says it in Landori, so we all know the depth of this betrayal.

I want to reach for her. I want to say it wasn't me. I don't know what it is, but I know it's terrible. Something Father would do in retribution, to remind this kingdom to stay on its knees.

My pleading gaze finds Ali.

She's temper wrapped in skin. Long, dark hair flutters around her face—wild and unkempt. Exhaustion lines her flaming eyes.

"He killed him!" she hurls, standing over me.

I back against the wall. I have nowhere to go.

"I don't understand the report," I say desperately.

"He's dead. Rahian is *dead*. Executed!"

I think she might actually kick me. Her leg is raised slightly, like it's a possibility. A drone hums outside in the morning air. Large propellers, possibly twin engines. I strain my ears, hoping for an end to this stale truce. Something to spring us from this prison.

"The General," Lady Havis whispers, peering out the window.

That's all I need.

I stand up without anyone's permission and break free, pushing out onto the tarmac, the drone settling across the airfield like a thunderous bird. The fox and swords flash by, the plane screeching to an impossible halt on the short runway. Nearly damn suicide for everyone, apparently.

I wait, brow wet in the heat. The door of the airplane opens and the first one out is Sinora Lehzar. I get out of her way fast, let her sweep by me, but her frantic eyes are only for her daughter.

I don't watch their reunion.

I hurry for the airplane and know only one thing.

My father has killed a king.

45

The General insists we come with him in his aeroplane, and I'm determined to refuse. Mother clutches my arm—a tight embrace—and I know she'd come in his plane to get to me. But never again. She won't go anywhere he asks, not now, and I acknowledge the very real fact that I've placed her in this trap, stranded in Resya.

Rahian.

Executed.

My mind still reels with this treachery. A king lined up for the gun like his rebellious officers. No trial, only a bullet in the midnight hour. The dishonour of those final moments is impossible to imagine, his body ripped open, his royal blood allowed to soak into the earth like spilt wine.

It should never have happened like *this*.

But Dakar has another card to play. "I suggest you come quickly," he informs Mother, his voice firm, a voice I once thought to trust. "It seems your son is struggling with critical concerns in Etania, and it would be best if you dealt with them straightaway."

A gentle, fatal threat.

Neither of us knows what ominous thing he's done with Reni, luring us into polite compliance, enough to compel us both onto his aeroplane. Besides, if we don't accept Dakar's offer, we'll only look suspicious, and Havis said we had to play innocent. He said it was the only way.

Standing on this runway, countless Resyan soldiers watching Dakar with seething anger, something in me shifts. I resented Mother for never intervening here, for letting her own brother build chaos. For staying away. But understanding crystallizes in this moment, as she stands before her greatest enemy. The realization that she may not be innocent—but she still *looks* innocent to the world, and no one can accuse her of a thing. To them, she's the beloved wife of a Northern king, a woman from a great noble family in Resya, and far more appealing than the ruthless General.

If she's going to defeat Dakar, she needs to keep it that way.

He the creature of war and she the star of peace.

As we climb into the large aeroplane, Athan's presence hovers somewhere in my vision, sitting in the far rear with Cyar and Trigg, but I refuse to look his way. I stay at my mother's side.

"What you did was wrong," I tell Dakar hotly. "You had no right to execute a king. No proof."

My words are bold, vicious, and I wait for the General's swift anger. I want to see it at last, the wickedness hiding behind this family—see it and know that I'm right. That nothing my mother has done could be worse than *him*.

But he doesn't rise to my provocation. He only tilts his head, listening closely as if I haven't just insulted him to his face. "But Rahian was guilty, Your Highness. I had all the proof I needed, from the one who would know."

I stare at him, not understanding.

"Jali Furswana," Mother explains quietly at my side. "She confessed Rahian's dealings with the Nahir revolt, and it was all true. Every document she offered."

I shut my eyes. Jali did it. She betrayed the king who rescued her, turned him over to men who have no respect for the titles they bear. Perhaps she thought she was saving herself. Little Teo. But in the end, all she's done is put another Southern royal in a grave.

She's a fool.

"You see," the General says to me, like we're at a tiny parley in the sky. "Rahian was guilty. He armed this Southern revolt in many places—planes, guns, shells. He kept this madness going for his own gain, to keep himself in power, but no longer. Anyone who dares aid the Nahir will think twice after our show of justice." His gaze holds mine. "There's nowhere to hide, Your Highness, not even behind a crown."

I feel cold. Not only from the chilly heights of the endless sky.

If he knows Mother's true connection to Seath, then he's waiting for the right time and place to reveal it, when it can do the most damage. And for some reason, I don't despise him for this. It only makes sense. It's what I would do, and now that I've breathed a fraction of the desperation that comes with hatred, felt that desire for *more*, I can't look at anyone the same. What did Dakar offer my mother long ago? What did she offer him?

I want to demand that of them both, but it's pointless. They'll never reveal the truth, and it's impossible to see any other version of this moment. I can imagine, and wonder, but this is all I have to work with—this fierce and lovely world with the choices already made, including my own. They wrote the past, but now I've written the present, with my pamphlets, and here we are.

This is what we have.

And so, I have to beat Dakar at his own game. He'll try to bring us down, by whatever means he's gathered, but I have my own, and I can ruin him first.

"What's happening in Madelan?" I ask calmly, not letting him see the dark resolve in me—nor my throbbing fear when I think of Tirza left behind with too many Safire boots prowling.

Dakar smiles. "Don't worry, Your Highness. My son, the Commander, is dealing with the problem there."

I feel, finally, as if I'm going to be sick.

46

I gather clues as we fly, listening to Evertal mutter with other officers. On this one night, revolts have surged across the South, from Madelan to Beraya to Havenspur and beyond. A concerted effort. A Nahir warning.

Directed right at my father.

Seath is damning us completely, proving to the world that we've kicked a hornet's nest of trouble by invading Resya. We've upset the frail balance of calm Landore has struggled to enforce for years. We've become the symbol of arrogance, the rallying cry for anger, just like those pamphlets vowed, and I have no idea what happens next.

Arrin's staying behind in Madelan to shove the city into order, and I'm well aware that won't be pretty. The guns will be burning hot today. Executions for any who dared join the insurrection—Nahir and Resyan alike. But that's the irony, isn't it? I'm not even sure we can tell the difference anymore. In one night, did half this kingdom become Nahir? Perhaps they weren't before. Perhaps they never imagined picking up a gun. But then the bombs fell and their sons and daughters were mutilated and, like magic, they became the danger in the shadows.

I understand their choice. I do. But when you make that kind of choice—as I've learned—there are inevitable consequences.

Five feet away, Ali and Sinora sit together, and Ali won't look at me. We're back to that game. The hours pass, an endless journey that feels like it has no end as they press together on their seats, Ali resting her head against Sinora's shoulder—pale in the grey light, dark hair a shield across her face. Eventually they both sleep, and I look on from some other world.

"What are you doing to her?" I ask.

Father doesn't need to clarify who I mean. "It's the end, at last. She knows it."

I don't let him see my heart flinch. I have no idea how he'll do it, but it seems possible finally—he's actually killed a king.

She'll be next.

"You might not be able to do this twice," I say, as if this logical fact might actually sway the man who just ordered a dozen bullets fired into Rahian's royal chest.

He glances back to where Sinora sleeps, unknowing of her fate. Or perhaps entirely knowing. "Oh no, Athan. It won't be me this time. It will be the Royal League—and I have her son to help me."

IX

BETRAYAL

47

Hathene, Etania

When Etania appears below the aeroplane, it looks different to me. The rolling mountains are leafless and dead, dusted with fresh snow, peaks stretching far—though not as far as I once imagined. No longer limitless and untouchable.

A mighty fortress that bombs can too easily turn to dust.

We made a brief stop in Madelan, where frantic servants brought our things from the palace, and for a breath, I was terrified someone might have searched my bags and found my pamphlets and photos. Mercifully, they were still there, evidence hidden away beneath silk blouses, unnoticed. As a few of the Safire officers disembarked, Trigg tried to smile at me on his way off the aeroplane. But even his strange humour couldn't lighten the moment. He knew it. I saw it in his eyes—a small, confused apology—and there was no time for any of us to witness the retribution being inflicted on Madelan by the Commander. I could only imagine the bloodshed.

People accused, lined up to be shot.

No rules, only vengeance.

And Tirza . . .

I close my eyes tightly. I refuse to think the worst.

As we land at our Etanian airfield, the frigid air shivers with apprehension, the haunted feeling that something has happened that cannot be undone. We walk the cold tarmac, lazy flakes drifting down, my mother marching for the palace without falter. She's wrapped in a wool jacket offered by Dakar, her long black hair catching flecks of white.

Betrayal.

It's on the servants' faces. In the courtiers' hurried pleasantries. Hathene Palace feels as stark and frozen as the mountains, guilty eyes occupied with marble floors. Dakar follows at a distance until Mother stops abruptly in the main hall. A warrior asking the battle to come to her. A mountain that cannot be passed. I stand behind her, my nausea growing, the realization that she expected this. Whatever has happened here with Reni, she knew it was waiting to happen.

She left for Resya anyway.

For me.

Reni appears at the top of the grand staircase, and his familiar face is a beacon of hope—a flare in the darkness, briefly rescuing. Then it's the exact opposite, a confirmation of treason as more Safire uniforms flank him, already here. Uncle Tanek as well.

"Do whatever you must to protect Etania."

"I will."

What the stars have I done?

"Mother," he says, so formally it insults the love between them. "Welcome home."

She glances over her shoulder at Dakar, then at the Safire uniforms up the stairs, standing at Reni's side in a show of alliance.

"Am I under arrest?" she asks bluntly.

"Not at all," Reni replies, still polite. "Let's speak together, shall we? It's not what you think, Mother. I promise we'll find the best resolution for all of us." He pauses. "As Father would want," he adds, softer.

"This is *nothing* your father would want," she hisses in Resyan.

Her words wound sufficiently, and Reni can only stare a moment. Uncle Tanek also looks stunned. I wonder who he really is. I always thought he was the enemy, sniffing out trouble, but perhaps he was only ever trying to protect us. Trying to keep Dakar away from our home, and Havis as well, impressing the danger of foreign interference on Reni at every turn.

My other uncle was the true trouble.

Dakar steps forward, his wicked voice remaining neutral. "Listen to your son, Majesty. We'll settle this in a civilized manner."

Mother laughs. It's loud in the echoing hall, a radiant defiance of the men before her, this false conversation, and everyone shifts uncomfortably, the maidservants watching in mute horror. The courtiers glance back and forth between their Prince, their Queen, and the uniformed General who just brutalized a kingdom and executed a king, and yet wishes to settle things in a "civilized" manner.

When Mother has recovered, she manages a smile that's equally defiant.

"Very well, General," she says. "Let's settle this once and for all."

My mother, I think. *A rifle in her hands.*

There's a long meeting after that—a respectable meeting, with the Royal Council to witness, yet it's all behind closed doors. Heathwyn whispers the full story to me, that Reni has uncovered proof of Mother's desire to hold his crown until her death. She wanted to keep it from him, to stay in power, and even Heathwyn shakes her head at this, like my mother's to be pitied for even considering it. But neither she nor anyone else knows the reason why.

Mother's sole protection, as Havis told me long ago.

It's flimsy armour, yet all she has. I see that now. As a Northern queen, there's little Dakar or Seath can do to exact their revenge, not while she wears it. Before the Royal League, she's greater and more formidable than the General—and if he was found guilty of hurting her it would only make things worse for his still-fragile grasp at power. And she's certainly more useful to Seath like this. A royal who could be threatened into helping like Rahian was, not just a traitorous sister to be punished.

In my room, I change out of my oil-stained dress, fabric crumpled from our desperate flight from Madelan, and Heathwyn offers me a stack of envelopes. "These are for you," she says hesitantly.

They're written with familiar, messy words, the kind that once made my heart swell with joy. I take them reluctantly, read them swiftly. So many words, so many fears, and at the end of it all, the truth. Athan did try to tell me. He tried to tell me right about the time he thought he might die.

I can't decide if I despise him or long for him.

My own traitorous heart.

As soon as there's opportunity, I hurl myself at Reni in his private wing. It's a righteous rage, and I'm calling him *fasiri*, over and over again, until I realize he has no clue what this means, a Resyan insult lost to his ears.

He holds me back from him, alarmed. "Ali, you need to let me explain."

"Explain? There's nothing to *explain*," I bite back. "You're ruining her. You're ruining her for your own gain!"

I'm spitting all of these things at him, because even if he doesn't know the truth—the General, Mother, Seath—he must at least see this.

But Reni appears pitying, the way Heathwyn looked earlier about Mother. It only infuriates me more. "Things are not what they seem," he tells me carefully. "You don't know what I know."

"And you don't know what *I* know."

"Don't I?"

His question stops me, his expression grim, hardly victorious. "Tell me, Ali. What you found in Resya, would it destroy everything? Would it damn each one of us—Mother, myself, even *you*?"

I have no answer.

It would.

"I've seen the world she left behind," I say hotly. "So many horrors, and not once has she spoken up. She was trying to protect us, to keep us innocent of her past, but I'm going to—"

"I know what you want, Ali," he interrupts, "and you're mad if you think I'm going to let our family burn for that. If we tell the truth, if we stand before the world and try to defend the Southern cause, it will be the end of our line. Mother's past would imprison her for life and steal my right to rule. Yours, too." He steps closer. "You want to throw our entire kingdom away for people who don't even know your name? Who will never care that you sacrificed *everything* for a chance—a very small, frail chance at that—of defending them? You can't change what's happened, Ali. You can't undo the past and bring back the dead. Whatever happened there with Mother and her family—it happened, it's done, and I swear to you I won't take the fall for her decisions."

I stare at him. He knows enough of her history, and he's not going to do a damn thing about it. Forget Mother and Dakar and the past. We are the new generation, the ones who have the chance to do things differently. And yet my brother's simply going to take his throne. He's going to defend his right to it and never mind anything else.

A gulf that separates us.

"I promised you I'd protect Etania and Mother," he continues, gentler, "and that's what I'm doing. Uncle Tanek said I have to let her go to the League. It's the only way she can defeat Dakar once and for all, before the entire world. Then it will be over."

I rub my hands across my face. I can't look at him. Traitors everywhere, it seems. Traitors I love so deeply that it hurts when I breathe.

"What are you planning?" Reni presses, uncertainty in his tone now.

"Oh, don't worry," I reply shortly. "Nothing that will reflect badly on *you*."

My viciousness works. His wounded gaze is confused, but I don't care. He's let Uncle Tanek talk him into this charade and I don't know what end they're envisioning. Perhaps Mother really can defeat Dakar at the League. Expose him for what he truly is, at last. She knows his secrets. But it's a selfish risk. And a dangerous one.

Reni's quest for his damn crown has fogged up all his good sense.

Frustrated, I march away from his imploring words, headed for the entranceway that leads to the eastern gardens, the mountains beyond that I need suddenly like air.

My hand is on the door when a Safire officer calls out, "No one's to leave the palace, Your Highness!"

He doesn't smile, his command frigid, and it adds evermore fury to the storm of my heart. He picked the wrong day to treat me like this, the wrong day to be in that rotten uniform.

I push the door open.

I see him reach for the weapon at his side, but I keep going, wondering if he'll actually shoot me and upend this whole madness, spark something larger.

Perhaps it might be worth it.

But no gun fires, and I continue through the gardens, shivering in my dress, past the bed of dead flowers, taking the path that leads to the stables. My cheeks and arms sting with the nipping breeze, and behind me, boots crunch through snow, rapidly gaining on my stride. I don't have to look to know who will be there. The one who certainly ordered the soldier to stand down.

Is there anywhere Athan won't follow me?

When I finally turn to face him, we're deep in the skeletal forest, only brown branches and a scattering of snow. He's still wearing the uniform from the reception, every bit the General's son. In a cap, no less. That damn fox sneaking through swords. He looks older, but perhaps he looked this way before, too, and I only see it now in light of the truth. I see Dakar in the angle of his nose. In his strong chin and grey eyes. In that smile he's always given me—slightly crooked, somehow calming.

A Dakar smile.

White peppers his grey uniform, his skin sun-golden in this colourless world. "Ali."

That's all he says, and I find an equal silence in myself. There's so much to share, and yet I don't even know where to begin. We've seen each other's nakedness, and surely there should be an intimacy between us now, an inherent familiarity. But in the winter woods, fully clothed, it's only an awkwardness left behind. The feeling of something unfinished.

I knew him.

I also didn't know him.

He strikes the first move anyway. With a few steps, he's before me, removing his cap, his rebellious hair falling free to brush his forehead, and he's a boy again, not an officer. Not Dakar's son. It happens so quickly, the transformation. Now I see only his eyes, the same ones that teased me as we hiked up our mountain, that adore entirely.

His coat is next, round my shoulders before I can protest.

Safire wool I don't want to wear.

"You're cold," he states, drawing me nearer.

I'm freezing. I wandered out into winter half-dressed, but there's also an entire sun bursting inside of me, and when he pulls me towards his warmth, his mouth finding mine, I surrender, wanting to see what will happen.

I kiss him as he is.

The General's youngest son.

My friend.

My enemy.

It tastes the same. Warm, gently hungry, his hands in my hair. That steady rising desire, all of me expanding at his touch. Wanting, wanting . . .

I pull away abruptly.

"No."

I sound hollow and sad even to myself, and his disappointment is a mirror.

His confusion, as well.

"Who is my uncle?" I ask him.

At least if he knows about Seath, I don't have to hide any longer. He'll know who I am. What I have to do next. It might even make sense to him.

But his confusion only deepens. "What?"

"Who is my uncle?" I repeat.

He stares at me, then shrugs towards the palace, towards Uncle Tanek, and I want to laugh at the whole calamity of us. He doesn't know—and I can't tell him. I can't admit who my uncle is aloud, not with his family about to take mine before the world, angling to expose our dark history once and for all. I can't admit that I hate his father for marching into the South no better than any Northern king, and his brother for the countless war crimes. That I helped rouse a revolt in Resya, killing so many in Safire uniform, and I'm not even fully ashamed of it. In fact, it felt right, watching those tanks burst to flame, and now I'm going to maneuver quicker than them, bring down his whole family before the Royal League. I'm going to ruin the Dakar name forever and save my mother.

So, where does that leave us?

Where does that leave me?

I'd love nothing more than to kiss him and kiss him and say nothing. To pretend I don't have these secrets inside of me. But that isn't fair to him, the same way it was never fair to me, and I see now how hard it is.

How easy, too.

His eyes plead with me to believe. "I didn't want to love you, Ali, but here I am." His warm hands cup my numb face. "What can I do? Tell me what to do, and I'll do it. Anything."

He needs some kind of answer. He deserves that at least, so I give him the one that has always been true, the one my mother understood months ago. "Take off your uniform," I reply softly, "and never wear it again."

I feel the wrongness of it as I say it.

You must stop being you is what I've asked.

But how else could I ever believe a Dakar? How else could I believe his love for me is greater than any loyalty to his family? I'm demanding of him the same thing that I now despise Reni for. I'm asking Athan to choose himself over them, and my command hangs in the air. I see his thoughts shifting in little loops, like a plane in the sky. He's considering it. He's truly considering it.

"I know you're not like them," I continue. "I know why you lied to me, and while I'm not sure I'll ever forget how much that hurts, the truth is, I don't hate you. I don't. You were right when you said there's too much about you I don't know, and that's the trouble. I can't . . ."

I trail off, unsure how to explain this expanse inside me. I preferred Athan when he was only a boy who flew an aeroplane. I thought I loved him, but perhaps I only loved the idea of him. Now he's too much, too complicated. And I don't know how to grapple with all of his pieces, the broken ones, the dangerous ones. How do you undo something that's been ruined since the beginning? How do you start over and make something better from that?

I don't know.

I hate this, but I don't hate him.

My limbs begin to shake, the cold as deep as my bones. As deep as my spirit. "My mother isn't innocent," I say honestly, "and no matter how we try, I'm simply not good for you. We're in opposite skies, you just don't see it now."

"You're not her," he insists.

"And you're not *him*. But we're still ourselves."

He reaches for me again. "I can be good for you. I don't care about any of this. Only you."

"You don't know me," I whisper, stepping away.

You don't know what I want from this world.

You don't know what I'm willing to do for it.

I hand his coat back, then turn away.

"Please, Ali. You're the only one who knows my heart!"

I believe him.

I do.

But he can't see my tears, and I keep walking for the palace.

48

Snow hovers like fog beneath the moon, Hathene Palace a graveyard as I walk the halls, a palace with no heartbeat, everyone hidden behind closed doors. Father's plane is being fueled on the tarmac for the long journey to the Royal League. Somewhere, a queen is preparing to face her fate. But I try to remember the way this place looked last summer, with the colour and light and laughter, how it felt like a home—a home Ali wanted to share with me. Something that held love.

It's too cold now. And she doesn't want me anymore.

"I won't bury you in hatred yet, Athan Dakar."

Sinora's voice follows me. It haunts my restless steps, firm, beckoning, and perhaps she planned it like this. Father said she was the master of confusion, that she could make an entire army wonder who was the enemy. She's done a damn good job with me, because even though I don't trust her, I still want to see her again. She told me lies, but she also told me the truth. And now she's like the end of a battle. She's like the end of a battle when my plane's shot to pieces and the runway appears at last. I never feel very victorious in that moment. I never feel like I've done a great thing. But I know I have to land and finish this thing. I have to feel the earth again.

The bump and jolt of reality.

"You don't have to live as a ghost."

I don't want to be one. I realized that somewhere over Resya, watching the world go up in flame. I realized that while kissing Ali and discovering that I was still precious to her—worth wanting, worth loving. It's new to me, a goal within reach, but Sinora saw it long before I ever did, last summer.

And maybe I don't want her to die anymore, either. It used to feel like justice, a target for my anger at Mother's death, but now it feels wrong. It simply feels wrong, like a thorn lodged in my ribs, reminding me with every step how wearying and pointless this unending rivalry is. All of this will destroy Ali and break her heart forever. It will ruin them. Ruin us.

My runway tonight is Sinora.

Because if I don't see her before we depart for the League, I'll go mad with her voice in my head, hearing it every day for the rest of my life.

But someone else finds me first.

"Lieutenant."

It's not the voice I want to hear, but I turn anyway. The Prince is graceful as he strides behind me in the shadowed hall. I expect a battle. The last time I saw him, a coup was being thwarted, a forest burning, and I have the sudden acute awareness that he would kill me here and now if he knew what Ali and I did in Resya. But he doesn't look leery of me, or even angry. He wears that calm, regal mask that feels indulgent of every muddy thing outside his royal sphere.

He doesn't speak, so I begin.

"Why?"

It's the only question that comes, the only one that matters now.

"Isn't it obvious?" he asks in return. "I'm on your side in this. You Safire have done an impressive thing. You secured a kingdom festering with corruption. I can admire that. And now, your father will help me secure the crown I deserve. The one that's rightfully mine."

"By betraying your own *mother*," I say, hoping all of the servants and footmen hear it, if they're eavesdropping. "And for what? A bit of gold on your head?"

He looks startled. "A bit of gold?" he intones.

And there it is. The eternal divide between our worlds. His expression changes, as if sensing my silent disgust. "Listen, Lieutenant. Do I admire the Safire? Yes. For a moment, I do. But you will never understand what a crown is. You will burn hot and bright for a day, but once that paper burns up, the fire will go back to its steady, constant flame. And gold melted is always gold. My right to rule was ordained by God himself. I've always had this crown. It was always mine."

He doesn't smile as he says this. There's no gleam of pleasure in his eye. It's simply his truth, unrolled before me with the steady certainty that he's absolutely right.

"And that's worth doing this?" I ask bitterly.

"You think I'm callous, Lieutenant, but I'm not overthrowing her, nor executing her. I'm simply using politics to remove her from the position she's too stubborn to surrender on her own. She's worn this crown for thirteen years and she's exhausted. This burden needn't be hers any longer."

This Prince is more vain and blind than I thought. He thinks he's going to depose his mother for the sake of family honour, but deposed to him means taking the crown from her peacefully, through political means.

Deposed to my father means something else entirely—a noose.

"Then you're doing her a favour," I say, unable to hide my sarcasm. "And will Ali appreciate it?"

Now I've touched a bruise of anger. His gaze flickers unkindly. "My sister will go along with whatever I say to go along with."

"Do you even know her?"

He narrows his eyes, and I've gone too far, but I don't stop. "I heard you're not even going to the League. You're letting your own mother wander into the wolf's den alone."

"I have to stay here," he replies defensively. "The real wolves wear Safire uniforms, and I won't leave an empty throne in Etania for their ambitious claws. Not after what happened in Resya."

He folds his arms, and for some reason, this admission makes me fear him a bit. He's part of the game now. Using my father to get what he needs, even knowing my father has an agenda of his own.

But this is not a match he can win.

He thinks this move will give him everything, but I can see the end he can't possibly envision—Sinora dead, Ali despising him forever. Left with a crown and a kingdom and nothing else.

There's only one right thing to do, and I take my chance, lowering my voice. "Don't do this, Prince. Don't trust my father. You'll regret it."

He stares at me.

"Renege now on whatever deal you've made, and let your mother keep the damn throne," I press. "Tell him you don't need his help and that you'll go to the League if he continues to cause your family trouble."

It's the only way they'll win. My father can't compete against royalty, against the entire League, not when Captain Merlant warned me we're on thin ice already. The Prince stiffens, ready to fight back. Then he seems to realize that I've just disparaged my own father, which I have no reason to do. It gains me nothing.

He looks at me a long moment, as if struggling to treat me like someone worthy of genuine conversation. "I had a vision," he explains, more hesitant now. "I know you Safire don't put stock in these things. You trust only in yourself. But I believe it's important to listen to divine signs, and I'm trying to do what's best."

I realize he's being honest. As honest as he can be with me.

"My father had a vision once," he continues, "of his own

death. He described it exactly as it happened, and I was there. I watched him the night he was poisoned, suffocating on his own bed. At the time, I didn't understand it was poison, but I begged God to kill him. To end the suffering. I prayed that prayer, and I won't wish the same for my mother if she falls into a similar trap." He straightens, as if embarrassed by his own vulnerability. His deeply human fear. "I'm going to listen to this revelation, Lieutenant, and I'm going to do what's best."

"And if your vision isn't right?" I ask.

"It will be," he replies. His voice is certain.

I'd like a vision too, I want to say. *Something clear and unmistakable to tell me what to do.*

But I don't have that. I only have this breath of a nudge inside my soul, and whatever he has . . . well, there's a rotten thing at the core of this royal world, and I want to be away from it—so far away it won't haunt me any longer. I want something else.

Gold of a different kind.

"Remember that I warned you," I say at last. "I tried."

"I will," he replies. Aversion weights his gaze again. "And you remember to stay away from my family—*all* of them—or your life will be forfeit in whatever comes tomorrow."

On that dramatic note, he leaves.

With no choice, I obey.

Outside, everyone in Safire uniform stamps their boots against the snowy, lamplit tarmac to stay warm, ready for our midnight trip eastwards. I stand with my father, waiting for Sinora to arrive for her final journey. I'm half listening to him, half thinking about Ali's lips, her hair, imagining us in a little wood hut on some evergreen mountainside. No uniforms, no crowns. Only a future that's clear and wide and holds love.

An endless sky.

Escape.

"Take off your uniform and never wear it again."

"Victory's very near," Father reveals to me quietly, his cigarette burning orange in the darkness. "Sinora will face her treachery at last."

I don't know why he's sharing this with me. I guess because Arrin isn't here, and I'm all he has, so I nod, like the good son I am now, the newly minted captain—not the star traitor—and listen to the larger plan at hand. Kalt has gone with our western fleet to lay siege to Hady, the port city which the Nahir captured last spring. Father gave Seath that city as a gift for his cooperation. A Free Thurn. But no longer.

I remember the way the Resyan coast lit up like fireworks beneath our battleship guns.

I remember Hady, a civilian city of men, women, children, life.

My stomach aches.

This is why I have to leave.

"They said we couldn't change the past," Father continues, "but we've done it. We've written our own legend."

"We're in opposite skies," Ali said. *"You just don't see it now."*

What can't I see? I try to search through every memory and find the secret she's hiding, but there's nothing there, only her smile, her joy in the world.

The Prince was right.

We all have visions, and I'm going to follow mine.

"Are you ready?" Father rests a hand on my shoulder. "I need you for this."

I look up at him, our airplane engines being tested nearby, snarling, and I know what he's going to ask of me, what he wants me to do before that Royal League in Elsandra.

"Yes," I say.

But I'll be gone.

I won't let him use me again.

49

Like Rahian in Madelan, Mother is now confined to her quarters, ordered to prepare quickly for her trip to the League, and I glare at the soldiers posted there—Etanian men, professing their loyalty to my brother by imprisoning the soon-to-be-deposed Queen. They allow me inside with a sheepish look.

Choices.

We're all making choices, from the smallest to the greatest. Helping to shift entire worlds. And tonight, there's only one person who might understand me—only one who knows what it means to want someone with you and away from you at once. To know that no matter how terrible they are, no matter how dark, they're still a piece of yourself, a mirror of your own soul.

I find Mother seated at her vanity, staring at the gold wedding ring on her finger. At once, I sense the endless grief we share, permeating this fractured home. She's scarcely packed a thing. Her traveling trunk remains open, its emptiness exposed. Eventually she says, "Do you want the truth? I should tell you before it's too late."

Too late?

That frightens me, because the last person to say this to me—to imply there would be no chance for a fair trial, for history to be written properly—was Rahian.

And in the end, his prediction came true.

But before I can ask I see the portrait on her vanity—the blonde woman.

Sapphie elski'han.

Athan's mother.

"I was in Masrah when that kingdom fell," she begins in Resyan, "when my brother helped topple that once-proud monarchy. It was his greatest victory, and I saw it all. I saw more than I ever wished to see, and that was the day I knew revolution could not come like this. Not like he wanted. I saw those two little girls escape the palace, those two princesses who had everything in life I'd been denied. I let them go. Because even they didn't deserve what happened that day. No one does. Certainly not children."

I sink onto the seat beside her.

She saw Callia and Jali escape?

She let them go.

The strands are too tangled, stories from every corner, crisscrossing in an intricate web, but she's not finished. "I've watched my brother lay a field full of mines for our enemies, but somehow, they never get the right boots. They get everyone else. The young. The old. The ones we never meant to kill." She turns, facing me at last. "And that's what you have to live with for the rest of your life, Aurelia. That is revolution. War. A deadly field that steals the innocent right along with the guilty, and those mines . . ." A tear falls, tracing her cheek. "No, I chose a rifle. My bullet only went exactly where it was meant to go. Every time."

Any lingering bitterness in me retreats. I've never seen her like this, never known her fully. But suddenly, with that one admission, I know her heart is wide and deep even in the face of darkness, that she took her hatred and tried to do right.

"I've never forgotten them," she whispers. "My brother, he burns for a cause I'll never surrender. It began the day our home was stolen, our father imprisoned for trying to feed his family. Seath had to care for us younger ones, shepherding us from camp to camp, working whatever job he could find. Somehow, he always made tomorrow seem like a better place. I worshipped him once. I thought he could do no wrong." Her voice catches. "And always, I have longed to show you and Reni both sides of this story, but you refused to see. You were suspicious of anything that came from my old world. And that's how it is. You can shout the truth until your voice is hoarse, but rarely will another soul listen until it strikes close to them."

She's right. She's always spoken of the necessary revolution in the South, but we refused to listen, to go deeper into her secret wounds. Perhaps she could have shared more. Or perhaps she did, and I was too blind to see it.

My eyes fall on the photograph.

"Did you love Dakar?" I ask, the question unexpected, unnerving.

I suddenly need her to deny it.

"Never," she replies. "Not in the way you think."

A shaky breath escapes my chest. I've learned to handle many things, but that might have been too much. "But you were friends?"

"Comrades. I knew his secrets, and he knew mine." She flexes her fingers, studying the wedding band again. "But he will kill me for what I did, my star. Even if he doesn't execute me, he won't stop until he hears what he wants from my lips, and I won't give him that. I'll keep you and Reni safe. Whatever I do, I do for you."

"Then why are you stealing Reni's crown?"

My question is stark, and she looks at me, her eyes regretful. "It was your father's idea. He wrote a decree to make it so, to allow me to reign to my death, and only Lord Marcin knew of it. But Marcin is dead, the sole witness. Now they'll simply say it was a declaration forged in my hand." She pauses, emotion suffusing her voice. Possibly grief, possibly rage. "Your father wanted to protect me, but the reality is, I'll die with or without the crown. It doesn't matter."

Someone knocks on the door. "Your Majesty," a muffled voice says. "It's time to depart."

We ignore the order. I put my hand on hers, longing to see her as the young woman in the photographs—fierce, unyielding, radiant. Sorrow made into courage. "Dakar knows who your brother is," I state, a fact that must be coming to haunt her. Soon.

As soon as she walks out that door and goes with Dakar.

"Yes, but he has no proof," she replies swiftly. "We burned the surviving records long ago, everything else lost in our displacement. Nothing to say who Seath is to me. It's Dakar's word against mine, and I am a queen. Who would believe him? No, that's not what he will use to bring me down. He wants me to confess another crime on my own. But do you know the best way to keep a proud man in a state of defeat?" I shake my head, and she leans closer. "It's to hold the thing he wants most—his own longed-for legend, his pride—just out of reach. That is what I will keep from him, to the end. And you will be a princess forever."

But what if I don't want to be a princess forever? Not if it means inheriting all of this.

"I'm going to protect you," I promise her. "I have a way."

She smiles, sadly. "Your brother has your father's heart, but you . . . I've always known that you have mine, and you must swear to me that no matter what happens at the League, you will always watch out for Renisala and keep his eyes open. He was meant to rule Etania—and he will."

"And me?" I ask. "Am I not meant to rule?"

In her silence is the answer I've always sought. The answer that's danced round the edge of conversations, in her resolve to marry me to Havis and send me to Resya even when everyone else claimed it was preposterous.

No.

She's never wanted a crown for me. She's always wanted

more—for me to see the South, to find the things she could never say, the things Reni will never understand.

She wanted me to learn her secrets.

She wanted me to know her true home.

Somewhere, beneath my bitterness and hurt, my love stirs fearfully for her again, because it's like looking at the horizon. I'm afraid of her, but I also want to follow. She's watched this sky change a thousand times, lived a story I only know the edges of, and she's still here. Entrusting her unwritten history to my hands.

I have to hold it forever.

"I want to go home," she says. "I want to see it again. I want to visit their graves and remind myself that it still exists. I can hear them calling to me. My father and mother. My sister. I hear them, and they want me to come, but I can't." She looks at me, fervent. "I won't. Not until I know you're safe."

Someone knocks on the door again, louder.

More insistent.

I stand and begin gathering gowns for her. "I'm going with you to the trial, Mother. I won't stay here."

"And if they imprison me?"

"I'll wait."

"My star, it could be years."

"Then I'll wait years!" I stop packing and turn to her, defying the tears in my eyes. "I'll wait as long as you need me."

Her gaze warms, and she doesn't protest. Perhaps she wants to keep me here with Reni, but knows better. She knows I won't obey. Or perhaps she's more frightened of all of this than she pretends, more alone than anyone can know.

"Then at least do one last thing for me," she says softly.

She has me bury a box of photographs and letters. Even her wedding band. She refuses to burn these remnants, perhaps unwilling to let her past—her old world—go to ash, but it can't stay here. It can't be found. Too much evidence, like the photograph album tucked in my bag. As she finally surrenders to Dakar's demanding men, escorted to the tarmac and aeroplane, I sneak her secrets out through the midnight doors, through the kitchens, and then lower them into the ground behind the stable, covered with earth.

Then I gather the weapons in my possession—Lark's photographs of the children shot in Beraya, my photographs of countless Safire crimes in Resya and beyond. I'll bring my battle—and Tirza's—to the Royal League as I vowed, and I won't let Dakar make the first move.

It will be me.

X

ESCAPE

50

⅗ AURELIA ⅗

Glorihall, Elsandra
Home of the Royal League

We arrive in Elsandra under cover of darkness. It's not yet dawn when the General's aeroplane touches down, a smattering of lights flashing past us in a sea of black, and I'm certain Dakar did this on purpose. I'm beginning to imagine the way the wheels of his deceptive mind work, the honourable image he must always broadcast before the world. It's the lie I believed for too long, that he was different from the Commander, that he was something new and admirable. The rising eastern sun.

But it was only a sharp glare, hiding shadows.

Now, he brings my mother to the Royal League at an empty hour when she can be whisked away—no cameras flashing or crowds to witness her arrival.

She's calm, a silent island of courage, but the first wrinkle of fear comes when we're asked to remain on the aeroplane while Dakar speaks with a handful of uniformed men gathered on the tarmac. It's a hushed moment, slithering with suspicion, and at last Mother's gaze shifts with concern.

When Dakar comes back inside, he wears a grave expression. "Your Majesty, I'm afraid the charges have changed. It seems you're not only to be tried for withholding your son's inheritance. Tomorrow, you're to be held to account for the murder of your husband."

It's a strange moment, because I'm not truly surprised. I

knew this was coming, somehow, and it's like being thrown into the frigid waters, falling forever towards the swells, knowing they're waiting to consume you whole, and that inevitability frightens me most.

It was always there.

"Then this will be quite a trial," Mother replies coldly, "since I am innocent."

With that, we're swept from the aeroplane and onto the runway, hidden by a herd of Safire uniforms.

51

ᴣ ATHAN ᴤ

Glorihall is freezing, even at high noon.

It's the frosted inverse of the kingdom we just conquered, chilled mist hanging across the city, brittle wind stabbing through my wool coat as I run the icy streets, gathering the pieces of our escape. Clothes, food, anything we'll need to get away. The train tickets alone are a small fortune, and my meagre pay is spent clean. I wish I could bring a plane, but I'd never afford the fuel, and it hits me then that I'm going to lose the sky. No more flying.

I tell myself it's worth it.

I can live without wings. I'll have her.

It still hurts somewhere deep.

The Royal League is a pristine building of white walls and grand chambers, nearly a palace itself, and in the small League apartment I'm sharing with Cyar, I write my letter to Ali. The pen shakes a bit with nerves and exhilaration, like taking off for a sortie. Adrenaline mixed with hysterical fear of the unknown.

"I know you shouldn't ever forgive me. I understand that. So what can I give you to prove I never wanted any of this? That I only want you? This is what I can give you, Ali. I'm giving up my name. For you. I'm leaving today and I'll never look back, as you asked. I'll never wear this uniform again. I'll forget the past, whatever they've done, whatever darkness I've inherited, and I'll think only of you—my future. Bright and perfect as dawn."

I say all of the things that have lived inside my head for too long. Perhaps they've been inside me my whole existence, a dream wanting to be known, struggling for breath, and I held it down. I ignored it and justified it and found a way to hide.

I won't anymore.

But first, I have to explain it to the one person who deserved to know all along. He walks in as I'm folding the letter, a bag open beside me, and I don't mince words. There's no point.

"I'm leaving," I tell Cyar.

It feels right saying it out loud, and I can see him trying to figure out if I mean going out for the day or the night or something more profound than that. "Leaving," he repeats.

"Tomorrow . . . for good. This isn't me. It never has been. All those years at the Academy, I wanted to fail." My confession feels clumsy, a lifetime of half truths tripping me up. He deserves this said to his face. But it's hard. "I mean, I didn't want to leave *you*, of course. But I've tried to be this person that he wants, and it's not me. It just isn't. So I'm leaving, with Ali."

This feels like the greatest and most terrible moment of my life, admitting this to Cyar. And the way he's looking at me now, I'm seeing another confession. An unexpected one.

"You think I didn't know that?" he asks.

I realize I did.

"Come on, Athan. Yes, you suddenly had a lot more reason to try last spring, but even that couldn't have changed your landings from shit-shows to perfection."

I don't know what to say. I always assumed he saw Top Flight the way the rest of them did. That Mother's death finally got my head on straight, got me to focus at last. Now I'm humbled by the truth. When we made Top Flight, he knew I'd been lying to him, that I'd been playing a game. And he never mentioned it once. He let me have that "secret" and followed me onwards anyway.

He's always believed in my best.

With a sigh, he sits down on his bed. "Where will the two of you go? Valon?"

"Hell no," I reply. "We're going as far from my family as we can get. Somewhere with mountains, I hope. And you should leave too. Not right away, but before anything else happens." I gesture at his uniform. "You don't belong here any more than I do."

His nose wrinkles in a familiar way. "Leave? *Me?*"

"Yes."

He has to come. I need someone who can look at me exactly like this, remind me when I'm being stupid, laugh with me, tell me I can be better. I need him. And he needs me. Because after seven years, the fact is we've hardly spent more than a handful of days not sharing the same room, the same fears, the same hope.

"Good God, Athan. They'd shoot me!"

I shake my head. "They wouldn't."

I can tell he doesn't believe me, but he doesn't understand— Father's never shot someone for desertion. To Father, they never deserved to be there to begin with. They're a weak link.

Like me.

I hold out the letter to him. "You have to make sure she gets this. No one else. I need—"

We both freeze as the door nudges open. Leannya stands there and I debate hiding the letter, but her narrowed eyes are already on us. She clears her throat in a sarcastic attempt at delayed protocol.

"There she is," I say lamely. "The hero of Irspen!"

She glares at me, as if it's my fault she was left behind to miss out on all the fun of war. "I'd have saved everyone a lot faster if I hadn't had to *bribe* Admiral Malek into letting me ride over on a damn destroyer." Her gaze darts to the letter. "What are you doing?"

"Nothing."

"Is that for your girlfriend?"

"Kalt," I say, the only name that comes to mind.

She's still suspicious as I fold the paper, away from her hawk eyes. But then she holds out her own letter. "It's from Katalin."

I make a face.

"Athan, you didn't write her once while you were away, so she just sent it to me instead."

"I was concussed!"

"Yet still flying planes?" She raises a brow. "Read this. It's important."

I look at her standing stubbornly in the doorway, her fair skin tanned, blonde hair hauled backwards, strands breaking free. She's an annoyed, scattered mess, and so much like Arrin it hurts. I'm going to leave her like this.

I'm going to leave.

I blink away the sting in my eyes. "Fine."

"She's smarter than you think," Leannya insists. "And actually a bit funny at times."

I take the letter and shove it into my bag, not feeling any overwhelming desire to read the words of the girl I don't love. I'd rather look at my sister and memorize every detail of her anger, to remind myself that I'm not leaving her here helpless. I'm leaving behind a little weapon, one that Arrin's spent years sharpening into his own image. The one he sat with on long-ago holidays at the beach, teaching her tank maneuvers with sea shells.

"You can forget sending that letter to Kalt," Leannya adds. "He's on his way back for the trial. We're all going to watch that bitch finally brought down."

It's Arrin, again. The casual way she speaks of death. The acerbic hint of a smile. It makes me feel desperate. "You don't always have to do what he wants," I say, struggling with these last words I'll say to her. "You have nothing to prove."

She frowns, clearly confused by the barrel roll in my thoughts. But she keeps up. She always does. "I don't do anything for him, Athan. I do it for *us*." Her voice is offended, like I've implied treason. "I won't watch all three of you die while I do nothing."

The buried pain in her voice scrapes at my heart. "No one's going to die, Leannya. It's not going to last that long."

Her eyes flicker again to my letter for Ali.

"No," she says. "I think it's only beginning."

Then she turns on her heel, disappearing back out the door, and that's going to be my last image of my sister—her furious and thinking everyone's already dead. The sister I swore I'd never abandon, no matter what.

I rub my head.

I need those painkillers right about now.

52

There's a knock at our doors late in the evening. A mostly untouched dinner sits on the carved oak table, and Mother stirs slightly in our bed. The "imperial suite" of the League is a lavish room of silk and satin, no bars on the windows, only luxe curtains and a view of the vast, frozen city drifting in snow.

It's my mother's gilded prison. A holding cell fit for a queen.

Closing the door to the antechamber, I tiptoe across the parlour, a tingle of fear trailing my skin. I'm certain I'll find Dakar there. It makes no sense, but suddenly he's a phantom ready to grab me and put me on the stand—force me to say the truth before the whole League, that my mother is Seath's own sister and guilty of murder.

My heart is in my throat as I open the door.

But it's Cyar. His familiar face is slightly embarrassed, and I'm so relieved, I fling my arms round him. He holds me. I'm sure the guards are perplexed by the sight of the Princess of Etania embracing a nameless Safire officer, but I welcome Cyar inside. He apologizes profusely, though his apology has no clear context. For everything, it seems, though none of this is his fault.

"Here," he says at last, holding out an envelope. "It's important."

It isn't difficult to imagine who it's from, but I don't take it. Instead, I sink onto the sofa that faces the window, waving Cyar to join me. He hesitates, but eventually surrenders and settles beside me. "I know you're upset," he begins after a moment, his Landori words spoken with their familiar, pronounced lilt. "And you have every right. You can be angry, Ali. But he does care about you. I promise you that."

I shut my eyes.

I can't be swayed, not even by Cyar, but he shifts beside me earnestly. "I'm not asking you to forgive him," he tries. "I'm only asking that you hear what I have to say. I have one brother in this world, and that's him. We've known each other since we were eleven. We've been together day in and day out ever since, and he doesn't always make good choices, I know. He can miss other people entirely. I say that as someone who's been there."

I open my eyes and look into Cyar's face. Still gentle, a bit hurt.

He means it.

"I told him not to do this"—he gestures at me—"but he didn't listen. And I'm telling you—I know when he's being honest and when he's lying. It isn't easy being in his position, in that family I mean. But he does care for you. I wouldn't lie about that. I have no reason to."

That lures a smile, since I can't imagine Cyar Hajari ever speaking a dishonest word in his life. But he's telling me this as if it's a sacred vow before God and heaven, a solemn profession that insists I listen and trust.

"I won't tell you what to do next," he finishes, "but I believe Athan's meant to be the best of his family, the one who can turn it around. I really do. He could do great things for Savient. For all of us. Please understand that one thing, if nothing else. I had to tell you before you read this letter."

I reach for his hand. "I believe you. I'll always believe you."

Relief smooths his features, his strained brow, and we sit like that for a few more moments, facing the night horizon of Glorihall. I wear our togetherness like a blanket, a soft thing that has no rhyme or reason, two people from faraway worlds, but we have something in common, and it's good.

There is hope.

When I glance at the day's newspaper on the table nearby, it rouses some other flicker of reassurance. My mother's story has made the front page, the high drama of a royal accused of murder, of stealing her son's inheritance, but on the third page, hidden away, is an entire spread dedicated to the siege of Hady and the quelling of violence in the South, battleship guns coughing smoke, the shore and city obliterated in the murky distance. And they're all Safire. Capturing a place that belongs to Landore.

It should be the grand story on the front page.

It's not.

My mother's trial is a welcome distraction. Gawain doesn't want his people to focus on his loss of control, the wave of fresh revolts in the South, Savient reclaiming his own territory for him. And Dakar certainly doesn't want anyone to question the sheer gall he's exposed in making this siege, by his own order. Without the Landorians.

It means something. And if Havis were here, he'd say there's an opportunity—both nations poised to potentially lose something irretrievable.

And I have a letter from a boy on the other side.

We have a chance.

Together.

I finally take the envelope from Cyar, ready to face it.

"I'll leave you alone," he offers quickly.

"Thank you," I say, and I mean it.

We stand and I kiss him on the cheek, this person who has kept Athan alive. I'm still grateful for that—eternally grateful. Then he's gone, and I stare at the envelope, willing myself to open it, to confront the truth. I do it very carefully, like I'm holding a living heart. The paper slides out.

"Dear Ali, I know you shouldn't ever forgive me. I understand that."

I can't help it—I smile. These are the neatest words he's ever written me, still half-scrawled, but more precise, like he was really trying for once. I want to want this.

I want to feel hope again, because anger is too hard.

Too exhausting.

"But we are not our parents, and we can do better. I have some-thing to give you, to prove I never wanted any of this, that I only want you."

I keep reading, my smile fading. I read the words over and over, until they've become a blur, caught in tears, and I sink onto the couch again. These little words have the power to up-root my whole world, to undo everything. Part of me wants to say yes. I believe Athan's words, the desperate offer written here. Perhaps in his trapped loyalties it makes sense, a way for us to escape and survive whatever is coming. Perhaps it would be the best thing. To do better than these old wounds we're forced to inherit and create a new life in Savient. To let him be the best of his family, as Cyar said, and wield that power side by side.

A princess from an ancient kingdom.

A general's son from a modern nation.

Old and new forged together, like glittering iron.

But to be with him, like this, would only betray everything I know about myself, my mother, the very world as it is.

"Come live with me in Valon and you'll be safe, I swear."

But "safe" is no longer good enough, Athan.

It's the end.

The place I can't follow.

53

The winter sun's barely up as I look into the mirror, wondering who the hell I am. It's been too long since I've seen myself in civilian clothes, and I look like a stranger. Brown jacket, tailored pants, crisp white shirt. It all makes me look younger. Tired, spent, but wholesome somehow, and I feel better already. A lightness jumping through my veins.

It feels right.

I head out onto the streets, bag in hand, aware of how reckless this really is. But it will never be as reckless as flying into a sky that wants to kill me. Leaving here, finding my way in an unknown world—it's infinitely safer than the other path.

Cyar said goodbye to me last night. He said it was better like that and he didn't want me to wake him in the morning. I made him swear to follow me when it's the right time. He agreed. He smiled, a bit off-kilter, a bit anxious, but he agreed, and that's the only way I could sleep, knowing that eventually everything will fall into place, the best path, the good path.

It's the direction we've always been headed, rising to meet us.

I cycle that thought through my head as I walk for the square by the train station, passing the clock tower and the promenade, the same as in so many other kingdoms. The same and yet also different, because this one is the last I'll walk through as the old me. *"I'm doing what you wanted,"* I tell Mother in my head. *"I'm being who you wanted me to be."*

I beg God I'm right. The truth is, I can't even remember what my mother told me almost a year ago, when I was drunk and terrified, after Father shot the traitor outside our home. I remember her face—the way she was looking at me, like I was already dead. She whispered things. She admonished me. I see it all, but I was too drunk, and the rest is lost in the haze of time, her words forever swept out of reach. I'd give anything to hear them again, to know what they were.

I'd give anything to have *her* here again.

Alone in the dawn chill, the stone steps are icy when I sit down to wait for Ali. I blow on my fingers, then fish gloves from my pocket. Arrin's watch flashes on my wrist. I couldn't bring myself to get rid of it, a small memory to steal for the new life. I'm certain that eventually they'll all forgive me—Leannya, Kalt. Maybe even Father. They'll accept my choice. It'll just take time, a bit of distance.

I sit and wait, staring at the clock looming above.

I know she's coming.

Early morning crowds surge past in suits and long coats. Women in fur and wool. They don't even notice me, a shivering boy huddled in a brown jacket. In my Safire uniform, people always stared—analytical, vaguely contemptuous. Like this, I blend into the horizon, and I love it. No more labels and ranks. No more boxes. Just me.

Seven o'clock comes and goes.

I distract myself by reading Katalin's letter. It still looks as though it were written by a kid learning grammar, but the message is loud and clear this time. A plea. Her last remaining brother has been arrested in Karkev and is set to be executed for fighting in the war against us—what feels like a lifetime ago now. Her own father signed the warrant for the sake of keeping the title of Governor my father bestowed on him. Katalin begs me to intervene, which certainly took some swallowed pride on her part. Begging me to get my father to do . . . something.

I hide the letter away again.

No wonder Leannya felt bad. She'd do the same if Arrin's life was on the line, but there's nothing I can do, not now. A girl passing by gives me a shy smile. I don't return it, because the girl I want isn't here yet, but she will be soon, and I try to imagine the smile on her face—the one that feels like mountains and dawn skies and *home*.

Seven thirty.

A train whistles from the other side of the station, bound north, and it's the one we should be on by now. I look at my watch, in case the one towering above isn't right. But Arrin's watch says the same thing.

For some reason, it's truly baffling to me. I sit there, wondering why she's late, why she'd tempt disaster on such an important morning. She needs to be here. She knows that, and I made it so clear in my letter.

I made it clear.

It's like my numb, concussed brain can't sift through thoughts any quicker. I'm jammed on this one idea—that she's supposed to be here and she's risking our escape. She's willfully being late. But then that muddle finally passes and the clock clangs seven forty-five, and I feel like my lungs aren't working. I'm only sitting there, a boy in a brown jacket, abandoned on the steps.

She's not here.

She's not here, because she doesn't *want* to be here.

I look down at myself—at the pants and shoes dusted with snow. I see a coward, running away yet again, surrendering to his smallness, forgetting everyone else. Did I actually think Ali would be like me? She's always been better than that, and of course she wouldn't leave her mother here alone. What the hell was I thinking? Don't I even know her?

It's the question I asked the Prince.

And like an idiot, I forgot to ask it of myself.

XI

TESTIMONY

54

Royal League

The morning of the trial, my mother's a powerful note of royal beauty—graceful, calm, dressed like a queen. She'll need it to defeat Dakar.

We enter the assembly room, escorted by Elsandrin guards, and there's an immediate hush in the babbling gossip. Last summer, the Commander gave his infamous speech here, condemning King Rahian and Resya before the world, and it doesn't look as large as it did on film. It's stately and grand, a rounded ceiling high above, stuffed with mahogany desks in a rising circle round the platform, smelling of leather and polish.

King Gawain begins the day's proceedings with a loud proclamation. "This isn't a trial," he informs the League stoically, his voice echoing in the auditorium. "This is a *royal* council to determine the truth."

It may not be a trial, but there's still a little witness stand at the center of it, and a special seat nearby where Mother's going to be forced to sit on her own, like a suspect. She's stared down by a half-filled room of representatives from each kingdom—royals and important nobles I've never met before. They're as strange to me as I am to them, the princess long sheltered behind Etanian mountains.

And of course, the General is there, the Commander at his side. Both look deceptively benign, their masks polite. Mother passes without a glance. I'm not that strong. I know Athan is with them, and I know what I'll find. Grey uniform, grey cap, grey eyes. Entirely a Dakar. His gaze is on the floor, but as I walk by, he looks up at me and his expression is a shadowed, exhausted thing—wounded.

I turn away quickly. The temptation is too great, to imagine another version of this moment. One where I've agreed to go to Savient with him and create something better.

How easy it could be.

Together.

I steel myself to those weakening thoughts, sitting down as Gawain continues. "Today we'll hear the case brought by General Dakar, a case which compels our thoughtful consideration. We'll also hear the words of our sister, Her Majesty Sinora Isendare, and we'll consider both with equal diligence. Our honour demands justice before God."

They're pretty words for this royal room, and he even covers Mother with the last name of our father, a shield of sorts, but I catch the Commander rolling his eyes.

Athan's brother.

I hold that fact tight, to avoid any regret when I look Athan's way. If he thought I'd go with him, willingly, and live in peace with the Commander, then he believes in my goodness too blindly.

The first witnesses brought forward are maidservants and footmen from our palace, here at the behest of the General. They stumble through the questioning, describing places and times they heard snippets of conversation that made it seem the Queen would keep her crown, rather than pass it to her son. Their stories are small and rather unconvincing, but then Dakar summons his better witnesses. Lord Jerig is one of them, the snake, and he's unwilling to even glance in our direction when he takes the stand. How I wish Reni could see this! This man has always been self-serving, and he claims the title thoroughly today. He declares Mother said from her own lips, to her Council, that she would bend tradition "to make the true choice." Clearly, he says, she was intending to keep the crown, a plot set in motion long ago, concocted after her husband died—or perhaps even before.

"And do you remember the day of Boreas Isendare's death?" Gawain asks. "Was there any reason to suspect foul play?"

"It was very sudden," Jerig replies, "and the body wasn't publicly viewed. He was a healthy man, keen to ride and hunt. I never believed his heart simply gave up, as they told us."

"That's not true," I interject, and I'm surprised at the echo of my voice in the large room. Mother's seated away from me, in her assigned place—exposed, set apart—and she gives me a gentle glance of warning. I ignore her, glaring at Jerig. "My father *never* hunted and you know it."

For a moment, Jerig appears caught by the lie, then he recovers. "Not often, Your Highness. But you didn't know him as I did before you were born. The point is simply that His Majesty loved the outdoors, and was a healthy man, and that you'd agree with, wouldn't you?"

Frustrated, I nod.

"Your Highness," Dakar says calmly. "I don't think you understand how a trial works. You can't speak as you please."

"I can when the claims are untrue," I reply. "And this isn't a trial. It's a *council*."

Dakar's eyes narrow, but he has no answer to that.

The next person called to the stand is none other than Jali Furswana. She glides up to the stage on her clicking heels and everyone appears stunned. She's certainly the first Southern princess to ever set foot in the League, and there's a tremor of awe. She's beautiful—beautiful and traitorous.

"As we all now understand," she declares in polished Landori, "my brother Rahian was corrupted by Seath of the Nahir and supported his violent revolution. This is a truth which cannot be denied. I have told General Dakar all that I know, the many times my brother did business with Seath, and I believe his execution was only just in light of the bloodshed and rebellion he supported."

Dakar smiles. Jali's working to remove any lingering foul scent round Rahian's death, and I wonder what he's promised her in return. I want to scream at her not to believe his lies.

But she continues. "My friends, the Nahir despise royalty. I watched them slaughter my own family, watched them put a gun to my father's head. And I know where Seath is. I know he's hiding in Masrah now, his safe haven after this fiery week of revolt. He must be stopped by whatever means."

"And," Dakar presses, "do you believe Rahian also had dealings with Sinora Lehzar? Might she have had Nahir motive to murder her husband—a Northern king?"

No, no, no.

Terror seizes me, realizing that Dakar might have just struck the killing blow already. Before I've even pulled out my evidence. Jali knows about our family, about Seath, and she will happily wield it for her own gain. Her gaze curves in our direction— beautiful, glittering, grand—and falls on Mother, who falters nearly imperceptibly. This is the girl she once let run free. The girl who now clutches her fate between vindictive hands.

But Jali faces the League again. She shrugs. "Of that," she says tonelessly, "I know nothing, General. I only know where Seath is now and that he needs to be stopped once and for all."

Relief floods me. Overwhelming gratitude, as well. I have no idea why Jali just chose to protect my mother, if she knows what my mother did for her long ago or if she simply can't bear to betray a Southern woman to a Northern court.

Dakar now appears dangerously vexed.

Jali didn't give him what he wanted, and I decide it's my time to speak.

I stand imperiously. "What an impossible thing to suggest, General. You have no proof of any of this, only meaningless rumours. But I do have proof. I have proof that can't be refuted. May I not testify as well?"

I'm appealing to Gawain, and his bushy brows rise. *"You have evidence?"*

"More than you can imagine."

My confidence seems to sway him—and my title. "Then by all means, Your Highness."

"The Princess?" Dakar interrupts. "Better to save the royal testimonies for—"

"No, General. I'll honour her request. Surely her words are worth more than the others'?"

I can tell Dakar doesn't agree—not at all—since I'm the daughter of the accused, a corrupted source. Perhaps if this were a proper trial, others would agree, but this isn't a trial. This is a "royal council" and I'm a royal. And so, I will speak.

He grudgingly takes his seat beside the Commander as I walk forward. Once at the stand, I face the entire League, feeling rather small suddenly, yet filled with startling courage. This is where I'm meant to be. The moment I chased with Lark long ago, and with Tirza these past months.

I'm ready to fight.

"First," I begin, "I must say this entire trial is a deep insult to my family, and sharply uncalled for. It is beyond belief that we're here to face the same baseless rumour from last summer, the one hurled at us by common agitators. That we should have endured that violent coup only to be brought here like this? It is *wrong*, and I am certain that everyone in this room sees it."

My tone has the desired effect. Gazes avert and heads tilt to listen.

Dakar's iron eyes fix on me.

"Furthermore," I continue, undaunted, "we're brought to account by men—crownless, not even royal—who pretend to share in our honour, when the truth is, they have none at all. They fight by the lowest means, with no thought for decency. I know this, Your Majesty, because I witnessed these shameful things myself in Resya."

Gawain glances round confused, evidently trying to determine who it is I'm glaring at. It's the Commander, and I hold his frosty gaze from across the room, his expression daring me to keep on, to say another word. And I will. As far as I can, with this platform. I'd always intended it to be a much more intricate case, with the General's naval son, with Reni. A show of alliance to compel a better world. But I can no longer wait. Today is about saving my mother—and I go alone.

"I was in Resya during the Safire campaign," I continue, "and great crimes happened there, crimes that have no place in an honourable fight. I even saw them with my own eyes, having survived the bombing of Madelan. Safire aeroplanes ravaged that royal city with fire. Innocent neighbourhoods destroyed. Civilian dead. How could anyone justify such a thing?"

There's a profound stir at this, and Gawain turns to the Commander again.

The Commander's glare is gone now, cleverly replaced by polite precision. "I believe," he says, "she refers to our careful targeting of airfields and army establishments in the northeast of the city. I understand that she—and those gathered here—are not well-versed in military strategy, but surely, Your Majesty, you know that this is no different than your own targeting of Nahir strongholds in Thurn? From a distance, it may have looked broad and callous. But it was in fact a very specific measure taken to avoid greater loss in our securing of the city. Such a measure is meant to end conflict, not prolong it."

Everyone looks back at me.

"And did you strike *only* military establishments?" I press. "You can stand here today and swear before us that your aeroplanes hit no one innocent?"

"I can't swear it," the Commander admits with false humility, "but I can tell you that it was never part of our objective. Our goals were honourable, and now Madelan is in much better hands. Would you have preferred a Nahir-loyal king continuing to cause trouble for his people? They should never have suffered for his traitorous ambition."

There are a few nods at that, and I want to scrub the perfectly decent expression from his face. He makes it sound very nice, very simple, but no one here has the memory of smoke in their nostrils, the feeling of the world shuddering beneath them. They haven't seen the tangled wreckage of his "specific measure."

"And what about the murder of prisoners?" I demand.

His decency switches to irritation. "I don't know what you're referring to, Your Highness."

"There were Resyan soldiers who wished to surrender—and you shot them right in the back."

Gawain appears stunned now. "And what proof do you have of *this*?"

I open my briefcase and hold up the photograph of the fallen prisoners. Then the mutilated Resyan pilot. Then all of the others in my possession, thanks to the kind and noble Officer Walez—one after another after another, my furious gaze fixed on the Commander as his expression changes to something almost fearful.

"God in heaven," Gawain breathes, taking the mutilated pilot from me.

He stares at the grainy image like it's blood in his hands, and I feel a bitter smile on my lips, because Gawain has no idea that he's next. The pamphlets from Tirza, from Thurn. I'm going to hold them all to account today, these leaders who have allowed darkness to run rampant beneath their banners, and everyone in the room is enraptured by me. They're listening. Truly listening.

And I hope, somewhere, Seath is listening too.

I want him to see his niece—brave as him, confronting this same evil.

And winning.

Are you seeing this, Lark? Are you watching?

"I have no reason to lie," I announce, holding up my notebook. "I was neutral in this war, but I recorded these things, for the sake of justice. I was even attacked by Safire fighters while in an unmarked plane. They have no care for the rules of war."

Weary triumph swells inside me as I wait for someone to haul the Commander off in chains or handcuffs or at least right out of this room.

He's a wicked fraud.

A criminal.

But Gawain frowns at me, still holding the photograph. "And you're certain these aren't lies?"

I lower my notebook. "Why would anyone lie?"

"When people lose a war, Your Highness, they might make many things up."

"So might the victors," I point out hotly.

The Commander stands at last. "And what if this is Nahir propaganda, Princess? You have no proof I had anything to do with this. I gave a specific order *against* shooting prisoners."

"Then your order wasn't good enough," I tell him bluntly. "As long as this happens under your watch, then the Safire cause is stained." I swing to Gawain, on fire with certainty. "In fact, I would say the same to you, Your Majesty, for I also uncovered evidence of crimes in Thurn, and I think you should know of those too."

Now, it's frighteningly silent in the room. Gawain doesn't seem to know what to do as I pull out Lark's photograph and hold it up so that everyone can see, at last, the children executed before the wall.

The Commander's rage transforms to disbelief as he stares at me, holding his shame high before all. "What the hell are you doing?"

"It's Beraya, Commander. Do you not remember what happened last summer? I believe you were there, weren't you?"

"This is ridiculous," he says, something rising in him too. His own desperation. "She's trying to distract us from her mother's trial with this—"

"*Liar,*" I hurl at him. "Admit to what you've done and save whatever honour you have left!" I turn to Gawain again. "Do you need to see more, Your Majesty? I have plenty to share. How about this pamphlet, describing how *your* pilots swooped down and killed an entire family, falsely believing them to be Nahir? Or how about—"

Gawain marches at me, snatching the photograph straight from my hand. "Commander, what is this?"

Of course he's going to spin this back round on the Safire, ensure they seem the guilty party, and I feel my first quiver of alarm—Lark's photograph in his hands. "I want that back," I say, reaching for it. "That's *my* evidence."

He holds it closer. "Your Highness, evidence belongs to no one. Please, let's settle this without hysterics." He turns to the Commander. "Who on God's earth did this?"

The General's son looks stuck—in his guilt, in his sin.

He has no answer.

"Give it back," I order Gawain again, and I don't care how I sound anymore, all I know is that I won't let Lark's photograph—the thing he died for—dissolve into the void of this League. "Give it back now!"

"Your *Highness,*" Dakar intervenes finally. "This is a ridiculous distraction you've concocted. We're not here to point fingers with hearsay, or debate the rules of warfare. We're here for the murder of a *king.*"

Gawain nods, clearly happy to return to the subject of my mother, not that of his own army. And in his quick assent, I realize my mistake.

"Indeed," he says firmly. "Now isn't the time for this, Aurelia. War is a complicated business, too complicated for those who aren't rightly involved."

I underestimated a Northern king's vain pride.

His pronouncement is fatherly scolding, so smooth it feels

like perfect courtesy, rather than the insult it is. He's saying this is too complicated for a little girl like me, and the children killed in Beraya don't matter, nor the ones in Thurn, or in Resya, and as I look round the room, at the League, at all of the baffled faces who've been watching our fierce exchange, entirely silent, entirely neutral, I see the truth.

They don't care.

I've offered them evidence, and no one here wants to look closer. This will never be about some worthless soldiers shot while trying to surrender, or some faraway cities burned up beneath night skies. These photographs will be filed away, contained, and all that will truly matter today is the high drama of a queen accused of murder—and the fact that the General of Savient now has an entire kingdom to control in the South.

I feel the emptiness of my hands.

My anger rising.

Perhaps I thought I could be like Lark's mother. She wanted to heal, to rescue, to care for everyone—Northern and Southern alike. But as I tremble on this stand, alone, I realize she died for that mission of neutrality, and it brought no lasting resolution. The world carried on. It didn't care.

We all have to choose sides. We have to, or nothing will ever change, and I know in this moment, looking at this room of cowards, I can't ever choose them.

I can't.

I rush at Gawain, trying to grab Lark's photograph back myself, but two guards seize me by the arms.

Gawain appears shocked at my outburst.

I struggle against their hold as he strides near. "Your Highness," he hisses, voice low. "Have you forgotten all rules of civility?"

"Civility?" I repeat. "Look at you!"

"No, you look at yourself, child! Bringing *Nahir* propaganda right into our League? You're not helping your mother's case. Not by any stretch of the imagination."

His threat silences me.

He's right, but I still want to slap his face for it. Has he listened to nothing I've said? Has he forgotten the photographs already? This isn't propaganda. This is *reality*. The world as it is for far too many people beyond this petty courtroom filled with fools.

"Perhaps we should adjourn for an hour?" Dakar suggests, maintaining some charade of perfect calm. "Let's not tarnish the integrity of this case with theatrics."

"Yes," Gawain agrees, nodding to the guards still holding me. "Take Her Highness back to her suite."

The men obey swiftly, and I want to protest, to run for Mother, but she only smiles faintly from her distant seat. I have no idea what she thinks of me right now—her daughter who's just failed on this stand, holding everyone to account. Perhaps it's the reason she never tried to do this. She knew they'd never listen.

"You can shout the truth until your voice is hoarse. . . ."

But what else is there to do? What hope do we have? I realize, very suddenly, that she's marched all of these many roads, wielded both weapons and words, fought in North and South, and I desperately want her to tell me what to do next, what chance remains.

But there's no time.

"I'm sorry, Aurelia," Gawain says to me as his guards lead me away, his voice gentle again. "You'll feel better once you've rested."

I don't say anything in reply.

I hate Dakar for his lies.

I hate Gawain equally for his weakness.

And like Lark warned, I'll never trust an ambitious Northerner ever again.

55

Tension ravages the room as the break wears on. Despite their best efforts to write Ali's proclamations off as propaganda, Gawain is clearly rattled, and Arrin looks about ready to shoot me—as if this is my fault. As soon as she raised those merciless pamphlets, we both knew. She was behind them somehow, collecting photographs, sabotaging his efforts a second time in less than a year, and it almost makes me laugh. This revelation might provoke Arrin to no end, but it strikes me as inordinately funny.

Of course she was behind them.

She's too clever for even him.

But now they've forced her away, an order that has the ring of formality, like they're only following reasonable rules and protocol. I'm going to get her back in here.

Somehow.

As I sit whirling through what move I can make, Kalt drops down beside me quietly. He's fresh off some ship from the siege at Hady. A little disheveled, for him, and there's a wary question in his eyes as he glances around. "What the hell did I miss?"

"Would you believe Arrin being accused of war crimes before the entire League?"

He raises a brow, but doesn't look quite as alarmed by that as he should.

This was supposed to be a trial for Sinora Lehzar and Ali made it a trial for the Dakars. A trial for *me*. It's the grand and divine judgment I've been waiting for, ever since those black marks started appearing on my plane, ever since I first lied to Ali, ever since I was born with escape in my heart, and it's time to make this right.

I'll start with the only person sitting alone.

Sinora.

I wind through those now gathered on the League floor, the endless mutterings, judgments, and stop before her dark gaze. She's endured this entire trial as gracefully as the sun going down, refusing to utter a single defense to the accusations, these rumours from the people who once served her. She's entirely at peace, unmoved in her seat, awaiting her turn.

We stare at each other a long minute.

"You came back to me, little fox," she says eventually.

I don't know what else to do. I cut right to the point. "Why did you never tell Ali my name?"

This is the question I've wanted to ask most. It was my fault for not admitting it to Ali, but it was also Sinora's fault, for pushing her own daughter into this without any kind of weapon.

Sinora smiles. "Did you ever consider that perhaps I wanted her to learn what betrayal feels like? To never trust the word of a Dakar?" She gestures at my uniform. "You're a greater lesson than any warning from me."

I stepped right into that trap, the obvious one, and my shame burns. I hate it. I'm tired of this, and I pull back on the mental throttle, getting out of the familiar dive. Here. Now. I stop seeing dragons and finally see Sinora—her lack of hatred even as she tells me this.

What did I even come to say?

She seems to sense my confusion. This woman who has outfoxed my father at every turn. "Did he ever tell you how we met?" she enquires.

I don't need to ask who she means. I shake my head.

"It was kindness."

The very word startles me.

"He picked me up on the side of the road in Thurn," she continues, "after every other person had passed me by. Landorian. Resyan. I was filthy, fleeing for my life, and I offered him nothing of value. But he gave me a ride still, because it was the right thing to do. It was simply right." She pauses. "You think your blood is corrupt, Athan Dakar, but the truth is there's no such thing as damnable blood. You hold every possibility."

I swear to God she's in my head, trying to make me believe the impossible.

Father wouldn't do this.

Nothing gains you nothing.

But she doesn't stop, no waver in her voice. "I'm not an innocent woman, and that's my confession. I am what your father has told you. I've lied. I've destroyed lives. I've buried hearts in the ground, hundreds of them. Same as him. It can all be true at once."

Her honesty is blunt and welcome, and I follow her lead. "He's putting me on that stand next. He's going to ask me if Ali said her father was murdered."

"Of course he's going to do that. And you'll tell the truth. You'll honour your family."

I struggle for the words to explain that I don't want to do it, that I'd rather have the thing she offered last summer—a life away from this, a life with Ali. I also want to apologize, but it doesn't feel earned. I can't redeem my entire family. I can't make this right. "I tried to leave here," I admit instead, "so I wouldn't have to do this."

Her lips twist to a frown. "Leave?"

"Yes."

"But why would you run from a chance to do what's right?"

"Last summer, you told me to escape. . . ."

She shrugs. "I thought you were the one, and I was wrong. That chance has passed."

Too slow.

Too late.

Wide off the barrel roll, and my expression must betray my helplessness.

"You're not the one," she explains, gentler, "but you're still here, and that says even more. When I looked into your eyes last summer, I saw someone trapped. Confused. But you're no good to anyone if you give in to that despair, little fox. If you disappear, you'll never change anything." She looks up at me, and her dark eyes are a perfect reflection of Ali's. Holding a night sky. "You can survive him, but you have to have a strength to match his, something he can't touch. And then you must understand that this is who you are. This was the world given you, and why would you leave it if you could do some good there?"

She makes it sound very obvious, and far more comforting than it should be, like I have a purpose, like I'm meant to be here in this family even when it makes no sense. And then I wonder if that's why she's still here. She could have disappeared long ago. She doesn't need to face my father—not with this public humiliation and his inevitable victory.

But she's here. Facing his strength with her own.

"You escaped your world though," I remind her, thinking of her as she once was in that photograph on Father's desk. Rifle on her shoulder. Southern to the bone. Now what is she? The vain pinnacle of Northern glory, with a crown on her head?

But her reply is swift. "No, I didn't escape. I made a choice. Don't you see the difference?"

Her courage anchors mine, and somewhere in her explanation, everything shifts for me. A hundred muddled thoughts becoming clear.

Choice.

Choice.

Choice.

I've never made my own choice. I went to Etania for revenge. Then Thurn. Then Resya. Diving, spinning, flick-rolling. Maneuvers of desperate retaliation. All of it to please Father, to avoid his gunsight, to get cards in the game. None of it was my choice. None of it was me. Leaving here wouldn't have been my choice either. I've never wanted to abandon Leannya or Cyar. It felt like me, but it was really still *him*. His ambition pushing my hand forever.

I feel myself nod.

"Good," she says, her gaze refusing to let me back down. "I have my own regrets. A thousand of them, all threatening to tear this world apart. The saddest part of living is the realization you only get to do it once. So please, don't make the same mistakes we did. I know you're both young, and young hearts change, but never forget her. My daughter loves honestly and you'll always know where you stand with her. Please trust that. Please trust her."

Ali.

I realize what she's asking, and I know these promises are dangerous, because I don't know where they'll take me. But it's my choice, a power I hold, and from now on, I'll use it. No more feeling small. No more running away. I'll take Ali exactly as she is—even if she can never take me again.

"I will," I promise.

As I say those words, this woman I once hated finally appears more at peace, and against all odds, it makes me feel better, too. If she wanted to play this last game—putting a loyal heart in her oldest enemy's household—she's done it well. I'm here. Willingly. "Give this to her," she says, handing me a letter. "There's no time to say goodbye."

"You'll see her when this is over."

Sinora doesn't agree. She only reaches out to touch my hand—warm, firm, slightly trembling. "I think," she says to me with a small smile, "that I'm rather afraid, Athan Dakar."

56

I shiver through my lonely break in the bitter wind of a balcony view. My chaperones allow me this moment outdoors, since I'm still a princess no matter what their orders are, and I pull on my wool coat and gloves, looking out at the expanse of snow-dusted city beyond. There are too many things for my thoughts to run through, too many fears and regrets and furies. But for some inexplicable reason, my heart settles on only one—one small thing that was said, unimportant and in passing.

"But you didn't know him as I did before you were born, Your Highness."

That's what Jerig said, and as I watch the distant streets, crowds of people plodding on with their little lives, I realize I have no idea who my father was before my life began. In fact, I scarcely know who he was for those few years given me. It's like a dream. A strange dream that I remember, and love, yet it's flimsy and shifting. What if he *did* hunt in the old days—and enjoyed it? What if he was an excellent shot with his rifle, and how could I even know? I was dropped into the middle of a story already being told. All of these years—these seventeen years—have felt like a beginning for me, a fresh world with new surprises, new revelations, new loves, but for my father and my mother, for Dakar and Gawain and Seath . . . for them, it's the middle of something already in motion. An intricate world already mangled. And their own beginning, when they were young, was the same as it was for me, the middle of something else, things they couldn't see or know.

The past does matter—because it's all a never-ending story.

My cheeks growing numb, I allow the guards to lead me back inside the warmth of the League, onward for my prison. I'm nearly down the hall when someone taps my arm. It's gently insistent, asking me to stop, and the uniformed men beside me appear bewildered. That's how I know it's him.

I turn.

Athan reaches out, but I back away, his hand left hovering in the air.

"I know you've made your choice," he says after a moment. "You don't want me, and I understand that. I've done too much wrong. But I'm going to do better, and I hope someday you'll understand my choice as well."

I try not to ache beneath the weight of his words. I want that other world, where the right and wrong are easy to see, where we only have to choose each other. Nothing else.

But when I look at him now, I can only see his father.

His brother.

Beraya.

"Please take this," he continues, offering me a letter, and I'm scared of it. Letters are twisting paths to dead-end hopes. "It's from your mother."

That revelation makes no sense, yet I still can't speak. I usually have words, so many words, but I feel like I've used them all up. I broke myself open before the world, and no one cared. All of my raw hope spilt out like blood and wasted on rock. There's nothing left, and I'm afraid Athan will see the dry well of my heart. I'm afraid he'll pity me, try to love me, try to apologize, but I don't want apologies. And his love is dangerous.

I want something *more*.

This dangling thread of my soul.

He looks at me, as honest as I've ever seen him. "Whatever

happens, Ali, please remember that I'm on your side. I always will be."

I take the letter at last. As the boy I adored and slept beside, I can't ignore the reality of us. He betrayed my family, betrayed my mother. He's been weak and helpless when he had great power in his hands. But as a boy in front of me with a weary heart made naked, offering me the only thing he can, I still care.

How could I not?

I offer my gloved hand to him. "I'll remember."

Warmth flickers across his face finally, from an old place, a place on the mountain, a place I won't forget. A place I'll always long for. He takes my hand and I squeeze his, my own apology, the best I can offer. "Perhaps it doesn't matter how I feel about you right now, Lieutenant," I say softly. "Perhaps we'll always be strung together like stars."

He follows us to my prison, silently a step behind, and I think he knows as well as I do what's going to happen when we get there. And we're right. At the doors of the suite, the guards announce that I'm to wait here until the afternoon. A polite way to inform me that I won't be present for my mother's testimony. I'd like to cry—or break something. But since I suspected it was coming, I simply slam the door on their neutral, apologetic faces. I hear Athan arguing with them all the way back down the hall.

I pace across the parlour, opening Mother's letter with furious fingers, wondering if I could crawl out the window. How far is it up here? Did Mother suspect this would happen? Does she have a plan already underway? It's still too impossible to think that she'd give this letter to Athan Dakar of all people, entrusting it to him, but it's in my hands now. He did what she asked.

Rallying my final shred of courage, I read the letter. The tears should come, but they don't, because I'm entirely dry. I simply read her words. This last story from her, holding far more than I ever imagined, and I press it into my heart like fragile hope. The only thing I'll take with me when I leave here, when I escape as she's begged.

"It is all for love, elski'han."

The words were never a threat.

Only love.

57

When the League reconvenes after the brief break, it happens exactly as I expect. Father wastes no time. He orders me forward, and I don't think I'd walk away alive if I disobeyed this time. But he doesn't need to worry. Sinora told me to be honest, so I walk for the stand. She nods at me and I don't know why, but that makes me feel braver.

We're both rather stuck in this together.

"Lieutenant, did Aurelia Isendare tell you that her father was murdered?"

Father's clearly eager to keep us moving forwards, not backwards, but I stop him.

"First," I say, "I'd like to address the earlier claims."

He pierces me with a deathly glare, but I forge onward anyway. "What the Princess said is true," I tell the entire League. "There were prisoners executed in Resya, by our forces. Perhaps there's truth in the other claims as well, though I can assure you that my brother *did* give an immediate order to stop it, once discovered. I also wouldn't doubt that the Nahir threw their own bloody work into the mix. Either way, Aurelia Isendare is right—these things are a stain on our honour and should be acknowledged."

Arrin stares at me—the blank kind, which might actually be the most dangerous—but I'm not done.

"You should, however, investigate your own as well," I inform

Gawain, which earns me a sharp warning from the Landorian corner, too. "Whatever's happening in Thurn doesn't look good, and no pilot should be accidentally killing innocents. It's confusing enough up there. Directions from the ground should be accurate, always, because no one deserves to live with the shame of a misplaced shell."

I'm looking at Arrin again and he won't meet my eye.

"You have your own reasons for dealing with the Nahir in Thurn," I finish, "but you also have a responsibility to do that well." I wave at the League generally, all the rich Northern suits who profit off their territory there. "Otherwise, you don't look any better than them. None of us will. And I should hope we're all in the business of seeking justice, since that's why we've even called this 'council' here today to begin with."

Silence.

Gawain appears slightly astounded, and Father asks, "Are you finished, Lieutenant?"

I shrug. "I am, sir."

I've just defended our family's reputation, reminded my brother that I won't blindly follow him, and held Landorian honour to account—all in under a minute.

That feels like an accomplishment.

A choice.

Father crosses his arms. "*Good.* Will you now answer the pertinent question?"

"Yes. Her Highness did tell me her father was murdered."

"She said it was hidden? Kept a secret?"

"Yes."

The fact that the Queen of Etania is now condemned by the word of her own daughter sends a ripple through the League, apparently far more compelling than my appeal for accountability.

"It was only kept quiet to avoid greater fear in the kingdom," I clarify, to make sure everyone sees that there's still no reason to assume it was Sinora.

But whatever I'm saying doesn't matter anymore.

Drama.

"Your Majesty," Father addresses Sinora. "Do you believe your daughter might have made such a confession to my son?"

There's no escape, and Sinora speaks honestly. "Yes."

With that, I'm moved out of the way and Sinora's ushered to the stand, ready for the main show. Declarations made. Stakes set. Her face remains serene, and Father meets her gaze with equal dispassion. They're both playing. Desperately. I sit between Arrin and Kalt, searching through everything I know— about her, about him—to find a reason for all of this that makes sense, and come up empty.

They've brought us here. Only they know why.

"Your Majesty," Gawain begins, attempting a formal smile at Sinora that falls short. "Have you any opening remarks to the charge?"

"I do," Sinora replies, "and it's to tell you that I am innocent. This rumour is baseless, spread by the instigators of the coup last summer."

The faces around no longer look so certain, and Gawain asks, "Did those instigators claim that *you* murdered Boreas Isendare?"

Sinora frowns, as if this is all beneath her. "Yes. But I loved my husband, and I would never have done such a thing." She turns to address the League at large, eloquent and lovely with her accent. "I tell you, I still grieve his death. There isn't a day that goes by that I do not wish he were here. There is no man, living or dead, whom I hold in higher esteem. A king with no match."

"But your husband *was* murdered?" Father intervenes, clearly trying to halt her beautiful poetics and get to the point.

"There were rumours, but even if they were true, it was never by my hand."

"That doesn't answer my question."

She pins Father with a look that's dangerously unyielding.

"However I answer, you'll find a way to condemn me. My guilt is already on your lips."

Gawain glances between them uncomfortably. "Your Majesty, that isn't true. We're not against you here."

I'm sure it sounds like a hollow assurance after all that's transpired this past hour, even to those who have no idea of the ageless enmity between them.

Father stands over Sinora, that towering presence that intimidates absolutely. "I see your guilt and your innocence at once," he announces. "I can imagine all possibilities. I also wonder if perhaps there's a reason you felt obligated to do this dark thing? Perhaps you knew something we do not?"

She tilts her head. "I don't understand."

"If Boreas Isendare was *not* the rightful ruler, then you might be justified in this necessary action."

He lets that sit, everyone around trying to catch up—and then I do. Very suddenly. Arrin's face changes to disbelief beside me.

Father's giving her a way out?

It's unfathomable, and Sinora, for her part, pauses carefully, perhaps also trying to comprehend this absurdity. "General, I'm afraid I don't know what you mean. My husband was King of Etania, his birthright."

Whatever Father's just offered, she rejects, and he darkens considerably.

Gawain clears his throat. "I'm not sure how—"

"If there was no reason to justify your action, then we need only one answer from you," Father ploughs on, ignoring Gawain. It's only he and Sinora now, facing off at the stand. "A 'yes' or 'no' will do. Did you murder your husband?"

She holds his brutal gaze. Tinier, but no less fierce. "I'll *never* answer to a man with no crown."

The room of royalty inhales sharply. Her implication is mesmerizing, and the tension hangs, palpable, while Father looks as if she's just stuck a gun in his face. I don't know much, but I know the laughable irony in this, that she, a woman retrieved from the side of the road in Thurn, has more power here than him. They both came from nowhere, but she's risen farther and higher than he ever dreamed.

It actually leaves my father speechless.

And in that space, I realize too late my brother is up and marching for Sinora. Kalt moves to stand, like he's going to chase Arrin down, but Arrin's already there.

"Quit your damn act!" Arrin growls at Sinora. "I won't let you play this game forever."

"I play no one," she replies, somehow still exquisitely calm. "Your father plays. He pretends to be one of them, but what is he truly? A little man with a little gun?"

"You don't know how this world works," Father declares hotly.

"No, I see exactly how it works. Kingdoms always fall from within. You know it too, and yet you ignore it even now. You think Savient is the exception."

If she isn't provoking him, then she's a fool. And Sinora Lehzar isn't a fool.

It's the dangerous point, the point where bad things happen, and no one else here seems to realize it, but I stiffen, as does Kalt. Arrin's hand inches towards his pistol.

"Goddamn it," Father says, nearly exasperated. "Is this what you're going to bring us to?"

"I've brought nothing."

"Lies! Will you look at me and say you didn't do that hateful thing?"

"I've done many hateful things. But not against my husband."

"I mean against my wife!"

There's a collective gasp in the room, and I'm sinking lower in my seat. Where the hell's Ali? I paid those guards the last of my scrapped-together savings so they'd let her out. She needs to be here. I don't know what's happening. The worst, a disaster, but someone has to stop it. I have nothing left to try. Even Kalt is frozen.

Ali's our only chance.

No one would lay a hand on her, not even Father.

"Ah," Sinora taunts Father with a knowing smile. "You want me to answer for that crime? Then yes. Yes, *that* was me. I killed her. I killed Sapphie, if it's what you want to believe. Now, will you live in peace? Will you let this end? I'll give you my neck. I'll give you my guilt and my blood, your victory. Is that enough? Is it?"

Arrin's pistol swings out.

It's there so suddenly, it's almost unnoticed. Then everyone sees. The entire room held hostage, silence quivering with terror as Sinora stares down the barrel, holding Arrin with an expression of pity—some maternal patience, like she faces a child holding a toy.

"You want to shoot me?" she asks in awkward Savien.

No one moves.

Father says to Arrin, also in Savien, "Put that away."

He says it slowly, like he's talking to someone about to leap off a pier.

Arrin doesn't listen. He's bent on Sinora, a strangled sound to his voice. "You took my sister from me first. Then my mother. You've made our lives into *hell*, and I'll never let you get away with that. Not while I breathe."

The League appears confused, the vast majority unable to understand Savien, but the image says enough. Sinora sits before the cold metal—defiant. "You can't shoot me, boy. I have what your father needs."

"You have nothing," Arrin snaps.

But Father doesn't deny her words, and she turns to him again. "I'm the only one who knows. You need me, Arsen."

"I don't need you," Father replies, dangerously quiet.

"You always have. I'm your back. Your comrade."

"You're a *liar.* A murderer and a traitor."

"Perhaps so," she says, rising from her seat at last, "but I am a mountain you cannot pass. Dead traitors will never speak your truth. You remember that the next time you line a victim before your gun. You remember that forever, Arsen Dakar, when your kingdom falls."

And then, suddenly, she has Arrin's pistol to her temple.

Arrin's hand empty.

Father appears horrified. "Sinora, you—"

The shot echoes.

She falls.

Then silence—empty, swelling, horrible silence.

58

I only see the final moments. I knew the guards would let me out. I knew Athan would make them do it. But by the time I'm standing in the League doorway again, it's only hateful shouts. Threats. A gun.

The excruciating *crack*.

It obliterates all sound in the domed room, overwhelming every frightened face, and I don't wait. I race for her, my heart already there as I fall down at her side, my knees cracking hard against the wood, the scratching wool against my skin. She's stretched out, limp. A flower of scarlet on her head.

"No," I whisper in Resyan. "No, not like this!"

My voice sounds like someone else's, someone far away, begging her to undo whatever has happened, begging her to love me enough to stay. I'm sweating in my coat, hot beneath the lights. Wet on my cheeks. No one comes for me. No one has the courage to face this evil thing, and they wait, simply staring at me like a pathetic spectacle, my mumbled Resyan words unknown to them. Somewhere a voice hisses, "Turn those cameras off!"

It doesn't matter. They can film this. They can remember it forever, because it's over. No more beginnings or middles for her. She made her ending. She didn't let him take it from her.

Her secrets go with her.

Her love, too.

My hands push the hair from her face, away from the blood, searching for something that won't come, some tiny breath of warmth, and it's a long while before footsteps approach me. I don't want to look. I refuse to. But the footsteps stop, waiting long enough that I glance right and find a pair of leather boots a few inches from my hands. They're polished. Safire perfect. A little trim of gold at the top. I look up and up, over dark grey pants and grey uniform and find, far above me, a familiar, narrow face staring down, pale with regret.

The General's second son.

The Captain.

He holds out a hand—one long, elegant hand—and I take it, unsure what else to do. Everyone else is too far. He's close. He brings me to my feet, and then his arm is against my shoulders, guiding me past the mute stares. Dakar. Gawain. All of them, fixated on me.

"Make way," the Captain orders, his voice firm, and everyone obeys. The nobles and princes, the cameramen and attendants.

They all move for him as he glides us out of the room.

I'm in a petrified daze as we walk back for my prison. The fog is all-consuming, the shock, but I do know that whatever's just happened to my mother, whatever she's just confessed, will leave me alone and in trouble—me, the girl who waved Nahir propaganda before the League, who called them all cowards.

She wanted me gone. Her letter told me to leave.

Once again, I stayed.

Her last wishes denied.

I hope they kill me, I think as the Captain takes me down the stairs.

Down.

Down.

I realize too late that it isn't right, how far down we're going, because we should be going up. I'm not sure where we are, and he's so tall. They're all tall in his family, but he might be the tallest, a tower with gentle and elegant hands. Pushing me forward.

"You need to disappear," he tells me as we go.

My throat hurts. "Where?"

"Anywhere."

He keeps talking, something about Athan, some kind of apology, but I can scarcely follow. I only know the words sound soft and firm with his Savien accent, distracting me from the grief threatening to overpower my entire being.

I clutch his arm. I have no one else. "Thank you."

He nods, not meeting my eye, and then he's opened a door and it's suddenly overwhelmingly bright. I squint into the light. Sun on snow. An empty park covered in white. It's lonely out here, the only footprints beginning and ending with ours.

I'm glad I'm wearing my coat.

"Go quickly," he says. "I'll stall them."

It dawns, at last, that we're not in my prison. I'm free—and it's because of him.

I can't form words. My frightened lips are half-numb, and none of this makes any sense. But then he lets out his breath, misting in the air between us. "You asked me two months ago what I would do to young boys who fought in battle."

Our conversation from another world, so long ago.

I nod.

"The truth is, Princess, my brother was a child of war, and look how he turned out. If I saw those boys on a battlefield, I'd do everything in my power to get them as far away as possible. *That* is my answer."

I try to say something, something to express the grateful turmoil inside me, this unexpected ending to our alliance that was never truly an alliance, but he stops me. "I don't want to see you again," he continues bluntly. "I want you to leave. I want you to go and try to . . ."

He stops.

Try to what?

To be happy? To live and forget what's happened this day?

He knows he can't fill that space with anything helpful, and so it gapes awkwardly between us, yet even in that, his honesty remains. Unwilling to fill this with false words that mean nothing.

"I will," I say to him, to save him from it.

Tears are freezing on my cheeks.

When did I start crying?

"Good," he replies, and he looks like he might be sad. His green eyes are very large and fragile in the light, an entire sea hidden away. The quick gleam of a wave before it turns over into the grey again.

For some reason I smile, because it's not just him. It's all of us.

Bright pieces turning over into the grey.

He looks confused at my strange smile, stepping away. He nods. Perhaps it's the only way he knows how to say goodbye, so I nod as well, to say yes, I see you. I understand. I'm going mad in the head, but don't ever forget me, please.

You're the best of them.

He disappears through the door, and I stand there in the spotless snow, realizing at once that I have nothing—nothing at all—except a letter from my mother, frozen tears, and a faraway home to reach.

XII

THE HORIZON

59

The world drifts beyond the train's window as a smudge of dull grey—snow and concrete and stone, the steady rattle taking me farther from Mother, farther from her body lying alone on the wooden floor, hour after hour, deeper into the Elsandrin countryside, heading south.

To the sea.

My spirit weeps as I stare out the glass, not really seeing anything beyond. I feel I've left her behind, abandoned her there, and I can't bear to imagine what they'll do. They'll say all the wrong things about her. Wild. Weak. Strong. Tragic. She'll be labeled too many words that aren't right. They won't see that she was a mountain they could never pass—full of love.

"O my enemy, my beloved."

"I offer myself."

I sift through my coat pockets again as the train clatters onwards. There was money in Mother's letter which gave me the ticket. I have Athan's necklace buried beneath a blue scarf and turquoise stones in my ears. I have a wool coat and gloves. That's all. That and Mother's words in my hand.

Havis will be waiting by the sea. Mother anticipated my escape, and she's done her best to whisk me away from whatever comes next. But when the Black appears beyond the window at last, grey as iron, empty as my heart, I feel my fragile courage giving way to despair.

It's all so very cold.

Alone.

A small crowd has gathered at the village wharf, murmuring together on the slushy docks—families, workers, tired-looking sailors—and evening fog hovers on the horizon. I stand there, my toes beginning to numb in my shoes, staring at the fishing boats in the harbour. There's no sign of Havis, and the grand star of this sleepy town is a small steamer with fresh paint.

I wait.

Mother wouldn't send me all the way to a tiny harbour only to have no one waiting.

Havis is here—somewhere.

I need to get home to Reni.

Minutes creak by, the sky turning violet, the little herd round me busy saying their private goodbyes, hiding tears as some venture up the ramps and onto the steamer. As the crowd thins, a familiar figure appears on the far side of the dock—solitary and hunched to the cold, shaved head exposed to the breeze. Cigarette lit.

Damir!

I push through the throng of hugs and farewells, desperate to get to him. If Havis has sent him to retrieve me, then perhaps he has news of Tirza. She's safe. She's waiting for me in Resya, and that's enough to give me some flare of hope.

Not alone.

Together.

But when Damir turns abruptly, his expression destroys that.

It's emotionless. Distant.

"Are you ready to go, Princess?" he asks, shuffling side to side, cheeks tinged pink by cold.

I'm suddenly scared to move. If Tirza were here, then some good would return to me. A goodness I'm greedy for. But Damir is still mostly a stranger, and what if Havis didn't send him? Is he even part of the plan?

"Where's Tirza?" I ask finally. "Please tell me she's safe. I need to—"

"She was arrested."

For a snowy breath, I think my heart ceases to beat. My grief pulses ever deeper, searing into my already worn heart as the ship engines shudder to life nearby. Above, night descends. A thousand stars in the darkening sky.

All of them strung together like stories unseen.

Damir shrugs a leather bag over his shoulder. "Let's go. We're headed to Havenspur."

"Etania."

He sighs. "We need to keep you safe, Princess. Do you want to march straight into the Safire again? Because they'll be headed for your home next."

He might be right. He might not be, and every word has come as if pulled between his teeth. He doesn't like me right now. Perhaps he blames me for Tirza's arrest. Perhaps he thinks I talked her into staying in the palace, right beneath the nose of the Safire. I don't know. I simply need to get away. I need the sun and the warmth and for none of this to be true, all of it buried in the earth, beside my mother, a piece of me dead and gone forever.

Damir holds out a steamer ticket.

I look at it, weighing the choice before me. I could run now on my own, return to Etania, to Reni. He'll be holding the kingdom together by a tenuous string. Always one mistake away from a truth that would destroy everything. Surely the Safire are breathing at his neck, waiting for a single blunder.

But my mother's sacrifice has bought us time. She was Dakar's enemy—not Reni—and without her in the picture, what point is there in chasing a cooperative Etanian prince? A prince who plays smoothly with both the Northern kingdoms and the Safire alike?

Perhaps I underestimated Reni.

He knows how this works.

And as I look at Damir, there's a sudden and profound tug within me to get on that boat, the realization that I have a far larger game to play than my brother. And only I can go chase it. Only I can honour my mother's heart beating fiercely in my chest.

She wanted *more* for me.

I take the ticket.

60

Glorihall, Elsandra

It takes just three days. Three days for the world to forget, to move on, to become even worse.

One.

Two.

Three.

The cover-up for Sinora's suicide is quick and efficient. As formal as everything else these royals do. The film is destroyed. The evidence erased. Everyone who witnessed it is stricken with guilt, saying that, yes, she died, admitting at least that much to the papers, but nothing else. No one reveals the last thing we all saw—a queen with a bullet in her head, bleeding on the floor of the Royal League.

I feel the danger of it.

Something's been lost, something my father was gambling on.

In this void, the disappearance of Ali demands my action. I tried to get to her on that League floor, but Kalt ordered me to stay. He was wiser than me in that moment. The last thing I need is Father's suspicious rage like a tracer on my back. Kalt had to be the one. But even Kalt couldn't keep her here, and he tells his story over and over, how he felt bad for her and left her in her room. And then she disappeared. She's gone.

Everyone assumes it's a temporary misplacement of a princess, a grieving girl too scared to show her face, but no one here knows Sinora's hidden past, her old enmity with Seath. Arrin said Seath would try to make Ali a target in Resya, a valuable pawn, and Father has always insisted Seath's quarrel with Sinora goes back longer than his own.

I'm terrified of what that means.

While I pace restlessly, soldiers roam the halls alongside me, Landorian and Savien and beyond. The League's gone from unofficial trial to military parley, a pack of finely uniformed animals drawn to the scent of blood. Their hushed whispers are loud in the silence. Questions. Concerns. Accusations. I just want to know where Ali is. If she's alive, safe, better off. I promised Sinora.

I turn a corner, ready to beg Kalt for the details one more time, to make sure I didn't miss anything important, and run right into a brooding huddle of Landorian naval uniforms. Rich blue with golden epaulets, the peaked caps of high admiralty. I halt in my tracks. It's the Rear Admiral of the *Northern Star* and the Commodore of its sister ship, the *Princess Everlasting*.

Only one uniform is Safire.

"My brother has a habit of shooting first and asking questions later," a familiar voice shares conversationally, "and my father often forgets he's no longer on the frontlines of a revolution. But I assure you, they'll be cowed after this unfortunate show."

I know I should say something. Speak up. Intervene. Maybe this is just Kalt being Kalt. This is what he does—quietly working to dull Arrin's glory, to make it look less alluring away from the light. He's been doing this for years, muttering critical opinions that aren't quite treasonous. But not with the Landorian Admiral of the *Northern Star*. Not outside our own ranks.

And not when Arrin really is on dangerously thin ice.

"You're a good man," the Admiral says, clapping Kalt's shoulder. "And fine work in Hady."

"Thank you, sir," Kalt replies, deferential.

Respectful.

It's nothing, I tell myself. Kalt's only doing what he can. We've taken a misstep—a very big misstep before the entire League—even though no one's said it aloud yet, the truth left to cower in the corner of every conversation. Kalt's just working his crowd with his usual vague charm, throwing them off the trail. And if he can shoulder his way past Arrin in the process, even better.

It's nothing.

On the fourth morning after Sinora's death, the silence ends.

"There's no sign of the princess anywhere," Gawain declares to us in a small office. "She's certainly been scared into hiding, what with that horrific show. Truly, what a tragic family. First the father murdered. Now this."

"It's regrettable," Father agrees, still clinging to the act, "but Sinora proved her guilt with this."

Gawain doesn't nod. He only taps his cigar with thick fingers. "Perhaps." He draws on the cigar. "Or perhaps you drove a fragile woman to her death."

"She admitted murder, Your Majesty. The murder of my own wife."

"But *why*? She clearly wasn't in a well state. She was afraid of you."

"And that's now an excuse for murder?"

"Not if you tell me her whole story. Why she would do this to you."

They don't know the final Savien conversation that took place—between Arrin's pistol and Sinora—and Father's hand is in a fist. Gawain is clearly smarter than he looks, because Father can't explain this. You pull one of Father's threads, the entire thing collapses. His brilliant cunning has also left him standing on an empire of quicksand. Especially now that Seath has betrayed us. One rumour about his dealings in the South and . . .

I shake away the thought. I don't even want to go there. Father will give in and talk his way out of this, somehow, whatever he needs to satisfy the Landorians. He's simply frustrated right now because even after confessing to murder, even after killing herself to destroy him, Sinora's found a way to remain a question mark. She's still sowing her confusion in the ranks of the enemy.

"I think she was simply mad with grief," Gawain finishes, and I actually wince at the condescending verdict. Maybe he's not so smart. "Your personal history has never been your strongest point, General, and I think it's best we forget what happened in that room."

"Agreed," Father replies swiftly.

Convenient.

Now we can all pretend a queen didn't kill herself, that Gawain didn't allow the perfect storm for it to happen, and that those dead kids Ali exposed never even existed.

"Though, General," Gawain adds, "while I admire your dedication to helping us deal with the Nahir problem, the facts do remain the same. Two royals are now dead under your watch, one who didn't even get a trial." The King stands. "That's an unflattering record."

I glance at Arrin's tense face, and I know he sees the same thing as me.

It's not good.

But Arrin really is cowed, as Kalt said in the hall, because he can't say anything here right now without inviting glowers. Only General Windom seems to still be on his side.

The rest look at him and see his pistol.

"I think for now," Gawain continues, "it would be best if my army occupies Resya. They are a royal kingdom, our brethren, and I'd prefer we settle the discord there ourselves."

I brace for Father's anger, since he's just been kicked out of the territory he won. I wait for his scathing critique, something like *"Oh? As effectively as you've settled the discord in Thurn?"*

But he only nods. "Of course. As you see best." Then he pauses, and I wait for the catch. Too easy. "The princess Jali mentioned Masrah, Your Majesty. What do you know of it?"

Shit.

Beside me, Arrin groans quietly as Gawain turns back to

Storm from the East   479

Father, brow cocked. "What's to know? They keep to themselves, isolationists, though they certainly aid the Nahir when they feel like it." His frown seems to sense the direction Father is headed. There's a reason Jali Furswana is still around. "Masrah is a dark void, General. We don't know their capabilities. We can only assume where they're at militarily—and that's not an assumption anyone should test lightly, not even if Seath is hiding there."

"I don't take anything lightly, I assure you," Father replies.

"And I'm not sure I'd trust the word of any Southerner either."

"Then perhaps that's been your trouble all along."

Hearing Father defend the South to this spoiled king almost redeems the plot brewing three feet from me. Almost. Jali's given Father a fresh opportunity. A new and greater chance at victory, in a place hiding both Seath and unknown glory. It isn't a kingdom connected to the North, like Resya. It isn't a territory the North has already claimed, like Thurn. It's something wealthy and untapped, something that might be ready for change. An old royal returned after twenty years in exile.

And with Seath now trying to kill us—we *need* a bigger friend in the South.

Sinora, what the hell am I supposed to do? You left us and now he has no one to hate!

It's like taking a huge weight off a scale. The balance has tipped too far, and my father can't survive without a goal, a sacrifice to make. He's going to do whatever he can to feel the cold precision of duty.

Gawain taps his cigar, watching Father carefully.

"Your Majesty," Father promises, a smile on his lips—the dangerous kind. "There are many riches waiting in Masrah and I assure you we will be eager to share the benefits with our greatest ally."

Dear God, the fact that this might work terrifies me.

Gawain finally appears intrigued—the promise of someone

else fighting a war he'll get the rewards from, no strings attached—and I glance at Arrin again, trying to figure out if he knew anything about this. He's watching Father and Gawain discuss logistics for the Safire exit from Resya, the passing off of occupation duties, something like alarm on his face.

He didn't know.

He wanted Resya to be his last war.

"Is this bad?" I whisper at him in Savien.

He pauses. "You know in a game, when you have a card that can change everything, and you hope it'll give you a shortcut to the end?"

I wait.

"You play it, but then everyone keeps staring at you, and you realize it was worthless, like you never played it at all." He swallows. "Sinora was that card for us. And Father just played it."

"Are you saying we've lost?"

I don't like the sound of that. Not from Arrin of all people.

"No. But I'm saying you need to play now like you mean to win. You play the next fifteen moves like your life depends on it." He jabs his elbow into my ribs, pretending to stretch. "No more idiot maneuvers."

"Don't worry, I know how to keep my gun in its damn holster," I reply.

That works.

He's effectively silenced, and the power feels good.

I don't tell him I've already made my choice. I'm here, for better or for worse, and if I ever make another traitorous move again, it will be when it counts. When I can save lives and change worlds. Nothing just for me anymore.

I rub my sore rib as Father departs Gawain's presence with a clipped bow. He doesn't say a word to us. He's already marching down the hall, to devise whatever comes next, and hope leaves with him. He won't come back with anything I'll like.

Kalt sweeps from the room last, but he's not quite quick

enough to avoid Arrin's hook. "Better get your fishing boat ready, Captain," Arrin snipes. "This smells like war."

Kalt doesn't look at him. "Believe me, Commander, it's already armed."

Then he's gone. Swimming off without a sound.

"Was that a threat?" Arrin asks me, astounded.

"You know it's never a good idea to read into Kalt," I say.

"True," Arrin replies.

But he doesn't look convinced.

It's nothing.

61

Havenspur, Thurn

My days at sea are listless. I'm bunked beside a boy who couldn't care less whether I slapped him on the face or cried myself to sleep every night. He sits like a stone in our tiny cabin, his lonely thoughts far from mine, both of us shifting with the endless swells, drinking watery tea that tastes mostly like milk.

Damir doesn't know we're closer than we ever were before. That perhaps I, too, now have this shining anger like a weapon— I'm simply too sad to pull the bitter strength up from the grave of my heart.

Silently, I read my mother's letter over and over, imagining her voice.

I hold her final secrets between my hands.

When we finally disembark, I know what I have to do, the power I hold. I may not be able to stop Dakar or Gawain, but I do have my own family. My own realm, and it revives me some-what. The bright sun as well. As we walk off the blistering docks and towards the city, we enter a place I've only ever seen in sketches and newspapers.

Havenspur.

It's exactly as Athan described. The busy promenade and old cannons. The colourful homes and seawater like a turquoise ribbon spreading down the coast. But it also holds the uncomfort-able tension of war, soldiers on every corner, uniforms mingling with sundresses. Out in the harbour, dozens of warships await their orders and aeroplanes growl overhead.

Unease tinges the balmy afternoon. It must be thanks to the revolts so recently suppressed, here in Havenspur and beyond, and I focus on keeping up to Damir, who threads through the crowds. There's no time to savour any of the views, and by the time we arrive at an apartment building far from the shoreline, the air hangs damp and heavy. No breeze able to squeeze down the narrow street.

Inside, an elevator creaks us up to the top floor and a stuffy hall.

He knocks at the last room on the left.

The door opens a crack and reveals a pair of amber eyes—so familiar I almost weep with relief. But then the door opens farther, and a stranger greets us. Heart-shaped chin, black curls. It's like Tirza.

But it isn't.

The stranger narrows her eyes at me, then glances at Damir, before hurrying us inside. I find myself hauled into a small, sparse home, an open window bringing a welcome breeze. There's a desk, a couch, a kettle on the tiny stove. Only one thing is in abundance—flowers. They spill from pots and trays, a dozen more on the little iron balcony, cheerful in the sun.

"You're staying here for a while," Damir reveals, and I don't protest.

My hopes for finding Havis vanished somewhere across the sea. And if I'm going to be kidnapped by the Nahir, I'd better learn why first. What my uncle wants from me.

"You can use any of this," the girl says in accented Landori, pointing half-heartedly at the kitchen and couch, then at the closet-sized washroom. "But these are mine." She pulls back a set of curtains, and there's no window behind them.

Only a wall of rifles.

Now that I'm taking her in fully, she looks less like Tirza after all. She's older and taller, with none of the repercussions of life under siege. Beneath her thread-worn red dress, she's all muscle and strength, built for resistance—and not the kind that hides in a basement, typing reports.

But there are still colourful bands on her wrists.

"I know who you are," I say, and she appears skeptical. She doesn't see how obvious it is. Another thread crossing, tightening this strange web. "You're Kaziah. The sniper."

Her empty silence proves it.

Damir finally chuckles. "Tirza adored her," he tells Kaziah, as if I'm not standing there.

The other girl appears deeply unimpressed by this fact.

"Take me to my uncle," I say sharply, to remind them both who I am.

Having a crown no longer counts for something.

But being Seath's niece might.

Kaziah only appears more annoyed by me. "No one sees him unless they're trusted. And you"—she raises a thick brow—"are definitely not trusted."

I stare at her, stunned, but she stabs deeper still. "Did you think your uncle would simply welcome you with open arms like a long-lost puppy? We all know what you've done, Princess. You're not only a lazy Northern royal, but your bedmates are not ones we feel warmly about. A damn Safire lieutenant? Yes, Tirza told Damir all about your special friend. I swear to you, the next time you see him, he will be *dead*. I'll make sure of it. Perhaps you could even trap him for me? Lure him right into my crosshairs?"

Her mocking words are expert weapons, slashing a tender wound. I believe this girl would kill Athan without question. Certainly if she knew he was the General's son, but possibly even just to get under my skin.

Don't you dare try to follow me, I tell Athan in my head. *Don't you dare this time!*

Kaziah isn't finished. Her bitterness towards me not yet spent. "You think you can come into this world and hold all the cards? You think you're untouchable, because of your name? That's only Northern arrogance, not yet cut from you. But it will be, because you are *nothing* here, and you won't be seeing your uncle until you've earned the damn right."

She steps away from the couch, arms crossing, as if suddenly realizing she's said far more than she intended. "I'm making tea."

She retreats for the kitchen and Damir watches me suspiciously, as if waiting for me to fly back out the door and escape, but where would I go? Swim across the Black? No, I have another mission now, and I try to settle my racing heart, sweat sticking to every inch of my body while Kaziah works. Her movements are quick and precise. Tirza galloped everywhere, bright and feathery. Kaziah simply looks like steel.

"What do I have to do?" I ask her finally.

"Hmm?"

"To see my uncle. What do I need to do?"

She curses, accidentally touching the hot kettle. When she returns, she places a steaming cup in front of me, real tea, properly steeped. Not a drop of milk. When she sits, I inch slightly away as her hand reaches under the cushion, retrieving a hidden folder. Stars, not another folder. The last one from Lark changed my life forever. It killed him. It led me here. But Kaziah doesn't know the disastrous mission I've already failed at, and throws a faded colour photograph on the table before us. I recognize the man there.

General Windom. The Butcher of Thurn.

"That's your target," she says.

"Windom?" I ask, confused.

She shakes her head, and her dark curls don't bounce like Tirza's. Hers are pulled back too tight. She gestures at the picture again. I realize she's not pointing at him, but beside him, at a young woman with faintly red hair. She wears a dress to the knees, green against ivory skin.

It's the girl who chased Captain Dakar in Norvenne.

"His daughter," Kaziah says. "She has secrets we need, and you're going to find them. I'll help, of course. But you know their Northern ways, and you'd do better than one of us ever could. This man"—her finger jabs the photograph—"is a *monster*. Every retribution in Thurn comes from him. He needs to be destroyed."

She means this, as much as anyone could, and Windom's face taunts us right back, severe even in a photograph. Something clicks together. All at once.

"Was Windom in Beraya?" I ask.

"He's everywhere, the bastard."

Of course . . . The Commander has always protested the crime. When I accused him last summer, he denied it and said it was the Landorians. I thought he was lying. I knew he was guilty. But what just happened before the League? I confronted him and he denied it again. And when pressed, he said nothing, not a word. Perhaps because he couldn't say who it truly was. Not with Gawain right there. And Gawain stole my photograph, because Gawain knew. He *knew* Windom was the true culprit I sought, ready to protect his own. He made sure the evidence disappeared. Forever.

A feral anger returns to my heart, familiar now, too many complicit in these crimes.

"Her name's Rahelle," Kaziah continues, "and she lives mostly here in Havenspur. If you do a good job with this, perhaps you'll meet your uncle."

I stare at the red-haired girl in the photo. "You swear it?"

"I wouldn't lie."

Her voice is blunt, but honest, like Tirza's, and I believe it. This is my chance, then. I have to ignore my mother's last warning to me. I have to go to Seath like I've always planned, except now I go with the dangerous awareness that he isn't weary at all. No, he's only getting started, and negotiation isn't his goal—it never was.

It was Lark's.

"The old want to wage war, but we aren't like them, Cousin."

A sadness wells for my cousin who defied his own father, who came to create his own future. Who went against the very blood in his veins to chase peace.

"Have you looked out the window yet, Princess?"

Kaziah's strange question startles me from my memories, and I glance at her.

Her gaze is a dare. "Go to the balcony and look."

I do what she says, to prove I'm not afraid of her, and as I step outside, light stings my eyes, the bright and searing glare of noon. Then my vision clears. The shadows fade, the world opening up from this high point, the stretches of Havenspur tumbling out below me, touching distant plains and an azure sea.

My breath catches.

Far beyond Havenspur, past the city's edge, a billowing cloud of dust hangs in the air, an endless line of tanks and trucks trudging in from the coast, aeroplanes splitting the sun above. Familiar grey steel with black swords.

Safire.

"They want to take Masrah," Kaziah says behind me. "To restore the throne."

"That's impossible," I protest.

"No, that's hell."

She's right, and I long for a radio address or a newspaper, something to explain this mad storm heading east, but what does it even matter? While I was stuck on that steamer sailing across the Black, these political stakes kept ticking and turning, marching ever forward, and now *this* spreads before us. Too many destroyers and cruisers dotting the sea, all designed to bring death. All of that firepower they marveled at in Norvenne. It's before us now with fierce intent, Safire ships ready for war, Landorian ones watching with churning impatience.

Kaziah hovers at my shoulder. "Those Safire soldiers may be dogs, but even a dog can be useful."

She shoves something at me, and I look down to find Damir's cartoon.

The lion. The *si'yah* cat.

The shadow of a fanged dog.

A dog.

"The lion needs its match," Kaziah continues. "A beast to fight another beast. Don't you agree?"

Now I stare at the sea in rising dread. The Landorian ships with their lion ensigns, the Safire destroyers in the distance, and it all makes sense, at once. The truth I was too distracted to see, the truth Rahian warned me about—an idea that could scarcely be believed.

This was never about isolated city revolts.

This was never about pitting the Nahir against the North.

The paper in my hand begins to tremble, because the scope of my uncle's ambition is far larger than they ever imagined. He's too clever for any king. Well aware the Nahir can't defeat their imperial occupiers on their own. It's too slow, too bloody, too costly. It's been going on too long.

But if Savient were to do it for them?

I'm horrified by the sheer mastery of it. A cunning maneuver that guarantees Southern independence at the end—because when these two mighty nations go to war, Norvenne and Valon will surely be decimated, unable to keep hold of the South. They'll destroy each other, forced to battle across every corner of earth and sea, thousands upon thousands of graves to fill, and it won't be over quick. It will linger. It will bleed out slow, the innocent trampled along with the guilty by these giants in their deathblows.

I realize I'm angry.

Wildly, desperately, righteously angry.

"What do you think, Princess?" Kaziah asks, hollow pleasure in her voice. "Are you going to help the cats?"

I hate the sound of "princess" on her tongue. Despise the very idea of it in her mind. It's not me. I don't know who I am anymore, but I'm not what she thinks, and as I look down at my empty right hand, where Athan held it last, I imagine his final promise captured in my palm, meant for a world that never was. I wanted that world. I believed in it. But they've stolen it from us, and now there's a darker dawn on the horizon.

Feeling utterly alone, I look away from the steel-filled sea, to where the southern horizon stretches clear and gold, beckoning like the tangled thread slipping between my fingers, pulling me deeper, asking me to make a difference in the only way I have left.

Somewhere, my uncle lies in wait. Somewhere, an eldest brother still fights inside of him—an eldest brother who protects, dreams, defends—and I will appeal to him. I will fight with the same fervor, for the nameless thousands, for the scattered family that sings in my blood.

"Yes," I say at last, mourning the beloved amber stone against my neck. "I am ready to help you."

War threatens to tear this world apart.

But there might be another way to freedom yet.

62

Valon, Savient

Father announces his next war to the sound of fireworks. Flames burn through the evening sky, a continuous thunder as he speaks about Masrah, the grand liberation to come, and it's far too easy. The crowd cheers. Faces shift with the colours and lights high above, the exiled princess Jali Furswana applauding him onwards. Everyone here is drunk on the promise of victory.

Savient.

The first nation in one hundred years to conquer a royal kingdom.

The first nation to take on the world, crownless.

To prove our triumph in the flesh, Father lines up heroes from the last campaign to be honoured with medals. Rahmeti soldiers who survived the cauldron. Brisali tank commanders who lurched through the deadly mountains. Even Evertal gives Leannya a special commendation for her feat with the cipher.

We air force officers are last. Garrick. Cyar. Thorn. Lilay.

And me—Captain Athan Dakar.

I've accepted that Athan Erelis is gone. He served his purpose, but now it's different. Now I've survived and returned, and it's time for me to take the name that's always been mine. My love for Ali is the closest thing that's ever come to my decision, but she has her own choices to make. And I have mine. This isn't about revenge or fear or guilt. It's simply my life—born as a Dakar, and all that comes with it, an entire sky of possibility.

It's frightening.

But it's real.

Katalin's in the crowd, and I've already promised her that I'll save her brother. I have a plan. Father's so distracted right now, it's a good time to move. I've learned how to bend around the edges of his vision, and I think that's the easiest part of my life now. The harder part is looking up.

Up into the sky I love.

I search for Mother in the colours, wanting to remember the last words she said to me, or even the exact shade of her eyes.

"Don't forget them. . . ."

It was something like that, and I think I'm doing the right thing, like she asked, if only I could see where—

"Athan," a voice whispers at my right.

I find Cyar looking at me. He's trying to say something without speaking. I can't read what it is. I should be able to, after all these years together, but I stare right back into his tense face, wondering, when someone stops before me. Father. Was he talking to me and I ignored it? Is that what Cyar was trying to warn me about? I don't know, but Father smiles, pinning the medal on me himself. The Adena Shield. A piece of stamped metal with crossed swords for my role in the cauldron, and it goes onto my lapel, his hand pressed above my still-beating heart.

I want to believe in him.

The man who once showed kindness.

I'm not sure I can anymore, and the spotlight swings, briefly blinding, over to Arrin. He gets the real prize. A golden fox studded in diamonds, then he's ushered to the podium, confronted by a sea of uniforms and civilians, all the drunken faces of victorious Valon.

Arrin wears his brilliant smile.

"The war in Masrah won't be easy," he declares. "We must—"

The sky bursts to flame again, far too low. Wrong timing. Someone hurries to stop the fireworks, and I stare up, enraptured by every earsplitting explosion only a few hundred feet overhead. Slivers of light. Sparks. Fire in the black. The microphone whines, a metallic ring, and I realize no one's talking.

Arrin's also turned to the sky.

Frozen.

It's been too long, an infinite stretch of nothing, and Kalt appears thoroughly mortified. On the other side of the stage, Father looks vexed. I almost laugh. Arrin silenced by fireworks. Then just as suddenly, it isn't funny. It's the exact opposite. It's wrong, everyone ghostly in the flickering lights, like corpses, and Arrin just standing there, staring up at the sky in fear.

"You took my sister from me first. Then my mother."

The memory lights up with a stray flash, like it's been there all along, unnoticed. The name tattooed on my brother's horribly scarred skin. The bitterness he spits. His unending devotion to only one person in this entire world—Leannya.

Sister.

Rozmarin.

That's the name inked on his skin forever, our *sister*, and Kalt finally acts, since no one else is. He walks right up and nudges Arrin, Arrin startling at the touch. He shakes himself. Realizes he has an audience and he'd better damn speak before Father does something to *make* him speak.

He takes a breath. "It won't be easy." He said that part already, but it doesn't matter. "We must not cower in the face of struggle, for struggle and sacrifice have given us a new world. We share the burden of Her Highness Jali Furswana, knowing she has lost her rightful home, knowing the ones who stole it now sow unrest in the South. Let us take it back for her. Let Savient and Masrah be united as a new sun rises across the sea. Freedom in the North—and in the South."

As I look up, my eyes on the horizon, his words echo into the empty night sky. Somewhere up there is Ali. She's waiting, wanting me to do the right thing until I can see her again. Until I can find her, hold her. Up there is Cyar and Leannya and Kalt and everyone else I need to protect. I'll go into the sky for them. Better me than someone else, as Thorn said. Below is hell, but I have a chance to do things right, and I'll do what I can even if it feels small, choosing this path, fighting for the peace this world desperately needs.

And if that doesn't work?

If I need to act?

Then flick-roll.

Star traitor.

Choice.

My dearest Aurelia,

I know you might think this letter should hold all of my secrets, all of the things I've never said to you, but the truth is—I have said it all to you. Everything I believe in, you know, and I feel at peace with that, because there's a point in every life where the words no longer matter. You will follow your own heart and perhaps, in the end, you'll only truly understand this—and me—once you've tasted it for yourself. The world as it is.

But there is one final thing you should know, and it is this—Sapphie Erelis was never my enemy. I never dreamt her death. No, she was my friend, Aurelia, a dear friend, and it was I who taught her how to undo Arsen Dakar's ambition. If he ever went too far, I knew she'd be the only one there to stop him. I was dead to him, after all. Our alliance shattered. But her? She was stronger than anyone realized, and I knew she could do it. She could place a traitor in the one place he'd never think to look—his own home. From his own blood. She must have distracted him quite well, because I don't think he sees it at all. That's her victory, in the end, not mine, and so I beg you now to always look beyond what seems obvious. Create your allies, everywhere, and only make an enemy when the survival of many depends on it. Every man-made cause has both beauty and disaster built into it, my star. From the royal to the freedom fighter. Chase the truth, chase justice. But be careful.

And most importantly—remember that kingdoms always fall from within. So do empires, armies, families. What's at the center of us is more powerful than any weapon, and I think you see that now. I learned very young the importance of autonomy. That change must come from within, not beyond, and I believe that entirely. The work of the heart can never be dictated by others.

Guard yours fiercely.

These, then, are my final wishes: that you be careful and be brave, my star. Stay far from your uncle Seath because he can't be trusted. I've included directions here. Havis will be waiting for you at the coast, to take you to safety. You may hold little love for Gref, but I promise he's the only one without a stake in this game. Judge that if you like, but it's the best place to be. For you. For now.

Aurelia, I've looked across the vast minefield of my life, and I've done my best.

It is all for love, elski'han.

Acknowledgments

Thank you, first and foremost, to my dear editor, Elayne Becker. It has been such an honour and a joy to work with you on these books, and I'm so blessed to have had your insight, enthusiasm, and friendship. I know our connection on this journey was meant to be. You are truly the best!

Thank you to all of my incredibly sharp and faithful writing partners. Radhika Sainath and Dylan Matthews, you have been with this story from its earliest days. I couldn't do this without you! Kamerhe Lane, Rosaria Munda, Gita Trelease, and my forever mentor, Katie Bucklein—you have each helped shape this book, and I am immensely grateful to have you in my life. Much gratitude, as well, to Mike Kern who has been a superb fount of wisdom for anything and everything warplane related.

All my love to the friends who have been close to me in a special way over the course of writing this book: Maggie Hathaway, Kristen Ciccarelli, Maura Milan, Hafsah Faizal, Brielle Khalar, and Lindsay Popovich. Much love, as well, to the brilliant and inspiring Marisa Aragón Ware, who not only created another beautiful cover, but who also offered me beautiful words of encouragement at the exact right moment.

Huge thank-you to everyone at Tor Teen for being absolutely wonderful: Ali Fisher (my excellent new captain!), Kristin Temple, Devi Pillai, Isa Caban, Peter Lutjen, Russell Trakhtenberg, Heather Saunders, Deborah Friedman, Kevin Sweeney, and Jim Kapp. Special thank-you to Laura Etzkorn and Lauren Levite for your dedication and enthusiasm, and for always making me smile!

Thanks to my brilliant and always patient agent, Steven Salpeter, along with Maddie Tavis, Sarah Perillo, Tim Knowlton, Holly Frederick, James Farrell, and the rest at Curtis Brown. I hope you all know how grateful I am for your continued guidance and unfailing support.

Thank you, as ever, to my family for being the perfect cheerleaders, critique partners, and wellsprings of matchless love: Mum, Dad, and Lily.

And finally, a huge and heartfelt thank you to my readers (who I truly think are the best in the world): you make this entire journey worth it!